WOLVES OF WAR

Martin Lake

Cover Design by Jenny Quinlan
Historical Fiction Covers

Interior by Michael Grossman

For Ollie

BOOKS BY MARTIN LAKE

NOVELS

The Flame of Resistance
Triumph and Catastrophe
Blood of Ironside
In Search of Glory
Land of Blood and Water
Blood Enemy
Outcasts
A Love Most Dangerous
Very Like a Queen
Cry of the Heart: A World War II Novel
Wings of Fire: A World War II Novel
A Dance of Pride and Peril
The Artful Dodger

SHORT STORIES

For King and Country
The Big School
Mr Toad's Wedding
Mr Toad to the Rescue
The Guy Fawkes Contest
Nuggets

Table Of Contents

THE CRUCIBLE

Leif worked the bellows furiously and watched the fire blaze stronger with each gush of air. Sparks from the flames leapt into the air, burnt bright for an instant and then died. Sigurd watched the fire intently, and the sword burning within it. Then he lifted the blade and turned it in the light of the forge.

'It's the finest sword I've ever made,' he said.

'Then it's wasted on that scoundrel, Eohric,' Leif said. 'He has an ill-favoured look.'

Sigurd shrugged. 'Eohric has given two thirds down-payment and that's enough for me. I don't care how a man looks as long as he pays.'

'It is no wonder you don't care about appearances, brother,' Leif said. 'You don't have to look at yourself as I have to every day.'

Sigurd grunted, his form of laugh.

Ever since they were children, people had commented on how different the brothers looked. If they had received a cup of ale every time they'd heard it they would have spent their days drunk.

Sigurd looked like Orm, their father. He was tall, broad-chested, round-faced and had a mass of golden yellow hair. Leif sometimes called him ox. He did not mind. He admired oxen for their stolid strength. He admired them for their endurance.

He followed his father's trade as well. But where Orm had been an accomplished smith, his son was more. Sigurd could work metal like a baker works bread. His swords were masterpieces of death and miracles of beauty. He was sought out by many to make their weapons.

Leif could not have been more different. He took after his mother who was a Moor from Seville. She claimed she was a princess but one of Orm's friends said she was the daughter of a spice merchant so incompetent he lost his money, his home and his pride and had to sell his only daughter to the Vikings. She was dark as a damson, small and lithe as a cat.

And she could tell tales to keep men enthralled. Leif learned every one of them, then added more from his own imagination. His friends called him a poet, his enemies a liar.

He acted as story-teller, a Skald to Klack, the head of the village though, in truth, Klack did nothing worthy of note, the village forever slept like an old dog and all Leif's tales were woven in his head.

Leif continued to pump, intently watching the flames darken as Sigurd plunged the blade back into the fire.

'What name does Eohric want for his sword?' Sigurd asked.

Leif shook his head. 'I couldn't find him this morning.'

'Then find him now. You might as well do something useful. You're pumping as feebly as a little girl.'

Leif grinned and headed out of the smithy.

He took a deep breath. It was a bright, cold morning but the air was heavy with the promise of spring. Sea birds cried loudly in the sky, vying for territory, boars snuffled amongst the huts, scenting females in heat, young men glanced swiftly at young women, hoping to see some sign of interest in return.

'Is the sword finished?' said a voice.

Leif turned towards it.

The stranger did, indeed, have an ill-favoured look. He was a young man, skinny as a ferret and had neither beard nor moustache. His face was narrow as if from a life-time of sneering. Now he stared at Leif with a hungry look.

'Almost,' Leif said. 'We need to know the name you wish to call it.'

Eohric glanced around, as if fearful his words would be overheard. 'It shall be called Havoc.'

Leif just managed to hide his grin. 'You choose an awe-inspiring name.'

'It is not my choice. It is not my sword.'

Leif stared at him intently then shrugged. 'It matters not. You have paid.' He paused. 'The final payment?'

Eohric untied a heavy purse from his belt.

Leif held out his hand and Eohric poured out half a dozen gold coins.

'Byzants,' Leif said in surprise. He weighed the coins in his hand. 'We agreed twenty.'

'You get the rest when the sword is finished.'

Leif nodded, reluctantly. He decided to ask friends to be close by when the exchange was made, in case Eohric chose to flee with both sword and purse.

'It is a fine sword,' he said. 'The best my brother's made. The weapon of a mighty warrior. I have to say that you do not look such a man.'

'The sword is not for me,' Eohric said. 'I was commanded to come here to see it made. By a very mighty warrior.'

'Who is he?' Leif asked, intrigued. 'Who will wield the sword? I must know this for the naming.'

Eohric shook his head. 'I cannot tell you.' He crossed his arms in a belligerent manner.

Leif sighed. 'As you wish. Though this will not help in the naming.'

He returned to the darkness of the smithy. Sigurd was pumping at the bellows, more strongly than Leif could ever hope to do.

'Well?' he asked. 'What's it to be called?'

'Havoc.'

Sigurd whistled. 'Eohric must think himself a famous warrior.'

'It's not Eohric's sword. He wouldn't tell me who will own it.'

Sigurd picked up his hammer. 'A shame. Do what you can.'

He pulled out the sword and began to beat upon the glowing metal, sharp blows running up and down the blade to give it the final tempering.

Leif watched for a little while, taking the rhythm of Sigurd's blows into himself, watching the sparks fly and die in the darkness.

And then he began to chant. 'All-Father Odin, you have given my brother Sigurd the power and skill to make mighty weapons. You have loaned him the strength of your son Thor to hammer out the steel and make it strong. Lend now the fierce valour of the war god, Tyr, that the sword may deal terror to the enemies of its lord.'

He fell silent, watching Sigurd beat the metal with ever more careful blows.

'All-Father Odin,' he continued. 'This weapon will be named Havoc and shall, if you will it, unleash havoc upon its adversaries. The wielder of the blade, whose name we don't unfortunately know…'

Sigurd glanced at him in surprise, pausing for an instant before continuing with his hammering.

'The wielder of this blade,' Leif continued, 'whose name is unknown to us but known, of course, to you, All-Father, this warrior will cleave to this sword as a brother and the sword will cleave unto him likewise. And so it will prove a stupendous sword, a blade of rumour and of legend. A blade worthy of Odin, Thor and Tyr.'

Sigurd gave the sword three final taps, gentle now, to seal the words of the spell within its heart. Then he plunged the blade into the water-trough.

The water crackled like a sea struck by lightning and steam surged up, a fierce mist which dimmed their sight.

But as Leif watched he thought he saw a shape within the mist. His heart almost failed him. He knew it to be the god Loki, lord of cunning and mischief. But a moment later Loki veiled himself as if he had not been.

'It is done,' Sigurd said.

He held the sword in front of him, eyeing it carefully. It was long, beautifully tapered, and the delicate tracery which ran down the blade glittered from the fusion of fire and steel.

'What do you think of it?' Sigurd asked.

Leif shook the image of the falsest god from his mind and bent closer to examine the sword. 'I'm glad it doesn't belong to Eohric,' he said. 'The man's not worthy of it.'

'But he's paid for it,' Sigurd said. 'So let's give it to him.'

He held the sword carefully as he walked towards the entrance of his forge, as if it were a new born child.

Eohric took a step towards them. 'I cannot take it from you,' he said. 'You must give it to the man who will wield it.'

'Then where is he?' Leif asked, irritably. 'My brother cannot hold it all day. Who is this mysterious man?'

'The man who commands those ships,' Eohric said, pointing towards the sea.

Leif gasped. A vast fleet of ships was heading towards the shore. They filled the sea, like a huge flock of seabirds, three score or more.

The villagers had ceased their labours and were staring, open-mouthed at the approaching host. Klack, the chief of the village, strode out of his hall and took a few steps towards the beach. He was trying to fasten his sword belt but his hands trembled too much to allow it. He looked around wildly for his hearth-warriors and they gathered to him, though reluctantly and with apprehension.

The ships were closing on the shore now and the measured beat of hundreds of oars drummed upon the ocean. Leif felt sick. He had not thought to die like this, so young, so pleased with life. He glanced at his brother who stood beside him, the sword still nestling in his hands. His face, as always, was inscrutable.

The foremost ship crashed against the shingle and a dozen warriors leapt out and dragged it up the strand to beach it.

They hurried to line the shore, drawing out their swords as they did so, facing towards the land.

The villagers were silent, as if every man, woman and child had forgotten how to breathe. An icy wind blew off the sea and Leif's eyes began to water. He wiped the wetness away swiftly, aware that they would look like tears. No one in village or ship moved.

Three men leapt from the ship and strode to the shore. One was huge, tall and broad, his arms like branches of a tree, his every stride immense. Beside him marched a younger man, smaller yet still broad and well-made, his gait confident, bold, almost a swagger.

The third man was very different. He was tall but lithe as a maiden, slight, skinny and fragile. And as he walked he seemed to bend, like a willow buckling before a tempest. Buckling but not breaking.

The air throbbed with menace.

The three men marched up the beach, the two larger men slowing to allow the thin man to keep up with them. When they were five yards distant from the villagers they halted.

The largest man's eyes roamed across the villagers and at once he saw a beautiful young woman at whom he stared. The second man fixed his eye upon Klack, having discerned from his raiment that he was the lord of the village.

But the eyes of the thin man darted everywhere, perceiving all as swiftly as a wolf marks out its prey.

Then he smiled. He had seen Sigurd and the sword and he walked towards him.

'This must be Havoc,' he said, holding out his hands.

'It is, my lord,' came Eohric's voice.

'Then give it to me, smith,' the man said to Sigurd. 'I have paid for it. The sword is mine.'

Sigurd was about to say that he had not yet received the final payment but Leif silenced him with a look. He passed the sword over.

The thin man took it, weighed it in his hands and studied it intently, almost hungrily, as if he were looking at the face and naked body of a woman. Then he swung it, once, twice, three times. The sound of the blade whistled in the air.

He seemed astonished, stared at it more closely, and ran his finger gently along the blade. Despite his care, the blade sliced his skin a little and a red line of blood appeared.

He grinned. 'This is a most marvellous sword.' He handed it to the other men to examine. 'What price did I agree, Eohric?' he asked.

Eohric mumbled an answer.

'Triple it,' the man said. 'It is worth every penny.'

Leif and Sigurd were astonished. Most great lords disputed the price already agreed, feigning disappointment at the quality of the work or pointing out non-existent flaws. They had never had such a generous reaction before.

Sigurd bowed his head. 'I am grateful, my lord.'

'Spare your thanks, smith,' he replied. 'You may yet come to regret them. And you may yet regret making such a marvel of a sword for me.'

He glanced at the other men. 'For these are my brothers, Halfdan of the Wide-Embrace and Ubbe the Swift.' He took back the sword and swung it through the air once again, his eyes gloating with lust for the weapon. Then he rested the blade against his shoulder and smiled with satisfaction.

'And I, my friends, am Ivar the Boneless. We are the sons of Ragnar Lothbrok. And with this fleet we mean to conquer the kingdoms of the Angles and the Saxons.'

Leif blinked, hoping that the importance of their mission meant these killers would turn and leave immediately. But something about him attracted Ivar's attention.

'Who are you, that stands weeping like a girl?'

'It's the keen wind, my lord,' Leif answered, hurriedly mopping his eyes.

'I did not ask about the weather. I asked your name.'

'Leif, Leif Ormson. I'm the brother of the man who made your sword.'

Ivar stared at him more intently, as if he had just discovered the answer to a puzzle. 'So it is you who chants spells when a sword is made? Who, or so I'm led to believe, thereby makes it a mightier weapon still.'

Leif swallowed. 'Not really. It's just foolish gossip. My spells are not what they are said to be. They're quite charmless in fact. They add a little embroidery to the blade, nothing more.'

Ivar looked at him dubiously. 'So you would say that all the power comes from the skill of the smith?'

'Absolutely. Definitely.'

Ivar stared at him, unblinking, until Leif thought he might expire on the spot.

'Is that truly so?' he asked. 'You are of no earthly use whatsoever?'

'Absolutely none.'

He had no sooner said this than he realised he may have made a terrible mistake. It was imperative that he divert Ivar's attention from him. He did not wish to be the first victim of his brother's work.

'My lord,' he continued, his voice as casual and disinterested as he could make it, 'you said earlier that the Smith, my brother Sigurd, might come to regret his words of thanks. What manner of jest was this?'

'No jest, spell-maker. I intend to take your brother as my Smith. He will come with me across the sea to war.'

Sigurd looked horrified at the thought. But before he could answer, Leif spoke once more.

'That is an excellent plan, my lord, save for one thing.'

Ivar stared at him, his eyes cold and unblinking.

'The one thing is that this sword, this truly marvellous sword Havoc, is the last great weapon my brother will ever make.'

'Why's that?' demanded the big man, Halfdan. 'Your brother's reputation is known from here to Hedeby.'

'It is,' Leif said. 'It is indeed. Yet, when he was born, a wise-woman prophesied that he would have the gift of making only a limited number of swords in his life-time. When that number was reached, his skill would forsake him. And thereafter, he'd make only farm tools and horse-shoes.'

'And how many swords is that?' Halfdan asked.

'Four score,' Leif said. 'Yes, that's the number. Four score wasn't it, Sigurd? And with this sword you have reached that number.'

'I don't know what you're talking about,' Sigurd said.

Leif cursed him under his breath and turned once more to Ivar.

'And, moreover,' he continued, 'the wise woman said that the last sword he made would be wielded by the greatest warrior of the age. A man not of great size but of great forethought, marvellous insight and a cunning which would astonish the world.

'She said that this man would be the friend of two worthy champions —' here he gestured towards the two men beside Ivar — 'And that they would together topple kingdoms and slaughter kings.'

'But these are not my friends,' Ivar said, darkly. 'They are my brothers.'

Leif placed his finger on his chin, to signify deep thought. 'Now that you say this, I seem to recall that the wise woman actually said that the two champions were the sword-owner's brothers.'

He took a deep breath and plunged on. 'So, you see, there's really no point in taking Sigurd with you. He'd just be a waste of space. Better to take a couple more barrels of ale. Or some pickled herrings.'

Ivar gave a dry chuckle and shook his head. 'It is a good story, spell-caster. But I don't believe a word of it. I commend you for trying to protect your brother but it will not work. He comes with me. From this day, forward, until his death, he is my Smith.'

'But the wise woman was most insistent —'

Ivar held up his hands to silence him. 'And whether your spells are as weak as you claim or not, I like your ability to tell a pack of lies to try to escape a situation you do not like. So be comforted, Leif Ormson. You will not be separated from your brother. You too shall come with me and be my minstrel, my Skald, my good-luck talisman.'

Leif swallowed. 'I wonder if this is the best use of my skills,' he said.

'Have no doubts, Leif. You will be in the thick of every battle and that will give you plenty of experiences on which to exercise your skills.'

'I beg you, lord, I think it best if I do not go.'

'And I tell you, Leif. You are my man, now. You go where I go and do as I command.'

A MARVELLOUS PLAN

'I have a plan,' Leif whispered to Sigurd that evening. 'A marvellous plan.'

Sigurd grunted but said nothing. The thought of leaving his home and his foundry had numbed him, body and mind. He sprawled upon the floor, his eyes unseeing, his mind as dull as a cow's in winter.

Leif felt the same. He loved his life. He'd got some standing in the village, friends, the occasional girl to share his bed, enough money to live a simple yet comfortable life. And Sigurd did all the hard work.

It was in marked contrast to their father who had left his smithy every summer to go raiding in whatever passing longship was looking for crew. He came back little richer, sometimes poorer, weary, often injured, always cursing his fate.

And then, one day, he never returned. Sigurd and Leif took over his foundry and began to work day and night. They had made a good life for themselves. Leif was determined that they would not follow the ill-fate of their father.

'We'll wait until dark,' Leif said, 'and then slip away from the village. We can reach the forest in a few heart-beats and Ivar and his brothers will never be able to find us. We know the forest and they don't.'

'It doesn't sound much of a plan to me.'

Leif bit back a curse. 'Have you a better one?'

Sigurd shook his head.

'Do you want to sail across the sea,' Leif continued, 'to go a-Viking and find your death in some hideous battle? To disappear from the world as father did?'

'No.'

'Nor do I.' He glared at Sigurd. 'And I told you not to make that sword.'

Sigurd shook his head wearily. 'Eohric offered too much money to refuse.'

'Well you could have made a poor sword. Then Ivar would have thought you a worthless smith and left us in peace.'

'I cannot make a poor sword. It's not in my nature.'

For once Leif had no reply to this. A man's nature and his skills were given to him at birth by Frigg, wife of Odin. A man who did not use the gifts she bestowed risked the wrath of all the gods of Asgard.

'Well, that's all in the past,' Leif continued. 'But if we want to have a future we must make our escape now.'

'But Ivar will track us down.'

'Do not think so highly of yourself, brother. Ivar has an invasion to undertake; he won't waste a moment on hunting you.'

Sigurd opened his mouth to argue but thought better of it. He had never yet won an argument with his younger brother and he doubted he ever would. He nodded his head wearily.

'Come on then,' Leif said. 'Before the moon rises.'

He peered out of the door and glanced up and down the village street. The men from the fleet were crowded onto the shore, squatting around cooking fires, eating and drinking and singing wild songs of battle. Leif shuddered at the thought of it.

He narrowed his eyes and searched out the headman's hall. He could just make it out in the light from the fires. Ivar and his brothers were being entertained by old Klack and his lustful young wife. With any luck she would already have bedded the big brute Halfdan while Klack would be boasting of the wealth of his village, too stupid to realise that this was an open invitation to Ivar to loot everything he and his people owned.

'Quickly,' Leif whispered. Sigurd slipped out after him.

'Where do you think you're going,' came a voice.

Leif cursed. He had not considered that Ivar would have posted a guard on the hut.

'Who are you, friend?' he asked lightly.

'You know who I am,' the man said, stepping into the light. 'My name is Eorhic, brother to Jarl Guthrum.' He pulled a sword from his belt and held it at Leif's throat.

Leif was puzzled. That a man of Eohric's rank should be sent to arrange for the making of a sword and now set to guard prisoners was very strange.

Sigurd grinned; he had the same thought. But he believed that it proved how valuable Ivar considered him.

'I feel honoured that the brother of a jarl should volunteer to guard us,' Leif said.

Eohric spat. 'It was none of my choosing.'

Leif smiled. Here was something to work on.

'Someone has a grudge against you?' he asked, feigning surprise.

'Ivar,' Eohric answered. 'He never liked me from the first.'

Leif nodded sympathetically and then glanced swiftly at Sigurd, nodding once towards Eohric. Sigurd merely looked blank.

'Perhaps he is fearful of you,' Leif continued. He signalled to Sigurd once more.

'Why would Ivar fear me?' Eohric asked. He gave a dismissive snort but, despite this, Leif sensed that he was curious to know more.

'It seems obvious to me,' Leif continued.

Eohric sheathed his sword and moved closer. 'Why obvious?'

'Because you're young,' Leif answered, 'clever, healthy and strong. And he is…what is wrong with him? Why does he look that way?'

Eohric gave a mirthless laugh. 'He is not called Boneless for nothing. He is made of gristle and spleen, nothing more. He blows in the wind, both in body and in heart.'

Leif gestured to Sigurd once again and, finally, he understood. He bent and searched for a stone.

'I have heard so,' Leif said. 'Perhaps Ivar is aware of his own weakness and fears that you are the man who will supplant him.'

'Who has told you this?' Eohric asked eagerly.

Sigurd struck and Eohric crumpled to the ground.

'Nobody you fool,' Leif said. 'It's only a story.'

He grabbed Sigurd by the arm and, silent as cats, they began to creep through the darkness.

They reached the end of the village and plunged into the greater gloom beyond the reach of the camp-fires. They took a few steps further and Leif began to realise that his plan was not quite so marvellous as he had imagined. They had brought no torch to light their way and they could see very little.

Leif went first, one step at a time, his hand groping in front of him as if he were a blind man. Sigurd had grabbed hold of his tunic and seemed to alternate between pushing Leif forward and holding him back.

'Let go,' Leif hissed.

'I won't. I might lose you.'

'If only the gods were so kind to me. Now, be quiet in case we're being tracked.'

They stumbled through the forest for most of the night until weariness overcame them. They flung themselves between the branches of an old beech tree, too tired to take heed of pursuit or danger from wild animals. Odin protect us, Leif thought and fell asleep.

He woke when a shaft of sunlight hit him in the face. For a moment he was befuddled and did not know where he was. Then the memory of the day before crashed into his mind. He felt sick at what had happened but, in a little while, he felt a huge sense of relief at their escape and an even bigger sense of self-congratulation at the success of his plan. They had escaped from an armed camp and would soon be free to return to their old life.

He shook Sigurd. 'Wake up. We need to put more miles between us and Ivar.'

They hurried through the forest for the rest of the day until the sky grew dark. They debated whether or not to continue but, in the end, decided it would be better to sleep through the night and start off again in the morning.

They woke shortly after dawn. They found a little stream to slake their thirst but nothing, not even the smallest fish, to satisfy their hunger.

'We need to find somewhere to get some food,' Sigurd said. 'Unless your plan was to make our escape and then to starve to death.'

'Feast on your own tongue, brother, if you plan to speak such nonsense. No forest goes on without end. We'll soon leave it and find a village with enough food and drink to satisfy even you.'

Sigurd gave him a doubtful look but followed him. Leif might be full of conceit but he was seldom proved wrong.

And nor was he this time. They walked a few miles longer and found themselves at the edge of the forest. A mile to the west they could just make out the haze in the sky which marked the sea. Leif narrowed his eyes. He thought he recognised the shape of the land before them. If he was right they were a good twenty miles south of their village and Ivar's fleet.

'There are houses,' Sigurd said, pointing to a settlement about half a mile to the west. 'We could get food there.'

Leif sighed. His brother was always hungry, though it was little wonder for he was big and expended a great deal of energy in his work. If he had been alone he might have searched for somewhere further east, more distant from the sea. But he knew Sigurd would not wait longer and so, advising him to be cautious, they headed towards the village.

It was a little smaller than their own village and the houses looked meaner and more unkempt. The women working in front of their houses eyed them suspiciously and one went running to the hall, a building little bigger than the rest of the huts, presumably to fetch the headman.

He appeared a few minutes later, wiping a mouth still greasy from the noonday meal. Sigurd's stomach rumbled at the smell of roast mutton.

'Good day, strangers,' the man said. His voice was thick with suspicion, his eyes nervous and alert. 'What brings such fine men to my home?'

'We are just common labourers,' Leif said, 'looking for the chance to work for food and a night's shelter.'

'Do you carry weapons?'

Leif and Sigurd shook their heads and the man appeared to relax a little.

'We have precious little food to spare,' he continued, 'It's been a hard winter. But a few of my men died in the coldest days so I could make use of you for a week or two.'

'We would be happy to do anything,' Leif said.

'The far meadow is overgrown with weeds and brambles and needs clearing.'

'Just give us the tools and we'll do the job,' Leif said.

'Good.'

Leif turned and gave Sigurd a satisfied wink.

'Follow me,' the headman said. Then he paused. 'There is one other job but I doubt you can do it.'

'Maybe we can,' Leif said.

'Our smith died a month ago and our horses are in desperate need of shoeing. And our tools could do with an overhaul.'

'I can do that,' Sigurd said, eagerly. 'I'm a smith, and a renowned one at that.'

The headman gave a cold smile and Leif felt a shiver of unease.

'It is good we have met up then, friends,' the headman said. 'You can stay here for as long as there's work to be done.'

He called to a woman to bring some food and ale. She hurried over with platters of mutton stew and thick chunks of bread. A younger woman brought a jug of good ale and some beakers. Leif's nerves calmed. The brothers squatted on the ground and began to devour the food eagerly. The headman left them to talk with a young man.

'We've struck lucky,' Leif said. 'The headman seems a sensible and honest fellow.'

Sigurd nodded, too intent upon his food to spare time for words.

In fact, they were both so engrossed that neither saw the headman step behind them, raise a heavy club and smash them on the head.

Leif lifted his head and instantly regretted it. There was a terrible pain in his skull and he thought he would vomit. He went to feel the back of his head but was unable to. His wrists were tightly bound.

'You won't get free,' Sigurd said. 'I've tried.'

Leif closed his eyes. 'What happened?'

'I don't know. One minute I was eating, the next I woke up trussed like a fowl and with my head aching like fury. And all the while you've been snoring peacefully.'

'Hardly peacefully. I think I might die.'

'I think you might both die,' said a voice from behind them. The headman stepped into view, his face a picture of delight.

'What have we done to you?' Leif asked. 'We offered to work for food and shelter.'

'Oh, it's not what you've done to me,' the headman said. He dragged them both to their feet and pushed them towards the door. 'See for yourselves.'

The day was drawing to a close but the dim light seared their throbbing heads. Leif forced his eyes to focus on a large shape in front of him. When they did he cried out in terror. A longship was drawn up on the riverbank and two figures were striding towards them.

The first was a huge man, in his middle twenties, with a large head, bull neck and wide shoulders. His long blond hair was plaited and his beard cut short beneath his chin. His face looked fierce.

His companion was younger and smaller. And familiar. Leif's heart sank. It was Eohric and he had a wild, dangerous look in his eye. Leif thought him more alarming than the giant beside him.

'Yes,' the big man said, his voice as solid as his shape. 'These are the runaways.' He threw a small bag of coins to the headman. 'You have earned the thanks of Ivar the Boneless.'

'I am honoured to have helped him,' the headman said, giving a ghastly grin which was made up more of fear than enthusiasm.

Eohric seized his hand and stroked it gently. 'As he grovels so abjectly, brother, perhaps we should keep the money.'

Leif gasped. So the giant was Jarl Guthrum, Eohric's brother?

Guthrum shook his head. 'No, Eohric. Ivar promised a rich reward for their capture.'

Eohric's face twisted in rage. A rage that could only be eased by violence and revenge.

He smashed his fist into Leif's stomach, making him double over. Then he chopped him on the back of the neck. Leif fell to the ground and tried in vain to protect himself from the rain of kicks which Eohric aimed at his head and chest.

'Enough,' cried Guthrum, dragging Eohric away by the scruff of his neck. 'Ivar wants them alive, you fool.'

'Oh, I would have left him alive, Guthrum. Broken-limbed but still alive.'

'You are not the one to decide upon his punishment.'

'A pity. I would so enjoy it.'

IVAR'S WELCOME

Leif expected Guthrum to head north to return to the village and Ivar's fleet. Instead he turned his longship to the south.

'We're in luck, Sigurd,' Leif said. 'This Guthrum is either a fool or he means to keep us for himself.'

'Why is that lucky?' Sigurd asked.

Leif shuddered. 'Do you want to meet up with Ivar the Boneless again?'

Ivar's reputation had long spread across the whole world. He had caused calamity in Ireland for both the native Irish and the Vikings who had settled there. He had returned to the north and wreaked havoc amongst the Danes, the Swedes and in Norway. Some claimed he had even travelled three thousand miles to Miklagard and crucified the Emperor of the Romans. Others said that he'd broiled him on a spit and served him up at a feast for his friends.

'I'm sure Guthrum isn't returning to Ivar,' Leif continued. 'Our luck still holds.'

'Good or ill-luck is in the hands of the Norns,' Sigurd said. 'They weaved our fate when we were born. There's nothing we can do about it.'

'They cursed my fate when they made me your brother,' Leif said. 'Of course, there's something we can do about it. We just have to use our wits.'

'Like you did when you decided to escape? That's hardly worked out well. The Norns will laugh to see us being dragged back to Ivar.'

'We are not returning to him, I tell you. Guthrum wants us for himself, to be his Smith and his Skald.'

Sigurd shook his head, wearily.

They sailed south for the rest of the day and set off early again the next morning. Leif noticed that Guthrum was making his men work hard at the oars and it was then that a sense of disquiet began to hit him.

All too soon he found out why. They turned into an inlet and Leif's heart went into his mouth. Ivar's fleet was waiting for them.

'Seen a ghost?' Eohric sneered. 'It's your own, I warrant.'

'If it is I won't have to listen to you anymore.'

Eohric smiled and punched him in the face.

'Another example of your wit?' Sigurd said to Leif, as he lay sprawling on the deck.

'Enough, Eohric' cried Guthrum. 'Ivar will be angry if you harm the goods.'

He strode over and pulled Leif to his feet. 'Have you no sense? Why do you antagonise my fool of a brother when you're up to your eyebrows in shit already?'

Leif smiled wanly. 'It is my nature.'

'Well it won't be your nature for much longer. Ivar is wroth because you fled and sent me in search of you. You won't be welcomed back with open arms.'

Sigurd cursed. The bile rose in Leif's throat. Guthrum gestured to them to leave the ship.

Ivar and his brothers were sitting by a campfire on the beach, deep in conversation. Ubbe saw them first and the other brothers turned to where he pointed.

Leif was horrified to see Ivar stare at them with grim joy.

'The runaways return,' he cried. 'Well done, Guthrum.'

Guthrum pushed Leif and Sigurd in front of the brothers.

Ubbe stared at Leif. 'I thought we told you not to harm them,' he said to Guthrum.

'They fought hard when we caught them,' Eohric said.

'We said you were not to harm them,' Ubbe repeated.

'We knocked them about the head a little but no more,' Guthrum said. 'The bruises were caused by the headman of the village. He didn't know you wanted them unharmed so he cannot be blamed for his zeal.'

Ivar looked at him doubtfully, uncoiling his legs like a snake waking up.

'It does you credit that you protect your brother so readily, Guthrum,' he said. 'Just be sure he is worth your concern.'

Guthrum inclined his head but did not answer.

'And so,' Ivar continued, 'I am left wondering what to do with you two.'

He got to his feet and placed a hand on Leif and Sigurd's shoulders. 'It is a puzzle. Some say that all men are free to choose their lord or leave him. In which case, you are guilty of no crime.'

He gave them a winning smile. Leif grinned back.

'But on the other hand,' he continued. 'some believe that any man who seeks to flee from a lord without even the courtesy of asking to be released is a miscreant of the worst kind and a coward into the bargain.'

Again, he smiled, although this time, Leif thought it wisest if he kept his own face straight.

'Now I puzzle which I believe?' He turned to his brothers. 'First let us hear from my kin.'

'I say that such a man is a criminal,' said Halfdan, 'and deserves death.'

'I think otherwise,' Ubbe said. 'All Vikings are free men. They have the right to choose their lord at any time. I agree that it was discourteous for them not to discuss it with you, Ivar, cowardly even. But it's not criminal. We should let them live. But as they have besmirched our reputation they should become our slaves.'

Ivar nodded thoughtfully, considering the recommendations of his brothers. He turned back to Leif and Sigurd, held his arms wide, gave a wry little smile and shrugged.

'You see, dear friends, how hard it is to come to a right conclusion?'

He sighed and put his finger to his temple, tapping it repeatedly as if he would cudgel out the best answer.

'I need longer to decide,' he said at last. 'But in the meanwhile, I will hang you up by your ankles. To keep you safe, you understand, while I think.'

Then he clapped his hand. 'And while you are hanging, Skald, you can conjure a tale for us. Once you have one, I will release you so you can recite it. It shall give me enough time to make up my mind about your fate.'

Four men dragged Leif and Sigurd to a nearby tree. They tied strong ropes to their ankles and cast the other end over a branch. Then they were hauled up and left dangling a dozen feet in the air.

'We shall soon see our father and mother,' Sigurd said. 'They will be disappointed to see us so soon.'

'Shut up,' Leif answered. 'I have to think up a tale.'

They hung from the branch while the sun descended to the west. A strong wind blew off the sea. It was this which kept the fleet from setting off. It also made Leif and Sigurd spin like onions drying in the wind.

At last, Leif clapped his hands and gestured towards a man who was sitting watching them. 'I have a tale,' he called. 'Go tell Ivar I have a tale.'

Ivar and his brothers sauntered up to the tree.

'You have a tale?' Ivar asked. 'Then let us hear it.'

'I can't tell you when I'm strung up like this,' Leif said.

'Why not?'

'Because it's blasphemous. Odin hung himself upon a tree to gain all knowledge. I cannot sing a song from such a position. It will look like I am mocking him.'

Ivar considered this for a moment and then ordered him cut loose. Sigurd, however, was left hanging.

Leif brushed himself down and bowed to the three brothers. 'I have my tale,' he said. 'A marvellous and honest tale.'

Ivar gestured for a bench to be brought and the three brothers sat at ease while Leif shuffled nervously in front of them. Two score other men came and sat on the ground close by.

'I tell the tale of Ivar the Boneless and the Emperor of Miklagard,' Leif began. He glanced at Ivar to see his reaction.

He nodded enthusiastically for Leif to continue.

Good, Leif thought, he likes himself well. Very good. He licked his dry lips and raised his voice high.

'Miklagard,' he said, 'the great city of the Romans, was ruled by the Emperor Michael, named Drunkard for his excesses. This foolish, weak lord grew angry in his palace for his people had heard rumour of the great warrior Ivar the Boneless and many whispered that he would be a better lord than Michael.'

Ivar nodded in appreciation. He knew that Leif was lying, of course, but he liked the lie.

'One day, Michael invited Ivar to come to Miklagard as an honoured guest,' Leif continued. 'The honest, trusting Ivar, journeyed there alone, confident that his good name and reputation would guarantee him a warm welcome. But, alas, the vile Michael imprisoned him the moment he set foot on the golden pavements of the city. Ivar was held prisoner in a fetid hole for half a year, trussed by cruel bonds and fed only on rotting bread, dead rodents and the water from the sewers.'

Here the audience gasped and Leif was pleased to see that Ivar was one of them.

'Weaker men, would have perished,' Leif said, 'any man would have done. But not the mighty Ivar. He kept himself alive by plotting how to escape and seek his revenge.

'It so happened that Ivar was not alone in his cell. Two rats of immense size had inhabited it for a while. Now Ivar fed them some of his bread until they grew to trust him. Little by little he enticed them closer by lying a trail of crumbs for them to follow. In the end, after many painstaking months, he laid the bread against the ropes about his wrists. And while the rats nibbled on the bread, perforce, they also bit upon his bonds. Eventually, after many more days, they gnawed through the ropes. The mighty Ivar was free.'

At this point the audience turned to Ivar to show their admiration at his cunning. He shrugged off their plaudits in a modest manner.

'Ivar strode to Michael the Drunkard's Palace,' Leif continued. 'The Emperor's naked slave girls fled at the approach of the wronged hero but crept after him to see how he would pay back their hated master. They did not have to wait long.

'The Emperor's guards flung down their weapons at the approach of the mighty Viking and loudly proclaimed that he would make a far worthier Emperor. But Ivar said that he was content to be the lord of free northern men, strong in battle, skilled in love and strong in honour. He did not wish for the Emperor's golden throne. But he did desire vengeance.'

At this point the audience fell silent. The only sound was the noise of Sigurd creaking in the wind above Leif's head.

'And what a vengeance he exacted,' Leif said quietly, turning to gaze at Ivar with adulation in his eyes.

'He gave the Emperor a choice. He would cut away one of his appendages: his ears with which he could hear the gong announcing the start of a feast, his nose with which he could smell his food and wine, his tongue by which he could taste them. Or, and this was Ivar's final choice, his prick with which he could service the thousand wives and slave girls he owned.

'The Emperor said this: "I need my ears to hear those who whisper sedition against me. I love my nose for it allows me to scent my food and nose out the stench of those ingrate beggars who would do me harm. I cherish my tongue for it is a worthy servant, allowing me to savour all wine and food and the delicate flesh of my women. But, as for my prick, I am so much a sot I have no more use for it. It will not rise, it will not harden. So take it and begone."

'And here the drunken Emperor pulled out his flaccid piece of flesh and handed Ivar a knife. Our intrepid hero wasted not a moment but immediately severed the useless ornament from the Emperor's groin. The Emperor pronounced Ivar his lord and master and suggested that his prick be broiled and served to the highest priest in the land who claimed it was the tastiest morsel he had ever eaten.'

Leif gave a deep bow to Ivar and basked in the storm of cheers and applause that followed.

'You are indeed a wonderful teller of tales,' Ivar said, clapping him on the shoulder. 'Because of this I will spare your life and that of your brother. But you must serve me until the end of your days. And you will. I forgive your foolish flight from me. I sense that you will be wise enough to remember never to do such a thing again.'

ACROSS THE WHALE ROAD

The prow of the longship sliced through the waves like a sword through flesh. It was now near the end of September, a foolish time to sail for the winds blew hard and fierce.

It was even more foolish to launch an attack upon an enemy country. Winter would soon settle upon the land and armies would find it difficult to move. Even worse, stores of food would dwindle and the people grow hungrier day by day. There was every likelihood that an army would starve to death. Yet Ivar, Halfdan and Ubbe appeared to have no worries about their expedition. Many of the warriors working the oars may have felt differently but, if they did, none dared show it.

Leif hung onto the gunwale and peered gloomily at the surf frothing on either side. They had been three days at sea and every hour had been a nightmare. He had been put to an oar on the second day out but he was so clumsy that Ivar had cuffed and cursed him and forbidden him to row anymore. He did not complain; the flesh on his hands had been shredded by the oar. Instead he had been put at the front of the ship and told to look out for danger.

'Any ships,' Ubbe explained to him, 'or a sandbank or rock.'

His eyes smarted from the sting of the salt sea but he comforted himself that it was better than rowing.

Sigurd, on the other hand, took to the oar like a babe to its mother's teat. He was used to hard physical labour and so familiar with the rhythm of the hammer upon the anvil that he found it no problem to row in time. Leif envied him but not for this. Sigurd readily accepted his lot in life and, now he had got over his initial shock, their change in fortune appeared not to distress him over-much.

Unlike Leif. He had too great an imagination. It was both a blessing and a curse. Now it proved a curse.

The fleet was sailing a few miles west of the coast to avoid treacherous sand-banks where even the shallow-draught longships might go aground. Leif grew convinced that the sand-banks were the coils of the world-serpent, fearsome enemy of Thor, and that at any moment it would writhe, leap out of the water and trap them. He muttered constant prayers to Thor to protect them until he suddenly realised that the great god might think he was invoking him and send a terrible tempest to his aid. A tempest which, far from aiding them, would sink and destroy the fleet.

He clamped his mouth shut. Many skalds feared that Loki, god of mischief would ensnare their voice. Such an event could prove their undoing. Leif was such a skald. When things grew difficult he readily blamed the deity, and then fell into fits of terror lest Loki heard and turned his baleful attention fully upon him. He whistled loudly, to keep any more words springing treacherously to his lips.

'Shut up that bloody whistling,' Ubbe cried from the rear.

'Let him,' Ivar said. 'It will keep the demons at bay.'

Leif whistled more loudly still. From the first hour of their journey he learned that, although Halfdan and Ubbe were older and more physically powerful, Ivar was the real leader of the army. It was his vision which had inspired them and now, his subtle will infused every warrior and made them row with relentless endurance. Each mile would bring them closer to the fabled land of the Angles where crops grew faster than a winter storm, where gold and jewels filled the coffers of the monks and where maidens outnumbered men three-fold and were the most lascivious in all the world.

Leif gave a grim smile. Good food, much gold and frolicsome women were all fine things but not if they were bought by sword blows or shattered bones. Thank the gods that I'm a skald and not a warrior, he thought.

It was at that moment that Ivar hailed him.

'Come here, Skald,' he cried.

Leif gulped and made his way unsteadily between the lines of rowers.

'Yes, my lord.'

Ivar thrust a spear at him. 'I realise you have no weapon. You cannot be part of my army without a weapon.'

'But I am your skald,' Leif said. 'I'm not a warrior.'

'That's abundantly clear. But if you're to sing about the deeds of warriors you must be close to them in battle. And then, even if not a warrior, you will be grateful for this spear.'

Leif looked at the weapon. A five-foot shaft of ash was topped with a gleaming iron tip as sharp as any knife. He imagined thrusting it into the body of an enemy and felt sick.

'Would I not be better with a sword?' he asked, trying to hide the nervousness in his voice.

'If you want to die,' Ivar said. 'A sword needs skill to wield it. Any fool can stick a foe with a spear.' He dismissed Leif with a gesture.

Leif trudged back to his post. He did not wish for any weapon, least of all a second rate one which he sensed he'd be unable to wield. He glanced suspiciously at the crewmen. He felt certain that one of them must be Loki in disguise.

But by the time he reached the prow he decided to make the best of things. He stood upright, spear by his side, and hoped that he would appear at least a little like a warrior. He knew that he would not fool any of the men in the ship and almost certainly would have as little success with any Saxon or Angle warrior. But he might, perhaps, dupe a young maiden and she would open her legs to him.

He spent the next few hours playing out such scenarios in his mind. Some of the girls were blonde, others with hair the flaming red of a setting sun, a few with tresses as black as jet. But all were virgins, although astonishingly expert in sexual matters. They were as naive as children in believing his claims to be a famous warrior, indeed, a prince or king of a far northern kingdom. But once he had inveigled them into bed they proved lovers of amazing skill, enthusiasm and physical prowess. And they were reckless, lewd and wanton to the most remarkable degree.

'Leif, what the hell are you doing?'

Asgrim, the oarsman closest to him had felt the pull on his oar which signified they were getting too close to a sandbank.

The helmsman also saw this and threw his weight against the steering board. The ship slewed to the right and freed itself from the monstrous grip of the sand-bank.

'Do you want us all killed?' Ivar yelled at him.

Not at all, Leif thought. Not with all those wonderful maidens waiting for me in England.

They sailed southwards for a little longer and then, after sniffing the wind, Ivar commanded the helmsman to turn and head for the setting sun. Leif felt sick with terror. Were they really going to sail across the open sea in the black of the night? And Ivar had accused him of wanting to get them killed. This was madness. Leif glanced behind. The whole fleet had turned in their wake and were following steadfastly. They might be doomed but they were not alone.

He sunk down to the deck and peered over the gunwale as the ship headed out into the vast black of the sea. Seagulls cried overhead, as if warning them of their folly. All too soon they fell back, no longer daring the risks which the Vikings seemed so keen to embrace.

The sun dipped towards the horizon, turning a bright, glowing red. A little later it settled upon the waters and it seemed to Leif that blood was leaching out of it to stain and poison the sea. Huge scarlet streaks surged into the sky, as if the whole sea were aflame. He closed his eyes at the horror of it but immediately opened them again, bewitched by the sunset's terrible beauty.

The wind from the land grew stronger and began to fill the sail. Ivar ordered the men to ship oars and there were many cries of relief at this.

The sky grew dim and, after a little while, all trace of light ebbed from the west. Leif glanced up. Stars began to appear in the deepening night, a wealth of jewels far richer than those that Ivar and his men were seeking. He shuddered at the chill beauty of them.

He glanced ahead and gasped in fear. He could barely see in front of him. But as his vision died so his other senses quickened. He felt the rise and fall of the ship, heard the hull crashing into the waves, the creak of the complaining timbers, the slap and crack of the sail. The scent of the sea grew strong in his nostrils, of waters full of sharp salt overlaid with a curiously clean yet bitter stink which gripped his nose and throat. But these senses could not show him the way and gave him no comfort. He was lost, blind, racing towards his doom.

He turned towards where Sigurd was sitting. He could not see him but could hear him snoring. He glared. It must be fortunate to go to one's death in such an unheeding manner. He aimed a kick at him but it did not wake him.

And then, out of the corner of his eye he saw a glint of silver on the eastern horizon. He breathed a sigh of thanks to Máni, god of the moon. He would be a lantern for them, he would lead the way to safety.

'Get some sleep,' Asgrim called to him. 'We reach land tomorrow and you'll need your wits about you.'

Leif settled himself down but sleep was slow in coming. Eventually his eyes began to droop. He glanced once more at the moon to be certain that it was still lighting the way and succumbed.

LANDFALL

Leif woke with a start. The sun had risen and was streaming onto his face. He glanced around. He was still in the longship, he had not drowned or been eaten by sea serpents. He sighed contentedly at his escape.

Most of the oarsmen were still asleep, Sigurd more deeply than most. For a moment he wondered whether to wake him but thought it better to let him get as much rest as possible. If there was going to be any trouble from the English he wanted his brother to be as strong and alert as possible.

His bladder was full and he could ignore it no longer. He climbed to his feet, unfastened his breeches and, clinging tightly to the gunwale, relieved himself in the sea.

'That won't increase it,' Asgrim said with a grin. He was wide awake and already chewing on a loaf of bread. He tore a lump from it and threw it to Leif who missed it and had to scramble to find it before it rolled into some inaccessible cranny.

'Thank you,' Leif said, gnawing on its hard crust. Asgrim was the only one of the crew who had given him anything other than curses and jeers.

'You've been friendly to me,' he said. 'I'm grateful.'

'Have I?' Asgrim said. 'I didn't mean to. I'll make sure not to do it again.' But he grinned as he said it, making clear it was a jest.

Asgrim was older than him, by twenty years or so. He was nick-named Traveller for even amongst the Vikings he was renowned for the seas he had sailed on and the lands he had crossed.

His face was burnt red by sea and sun, his hair beginning to turn white. His eyes were weary and wary, as if they had witnessed too many disquieting things. Leif suspected that he was the cause of many of them.

His arms were massive from pulling on an oar and wielding a sword in battle and they showed the scars of many wounds. His long questing nose had been broken more than once.

'How many times have you gone a-Viking?' Leif asked.

Asgrim opened his left hand five times. 'At least that,' he said.

He looked at his hand thoughtfully, as if trying to recall each of the raids he had been on. 'But never one as late in the year as this.'

Leif felt the grip of unease. 'Does this alarm you?'

Asgrim shrugged. 'The Norns will decide my fate and that of every man on this ship.'

'And you don't think that Ivar had a part to play in it? He's the one who decided to sail so late in the year.'

'Maybe that's because the Norns have decided his fate also.'

Leif sighed. Sometimes he wondered about the point of doing anything, what the use of making choices, having plans. He hated the idea of being the plaything of the gods.

'But sailing this late in the season?' Leif continued. 'Why do you think we're doing it?'

'For our advantage,' Asgrim said with a chuckle. 'I don't think Ivar gives a fuck about the Norns. He is his own man

46

and rules his own destiny. You should know that after telling us what he did to the Emperor of Miklagard.'

Leif almost told him that he had made the whole story up but thought better of it. A good story could be ruined by explanation.

Asgrim pointed to the west. 'There's the coast of England. We'll be there soon enough. Grab your spear and a shield.'

'I don't mean to do any fighting. I'm Ivar's Skald.'

'You know that and I know that. But I don't think an English warrior will realise.' He unhooked a shield from the gunwale and passed it to Leif. 'And wake your oaf of a brother. He may lack your wits but he's got enough strength and courage for the both of you.'

'He has,' Leif said absently as he stared anxiously at the coastline. 'We swapped our virtues with each other when we were children.'

'I think you may have made a bad choice. We always tell ourselves that the English are weak and cowardly but I've found it isn't the case. They're kin to us, you see, from long ago.'

'I've heard so. Is it true they can understand our speech?'

Asgrim nodded. 'And we their words, or at least most of them.'

Leif pondered this a moment, wondering if this would prove useful or not. Then he aimed a kick at Sigurd to wake him.

The coastline was low and flat, with a shingle beach good for securing the boats. Just behind lay a line of low sand-dunes. Two men sat on horseback on the largest dune, watching them approach. Then, as the fleet grew closer, they turned and rode off.

'Going to tell their lord, no doubt,' said Asgrim.

'Where are we?' Leif asked. 'Do you know?'

Asgrim studied the landscape for a moment. 'Judging by its look and our journey hither I would say we are in the Kingdom of the East Anglefolk, probably on the borders of the land of the south and north folk.'

'You're right, Asgrim,' said Ivar, hunkering down beside him. 'It was a deliberate choice. Most chieftains go for the richest targets, the churches, the fat towns. I go for the most useful.'

He pointed to the river in front of them. 'That's the river Waveney. It stretches a hundred miles inland and is the border between the north and the south folk. They may have been part of one kingdom for hundreds of years but they still think themselves different from each other.

'When terrible things happen, those differences grow stronger. And what can be more terrible than Ivar the Boneless and his brothers?' He gave a good-humoured laugh.

'We will sail up river, attacking settlements on either bank. The north folk will believe they have suffered the greatest harm and the south folk likewise. And in this way we will spread discord amongst them.'

'And presumably,' Leif said, 'if things go ill with us we can simply cross to the other bank.'

Ivar gave him an angry look. 'How can things go wrong for Ivar? How can the Christ followers stand against him?'

Then his anger subsided, so abruptly it seemed to have been fabricated.

He stared at the river thoughtfully. Then he gripped Leif firmly on the arm and lowered his voice. 'You're right, of course,

Skald,' he said. 'This too is part of my reason for attacking here. But don't ever tell anyone, not even my brothers.'

Leif shook his head. From now on, he thought, it might be wiser to keep his opinions to myself.

Or perhaps not. Ivar had obviously been surprised by his words. Perhaps it was no bad thing for him to realise he was not the only cunning and far-sighted man in the army, that Leif could do more than merely tell tales.

Not that Ivar seemed impressed for more than an instant. He pushed Leif out of the way without a word and took up position by the dragon-headed prow. The ship was now approaching the shore and two men readied themselves by the mast. Ivar watched the shore carefully and raised his hand. The sail was struck, the ship slowed and a moment later slid up the beach, sending shingle flying everywhere.

Ivar leapt to the shore and yelled in a huge voice: 'I am Ivar the Boneless and my brothers are Halfdan and Ubbe. We claim this kingdom for ourselves.'

Asgrim exchanged a look with Leif. 'I've never heard that before. I thought this was just another raid.'

'Ivar is not a normal Viking, then?' Leif said.

'Oh no. But I had not thought he wanted to conquer a kingdom.'

The rest of the crew followed the brothers off the ship. On either side more longships rode up onto the beach, halting abruptly like cats which have caught sight of a mouse. Their crews leapt onto the shingle and formed into ranks, shield high and spears thrusting, ready for trouble.

Ivar and his brothers seemed pleased with this display and immediately led the way up the dunes. Leif, Sigurd and Asgrim and the rest of the crew followed.

The morning sun lit up the land ahead of them. It looked a rich place, with rolling meadows dotted with flocks and herds, and many, many fields ripe with crops ready for harvest. A fat village was to the north and they could see that people were already streaming from it at the news of their landing.

'Do you think they will make good slaves?' Halfdan asked.

'Better than the Irish, so I hear,' said Ivar. 'Sullen and resentful at their plight but strong and hardy.'

'Then we should capture them,' Ubbe said.

Ivar shook his head. 'No. I don't want slaves, not yet. I want horses and supplies. And to do that we must judge our attacks to a nicety. We want to cause enough of a problem for the East Angles to choose to make peace rather than fight.'

'But the men are spoiling for a fight,' Halfdan said.

'There will be plenty of opportunities for that,' Ivar said. 'This is no raid for plunder, brothers, this is far, far more.'

His eyes opened wide with lust. Asgrim grinned with approval. Sigurd thought about horses and horse-shoes.

Leif felt sick.

'How many men does Ivar command?' he asked Asgrim, hoping that there would be more than enough to keep Sigurd and him safe.

'As many as you see,' Asgrim answered. 'I have not the skill to count them.'

Leif gave a look of surprise and turned to the fleet. He calculated that there were over sixty ships drawn up on the shore. Each had about thirty warriors so that meant Ivar's army numbered many more than a thousand, a truly immense number. He wondered whether the King of the East Angles would be able to speedily gather such a host.

He was soon to find out. Ivar led the men across the dunes to the nearby village.

It was deserted when they got there, even the most elderly and lame had managed to hobble to hiding places in the nearby woods.

The warriors went from house to house, stripping them bare. There was little of value: pots, pans, tools and knives with the occasional trinket, keepsake or coin. Discarded clothes were taken for the winter, whatever food or drink could be found, and some small wooden items which would do for swift-burning fire-wood. Only the hall provided anything of real value, some goodly clothing, three fine swords, some spears, jewels and coins in a strong box.

There was a small church at the far end of the village and this proved more profitable, as churches usually did. The men made off with a good haul of gold and jewels, together with fine fabrics. Ivar was most pleased with a sacred book decorated with lavish pictures of demons, flying women and tortured and dying holy men. 'It must be about a Viking attack,' he mused, stuffing the book into a sack.

A little after this a sudden wind blew in from the west and within minutes a fierce storm lashed the land. Although it was still only a few hours after noon, Ivar decided to spend the night in the village. The three lords and their chieftains settled into the hall with their closest companions. The rest found what shelter they could in the remaining huts, pig-sties and cow-sheds.

Leif and Sigurd had the good fortune to count as members of Ivar's crew and were allocated space within the hall. The warriors feasted well on the food that was found in the larders and drank even better of the good ale they found there.

Leif felt only relief at no longer being thrown around by the terrible sea and soon began to drift towards sleep. He searched out a space far from the cold air of the windows and lay down with his cloak wrapped around him, watching Sigurd taking part in a drinking contest.

So far, he thought, his new life was proving not so bad as he had feared.

THE KINGDOM OF THE EAST ANGLES

'Wake up,' Sigurd whispered into Leif's ear next morning. Leif struggled out of a deep sleep and looked around, uncertain for a moment where he was. He began to drift back to sleep but Sigurd shook him vigorously. 'Ivar has summoned us,' he said.

This woke Leif up. What could Ivar the Boneless want with them? He suspected it boded ill.

He pissed into an empty ale jug and followed Sigurd out of the hall.

They trudged through the cold dawn to the edge of the village, overlooking the river. The piercing cries of crows rang out from nearby trees. Leif shuddered. Too often these birds proved harbingers of disaster.

Ivar, Halfdan and Ubbe were deep in conversation with Guthrum. Leif's eyes narrowed. If Guthrum had not found them they would still be snug in their homeland instead of cast adrift on this dangerous venture.

'Welcome Skald,' Ivar said to Leif. 'I have good news for you.'

Leif cocked his head, careful to seem neither interested nor dismissive.

'I have decided to wait here with the fleet for a little while,' Ivar continued.

'That is good, my lord,' Leif said. 'I will be delighted to entertain you with tales and songs.'

'You won't have the chance,' Ivar said. 'I am sending Guthrum to seek out the King of the Angles. I need someone to bear witness to all that is said and done at their meeting. Guthrum will have to keep his wits about him while he negotiates with the king. I need somebody to remember all that is agreed. That will be you.'

Leif opened his mouth to argue but Ivar continued without noticing or taking breath. 'More importantly, I want you to try to listen beyond what their king says. In my experience frightened lords speak honeyed words which are coated with venom. I need you to detect the poison and tell me about it.'

'But I have no experience of such things, lord —'

'I care not for your excuses,' Ivar said. 'You leave immediately. As sign of my favour you may take your brother with you.' He stared at Guthrum. 'As may you, Guthrum. But remind Eohric that Leif and Sigurd are my men now. I will not have any harm come to them.'

'You can rely on me,' Guthrum said.

'I hope I can.' Ivar smiled but it was as cold as a winter frost.

'We go within the hour,' Guthrum said. 'Get your things.'

Asgrim was sympathetic at their plight and pressed a long knife into Leif's hand. 'In case of enemies,' he said.

'But surely the English will not dare to harm us.'

'I was talking about Eohric,' he said. 'I deem he has a strange madness and, for whatever reason, he has taken against you.'

'I could not fight Eohric.'

'No. But the knife may give him second thoughts about attacking you.' He gave Sigurd a skin of ale. 'For the journey,' he said.

The brothers headed outside but Asgrim called once more. 'Your spear, Leif. Don't forget your spear.'

Guthrum stood by the river watching his ship approach. Eohric turned and gave Leif a mocking smile but contented himself with that. Leif was grateful for Asgrim's gift of a knife. He hoped that Ivar's warning would be enough to constrain Eohric but the knife would be a good back up.

'I hear you're no oarsman,' Guthrum said to Leif. 'What can you do?'

'I'm a lookout,' Leif said, 'a good one.' He hoped that Guthrum had not heard otherwise.

'We'll soon find out the truth of it,' Guthrum said. 'We're heading to Norwic which is the biggest town in the kingdom. If the king of the Angles isn't there our arrival will be sure to draw him.'

Leif nodded, impressed by Guthrum's grasp of tactics.

'The rivers we travel will grow narrow,' he continued, 'so I need you to watch out for danger on either bank. I have no doubt we will be shadowed by English warriors so I want you to watch them closely. A few men are not to be feared. But if they act suspiciously let me know. I want forewarning of any trap up ahead.'

Leif forced down the sickness in his throat and nodded enthusiastically.

'What does he mean by the English acting suspiciously?' he hissed at Sigurd. It was a bad sign when he was forced to seek advice of his brother.

'When they gloat, I suppose.'

'When they gloat?'

Sigurd nodded. 'Knowing that we're about to die.'

Leif shook his head wearily. But maybe, just maybe, there was some wisdom in Sigurd's words.

They clambered onto the ship. Sigurd was directed to take an oar and Leif settled himself in the prow. 'When they gloat,' he muttered under his breath. 'It's more likely the first suspicious sign will be an arrow in my throat.'

His fears grew as the ship moved up river. The land was flat, the current was slow and the river meandered in great loops, turning from west to east and then to north and back to west again. But little by little they moved deeper into the kingdom.

As the day wore on the river began to narrow. Leif's neck grew stiff from constant turning to look at either bank, his eyes ached from peering so intently for any sign of danger. Occasionally he would spy horsemen on one side of the bank or the other. At first he alerted Guthrum every time he saw this and Guthrum would join him in the prow to watch intently for a while. But eventually, seeing they made no move other than to shadow them, and being too far away to know whether their faces were gloating, bored or fearful, Leif stopped raising the alarm.

At length as the daylight began to fail, the river turned straight towards the north. On the eastern bank stood a line of stone walls, perhaps a dozen feet high, with round towers at regular intervals.

'What's that?' Leif asked in amazement.

One of the oarsmen spat into the water. 'A fortress built by demons,' he said. 'A deadly place.'

Leif was surprised at his words. A fortress seemed to him the safest place to spend the night.

But as the longship passed beneath the walls many of the men grasped the hammer-shaped amulets they wore about their neck and breathed prayers to Thor to protect them. Even Guthrum's hand went to an amulet although, apart from Leif, he was the only one to scrutinise the walls.

The ship suddenly entered a wider expanse of water, silent and tranquil, shimmering in the last of the sunlight, dotted with ducks and geese. Guthrum signalled to his men to stop rowing. They obeyed the moment the words had left his mouth. It had been a gruelling day of constant oar-work.

Guthrum strode towards the prow of the ship and glanced across the waters. 'What think you, lookout?' he asked. 'Do you smell the sea?'

Leif sniffed and thought he could just detect a hint of salt on the air. 'Perhaps, my lord,' he said. 'But I think they may be a truer sign.' He pointed east to where a flock of seagulls swooped and banked.

Guthrum grunted. 'We don't want to go that way.' He peered across the waters more intently. 'The river grows wider here which suggests it will soon empty into the ocean.'

'There's another river there,' Leif said, pointing to the west.

A second river, wider than the one they had journeyed on, emptied into the river basin.

Guthrum followed his gaze and smiled. 'That would appear the way we should take although these rivers twist and turn more than a liar's tales.'

He fell silent for a moment longer and then made up his mind. 'We will rest here for the night and decide tomorrow.'

'Perhaps we could find a villager,' Leif said. 'Ask him the way.'

Guthrum frowned. 'Why would an Englishman speak truthfully to us? Unless he is suffering torment.'

They slept fitfully under the stars. A cold wind blew from the waters to the north, and Leif found his cloak too thin to keep the piercing blasts from his flesh. He was glad when the sun rose, tinting the waters the red of a robin's winter breast.

His pleasure lasted no more than a few heartbeats. Two hundred yards away stood scores of men, staring at him with vicious, angry faces.

'Wake up,' he cried. 'Wake up.'

Guthrum was the first to respond, leaping up as soon as his eyes opened. He cursed aloud and drew his sword. The rest of the men scrambled to their feet.

'Where are the pickets?' Eohric yelled.

Guthrum shook his head. 'Overwhelmed, I guess. Before they could shout warning.'

'Do we fight them?' Leif asked nervously.

Guthrum looked at him with contempt. 'Do you think I'm mad. There are four times our number.'

'But peasants most of them,' Eohric said. 'Maybe a score of well -warriors.'

He was right. The first rank of men bore shields, spears and wore mail or leather breast-plates. The rest were farmers and field workers and had no armour. Some bore spears or knives but most wielded staffs or sickles or cudgels. They looked terrified.

'Most of them are armed with clubs,' Eohric sneered.

'A club wielded even by a peasant can smash your skull,' Guthrum said angrily. He glanced from the men to the ship.

'I want a shield wall of a dozen men while the rest prepare the ship.'

Twenty men scrambled aboard the longship, grabbing oars and unhitching the ropes which held it fast to the bank. At the same moment the English yelled in fury and began to advance.

'Can we hold them?' Leif asked.

'Long enough to get the ship ready,' Guthrum said.

'Then what?'

'Then the rest of us wade out to get on board. And if you don't stop your half-wit questions I'll leave you behind to protect our rear.'

Leif turned to watch the men on the ship feverishly making ready to leave. But then something else caught his eye. Flaming arrows flew from beyond the English line and thudded onto the ship. Some caught in the blankets and ropes upon the deck. One lodged in the furled sail and begin to smoulder.

'Shit,' cried Guthrum. 'We have a clever foe.'

'And there he is,' Leif yelled.

To the rear of the English was a man beside a small fire. It was he who was overseeing the bowmen, pushing them to the fire to light their arrows and then directing them where to aim. He saw that Leif had spotted him and directed his men to shoot more swiftly.

'The ship, Guthrum,' called the helmsman. 'The ship will soon be aflame.'

Guthrum turned at his call. The crewmen were using buckets to draw water from the river and just about managing to keep the flames from spreading. But ever more arrows thudded onto the ship and it was clear they would soon lose the battle.

Guthrum made up his mind. 'A dozen of you back to the shield-wall,' he bellowed. 'The rest take the ship out of reach of the arrows.'

'You don't mean to try to hold this ground with two dozen men?' Leif asked in horror.

'No,' he answered. 'I intend to slaughter these bastards.'

The rest of the crew joined them in the shield-wall. Guthrum strode a yard or two in front of them and flung his arm towards the Englishmen.

'There's four score men out there,' he cried. 'Four men to every one of us. If they were warriors, we would be sore put to battle them. But they're not. They are peasants, thralls and young boys. Little better than the sheep or cows they tend to.'

He laughed aloud. 'Are Vikings frightened of sheep and cows?'

'No,' yelled some of his men, laughing along with him.

'Then let us slaughter these beasts as we would do in readiness for the winter months.'

And with that he charged.

A low groan of fear rose from the English ranks. They saw well enough that they were being attacked by one lone warrior but he was huge and strong looking and a Viking with a grim and ferocious mien. Their courage wavered and they glanced at each other to see what they should do.

And then Guthrum reached them.

He smashed into the front rank of warriors. They may have been well-armed but few had ever fought in a battle before. Two men fell beneath his onslaught, battered by the force of impact. He slashed open the neck of a third man and hacked the sword arm of a fourth before he could take a swing.

But then a cry came from the rear of his enemies. 'He's only one man. Kill him, kill him.'

Guthrum glanced up. The cry came from the man who was directing the bowmen. Now he grabbed a spear and charged down the hill towards him.

His words put heart into the English and they began to jab their spears at Guthrum. He parried them as swiftly as he could but he realised he would soon be overwhelmed.

But then, with a mighty roar, the rest of his men crashed into the English line. They may have been only twenty men against near a hundred but they were experienced, deadly and the danger to their lord had made them furious and vengeful. Swords rose and fell, spears thrust home and the Englishmen fell like wheat before autumn harvesters.

Even Leif felt the fire of combat rage in him and as he jabbed with his spear he marvelled at it. He had no liking for Guthrum and a mighty liking for himself but he pushed forward with the rest of the warriors as if heedless at the thought of death.

A spear graze to his cheek ended this brief blaze of courage. The man who had made the thrust stared at him, his eyes wide with fear or fury, and made another lunge. Leif side-stepped in terror, and then he saw Sigurd's spear plunge into the neck of his enemy. Blood spurted from the wound and the man fell.

A second man replaced the spearman and squared up to the brothers. He was larger even than Sigurd and he bore a club so huge that Leif wondered at its purpose. Killing bulls, perhaps.

But he had no time to ponder more for the man raised his club and brought it down on them. Sigurd managed to raise his shield in time but the blow knocked him to his knees.

Leif yelled, part-warning, part-alarm at his brother's plight, part-terror. He turned towards the giant, spear thrusting feebly towards him. The man gave a contemptuous laugh and raised his club above Leif's head.

But before he had time to strike, a sword blade pierced his chest. He looked down in surprise as blood belched around the wound. Then Guthrum withdrew his blade and slashed the man across his waist, opening the flesh so deep Leif could see the coils of his guts. The Englishman shook his head ruefully as if he had been bested at a game and slid to the ground.

Leif nodded his thanks to Guthrum.

'Couldn't let Ivar's Skald die,' he said, and returned to the attack once again.

It was over a few moments later. The peasants lost all heart for further battle and fled hotfoot from the fray.

Guthrum yelled to his men to hold fast. But then he spied the man who had directed the arrows against his ship.

The man stood hesitant as the rest of his friends raced past him, almost as if he had a mind to stand and fight alone. But then he turned and began to stride after them.

Furious at the man who had almost destroyed his ship, heedless of his own command, Guthrum leapt after him.

Although a huge man he was astonishingly fast. Within moments he had closed the distance to his foe.

The man must have heard for he suddenly glanced over his shoulder and saw Guthrum. His eyes widened in horror. He started to run.

Guthrum forced his legs even faster but the Englishman, unwearied by battle and with the goad of terror, began to outstrip him. The Vikings cheered on their chieftain although a few offered bets that he would not win and yelled in support of the Englishman.

It seemed for a short while that they would win the wager for the space between hunter and prey widened. Then something shot from Guthrum's hand, a throwing axe, and hammered into the Englishman's back. His legs buckled and he fell.

Guthrum was on him in an instant and hauled him to his feet. He laughed in triumph and dragged the man back towards his waiting crew.

PLANS GONE AWRY

The English captive was thrown onto the ship, his arms and legs bound by thick cords. He struggled to get free but Eohric smashed him in the face and he decided to keep still.

The longship headed into the river which Leif had spied earlier. There was no sign of anyone on either bank, the land appeared deserted. Guthrum stared about him cautiously for a little while and decided that they were in no immediate danger.

'Come here, Skald,' he called. 'I would have your ears for my questioning of the prisoner.'

Leif hurried to him, thankful to no longer bear the responsibility of spying out the land.

Guthrum kicked the captive in the side and hunkered down beside him.

'Who are you?' he asked. 'A jarl, one of the King's captains?'

The man gave a mocking laugh and shook his head. 'I am a Leech, a humble healer, nothing more.'

Guthrum and Leif exchanged glances.

'A healer,' Guthrum said. 'You've done more harm than healing this day.'

'It is you who did harm,' the man replied. 'You have come with fire and sword into our land.'

'It was your fire which nearly did for my ship.'

The man chuckled. 'A little longer and it would have been consumed.'

Leif glanced up at the mast. The sail was still furled but he could see holes where the fire had taken. He wondered if it would be able to take the wind any more.

'So, tell me why a leech was directing the battle,' Guthrum continued. 'Why not the lord of these parts?'

'Because Lulla is a fool. And a coward as well.'

'So he told you to direct the battle?'

The leech shook his head. 'He had no idea of the danger. He can barely tell a cloud from a tree.'

Guthrum folded his arms. He did not like men who were contemptuous of their lord. But neither did he like lords who were stupid or cowardly.

'What is your name, Leech?' he asked.

'Tell me yours and I will tell you mine.'

Guthrum buffeted the man across the head. 'You're in no position to demand anything, thrall. I asked you a question. What is your name?'

The man remained silent for a while. 'Deor,' he said eventually. He gazed into Guthrum's face, his eyes unblinking and unafraid.

Guthrum glanced up at Leif who merely shrugged in a non-committal manner.

'And I am Guthrum.' He said it with a mixture of grudge and respect. 'I am chieftain of these men and a hundred more.'

'You won't be much longer,' Deor said.

'Why so?' Guthrum's eyes flashed angrily.

Deor nodded towards Guthrum's left arm. A long, ugly gash went from wrist to elbow, the blood still seeping red.

'It is nothing,' Guthrum said. 'A scratch does not kill a man.'

'That one will,' Deor said. 'I see signs of pus already, the start of wound-rot. If the arm is cut off in the next few days you may live, perhaps. But if it's not cut off, you're a walking corpse.'

Guthrum scoffed at his words but Leif could tell he was concerned, although unwilling to show it.

'Enough of your prattle, Leech,' he continued. 'I would know where your king is. Does such an accomplished healer and warrior have an idea of his whereabouts?'

'I do.' Deor sighed. 'Edmund is at Norwic, dallying with his churchmen and his women.'

'He likes both?' Guthrum said. 'I thought the Christ-followers despised women-folk.'

'If they did,' Deor said, 'they would disappear from the world. Christ-followers are keen to breed offspring to follow the faith. A man can kneel both to pray to God and to enter a woman. Edmund is proof of that.'

'You don't like the king, it seems,' said Leif.

Deor shrugged. 'Why should I care for any man who rules over others?'

'There have to be lords,' said Guthrum.

'Do there?' Deor gave a dismissive shrug. 'Lords like Lulla and King Edmund we can do without.' He gave a sidelong look at Guthrum. 'As we can do without Guthrum and his wolves.'

Guthrum laughed aloud. 'You have courage, Leech, I give you that.'

'Dead men can afford to be brave.'

Leif frowned. 'What makes you think you're a dead man.'

'I'm a captive of the Vikings,' Deor said. 'I now measure my life in breaths not days.'

'You shall live a while longer yet,' said Guthrum. 'I need to know all I can about this kingdom and its king.'

'What is to tell?' Deor said. 'East Anglia was once the greatest kingdom in this island. Then the Mercian king attacked, conquered us and stole our wealth and pride. We have our independence once again, but Edmund bows his knee to the Saxon king of the far west.'

'Saxon king?'

'Æthelred of Wessex and his pup of a brother.'

'And King Edmund? Will he prove a strong foe to us?'

'He's a young man but not, I deem, a warrior. As I said, he worships God and the cunny in equal measure.'

Guthrum clapped him on the shoulder. 'He sounds like a man I can deal honestly with.'

Deor laughed. 'Can a wolf be honest?'

'As honest as a leech, I deem.'

Guthrum stood up and stared at Leif. 'Did you hear all this? And do you reckon the leech speaks true?'

Leif swallowed, nervous at giving the wrong answer. 'I heard it all. Whether he speaks truth or not, only Odin can be certain.'

'A clever answer but a craven one. Come man, tell me what you think. Ivar tells me you have great intelligence and greater cunning. I don't want your cunning now. I want your intelligence and your honesty.'

Leif sighed and turned to stare at the captive. 'I think he speaks truthfully,' he said. 'He has no reason to tell us the shameful history of this kingdom and no reason to deride his king. He is a man who sees much and is not afraid to think for himself.'

'Then he should be an inspiration for you, Leif. You'll never be a warrior but if you use your brains you may yet prove of service to Ivar. And to me.'

He dismissed Leif but he remained a moment longer.

'One thing, more, my lord,' he said. 'You would do well to ask Deor if this river leads to Norwic.'

Guthrum laughed. 'Already learnt the lesson, I see. But fear not, Skald, I had thought to ask this without your prompting.'

Leif's insides squirmed but Guthrum did not seem angered by his presumption, merely amused. Not so his brother. He had been listening all the while and now shot a vicious look at Leif as he returned to the prow.

Guthrum sent two parties of men to scout up the river in search of enemies. They returned just before noon. There was no sign of any on either bank.

Deor told them that the river was called the Yare. It headed in long, meandering loops towards the west where another river, the Wensum, flowed into it. The town of Norwic lay two miles west of where the two rivers joined.

The Vikings rowed up the river at a slower pace than the previous day. Guthrum wanted to rest the men after the recent battle and to regain their strength for any future ones. They were more than content to set a slower pace.

Guthrum seemed restless and walked continually from one end of the ship to the other. Leif noticed that whenever he stopped he would hold up his arm and examine the wound. The Leech would smile grimly at this.

An hour before daylight fell, Guthrum ordered a halt. Here the River Wensum flowed into the Yare, creating a small islet where the Vikings made camp. This time, Guthrum doubled the number of pickets and threatened to slay any one of them who fell asleep. None of the men complained.

He questioned Deor thoroughly about Norwic. He said it was a huge town, spreading along either bank of the river Wensum, with four thousand people dwelling there.

Guthrum scoffed at this figure. 'That's three times larger than our war-host. Bigger than any settlement in Denmark.'

'It will provide plenty of warriors to fight you,' Deor said. 'More than enough to destroy you and all your men.'

Guthrum rubbed his wound anxiously for a moment.

'Does the city have any fortifications?' he asked.

'A wooden palisade on the northern bank of the river.'

'And churches, monasteries?' Eohric asked, his eyes glinting in the light of the fire.

'Four churches and two monasteries.'

Eohric rubbed his hands with glee.

'We're not here for plunder,' Guthrum growled. 'Ivar told us to seek out King Edmund and discuss how he would accommodate the war-host.'

'We ask a favour of him?' Eohric asked. 'We beg instead of take?'

Guthrum gave him a thoughtful look. 'Do you question the sons of Ragnar Lothbrok?'

Eohric's eyes narrowed and he shook his head, nervously.

'And do you question me?'

Eohric paused a little before mumbling no.

'Make sure of it. Blood is thicker than water but blood is easily spilt.'

The next morning proved the truth of his words.

Guthrum woke from a sleepless night. He had flung off his cloak, despite the chill of night, and complained of feeling hot. He climbed to his feet but staggered and snatched up a spear to keep himself upright.

'Does something ail, you lord?' Leif asked anxiously. He realised that Guthrum was the only thing standing between him and Eohric's malice.

Guthrum shook his head. 'Just the night airs and bites from river midges.'

Leif nodded but then took a sudden step forward. 'Guthrum, your arm.'

Guthrum lifted his arm and screwed up his face in distaste. The wound was hectic red and running with yellow pus. The skin around it was dark blue in colour, raised up and covered with angry blisters.

Leif stepped forward to examine it and recoiled immediately. The stench from the wound almost made him vomit.

'I'll get the Leech,' he said.

Guthrum started to argue, fearing the impression this would give to his men, but felt too weary to do so. He slid down upon the floor and bowed his head as Leif ran to fetch Deor.

'It's wound-rot,' the Leech said, after the most cursory glance. 'I warned him yesterday.'

'Can you do anything?'

Deor shrugged. 'I might be able to. But why should I?

'Because we will free you, give you your life.'

Deor stared into his eyes. 'Can you make such a promise? You do not seem a great warrior, nor does your leader treat you with respect. His men even less so.'

'I can make this promise,' Leif said with more confidence than he felt. 'I am the Skald of Ivar the Boneless, highly placed in his service.'

Deor looked doubtful for a moment. But he had little to lose and much to gain.

'I cannot swear to heal him,' he said. 'But he's a strong man and the wound is just beginning to fester so there may be some chance. Fetch me two strong men and the sharpest knife you can find.'

Leif remembered the only other wound-rot he had seen and shuddered. 'You mean to cut off his arm?'

'If I did, I would ask for an axe. No, I intend to cut away the source of the poison. Now hurry.'

Leif returned with Sigurd, Thorvald the helmsman, and a very sharp knife.

Eohric was squatting by his brother, glaring murderously at the Leech. 'If he dies, I shall flay you alive,' he hissed.

'No you won't,' said Guthrum. 'The man is a healer and his pride will make him do his utmost.'

Deor laughed. 'You are wiser than I thought possible for a Dane.'

'Get on and do what you must.'

Two men returned from the river bearing buckets of water. Deor sniffed at it, plunged in a rag and began to wipe at the wound. They could hear a faint sound of ulcers popping and the stench wafted towards them like the wind from a midden. Leif gagged. Eohric shuffled back a little.

Deor gestured to Sigurd and Thorvald.

Thorvald was smaller than Sigurd but stocky and with massive arms. He had the bull neck and face of a mastiff. He looked every bit as strong as Sigurd.

'Hold him down,' Deor said. 'As firmly as you can.'

Then he took the knife and began to scrape away at the wound. Guthrum's strength and courage almost failed him but he managed to clamp his mouth shut and make no noise.

Deor worked swiftly, gouging out the most discoloured flesh and slicing off the blisters. Blood ran everywhere and he allowed it to do so. 'A little like flaying, isn't it?' he said to Eohric with a chuckle.

Eohric cursed him but did not move.

At last, with Guthrum's arm awash with blood and his head lolling with pain, Deor stopped his butchery work. He reached into his bag and pulled out a jar with a wooden stopper, some leaves and a long, narrow piece of cloth.

Swiftly he wiped Guthrum's arm with the wet rag, revealing how deeply he had cut. Then he reached into the jar and pulled out a fistful of maggots. He slapped these into the wound, placed the leaves on top of them and then wound the cloth around Guthrum's arm, fastening it with a knot and a couple of pins. He leaned back on his haunches and pronounced himself satisfied.

'Will he live?' Eohric asked.

Deor shrugged. 'He might. But I would pray to your gods if I were you. If the wound gets worse I shall have to remove his arm. And then...' He left the rest of the sentence unspoken.

'We cannot go to Norwic now,' Thorvald said.

'Why not?' said Eohric. 'My brother will recover or not as much in his longship as in this fetid isle.'

'I didn't mean that,' Thorvald said. 'We need him to talk with the king.'

'I can do that,' Eohric replied.

Thorvald stared at him silently for a little while. Then he shook his head. 'I don't think so. Such talk calls for a calmer man than you, a man more far-seeing and subtle. We shall have to wait until Guthrum recovers.'

'That will take many days,' Deor said. 'The fever has already begun to take him and will grow worse. He will begin to ramble and talk nonsense, hardly the display you wish to give to King Edmund.'

'Then we shall have to wait here,' Thorvald said. 'Unless…' And he turned to Leif and put his hand on his shoulder.

KING EDMUND

King Edmund's hall was situated on the north bank of the River Wensum, on the eastern edge of Norwic, close to the palisade. It was bigger than any hall Leif or Sigurd had seen, large enough to feast a hundred men with ease.

They exchanged nervous looks. Their dealings with wealthy men had rarely been easy, forced to endure a continual series of complaints about the quality of their work and haggling over price. And now they were entering the hall of the wealthiest man they could ever imagine.

'Are you sure about having me speak to the English king?' Leif asked Thorvald anxiously.

The helmsman smiled grimly. 'More sure than having Eohric do it. We wouldn't leave the hall alive if he were to speak for us.'

'Should I pretend to be Guthrum? To give myself more authority?'

'You claimed the authority of Ivar when you promised the Leech his life. You can boast the same here.' And with that he pushed Leif towards the door-wards.

'Vikings,' said one of the men, suspiciously. 'Some of your kin are traders in our city. Do you wish to negotiate such rights? Do you come in war or in peace?'

His speech sounded strange to their ears, with less iron and strength than their own tongue, but they could understand it well enough.

'We come for many purposes,' said Thorvald. 'But our leader will talk with your king, not with you.' He gestured towards Leif who gave a sick smile.

'Have you weapons?' the door-ward asked.

Thorvald pulled his sword from its scabbard and handed it to the guard. Leif and Sigurd gave over their knives.

The door-ward considered them for a little longer. 'This seems strange,' he said to Thorvald at last. 'You have the sword and the manner of a warrior. Yet your companions act like common tradesmen and you say that one of them is your leader.'

Thorvald did not reply. The man gave them a final, puzzled look before opening the doors.

The hall appeared larger inside than out. This was because it was astonishingly bright. There were dozens of windows with shutters wide-open, rush-lights burned on every bench and torches flickered upon the walls. And the walls were white, covered with lime-wash to catch every last drop of light from sun and flame.

Leif could not imagine the wealth and power of a king who owned a hall so splendid. Richer than the kings of Denmark and of Frankland. Richer perhaps than even the Emperor of golden Miklagard? And now he had to barter with him.

Half a dozen men sat at a high table at the rear of the hall. From their age and apparel they appeared to be powerful lords, perhaps advisers to the king. They watched with curious, wary eyes as the three men approached.

'Who are you?' one called as they got close. 'What do Vikings seek from King Edmund?'

Thorvald pushed Leif forward.

'My name is Leif Ormson,' he said. Even to his own ears his voice sounded weak and tremulous. 'I am Skald and adviser to the great Viking lord, Ivar the Boneless.'

The English lords gasped at the name of Ivar. They stared at one another, words failing them, their eyes resting finally on the youngest man amongst them.

He wore a simple tunic adorned with a single golden jewel upon his chest. His eyes had widened considerably at Leif's words and now he chewed on his bottom lip. Finally, he clenched his hands and leaned forward.

'I am Edmund, King of East Anglia,' he said. 'Step closer and say what you must.'

He gave a swift signal. Two dozen warriors appeared on either side, swords unsheathed and pointing at the Vikings.

Leif coughed to clear what felt like rocks clogging his throat. When he spoke, his voice was little more than a croak. 'Lord Ivar and his brothers Halfdan and Ubbe have arrived on your shores in a fleet of sixty ships.' He paused, uncertain what to say next.

He had no need for concern. The name of Ivar had caused dismay amongst the Angles. The size of the fleet threw them into state of consternation.

Edmund was the first to control himself and raised his hand for silence. 'Sixty ships do not come to trade,' he said.

'Sixty ships hold more twelve hundred warriors,' Leif said. He could sense the panic flowing from the king's advisers.

But Edmund shrugged, as if unconcerned. 'I can put four times that number of thegns into battle, ten times that number of fyrdmen.'

'Which is why we have come to talk,' Leif said.

But, in contradiction to these words, he fell silent once more, desperately wondering what to say. He had not realised that Edmund's kingdom was so powerful and wondered if Ivar had either. Any threat he could make seemed pointless and futile against such a mighty power.

The silence grew longer, unbearably longer.

Leif began to panic, uncertain how to respond and believing his silence marked him as a fool. At the same time, Edmund and his advisers grew apprehensive, ascribing all manner of threat and disaster to his silence. Ivar could never wreak havoc as dreadful as the doom their imaginations began to conjure up.

'Then talk,' Edmund said from behind gritted teeth. 'Say what your master bids you.'

Leif swallowed, having no idea what Ivar wanted. Only Guthrum knew this and he was in his ship, fighting a losing battle with his wound and fever.

'Ivar wants winter quarters for his men,' Leif said, desperately clutching at any straw. 'Food, lodging, and servants.'

Edmund did not respond for a moment. The man to his right bent and whispered something in his ear.

'I can give this,' Edmund said at last, 'for three months. Until after the Christmas feast.'

Leif glanced at Thorvald who refused to give him eye-contact. The helmsman was as much at a loss as Leif, it seemed.

He looked at his brother who seemed equally baffled. But looking at Sigurd made him suddenly realise something. This was just like bargaining for the price of a sword or a scythe. On a grander scale but, in essence, just the same.

'Three months is not long enough,' Leif said.

He took a deep breath, feeling himself on familiar ground now. 'Three months will take us to the coldest, bleakest months of the year. We need quarters until the spring.'

Edmund and his advisers huddled together, their voices hissing like angry cats. Thorvald glanced at Leif doubtfully, his face showing he thought that he had over-played his hand.

Finally, the Englishmen grew silent. Edmund drew back his shoulders. 'Quarters until the spring, it is' he said. 'But I insist that your army be divided into four divisions. And I will decide where they are settled.'

'That is satisfactory,' Leif said. 'You know where your best pastures lie. We ask only that they are close to rivers so our ships can come and go.'

Edmund's face grew grim but eventually he gave a curt nod. 'Is that all you desire?' he asked, his voice thick with sarcasm.

Leif blinked in surprise. So, the king's barbed words were the strongest weapon he dared to wield. And, moreover, these words had given Leif an opening.

'I'm glad you asked,' he said with a winning smile. 'When we leave your kingdom in the spring we will need horses for all our warriors.'

The faces of King and advisers turned to stone.

'For all your warriors?' said the man to the king's right.

'For all twelve hundred.'

'Preposterous,' cried the man. 'We could not provide so many mounts.'

Leif shrugged. 'In that case, we shall be forced to remain here for longer.'

He made to leave but Edmund raised his hand to stop him.

'I agree,' he said. His voice was little more than a whisper. 'But you must swear oaths that you will leave by two months after twelfth night.'

'I accept,' said Leif. He turned on his heel and marched down the hall, followed by the others.

'When's twelfth night?' he asked Thorvald as they collected their weapons.

'It's twelve days after Yule,' he said. 'Which means we stay until the beginning of March.'

He slapped Leif on the shoulder with delight. 'I'm proud of you, my friend. And I think Ivar will be as well. I doubt Guthrum could have done better.'

Leif beamed with pleasure. His mind leapt with thoughts of a bountiful future. He would, indeed, become Ivar's chief adviser, he would receive much treasure, fine clothes, a comely hall and beautiful women to share his bed. Maybe his new life would not be as bad as he feared.

He glanced in triumph at his brother. Sigurd merely scowled.

RETURN TO IVAR

Guthrum was still raving in his fever when they returned to the longship. Eohric claimed leadership of the men but there was immediate dissent and Thorvald was chosen in his stead. Eohric raged and refused to take his oar, standing beside the helm as Guthrum had done. There was much anger at this but none dared challenge him too openly. In the end, Thorvald took the helm with a dark look at Eohric and steered the ship back down the river.

They made better time now as the current of the river aided their progress and a westerly wind enabled them to use the sail. Within a day they reached the place where they had been attacked.

'We should camp in that great fortress,' Leif said to Thorvald. 'We would be safe from attack there.'

'So speaks the great Skald and spokesman for Boneless,' sneered Eohric. He spat at Leif's foot. 'Demons and monsters dwell in such places. We would be mad to go there.'

Thorvald looked thoughtful but, in the end, shook his head. 'It's too risky,' he said. 'We do not want to incur the wrath of any gods or demons so deliberately.'

Later, as they camped by the river, he approached Leif and squatted beside him. He stared into the darkness for a while and then sighed. 'You may have been right about the fortress,' he said. 'I almost ordered the men to camp there.'

'Why didn't you?'

'I am not their lord,' he said, 'except for a little while. I doubt I would have been able to persuade them. And if I had done so and demons appeared…' He fell silent as he contemplated such a dread situation.

'You're clever, Leif,' he continued, at last. 'Wise men such as Ivar and Guthrum will make use of your wits. But fools, and especially arrogant fools like Eohric, will resent your wisdom and seek to harm you. Remember this.'

He got up to leave.

'And are you a wise man, Thorvald?' Leif asked.

Thorvald chuckled. 'Wiser than most. Which is why I choose you as my friend.'

Sigurd grunted when the helmsman was out of hearing. 'I wouldn't trust him, little brother. He is too watchful. Just like Eohric.'

Leif shook his head. 'I don' t think so, Sigurd. Some men watch others to protect themselves from attack or purely out of curiosity. I think Thorvald is one of these. Others, like Eohric, watch only to find the opportunity for malice and cruelty.'

'And they, as often as not, are our masters.'

Leif did not answer for a while. 'I don't intend that to be the case for us anymore,' he said finally. His voice bore a new, determined tone.

The next morning, Thorvald sniffed the air and made the decision not to return by the winding river they had taken before but to head to the open sea a few miles east and then sail down the coast to join Ivar's fleet.

They were followed by a mob of seagulls as they left the calm of the river and breasted the waves. A stiff northerly breeze filled the sail and they swept down the coast at speed, arriving at the fleet before noon.

The longships still lay where they had beached and a wooden fortification had been thrown up beside it. Inside stood half a dozen tents.

Thorvald steered the longship close to the fortress and the crew disembarked to loud shouts of welcome. These shouts turned to groans at the sight of Guthrum.

He was placed on a make-shift stretcher of oars and shields and carried up the slope to the fortress. He was still locked in a fierce fever but his raving had grown quieter and more intermittent.

Deor the Leech walked beside the stretcher, his face full of foreboding. He had confided in Thorvald only that morning that he believed that Guthrum's arm would have to be amputated. He prayed that he was not the one to do the job. If anything went wrong he knew that he would be slain.

Ivar and his brothers had seen the longship return and hurried down to greet them. They looked alarmed at Guthrum's condition. Thorvald swiftly told them all that had happened.

'Will he survive?' Ivar asked Deor. His voice was icy with threat.

'That is in the hands of your gods,' Deor answered.

Leif glanced at him, surprised that he should speak of Norse gods instead of the Christ.

'Then we must pray to Eir to heal him,' Ivar said. 'Take him to my tent. Go with him, Leech. If he dies, I'll throttle you with my own hands.'

Eohric grinned at the thought of this, although he would prefer to be the one doing the throttling.

'Why are you smiling, boy?' Ivar said. 'You should be fretting about your brother. And fretting even more about what will become of you, should he die.'

Eohric's smile was replaced by a look of terror.

Leif glanced away, worried that Ivar would notice his pleasure at how he had dealt with Eohric. He was not swift enough.

'You two are still the best of comrades, then?' Ivar said, punching him on the shoulder. His voice, however, held no trace of condemnation.

He looked from Leif to Eohric and back again, his eyes growing more thoughtful. 'My advice to you, Leif, is to keep clear of Eohric,' he said, 'even more so if Guthrum dies. Guthrum can keep his brother in check. I do not have the time.'

He turned to Thorvald. 'Did Guthrum speak with the English king?'

Thorvald shook his head. 'He was already too far gone in his fever. We left him on the ship. The men chose me to take his place.'

'Not Eohric?' asked Ubbe in surprise.

Thorvald shook his head.

'The men were wise,' Ivar said. 'You shall remain leader of Guthrum's men until he recovers. And thereafter, if he doesn't.'

Eohric cried out and stepped close to Ivar, his fists clenched.

Ivar turned to face him, his face calm yet threatening. 'You seek to dispute my decision? You may be a jarl's son but I am Ivar the Boneless.'

Eohric glared at him a moment longer, then hung his head.

'Get out of my sight, boy. Go to your brother's side. And if the leech asks for anything make sure you fetch it.'

Eohric slunk off after the stretcher.

'So,' Halfdan asked Thorvald. 'Did anybody speak to the king?'

'I went to his hall,' Thorvald said. 'But I deem I am a man of few words and they are rough-hewn. I took the skald Leif with me and he spoke for us.'

The brothers exchanged astonished looks. Leif began to shiver with fear.

'He did well,' Sigurd said suddenly. 'My brother did well.'

Ivar glanced at him a moment, then folded his arms and stared at Leif. His eyes twinkled with amusement.

'Tell me, Leif,' he said, 'exactly how did you do well?'

Leif went red in the face. 'I struck a bargain with the English king.'

Halfdan went to speak but Ivar silenced him with a look.

'Tell us more.'

'Neither Thorvald nor I knew what Guthrum was going to say to Edmund,' Leif said. 'Did not know what you had commanded him. So I had to decide for myself.'

'You had no right —' Halfdan cried.

'Peace, brother,' Ivar said. 'Let us not condemn the man before we hear all of his tale.'

Leif gulped and forced himself to continue.

'I told the king that we wanted quarters, secure quarters with good shelter and plenty of food.'

'We can take all that for ourselves,' Halfdan cried. 'We told Guthrum to demand treasure: coins, gold, jewels, precious books, slaves.'

'We did not know that,' Leif answered.

'A Viking would know it. But not a ceorl such as you.'

Ivar held up his hand for silence. 'Continue your tale, Leif,' he commanded.

'Edmund agreed to my request very quickly,' he said, 'but offered to quarter us for only two months. I demanded he provide for us for two months after Yule. And he agreed.'

Ivar's eyes widened with respect.

'You did well,' Ubbe said. 'That will take us to the spring.'

'And then what?' Halfdan asked. 'This will only give the Angles time to ready their forces and we will be slaughtered in our tents.'

Leif swallowed hard. 'I assume that wise leaders will guard against such a danger,' he said.

He felt Thorvald's fingers dig into his shoulder, a warning to control his tongue.

'There is more,' the helmsman said. 'Leif bargained for more.' He gave Leif a little shove.

'Horses,' Leif continued. 'I demanded that the Angles provide a thousand horses for our warriors.'

Halfdan looked bemused. 'Why? We have our ships.'

'English lands are vast,' Leif said. 'I have heard from Asgrim the Traveller that you can sail only so far in them. Horses will enable you to cross every kingdom in the island. They are the longships of the land.'

Ivar clapped his hands with pleasure and thumped Leif on the shoulder.

'You did well, Leif.' He pulled a thick gold ring from off his arm and handed it to Leif. 'This may prove the first of many. You have earned it. And I name you Spokesman to the sons of Ragnar. This shall be proclaimed amongst the men.'

Leif grinned with delight. He saw ahead of him a path as glittering as Bifrost, the rainbow bridge which led to the Gods.

The rest of Guthrum's crew soon spread news of the events in Norwic and Leif was celebrated by the warriors. Pillage and plunder were attractive but the thought of safe quarters throughout the harsh winter months was even more so.

The only thing to spoil Leif's pleasure was the unremitting animosity of Eohric. Whenever Ivar was near he spent most of his time at Guthrum's bedside. But when Ivar was away he slipped outside of the tent and wasted no time in spreading discontent about Leif's agreement with Edmund.

His tactic worked; the army began to take sides. The older, more experienced men liked the notion of waiting out the winter months in comfort. Some, the younger men who had been on few campaigns, began to complain that Leif had deprived them of plunder.

He began to worry and sought out Thorvald for counsel.

'It's only the young hotheads,' Thorvald told him. 'Nothing to worry about from them.'

'Hotheads are hot-tempered,' Leif said miserably. 'If they can't kill Angles they might choose to kill me instead.'

'You're safe while Ivar and his brothers smile upon you.'

'Except for a stab in the dark,' said Sigurd.

'No man is safe from a stab in the dark,' Thorvald said. 'That is why he needs good friends.'

'Do friends have cat's eyes then?' Leif asked. 'To keep watch over him?'

'No. But they can avenge a murdered friend.'

'Small comfort, Thorvald, small comfort.'

He pulled out his knife and began to sharpen it on a whetstone.

'That's a sensible move,' Thorvald said. 'I wonder how long Eohric will bow to Ivar's command to leave you well alone. If he thinks he can slay you in secret he'll do so. You may have need for a sharp blade.'

Leif stopped his work. 'Why does Eohric hate me? I've never done him any harm.'

'Because he's mad,' Sigurd said. He thought it best not to tell Thorvald how Leif had duped Eohric when they tried to escape from Ivar. He took the knife and whet-stone from Leif's hands and began to sharpen with more skill than his brother could ever hope to muster.

'Sigurd has the truth of it,' Thorvald said. 'I've known Eohric since he was a young boy. He had a vicious streak from the first. He loved to taunt and bully other boys, always when Guthrum was near to protect him from retribution. And he delighted to pull the legs off spiders and beat his puppy.'

'Cursed by Loki,' Sigurd said.

Leif shuddered at the name. He had grown warier of the god of mischief since the day he glimpsed him in the smithy. He was beginning to think that Loki had cursed him, angered at his catching sight of him.

'I think you're right,' Thorvald said. 'But Eohric's grudge against Leif has other causes as well.'

Leif stared at him intently, his heart hammering. If he could understand, he might be able to defend himself better.

'You look like their older brother, Arnbjorn,' Thorvald explained. 'He was about my age and a man destined for great things, including inheriting his father's wealth, hall and hearth-warriors. He was a strong and determined man, a brave warrior, and he and Guthrum were as close as brothers could be.

'But Arnbjorn had no great liking for Eohric, despising him for his cruel nature and air of mischief. As the years went by he made no secret of his scorn. So, while Guthrum loved Arnbjorn, Eohric came to hate him. It is unfortunate for you that you resemble him. Every time Eohric sees you he is reminded of the brother who detested him. The brother he loathed and feared.'

'So where is Arnbjorn now?' Leif asked.

'Dead.'

Thorvald glanced around as if searching for unwelcome listeners.

'He went out trapping foxes one winter morning,' he continued. 'But he did not return. He was found four days later, dead at the bottom of a steep river bank, his leg shattered by the fall, his skull cracked open to reveal his brain. We were not sure if he died from bleeding or from the cold. It was a terrible winter.'

'He must not have been a skilled hunter,' Sigurd said, 'falling down a bank like that.'

'He was the best hunter in the village,' Thorvald said. 'He would not have fallen. Though he may have been pushed. After having his skull smashed open.'

He gave Leif a grim smile. 'So, keep your blade sharp and your eyes peeled, Leif.' He got to his feet. 'You can count me as a friend. But take my advice, make as many more as you can, and swiftly.'

BIDING TIME

Emissaries came from King Edmund a week later, bearing the Vikings great gifts and with details of where they were to over-winter.

But the sons of Ragnar would not be told where to go.

Ivar had investigated the great fortress which Thorvald had described to him. Now he demanded that one of the encampments should be within the fort and that the others should be along the river system which led from it.

The emissaries argued against this at first, intent on settling the Vikings on the margins of the kingdom and far from access to any rivers. But Halfdan's threats to ravage the land persuaded them otherwise and they hurried back to Norwic to tell King Edmund.

They returned to say that they could use the fortress and naming three other places for them to be quartered. They had chosen the most distant parts of the kingdom, desolate and bleak with little shelter or pasture.

The brothers demanded better.

'You'll come with me to the ancient fortress, Cnobheresburg,' Ivar told Leif a few days later. 'Ubbe goes to Thetford, Halfdan to Exning in the far west and Jarl Sidrac to Eye in the centre of the territory of the south folk.'

Halfdan gave a savage laugh. 'Edmund must take us for fools, trying to settle us in the forsaken parts of his kingdom. He'll soon realise that he's the fool.'

'We're placing our armies where we want them,' Ivar explained. 'We're cutting Edmund's kingdom in two and each camp will be in reach of the others by river.'

The Viking armies would be strung across the centre of the kingdom, a threat to the north, the south and the heart.

'And when we get their horses, what then?' Leif asked.

'We'll be able to go where we please.'

That afternoon, Guthrum's fever broke and he sat up and demanded meat and ale. Thorvald sent for Deor.

'He's a strong man,' the Leech said in admiration.

'He's a Viking,' Eohric said, 'and my brother. What did you expect?'

'I expected nothing,' Deor answered, 'although I thought he might die.'

He bent closer to Guthrum's wounded arm. 'Now I shall find out if I must saw his arm off.'

He slowly undid the bandage, sniffing all the while. 'No stench of wound-rot,' he said.

Guthrum nodded, almost casually, unwilling to admit the sense of hope which was etched upon his face.

At last, Deor unwound the final piece of the bandage. The leaves he had placed there a week before were still in place, although brown with blood and torn and shredded.

'Does it itch?' Deor asked.

'A little.'

'Good. That is probably our little friends still doing their work.' He pulled off the leaves and smiled. Swarming on the wound were a mass of maggots, bloated, slow-moving, full feasted on the foulness of the wound. Carefully, Deor brushed them away. The arm was dark but flesh-coloured, not the charcoal black he had feared.

'You'll live,' he said, straightening up. 'And you'll keep your arm.'

Guthrum grinned in relief. 'Thorvald,' he said. 'Fetch me an arm-ring. I would reward this excellent leech.'

'You can reward me better by letting me go back to my people,' Deor said.

Guthrum laughed. 'Do you think I will let a healer as good as you desert me? No. You will remain in my service. I will reward you well for it. You'll have no cause for complaint.'

Deor scowled but thought it wisest not to argue.

'And now,' Guthrum continued, 'we must make our way to King Edmund's hall to strike our bargain.'

Thorvald and Deor exchanged glances.

'There's no need,' Thorvald told Guthrum. 'You've been lost in a fever. The bargain was struck a week ago.'

Guthrum looked astonished. 'I have lost a week?'

Deor nodded.

Guthrum tensed. 'Who bargained for me?' He stared at Eohric. 'Not you?'

'No brother. The rats you feed deserted me in favour of our helmsman.'

'Good,' Guthrum said. 'I also would have chosen him to speak in my place.'

'Except he didn't,' Eohric said. 'He was too fearful to open his mouth. The blacksmith's lackey spoke for you instead. And for Ivar.'

Guthrum glanced at Thorvald. 'I was not afraid to speak,' he said. 'But I deemed that Leif would have a smoother tongue.'

'You're probably right,' Guthrum said. 'Where is Leif now?'

'I can send a man in search for him,' Thorvald asked.

'He won't be hard to find,' Eohric said. 'His smooth tongue will be up Ivar's arse.'

'And yours will be wrenched from your mouth if Ivar hears this,' Thorvald said.

Eohric stepped closer to Thorvald, his face in a fury.

Thorvald merely laughed and turned to Guthrum. 'I'll send for Leif. He will tell you more about our meeting with Edmund.'

'Come eat with me, Thorvald,' said Guthrum, 'and tell me about how you brought my ship back here.' He gave Eohric a suspicious look.

Leif arrived shortly after, and not alone. Ivar was with him.

Eohric went deadly pale, he licked his dust-dry lips and he looked about to bolt from the tent.

'What's troubling you?' Ivar sneered. 'Disappointed that your brother didn't die?'

'I love my brother,' Eohric mumbled.

Ivar ignored him and went to Guthrum. 'You're as tough as a mule. I'm glad of it.'

'I think the healer may have helped,' Guthrum said.

Ivar stared at Deor. 'Has Guthrum rewarded you?' he asked.

'He has promised me a gold arm-ring.'

'Which gives you reward but also makes you his man.'

'So it seems.'

Ivar held his gaze for a few minutes. 'And I shall reward you. Guthrum is a not the sort of man I wish to lose.'

'And what reward will you give to me?' Deor asked.

'Your life and a purse of golden byzants.'

'Both are acceptable to me.'

Ivar laughed and clapped Deor on the shoulder. 'You have guts and a dry wit, Englishman. I might even come to like you.'

'Come sit with me,' Guthrum told Leif. 'I would hear your tale of how you spoke for me to Edmund.'

The following day, Leif was summoned by Ivar. He found him with his brothers staring at the river.

'We are having a feast tonight,' Ivar said, 'to celebrate Guthrum's recovery. I want you to tell a tale about the fight where he got injured. Make it honest but put in a few laughs at Guthrum's expense.'

Leif looked horrified. 'Put in a few laughs. But isn't that risky? For me?'

'Guthrum in not the sort to bear a grudge,' Halfdan said.

'Unlike his brother,' added Ivar. 'You would be wise not to mock Eohric in any way.'

'I don't need telling that, my lord,' Leif said.

He was about to leave but then hesitated, trying to formulate a question which had been nagging at him.

'We're still at the camp,' he began. 'We've not moved to our quarters. Why is this?'

Ivar stared at Leif, shrewdly. 'Because Edmund hasn't agreed to our demands yet. We need his promise to be certain that he provides food and shelter for us. Otherwise all is pointless.'

Leif stared into the distance, towards where he guessed that Edmund and his advisers would be arguing whether or not to agree with Ivar's demands.

'But what if Edmund doesn't agree with you? What if he insists that we go where he chooses.'

'Then we persuade him,' Ivar said. 'By tearing at his guts.' He pointed to the north. A dozen warriors were heading to the camp, driving before them a couple of score of people, sheep being herded not by shepherds but by wolves.

'Slaves for the camp,' Ivar said. 'If we mount more raids like this, Edmund will agree to our terms.'

The people were in their prime, mostly in their twenties, chosen for their strength and likelihood to toil for a good many years. They were sullen and frightened, their eyes widening in horror as they trudged ever closer to the huge army. They were burdened with sacks containing grain, pulses, smoked meats; food looted from their villages to feed the Viking horde. There were also a dozen donkeys, laden down with ale and mead.

'Strong men,' Ivar said approvingly as they passed by.

'And lovely women,' said Halfdan. Then he bellowed, 'Bring the women over here.'

With much wailing and resistance, the women were separated from the men. A few of the younger men tried to prevent this but were beaten savagely by the guards. Finally, the women were pushed forward and stood, terrified, in front of the brothers and Leif.

'I'll have that one,' Ubbe said, indicating a woman with flaming red hair.

'Those two for me,' Halfdan said. 'The buxom ones.'

'What about you, Leif?' Ivar asked. 'You did us a great service. Take a woman for your bed-slave as your reward.'

Leif was shocked. He was not considered a great success with women back home. He would often fall smitten by a beautiful or kindly girl and then spend too much time wondering how best to approach her, if she would accept him, and then if she'd be satisfied with him, throw him over or ask to be his wife. In the meanwhile, a less imaginative man would move more swiftly and snatch the prize from under his nose.

And now, he was given a chance to choose a woman who had no say whether or not to accept him.

'I'm not sure...' he began. What if the women he chose hated or despised him?

'Not sure which one?' Ivar asked, not realising Leif's dilemma. 'Take the one that stirs your balls.'

Leif gulped and stared at the women. They were all comely, all desirable. In the end he narrowed his choice to three, his eyes travelling over the face and figure of each of them.

'Make your mind up,' Halfdan said. 'If one doesn't suit, you can swap her for another.'

'That one,' Leif said, pointing to a dark-haired girl at the end of the line.

Ivar gestured to her and she walked nervously towards them.

'What's your name, girl?' he demanded.

'Aebbe,' she said. She began to bite her lip, anxiously.

'This is your new master,' Ivar said, shoving Leif towards her. 'You do whatever he demands. You're his to do as he wishes with.'

The girl looked horrified and then began to weep silently.

Leif reached out and touched her on the shoulder. 'I won't hurt you,' he said.

She wept even more.

OF GODS AND GODDESSES

Ivar was right in saying that attacking the nearby villages would influence Edmund. For the next few days the Vikings systematically destroyed everything in the vicinity. A day later Edmund sent word that the army could over-winter in the locations they preferred.

With the same speed with which they attacked their enemies, the great army struck camp and headed for their separate destinations.

Leif was unhappy that Guthrum and Eohric were also going to the fortress at Cnobheresburg. He'd hoped that they would be sent with Ubbe to the far west, as far as possible from him. His one consolation was that Thorvald would also be coming with them to the fortress.

'Don't worry about Eohric,' Sigurd said. 'He's been warned off by Ivar and Guthrum will make sure the little shit keeps his distance. And besides, you've got your bed-slave to take your mind off things.'

Leif nodded enthusiastically. But the truth about his bed-slave was very different.

He had owned Aebbe for three days and three nights. She was a willing enough worker in the day but at night, as he got into bed with her, she grew rigid with fright. He had tried to kiss her but she would start to weep and he felt too disheartened to do more. He spent the nights restless with frustration, hot with desire yet not caring to force himself upon her.

Each morning he received the jests of the other men with good humour, agreeing with them that she was a voracious lover and would wear him out. But inwardly he squirmed. On the previous night he had gone to bed long after his friends, waiting until they slept so they would not notice the silence coming from his own bed.

Now, as the longships headed north towards the fortress, Aebbe approached him and rested her hand lightly upon his.

'Where are we going, lord?' she asked.

Leif brightened at her words. This was the first time she had spoken to him except in response to his own words.

'To the fortress at Cnobheresburg,' he said. 'We'll spend the winter there.'

She nodded but did not say more.

'Do you know the fortress?' Leif asked, at last.

'Yes. I am from Fritton which is a mile from there.'

Leif wondered whether he should ask the next question, fearful that it would diminish him in her eyes. 'Some of the men think the fortress was built by demons and that ghosts dwell there still.'

'I have heard the same.'

He gave a quick laugh. 'That's not very encouraging.'

'Who am I to encourage you?' she replied with sorrowful voice. 'You are my master and I am your slave.'

'But you've not always been a slave.'

'No. Until a few days ago I was free. I had a father and a mother, and two little sisters. And now they are dead, slaughtered by your friends.'

'I'm sorry about that.'

She turned towards him, her eyes contemptuous. 'Are you?' She shook her head. 'I very much doubt it. For what Viking is ever sorry for another person?'

'I am,' he said, hesitantly. 'I am for you.'

She turned to look at him, her eyes big with suspicion but also, perhaps, a growing hope. The moment was all too fleeting. She turned away once more and stared at the river foaming as the longship sliced through its waters.

They reached Cnobheresburg at noon and Ivar wasted no time in securing the fortress. The walls were fifteen feet high and sentries were allocated to the walls for Ivar had as little trust of the Angles as they had of him and assumed that an army might appear at any time. He gave his captains responsibility for the bastions which were sited at each corner of the fortress and at intervals along the wall. He himself took over the large gatehouse to the east which was the most likely point of attack. Tents were erected and a beginning made to the construction of wooden huts.

Leif was allocated a place in the gatehouse so that he could entertain Ivar with song and stories. Sigurd was sent to Guthrum who had been given command of the south-west bastion and told to organise a smithy.

Thorvald, Leif and Asgrim helped him unload his anvil from the ship and drag it to the crude wooden shed slaves were constructing close to the bastion.

'You should have made the slaves carry this great weight,' Asgrim said as they positioned the anvil in the centre of the shed.

'I wouldn't trust them,' Sigurd said. 'This anvil is centuries old and has come down to me from my forefathers.'

'All the way back to Wayland the Smith,' Leif added.

'Wayland was your ancestor?' Asgrim asked in an awed voice.

Leif adopted a stern and serious face. 'Father to son, a line unbroken.'

Asgrim turned to Sigurd. 'And you learned your skills from your father?'

Sigurd nodded.

'He was a famous man,' Leif continued. 'He was Smith to the great warlord Hæstenn and journeyed with him to the kingdom of the Moors, to Rome and to Frankland. In each of them he sought out the most famous sword-makers, worked alongside them and thereby enhanced his craft and knowledge still further. And those skills he passed on to my brother.'

'It's no wonder that Ivar sought you out to make his sword, then,' Asgrim said.

Sigurd gave a fleeting smile. 'Havoc is a good sword, despite what my brother thinks.'

Asgrim and Thorvald turned to him, their eyes bright with curiosity.

'What do you mean?'

Leif refused to say more so Sigurd explained. 'Leif claims he saw Loki hiding in the steam when the sword was being quenched.'

Leif gave him dagger looks, not wishing this to be common knowledge.

'I may have been mistaken,' he said. 'Perhaps it was only the shifting shape of the steam.'

'But Loki is a shape-shifter,' said Thorvald, clutching his hammer amulet to ward off evil. 'It must have been him.' Asgrim nodded in agreement.

Leif groaned. Both men were now convinced about the story and there was every danger that it would spread around the camp until it reached Ivar. There was no telling what he might do when he found out that the god of mischief had been present at his sword's making. And that Leif and Sigurd had kept this information from him.

'What does the appearance of Loki mean?' Asgrim asked. 'Is the sword cursed?'

Leif raised his hands in an ambiguous gesture. 'In one way only,' he said, inventing desperately. 'Loki said that the sword would prove the doom of any man who stole it from its rightful owner and sought to use it in battle.'

The men, even Sigurd, looked astounded at his words.

'But Loki was not the only god I saw in the dark of the smithy,' Leif continued.

He glanced around as if to see anyone who might overhear. Then he gestured the three men closer.

'You must swear not to tell anyone of this,' he breathed.

They swore.

Leif lowered his voice. 'I also saw the great god, Thor. He appeared at the anvil, his hammer Mjollnir in his mighty grip and made a second prophesy. He said that the true bearer of this sword would never be vanquished in battle, would be the slayer of kings and destroyer of kingdoms. That he would become the mightiest ruler in all the world.'

'We should tell Ivar this,' Asgrim said.

Leif held up his hands nervously. 'We must not. For Thor also said that his prophesy would work best if the wielder of the sword had no knowledge of it.'

'Why would that be?' Thorvald asked.

'I don't know,' Leif said irritably. 'I'm not privy to the thoughts of the god. I merely report what he said to me.'

At that moment Leif was rescued from any more debate by a mighty roar from the eastern gate. But it was not a cry of dismay at sight of an enemy army. It was a cry of welcome. Entering through the gate were four large carts pulled by oxen. Each cart contained half a dozen women, dressed in the finest clothes.

'Whores,' breathed Asgrim. 'It's like a prayer from the gods.' He led the way to see them.

News of the whores spread swiftly across the fortress and the four carts were soon surrounded by laughing warriors. But when one attempted to clamber onto the foremost waggon a tall young woman kicked him in the chin, sending him sprawling to the ground.

'Get your filthy hands off,' the woman cried. 'These are my girls and I'll tell you when you get to touch them. And for what price.'

'How much?' cried one of the warriors.

'More than an ugly fool like you can afford, I warrant,' she answered. The men cheered her loudly for this reply.

'Now, where's your leader?' the woman continued. Her eyes lit on Sigurd. 'You have big arms and strong thighs. Are you Ivar? Are you the fearsome heathen lord?'

'No,' shouted one of the men. 'He's only a blacksmith.'

'Better a blacksmith than a piece of shit like you,' she said to him. 'I happen to love blacksmiths; my father was one. I'll take him into my bed, little turd, but you'll never get as much as a touch or a sniff of me.'

She glanced around the camp. 'So? Where is your lord?'

'He's here,' came a loud cry. The throng made way for Ivar to approach the whores. 'And who may you be?'

'My name is Nerienda,' the woman answered, 'and I bring my girls to keep you and your men warm this winter. They're the finest whores in the kingdom and they don't come cheap.' She smiled. 'But then I've always heard that you Vikings desire the costliest treasures.'

'That we do, Nerienda. And you are welcome to spend the winter here. I am Ivar the Boneless, lord of this host.'

'I hope one part of you isn't boneless,' she said. 'I can promise it won't be once I begin work on you.'

Some of the warriors cheered at her words, but not those who knew Ivar best.

A slow smile came across his face. 'And how much do you charge?' he asked.

'More than any of your warriors can afford,' she answered. 'But I'm sure you have enough about you to satisfy even my appetites.'

He reached up and helped her jump to the ground. 'You're welcome, Nerienda. You and your whores.'

She looked around the fortress intently, her eyes taking in everything in moments. 'Well, there's nowhere quite good enough for my girls,' she said, 'but we'll have to make do for a little while.'

'Not you, Nerienda,' Ivar said, pointing to the gatehouse. 'These are my quarters.'

She gave him a little pout, enticing and challenging, and strolled off to the gatehouse.

'You know your price, girls,' she said. 'Don't let these robbers try to pay a farthing less.'

The women climbed off the waggons and the most powerful men each led one of them away.

Leif and Sigurd were not amongst them, although neither seemed disappointed at this. Sigurd's eyes followed Nerienda as she entered the gatehouse.

Leif caught a glimpse of Aebbe. She was standing by the well, unmoving, her eyes fixed upon him. For a moment he did not move, then he began to walk towards her, his pace increasing with every stride.

'Am I a good slave?' she asked as she reached him.

'I do not want you as a slave,' he answered.

She stared into his eyes and then, very slowly, reached out and took his hand. 'Then what do you want me to be?' she asked.

'My woman.'

Her eyes relaxed although she did not yet smile. 'Come then,' she said, leading him back to their hut.

THE GREAT ENDEAVOUR

The Vikings had barely finished building their dwellings when winter descended with a month of fierce storms and tempests. They hauled their ships up high on the river-bank, fearful that the gales would damage them, or worse yet, sink them or cast them adrift. Roofs that had been built too hastily blew away and the ground in the fortress became a quagmire. Men walked hurriedly in ceaseless rain, heads bowed, wet as water rats.

Sigurd and Leif spent the month making horse-shoes for the mounts which were to be given to the chieftains of the army. The rest of the army would have to make do with unshod beasts with all the dangers of them going lame. Iron was precious and once enough shoes had been made they turned their attention to making more spears and swords.

Leif and Aebbe grew more comfortable with each other although she sometimes made it very clear that she was with him only under duress. Leif did not mind. He delighted in her good looks and soft body and the fact that now she rarely refused him in bed.

'You're strutting like a cockerel,' Sigurd said to him one morning. 'A man can get tired of seeing this.'

'Then do something about it,' Leif said. 'Go to one of the whores. Choose one you like and make her something pretty as payment.'

Sigurd did not answer other than to hammer with extra strength upon the anvil.

'I see,' Leif said, light dawning on him. 'You are hot for a whore. But it's the one whore who's not available.'

Sigurd brandished his hammer in anger. 'Do not talk of her,' he said.

Leif smirked. 'You lust for Nerienda. That's very foolish. She belongs to Ivar.'

'She belongs to no man,' Sigurd answered. 'She has made that very plain.'

Leif frowned. 'You've spoken with her?'

Sigurd nodded. 'We talk sometimes, in the evenings. She seeks me out.'

Leif touched him on the arm. 'That's very dangerous. Ivar will show no mercy if you seek to take her.'

Sigurd sighed. 'That's true. I'm no fool. I will not touch forbidden goods.'

He glanced around and when he spoke again it was with lowered voice. 'But Nerienda says that Ivar has little interest in her anymore. His mind is full of battle plans and bold dreams. I will be patient and, when he tires of her, she will come to me.'

'Let's hope so,' Leif said. 'But just remember that although a man may lose interest in his woman he may not be happy for others to take his place.'

Sigurd shrugged. Such ideas were not worth wasting thought on.

The storms ended at last and the days grew bright but bitter cold. Frost gripped the land until late each morning and a sharp wind needled beneath cloak, tunic and even fur. Ponds began to ice over and the only birds noticeable were crows and rooks. Their mocking cries floated from the nearby trees, making the men miserable and ill at ease.

Despite the bitter weather, carts arrived each day bearing provisions sent by Edmund. But as the days drew short and Yule approached, the carts diminished in number and carried fewer goods.

Ivar summoned his chieftains to him and announced that he was losing patience over this and would go to see the king.

'And you come with me,' he said to Leif. 'Let's see if your honey tongue can work your wiles upon him once again. And if you have to give him your arse for more meat, then so be it.'

'I think he likes women,' Leif said, nervously.

'The leech tells me he likes anything with a hole he can thrust into. So be prepared.'

The next day Ivar, Thorvald and Leif marched up to the walls surrounding Norwic and demanded entry. The gates opened silently and they strode inside.

Ivar's eyes darted everywhere, taking in the clothes of the townsfolk, the goods on display on the market stalls, the beauty of the women and the robust looks of the men.

'Good pickings here,' he said to Thorvald. 'And we may yet have to come and get them.'

Edmund had heard word of their arrival and welcomed them courteously in his hall. Yet, despite his affability, he had placed twenty of his household warriors close to hand.

'Welcome, Lord Ivar,' he said. He picked up a goblet of wine and himself approached Ivar and placed it in his hands.

Ivar drained it in one gulp and handed the empty vessel to Leif.

'I shall get you a sack for that,' Edmund said, his voice betraying not a shred of the disgust he felt at such naked thieving.

'Good,' Ivar said. 'But I did not come for wine cups. I came to find out why the supplies you send me are dwindling. And to see how many horses are being gathered for my men.'

Edmund indicated an empty seat by his throne. His advisers shuffled nervously as Ivar took his seat.

'Supplies,' Edmund began, 'are dwindling because they are being depleted by the appetites of your men.'

'That's not my concern,' Ivar said.

'But my people are going hungry in order to feed you.'

'Also, not my concern.'

'If the fox eats all the hens,' said Hwita, Edmund's young adviser, 'there will be no eggs to last through winter.'

'A fox?' said Ivar, his voice growing harder. 'I'm a wolf and if I eat all the hens I move on to tastier meats. I care nothing for eggs.'

Edmund could barely hide a shudder.

'We are endeavouring to find food from further afield,' said the old adviser, Oswald, his voice calm and soothing. 'This will take a little time for the paths across the kingdom are sodden by the recent rains. But come they will, be assured of this.'

'And the horses?'

'They have been earmarked for your warriors, have no fear. But we are keeping them in their pastures until the spring when you need them.'

'A man who talks sense,' Ivar said. 'I congratulate you, Edmund, on having at least one adviser who is not a braggart or hothead.' He gave a ghastly grin at Hwita who blanched under his gaze.

'As I congratulate you on yours,' Edmund said, gesturing to Leif. 'When first we met, and he spoke for you, I assumed he was a jarl. But now I hear that he is your Skald.'

'Who told you this?' Ivar asked suspiciously.

'My men come and go with supplies to your camp,' Edmund said in an innocent tone. 'They hear gossip and sometimes that gossip comes to my ears.'

Ivar's eyes narrowed dangerously. 'A wise lord does not listen to gossip.' His voice was a warning hiss.

'But I like the news that your man, Leif, is a Skald,' Edmund said. 'I like him and wish him to be mine. As a gesture of good faith, a seal to our brotherly bargain.'

Leif swallowed, wondering if Ivar's earlier jest had contained some truth. Edmund would not be the first lord to bed men as well as women.

'And what would you do to him if I give him to you? Will he be hamstrung or slain?'

'Certainly not slain,' Edmund said. 'Where is the profit in a dead Skald? And he will only be hamstrung if he's foolish enough to try to flee.'

Ivar shook his head. 'He's my Skald and I keep him.' He paused. 'You can have my whore, though. I grow tired of her.'

'Nerienda?'

Ivar laughed. 'Your spies are well informed. Yes, Nerienda. She is a marvel in bed but she prattles too much for my liking.'

'And for mine,' Edmund said. 'You are welcome to her.'

Guthrum and Thorvald exchanged glances at the news that Nerienda had serviced more than one great lord. Ivar did not even blink.

'But I still desire your Skald,' Edmund continued.

Ivar turned to Leif. 'You're a free man, Leif. Do you wish to be Skald to a king? I'm sure your English woman would prefer it if she came back to her people.'

'I dwell with my people and my lord,' Leif said, bowing his head. 'That is all I desire.'

'Then there's your answer,' Ivar told Edmund. 'Find yourself another boy to bugger.'

Edmund's face grew ugly with loathing but he hid it in an instant. 'I desired only the occasional good tale,' he said. 'But if the Skald is unwilling…'

'He is,' said Leif, quickly.

Edmund waved his hand in the air to suggest he had no further interest in the matter.

'And the food?' Ivar asked.

'It will come shortly,' Oswald answered.

'Make it sooner,' Ivar said. 'And in the meanwhile, I shall not restrain my men from seeking extra provisions from your people.'

'But —' began Oswald.

'Don't but me,' Ivar said, and strode from the hall.

'How can such a wretch be a king?' he fumed as they walked through the gates. 'He scorns my woman and lusts after my Skald. Well, he will rue his words.'

He wasted no time when they returned to the fortress. Scavenging parties were sent out to plunder and despoil the surrounding villages, to teach people and king that Ivar the Boneless brooked no opposition to his demands.

Edmund's words had been correct. The nearby villages had been denuded of much of their harvest to feed the Vikings. But Ivar's men were skilful and cunning thieves. They searched every hut and cott, every church and every plot of land for hidden food and treasure. The savagery and violence of their search demolished many of the worst constructed homes.

Villagers pleaded to keep their last ox for plough work, to no avail. They begged to keep one cup, one cooking pot, one spoon for every family, to no avail. Priests hung on to their holy books and relics, to no avail.

The villagers drove their pigs into the forest but the Vikings found and slaughtered them. The last remaining sheep or mules were taken back to the fortress. Anyone who resisted too strongly was slain. And when each village had been completely ransacked, the strongest sons and prettiest daughters were taken as slaves.

Ivar completed his lesson to the English by sending Nerienda from his bed; he wanted no cast-offs from an English lord. Instead he took a comely nun from a nearby convent, raped her in front of his assembled warriors and cut out her tongue to keep her from annoying him with any talk.

Nerienda kept herself to herself for seven nights and then asked him if she was free to choose another man. Ivar gave a casual shrug, part indifference, part assent and she went to Sigurd.

And on that day, twice the usual number of waggons trundled into the fortress, all heavily laden with food, ale, wine and warm furs for winter.

WEST AND NORTH

It continued a savage winter but finally, two months after Yule, the sun grew warm and the men grew hot for action. Ivar sent the swiftest longships up river to check that the other three camps were ready to move. And then, at the beginning of spring month, the horses arrived at the fortress.

The finest steeds were chosen by Ivar and his chief men: the ten ship captains, their helmsmen and the most renowned warriors, fifty in all. Sigurd spent two days fitting the iron shoes he had made earlier in the winter. The rest of the mounts were given leather hoof-boots, not as hard-wearing but sufficient if they were ridden carefully.

That proved a problem at first for few of the men were used to riding horses. Many could not keep their seats and those that did rode with all the grace of sacks of meal. There were many bruises and several broken limbs in the first weeks after the horses arrived. But Ivar insisted that the men grew skilful in riding their mounts and it seemed that they would remain in the fortress for ever.

In the end, Jarl Frene sought Ivar out. He was captain of half a dozen ships, the son of a wealthy man from the island of Borghund, although this was the first time he had sailed on a raid to the west.

'The men feel like fools,' he said. 'We are not merchants or farmers, content to trudge on broken-winded nags across fields and fens. We are made to ride the waters. Why can't we keep to our ships?'

'Because we need to go inland,' Ivar said.

'The rivers go inland.'

'But not everywhere. And many grow narrow which makes our ships vulnerable to attack.'

'Attack by who? The English?'

'Don't underestimate them. We Northmen have only struck at easy prey in the past, villages and little towns, isolated monasteries, most of them close to the coast. But the English kings are powerful and once they have the time to gather their forces will prove fitting adversaries.'

Frene looked dubious. 'And what of our ships?'

'I will send them by sea to the northern kingdom of Northumbria.'

'Why there?'

Ivar turned to Guthrum who had been quietly listening to the conversation. 'Why there, do you think, young Guthrum?'

'Because they have great wealth?'

'The Mercians and the West Saxons have greater.'

'Then we should attack one of them,' Frene said.

'No, we shouldn't,' Ivar said. 'Because Wessex and Mercia have more than just greater wealth. They are the most powerful kingdoms. Their kings have more people, more warriors, more resources to pit against us. But Northumbria is divided between two enemies who both claim kingship. Fatally divided, I hope.'

Ivar was a great war-captain, not so much for his prowess in battle as for his cunning and command of the issues which led for victory. Nevertheless, Frene remained unconvinced and did not attempt to hide his doubt and dissent, giving Ivar a look of contempt before walking away, shaking his head all the while.

That night Ivar ordered an especially lavish feast. It was partly to use up the supplies before they left, partly to remind the warriors that Ivar was in command and was a man of great wealth and largess. But it soon became clear that there was another reason.

The feast was well underway and yet there was no sign of Ivar. Leif wondered at this for he had been at all previous feasts, allowing himself to be relaxed and at ease with his men, less the unquestioned leader than the first among equals.

'Why isn't Ivar here?' he asked Asgrim.

He shrugged. 'Maybe the murmurings against him have diminished his appetite.'

The idea surprised Leif and he sipped at his ale as he pondered it.

At that moment a shape leapt up on the table to his left. At first he thought it was a cat but then he realised his mistake. It was Ivar but not as he normally appeared.

He had folded himself up as a washer-woman might fold a bulky garment. His chin rested on his knees, his knees touched his chest and his feet were tucked away, completely hidden. He was the size of a child, no bigger.

And then he moved along the table with a curious waddling gait and Leif saw that he was walking on his hands. His head turned from side to side as he approached, as if he were searching for something or someone. Men drew back as he neared them for he was hideous, a monster lurking in a nightmare, a thing of terror made flesh.

At last he found what he was looking for. He stopped in front of Jarl Frene and turned, crabwise to look at him. He said not a word but stared directly into his face, not moving, not speaking, unblinking.

How long he remained like that no one could tell. Leif felt it was as long as winter. The hall fell silent, the eyes of every warrior, slave and servant straining to see what would happen.

Jarl Frene suddenly lifted his hand to shield his eyes, almost retched, then staggered up and fled from the hall.

Ivar gave a ghastly smile, leapt from the table and disappeared.

'I feel sick,' Leif whispered to Asgrim.

'Not as much as Frene does, I warrant,' he replied.

The longships from inland returned and, together with the ships at the fortress, were crammed with supplies: salted meats, pickled fish, grain, ale and spare weapons. Some of the women, the best slaves and the whores, were also selected to go on them. Leif and Sigurd were relieved that this included Aebbe and Nerienda. Northumbria was said to be cold and bleak and their warm bodies would prove comfort indeed.

Skeleton crews were selected and the ships headed out to sea. Leif stood by the shore and watched them depart. He felt a pain in his heart at being separated from Aebbe although he very much doubted she felt the same. She acted more pleasantly towards him with every day, it was true, but he sensed no real affection from her. It was only then that he wondered if she had been fond of any man before she was enslaved.

Sigurd met him as he trudged back into the fortress. He held out a clean, new scabbard.

'What's this?' he asked.

'What's it look like?' Sigurd answered, his voice gruff.

Leif took the scabbard and withdrew a new-made sword. It was magnificent. The blade was sturdy and highly polished, the hilt was covered in shark skin and the pommel decorated with runes for luck.

'This is the sword of a great warrior, a captain,' he breathed. 'Not for a man such as me.'

'Why should only wealthy men have the finest weapons?' Sigurd said. 'I want you to bear a sword to make Eohric grind his teeth in rage and envy.'

Leif grinned but then his face grew more serious. 'Perhaps I will grow to be worthy of it,' he said, as much to himself as to his brother.

'You talk nonsense, as always,' Sigurd answered. 'I give you this to protect yourself from harm, not to try to become the warrior you'll never be.'

Leif laughed and slapped Sigurd on the shoulder. 'It is a marvellous gift. I thank you for it.'

'Just don't get yourself killed. Practise with it. Thorvald will help.'

'And did you make yourself a fine sword?' Leif asked.

For answer, Sigurd led him to the smithy. On the anvil was a large hammer, one side like a heavy club, the other shaped like an axe with sharp and deadly blade.

'That's not a sword,' Leif said. 'You'll look like Thor with his hammer.'

'I have no skill with a sword,' Sigurd said. 'It was Guthrum who gave me the idea when he told Eohric that a peasant could crush a man's skull with a club. I've spent my life hammering iron and steel. I think I should be able to hammer English limbs and heads.'

The army moved out a few days later. The horsemen were not encumbered by carts or pack-animals; Ivar meant to plunder the lands they passed through.

They journeyed to Eye to pick up Jarl Sidrac and his men, on to Thetford where Ubbe awaited them and finally on to Exning to join with Halfdan and the last of the army.

They crossed over the earthwork called Devil's Dyke, headed west to the river Granta and then onward until they struck the ancient road of Ermine Street. They were now within the Kingdom of Mercia and it was not long before they were being shadowed by an army.

Ubbe rode his horse close to Ivar. 'Will they fight?' he asked.

'I doubt it. They are only half our number.'

'But if they're joined by others?'

'Then we may have a fight on our hands. The Mercians are not like the men of East Anglia who are more interested in farming and trade. Mercia was once the greatest kingdom in the land. The mere name of it inspired fear from north to south. The Mercians will not idly let a challenge to them go unanswered.'

'So we fight?'

'I would prefer not. Northumbria makes an easier target. It's not the land it once was and is riven by the ambition of two wretches who seek to be king.' He clapped his brother on the shoulder. 'Fear not, Ubbe, in the far north there will be meat enough for our swords to feast on.'

And with these words he pulled Havoc from its scabbard and gazed on it lovingly.

'It's not yet tasted blood,' Ubbe said.

'That is good,' Ivar said. 'The longer it grows hungry the better it will feed.'

The Vikings continued north, followed every mile of the way by the Mercian army. The men began to feel that they were prey being stalked by a pack of wolves and seven days after crossing into Mercia the jarls demanded a meeting with Ivar and his brothers.

The warriors sat on either side of the road with the three leaders on a pile of furs which raised them high enough to enable them to be seen by all.

Many voices called out in a tumult of noise until Halfdan yelled for silence. 'We cannot make decisions with so many voices,' he cried. 'Let us hear from some spokesmen.'

The venerable Jarl Sidrac stepped forward accompanied by Jarl Frene. Frene had been terrified by Ivar's appearance on the feast table and was haunted by it. But now it made him the more determined.

'Wisdom and vigour, I see,' said Ivar with a smile. 'Speak, friends, we would hear your counsel.'

'We are tired of being hunted by the Mercians,' Sidrac said. 'They are less than half our number. I say we should attack and destroy them. They're getting on my nerves.'

There was much laughter from those who knew Sidrac. A man more cold, calm and calculating could not be found, a reputation of which he was justly proud.

'I know what he means,' Leif whispered to his brother, with a shudder. 'The Mercians are like the nightmare which haunts you every time you fall asleep.'

'As long as they don't attack us,' Sigurd said with a shrug. He put his fingers to his lips to quieten Leif.

Now Frene stood forward, until he was beside the pile of furs, where he turned as if to address the army rather than its leaders.

'I agree with Sidrac,' he said. 'To ignore the Mercians is craven.'

The assembled warriors shot nervous glances at the three sons of Ragnar, wondering how they would react to such inflammatory words. They seemed unconcerned.

'What seems craven to a spear-man,' Ivar said, 'is wisdom to a chieftain.'

'I am not a spear-man,' Frene cried, angrily. 'I am a Jarl.'

'Indeed you are,' Ivar said, smoothly. 'You brought six ships to this enterprise, one hundred and twenty warriors.' He gestured to the army. 'One hundred and twenty out of an army of more than a thousand, and all here following my brothers and me.'

'A thousand warriors who are sick of being held on a leash,' Frene said. 'Like hunting dogs refused their quarry.'

'Ivar won't like that,' Thorvald muttered.

'I agree with Frene,' Eohric called. 'We are twice the Mercians' number and twice the men they are.'

'So says the boy, Eohric,' Ivar said, his face grown suddenly cold. 'When I wish to speak to one of your family it will be to Guthrum.'

He dismissed Eohric like a man swats a fly and turned his gaze to Guthrum who reluctantly climbed to his feet.

'And I wish to hear why we abide being followed.' His eyes swept over the army and then turned to rest on the brothers. 'As Ivar said, there may be reasons which are obscure to us.'

Ivar held his gaze before turning to address the warriors.

'Of course we could attack the Mercian army,' he said, 'and of course we could destroy them. At worst we will be mauled but we will win the battle. Or things may go even better for us and we will destroy them completely and congratulate ourselves. Why we can even get Leif the Skald to tell a brave tale about it. But what then?

'I'll tell you, what then. The King of Mercia will simply raise another army, one much larger, and attack us. And then it will be our corpses that are left to rot on the battlefield.'

The men murmured at this, undecided at the choices before them.

'But surely they will attack us anyway,' Sidrac said. 'They are merely waiting for more favourable ground.'

'I think not,' Ivar said. 'They would prefer it if we leave Mercia behind and attack their ancient enemies to the north.'

'You cannot be sure of that.'

'I think I can.'

The warriors watched the two men for a moment longer. But then Sidrac lowered his head in acquiescence and Ivar bade the army disperse.

He decided to demonstrate his reasoning the very next day. He sent a large attachment to the west of the road with orders to ransack a nearby village. They did so with dreadful ferocity. The Mercian army looked on, unmoved by their depredations.

It appeared that Ivar was right. The Mercian commander must have been ordered to do nothing other than watch the Vikings as they made their way across the kingdom. The occasional sacked village was a price worth paying as long as they kept moving northward.

After a few more days they entered a flat plain which seemed to go on endlessly. There were no longer any heights to the west to offer the Mercians a vantage point and they withdrew. But the next morning the Vikings awoke to find that their enemies had increased mightily overnight, with near a thousand on the road ahead of them and another thousand behind.

'They're going to attack us,' Thorvald muttered. 'What will Ivar do?'

He did something quite surprising. He sent Leif and Deor to seek out the Mercian commander.

'What will I say to him?' Leif asked.

'Whatever it takes to prevent him attacking us on this open plain.'

The Mercian commander was a seasoned warrior by the name of Ceolred, hair grey with age but with eyes as sharp as those of a young man.

'You come to treat?' he asked. It seemed to Leif that, despite his words, he had no interest in what they had to say.

'Not to treat,' Leif answered, 'but to ask advice.'

Ceolred's suspicion changed to curiosity. 'Say on.'

'My leaders, Ivar the Boneless, and his brothers, Halfdan and Ubbe wish to know the swiftest way to get to Northumbria. Do we stay on this road and go north until we cross the River Humber or head west?'

Ceolred's look changed back to one of deep suspicion. His eyes flickered towards the Viking army, pondering their numbers and strength.

'I had not thought the Danes to be horsemen,' he said at length.

'They're not,' Deor said. 'They hate the beasts.'

Leif glared at him. It was unwise to give any information of weakness to a foe such as Ceolred.

'They?' Ceolred said. 'Are you not a Dane?'

'A man of East Anglia,' Deor answered. 'Held captive by them.'

Ceolred sniffed. 'If you wish, you can cease being their captive and come to me.'

Deor gnawed at his lip, uncertain how to answer. The Mercians had been the mortal enemy of his people for a hundred years and more. He doubted he could trust them overmuch. And with them he would be a nothing, just a man who owed them a debt. With the Vikings, it was he who was owed a debt of gratitude by Guthrum.

'I think it best if I stay with the Danes,' he said at last.

Ceolred's lips curled with distaste but he said nothing more to him.

He raised himself in his stirrups and gazed to the north and to the west, calculating the shortest distance the army could take to leave Mercia. He summoned one of his thegns and they conversed together a while.

'How will you cross the Humber?' Ceolred asked at last.

'We have a fleet waiting for us,' Leif answered. 'They will ferry us across.'

'Or ferry you back down the Trent,' said a thegn.

'Silence,' cried Ceolred. Like a fool the man had pointed out the best route to attack the heartlands of Mercia.

'Your warships will not easily take horses.' Ceolred spoke swiftly to distract attention from the thegn's words. 'But we would allow you to use our ferries.'

Leif watched the Mercian intently as he appeared to ponder the best choice. At last he made a decision. 'On balance,' he said, 'I think you should go thither.' He pointed to the north-west.

The thegn looked astonished at his words, a look which was not lost on Leif.

Ceolred, however, ignored the thegn and carried on. 'Another Roman Road goes that way. It will take you to the river Don. Once you cross that you are in Northumbria. I will escort you that way. If you keep to this path you need have no fear of us. If you seek to go any other way, we will slaughter you.'

Leif bowed and returned to the camp with the news. The brothers and the captains listened to him carefully.

'I think it's a trap,' Ubbe said. 'Why else would he want us to go that way?'

'I agree,' Halfdan said. 'The road directly to the north is shorter and the Mercian says he will allow us to use their ferries.'

Ivar did not respond for a moment.

'And what does our emissary think?' he asked Leif. 'You were with the man.'

Leif swallowed, unhappy at being asked for his opinion. Fortunately, he had given it a lot of thought on the road back.

'I think the Mercian is an experienced commander,' he said. 'He knows how to tempt and trick. I agree with Ubbe that he is laying a trap but I disagree as to where.'

The captains leaned forward, intrigued by his words.

'He mentioned the direct route,' he continued, 'and said we could use the ferries. But then, without giving a reason, he changed his mind. This raises our suspicions and we do right to conclude that he is luring us into a trap.

'But consider this. The English think we Northmen are cunning and deceitful fighters, more given to setting traps than walking into them. I think that Ceolred has suggested the western route expecting we will immediately suspect it to be a trap.'

'Why would he do that?' Ubbe said.

'Because he thinks that, fearing such a trap, we'll decide to take the other route, direct to the ferries. And that, I believe, is the way he really wishes us to go. Because that is where he has actually laid his trap.'

'This is just an opinion,' Halfdan said. 'What if the Mercian is not as subtle as you believe?'

'I think he is,' Leif said, quietly.

'Leif's words make sense,' said Ivar. 'The Mercians would not send a fool to negotiate with us. We must weigh his words very carefully.

'And let's consider the situation at the ferries. It will take days for us to cross with all our mounts. This Mercian can bide his time until the odds are in his favour, until half our army are left on this side of the river and half on the north. He will attack and destroy the men remaining on the southern bank. Who knows, he may even have another army lying in wait on the northern one.'

The captains were alarmed and confused at the same time. Ivar seized the moment, ignored the notion of weighing Ceolred's words and decided that they would take the western road.

An hour later, two horsemen trotted back from Ceolred. They gave the brothers a sack of silver pennies, as payment for their acquiescence.

The army cheered. Ivar and his brothers were considered lucky commanders and luck was the most valuable of any man's attributes.

Ivar took Leif on one side. 'I hope you're right about the advice you gave us.'

'If I'm wrong, then we're all dead men,' Leif said.

Ivar laughed and clapped him on the shoulder.

INTO THE NORTH

They made good progress from then onwards and came at last to a river which flowed swiftly from east to west. Ceolred deigned to ride back to the assembled Vikings to speak with Ivar and his brothers.

'This is the river Don,' he said. 'North of it lies Northumbria. I cannot tell you who is king there for cousins and friends feud eternally for the crown. The last I heard, Aelle had seized the throne from the previous king, Osberht, and they are now in contention. So, two hounds fight over the carcase of a pig.' He gave a grim smile. 'May you have good fortune in Northumbria.'

The Mercian warriors stood to one side and watched the Vikings as they made ready to cross the river. The Vikings cast anxious looks at the mounted warriors, fearing they would attack them mid-stream and at a disadvantage in any fight. But the Mercians made no move, merely watched as the Viking horses picked their way across, content to let them leave and go on their way to Northumbria.

The river was fast flowing but shallow and they forded it without mishap. The brothers remained on the Mercian bank until the last of the army had crossed over. Then, with a cheery wave to Ceolred, they trotted across the river.

'That was a dangerous time,' Halfdan said. 'I thought they might fall upon us as we crossed.'

'They would have if they'd intended to slaughter us,' Ivar said. 'But they're happy for us leave. I suspect they want us to cause problems for the Northumbrians.'

He called Asgrim over. 'So, Traveller, what do you know of this kingdom?'

Asgrim chewed on his bottom lip, searching his memory. 'I've been here only a few times, Ivar. The first time was a dozen years ago when King Osberht was the king. I returned three years ago. Osberht had been deposed by Aelle who is some relative of his, brother or cousin, perhaps. Osberht had retreated to the far north to try to raise an army to win back his throne. The Northumbrians are ever like this, a pack of wild dogs fighting over a corpse.'

'Is the corpse of any profit to us, then?' Halfdan said. 'Will there be pickings enough for us?'

'Even though it's not as wealthy as Mercia, Northumbria's still a rich land,' Ivar said. 'And it's especially rich in churches and monasteries. While its kings and nobles fight each other incessantly the Christ followers quietly pile up their wealth and jewels. There will be pickings enough even for you, brother.'

'And women?' Halfdan asked.

'Small in the main,' Asgrim said. 'But frisky in bed, it's said.'

Halfdan rubbed his hands together. 'Then let's find some.'

They set about this in earnest the next day. Two villages lay a little to the west of the road and as dawn stole over the land, the host surrounded the larger of the two.

'I don't like the idea of attacking defenceless villagers,' Leif whispered to Asgrim.

'They won't be defenceless when they wake up. And when a villager fights you, even with only a knife or a scythe, you'd better fight back. Either that or be prepared to die.'

'I don't like it, is all I'm saying.'

'You want to eat, don't you,' said Thorvald grimly. 'Either the English fill their bellies or we fill ours.'

I wish I hadn't come, Leif wanted to say, but dare not. It would do no good to admit that he'd been forced to come on the expedition. And Ivar, he felt sure, would be angry if he did so.

He pulled his sword part way from the sheath and stared at it.

'I haven't even got a name for it,' he said. He was suddenly alarmed at the thought that it had not been given a name at the proper time, at its forging.

'Don't worry,' Sigurd said. 'I named it for you. Sharp-Tongue, I called it. I thought it would suit you.' The laughter rumbled in his throat.

'Just be thankful that my sharp tongue has got you out of many difficult situations.'

'It has got me into far more,' Sigurd said, although without rancour.

Guthrum slipped through the men and crouched beside them. 'Ivar says we are to search for food, ale and pack-horses.'

'Not slaves?' Thorvald asked.

'We're too far from the sea to transport captives to the slave markets. So, we're only to take women ripe for fucking and young lads who can carry supplies for us. No old folk, no men, no children.'

At that moment, Ivar and his brothers strode out in front of the massed troops and began to lope towards the village.

'Stay close together,' Thorvald said to Leif and Sigurd. Leif nodded mutely and followed him at a fast stride.

The village dogs were the first to notice the onslaught, giving vent to howls and barks. Moments later the villagers piled out of their homes in consternation. Some of the men bore paltry weapons: knives, hunting spears and clubs but they were no match for the well-armed Vikings. They fell on the villagers with a horrendous roar.

Leif was between Sigurd and Thorvald, his gorge rising in fear. A tall, gangling villager, stood in their path. Sigurd smashed the man's shoulder with his hammer then, as he staggered, gave a second blow which stoved his skull in. Leif grimaced but Sigurd laughed, part pleasure, part relief that he had won the contest.

Thorvald leapt into a handful of men who parried him with feeble thrusts of their knives. He slashed open the arms of two of the men and drove his sword-point into the stomach of a third. But a fourth man, unscathed, leapt on him, wildly slashing with his blade.

Leif did not think, he stepped in and hacked with his sword, a clumsy, idiot movement more akin to chopping fire-wood. But it was enough. The sharp-honed edge of his sword cut through the man's tunic and sliced a huge gash in his side. He looked down at the wound in horror and fell to his knees. Leif wondered whether to stab him but he had no need. The man collapsed on the ground, blood flowing from him like melt-water.

'Thanks,' Thorvald grunted. 'Let's go.'

He led the way into a hut which stank of cows and bodies. A woman cowered in the corner, trying in vain to hide her children from their eyes. Thorvald seized her face in his hands and turned it to get a better look. 'Good enough for fucking,' he said and hauled her towards Leif. 'Keep hold of her and stay out of trouble.'

'What about the children?' Sigurd asked.

Thorvald glanced at them. 'Too young to carry supplies,' he said.

'Then are we to kill them?' Leif stuttered.

'I won't,' Thorvald said. 'I have no stomach for such work but plenty of others do.' He glanced at the eldest girl, who was perhaps ten years old, then stepped forward and sliced open her neck. She fell without a gasp.

'I thought you had no stomach for killing children,' Leif cried angrily.

'But even less for little girls being raped to death.' He said no more and hurried from the hut.

The woman struggled from Leif's grasp and cradled her dead child in her arms. Leif felt sick. Out of the corner of his eye he thought he saw a shape lurking in the shadows. He turned, his sword shaking in his hand. And then he gasped. It was Loki, god of ill-deeds, delighting to see what had just occurred. He seemed to raise his hand as if to bless Leif and then faded from earthly view.

Leif staggered against a stool, barely keeping his feet. He had to do something, anything to try to master himself. 'Come with me,' he ordered the woman.

'Don't kill me,' she cried.

'I won't. I promise.'

'My children. Can they come with us?'

Leif hesitated for a moment. 'No. But I can take them to the edge of the village, away from this slaughter. If they can get away they might yet live.'

'I want to go with them,' the woman cried.

Leif considered this for a moment but shook his head. Thorvald had made him responsible for her and he needed to keep her safe. Besides, she was comely, and Thorvald would want first use of her. 'They flee or they die,' he said. 'But you must stay.'

He felt sick as he said it. The youngest was only two or three years old, the others, a boy and a girl must have been six or seven at most.

'It's up to you,' he gasped, his voice so thick he could hardly force out the words.

She stared at him, eyes wide with horror.

Leif's determination wavered at the sight of this. 'I'll take them, then,' he said. 'But if they're killed, I bear no blame.'

The woman nodded and pulled the children close.

He led the way out of the hut and to the side of the village where the women and young lads were being gathered.

'We don't want children,' cried one of the guards, an older man with thin hair and skinny arms. He drew his knife and advanced upon them. The woman grabbed her children and used her body to shield them. The man cursed and tried to stab them but she twisted and turned so much every blow missed.

'You'll harm the woman,' Leif cried. 'And Thorvald has taken her for Guthrum.'

The man stopped and stared at him suspiciously. 'And the children?'

'That's for Guthrum to decide. Perhaps he'll sell them to some monks.'

The man cursed and spat at Leif's feet.

'Bring them here,' Leif said to the woman and helped her drag the children to the edge of the crowd.

The village now echoed with the screams of children and old people as those less fastidious than Thorvald went to work, slaying without pity. Others walked out of huts bearing the tiny scraps of food they had find there. A few smirked with triumph, jangling a couple of silver pennies from the richer peasants, or a choice trinket or knife. But overall the pickings were poor.

Thorvald, Sigurd, Guthrum and Eohric appeared and made their way towards him.

'It was barely worth doing,' Guthrum said to Thorvald. 'Where's the woman?'

Thorvald pointed her out and Leif pushed her forward. 'Pretty enough and a good body,' Guthrum said to Thorvald. 'Have her and good pleasure of her.'

The old guard gestured to Leif. 'This little bastard said she was to be yours.'

'What's it to you?' Guthrum said, his voice dangerous and threatening.

'And Ivar said we weren't to take children,' the man continued.

'What children?'

The man gestured angrily at them. 'I tried to kill them but this bitch got in the way. And the Skald said you wanted her unharmed.'

'Of course I want her unharmed,' Guthrum said.

The woman began to weep.

'Are these your children?' he asked, roughly.

She nodded.

'Then they can live.'

He grabbed hold of her and passed her to Thorvald. 'We can sell them at the next monastery,' he muttered to him.

'I think we should kill them,' Eohric said, drawing his knife. 'It's what Ivar commanded.' His eyes glittered with blood-lust.

'I've decided,' Guthrum said. 'The children live and we'll sell them.'

'They'll slow us down,' Eohric said. 'And the bitch will try to escape with them.'

'I'll answer for that,' Leif said.

'Ah,' Eohric said. 'So your cock is hungry for this bitch as well.' He spat on Leif's groin.

'Enough,' Guthrum said. 'Come with me, Eohric. Ivar and Halfdan will want to hear our report.'

Eohric gave a spiteful look at the woman and her children before turning and hurrying after his brother.

Thorvald cursed. 'I wish I could sell him into slavery,' he said.

'Don't let Guthrum hear you say that,' Leif said.

'Have no fear of that. I will not speak ill of Eohric unless I must. Guthrum knows well his faults but he's still his brother.'

Leif and Sigurd exchanged a glance and then looked away.

Thorvald gestured to the woman. 'What's your name?'

'Eawynn.'

'And your man?'

She shrugged. 'He died a year ago when hunting.'

Despite her thick accent, they could understand her well enough. She reached out and touched Thorvald's hand. 'Will you really sell my children?'

'To your Christ-men. It will be better than to some Khazar whore-master.'

'And me?'

'You're mine. My bed-slave.'

She began to weep. Leif turned away in shame.

NORTHUMBRIA

The army stayed close to the river crossing for a couple of weeks. Ivar was wary of the Mercians and wished to make sure they were not going to attack from behind. He sent spies back across the border and they made their way south for twenty miles without seeing any signs of military preparations. The Mercian king, Burgred, appeared to believe that the Vikings were no longer a threat to his kingdom.

He was right. Northumbria was already proving easier pickings. The army roved west and east for thirty miles, looting every village and hamlet in sight. A few thegns resisted but with laughable forces of a couple of dozen men at most. Those who survived the battle died on gibbets as warning to others who felt themselves courageous.

The land to the west of the Roman Road rose in folds to high hills and bleak moors where skinny sheep and wiry goats roamed. The meat was tough yet tasty and hunting expeditions went out daily. The land to the east was more fertile. The villages had stocks of grain and the earliest crops of kale, cabbage, carrots and onions as well as plentiful supplies of apples. Despite passionate appeals from the villagers, the Vikings slaughtered most of the cows and pigs and fished the ponds dry.

The army moved north as May was ending and settled themselves in a small port town on the River Ouse. Asgrim was sent down the river on a fishing boat to make contact with the fleet. It took two weeks for a favourable wind before it could sail to join them.

Leif and Sigurd joined the throng of warriors gathering on the riverbank. Two miles down river the first of the longships appeared, sails bellying in the easterly wind. A cheer went up from the men. The ships contained food, ale, women and spare weapons. More important, they provided a haven and a better means of escape than the horses they could not bring themselves to love.

The ships drew up and dropped anchor stones. Many warriors waded into the water to help unload them. From the third ship a shrill female voice called out, 'Sigurd, you big oaf. Come and get me.'

Sigurd grinned at Leif and trotted along the bank towards the ship. Nerienda stood in the prow of the ship, her whores in a gaggle behind her.

Sigurd plunged into the water and held out his arms. Nerienda leapt from the ship, to a great cheer from the men. The rest of the whores showed no such spirit and insisted that the ship be dragged close enough to the bank for them to alight with more dignity. Among them was Aebbe.

Leif approached her with some trepidation. He was still not sure how she felt about him and although she was his slave, to do with as he wished, he wanted more. He took a deep breath and marched towards her.

His heart began to hammer and he felt his face grow hot. She blushed and looked at him shyly. Nothing else she could have done would have made him desire her more. He started to speak but for once his silver tongue betrayed him. He could not manage a coherent phrase.

She took his hand in hers, glanced at the ground and then, after a moment, looked up and stared into his face. The look was challenging, accepting, and yielding, all at the same time. He gasped and gave a feeble smile.

'Come with me,' he mumbled.

He led her away from the river to a place he had discovered only a few days before. A little way into a forest there was a small glade, open to the skies. Most of the ground was made up of rough little bushes but a large pine tree had shed many of its needles and here Leif laid Aebbe down.

She folded her arms around him, pulling him close to her. Her mouth reached for his and he felt her tongue tickle his lips. He realised, with a pang, that it was the first time they had kissed. He pulled her closer and closed his eyes, all his awareness on his mouth and hers. He felt an overwhelming desire to laugh but the joy of her kisses prevented him. At last, he could contain himself no longer and began to undo his breeches. She opened her legs and guided him into her.

Now he opened his eyes and stared into hers. He had never realised how bright they were before, like a spring sky in the morning.

She smiled and murmured, 'This is good.'

He nodded, unable to find fitting words.

Afterwards they lay cradled in each other's arms. He felt stunned, a master of the world and, at the same time, as inconsequential as a pebble on a beach. He tried to make sense of his feelings but could not. He sighed and decided he would be wise not to try any longer.

She reached out and stroked his hair.

'I came to realise I missed you,' she said quietly. 'On the voyage north we hit a sudden storm and I thought the ship might sink and I would die. It was then that I realised how much I missed you.'

He did not reply but she did not feel concerned at this, knowing he had not the words to answer. He squeezed her hand softly and she stroked his hair more gently still. The sun dappled their faces and life felt good.

On the fringes of the forest a pair of eyes watched them bitterly.

They remained at the camp for another week. Ivar used the time well, feasting the warriors, spending time with all and sundry and debating the next moves with his brothers and the greater chieftains. The followers of each chieftain received gifts, reinforcing their loyalty before the coming battles. A sense of anticipation and excitement slithered serpent-like throughout the camp. The leaves were starting to fall and the men knew that they needed to secure strong quarters for the cold months ahead.

At last, when everyone's nerves were strung tight, the command to move north was given. Half of the men rode, each with a second horse on a leash behind. The other half of the men took to the ships in order to man the oars and ensure that the ships were no longer reliant on the wind.

Their path followed the bank of the Ouse and eventually they neared the city of York.

Leif rose in his saddle as they approached. Townsfolk were streaming out of the northern gates, terrified by the sight of the longships. Few had ever seen them for no Viking war-fleet had sailed so far inland before, but rumour of them was enough to provoke despair and flight.

Ivar turned to him and laughed. 'Remark this well, Leif,' he said. 'I require a song telling how the brave folk of Northumbria turned tail and fled at the mere sight of our army.'

'You shall have it, lord,' Leif answered. 'I shall not mention that most of those who fled were shopkeepers and their wives.'

Ivar gave him a sardonic look. 'It's a good job I like you, Skald,' he said. 'You sail very close to the wind. Just be sure you have the skill to avoid coming to grief.'

York was built at the confluence of the rivers Ouse and Foss and the Viking army camped on the spit of land between the two streams. Ancient walls loomed to the north and Ivar and Halfdan eyed them speculatively.

'The walls are high,' Halfdan said, 'and there are many warriors. We'll lose a lot of men if we attempt to storm it.'

'We may have to,' Ivar said. 'But let's give them the opportunity to flee.'

'They've had that already but they didn't take it.'

'Then let's give them an incentive as well. Send horsemen to capture some of the fleeing townsfolk. Men, women and children. And make sure that some of them are wealthy.'

Halfdan grinned. He knew well what Ivar had in mind.

The horsemen returned a few hours later, dragging behind them two score of townspeople.

They were shepherded south of the walls to where the Vikings had already flung down a pile of long poles, the purpose of which was not clear to the Northumbrians.

Ivar strode towards the walls, making sure to keep out of reach of any arrows.

'I guess you are all worshippers of the Christ-god,' he cried. 'Well I am not. I follow Odin the All-Father and his son, Thor.'

He reached for the Thor hammer talisman about his neck and displayed it to the onlookers on the walls although none could see it from such a distance.

'You might think,' Ivar continued, 'that if I were to execute your friends here, that I would have their skulls crushed by hammers in honour of Thor.'

A cry of rage and horror came from the warriors on the walls and from the townspeople behind him.

'But I am a civilised man,' Ivar continued. 'I shall not execute these people in honour of my god.'

The townsfolk gave a collective sigh.

'No,' Ivar continued. 'I shall execute them in honour of yours.'

He turned towards his warriors who immediately seized the townsfolk, threw them onto the poles and proceeded to hammer long nails through their wrists and into the timber. Then they hauled the crosses up and allowed them to drop into ready prepared holes.

The screams of the victims echoed against the walls. But none of the Northumbrian warriors made a sound. They were too shocked and horrified.

'I don't know how long they will take to die,' Ivar yelled at the Northumbrians. 'But it will give you something to watch while we make our preparations to come for you.'

CHALLENGING THE KINGS

Leif, Sigurd and Asgrim were amongst the men ordered to watch the walls that night. The agonised cries of the townsfolk hanging on the crosses unnerved them and they were glad they had been ordered to one of the northern gates where they would no longer see them and the noise of their pain would be muted.

'How long will it take them to die?' Sigurd asked, averting his eyes as they passed by.

Asgrim shrugged. 'I've seen a strong man last three days,' he said. 'The children will be dead by morning at the latest.'

Leif shuddered. He could almost feel the nails through his own wrists and the dreadful torment of the body as it dragged downward. 'Somebody should put them out of their misery,' he said.

'Ivar wants the Northumbrian warriors in the town to see it,' Asgrim said. 'He's hoping it will make them flee.'

'It would just make me fight the harder,' Leif said.

'There talks a man who is a tale-teller, not a warrior,' Asgrim said with a good-natured chuckle.

'I doubt I could find words for this,' Leif said, glancing up at the figures on the crosses. 'Come on, let's go.'

They hurried around to the northern side of the wall and were directed to keep watch on the north-eastern gate. They were to go to the woodlands nearby, out of sight of the walls.

Leif looked around. He could just make out other men in the trees to the west of them.

The he groaned. 'Here comes grief,' he said, gesturing at the approaching figure.

'Eohric,' snarled Sigurd. 'And he's coming this way.'

'Skulking in the bushes?' Eohric said. 'Frightened of a few arrows?'

'Where are you going?' Asgrim demanded.

'I asked to be sent over to the southern walls,' he answered. 'If it's any concern of yours.'

'I can guess why,' Leif said. 'You want to listen to the screams of the people hanging on the crosses.'

Eohric did not trouble to hide the smirk from his face.

But then he folded his arms and gave Leif a look of contempt. 'Was your whore good today, Skald?' he said. 'I imagine that she bewitched you the day she took you into the forest.'

A feeling of unease slithered down Leif's back.

'It's only envy, Leif,' Sigurd said. 'No woman would willingly take such a loathsome youth to bed. Even a slave would cross her legs.'

'As your brother's bitch crosses hers around his back,' Eohric sneered.

'That's a poor insult, boy,' Asgrim said. 'It shows the girl's passion. And it proves that, despite your boasts, you know nothing of women or of fucking.'

Leif stared at Eohric. 'Were you watching us?' he asked. His voice was taut with cold fury. 'Did you follow us to the forest?'

'Why would I do that?' Eohric answered. 'I have better things to do. But I saw you being led like a cur towards the trees.' He laughed. 'Good dog, Skald.'

Leif stepped forwards, fists bunched, but Sigurd held him back.

'It's late to be out, boy,' Asgrim said. 'Night will fall and then you might fall a victim.'

'But not of witches,' Sigurd said, ominously.

Eohric forced a laugh but he looked alarmed and strode off without reply.

'You were unwise to threaten him,' Asgrim said to Sigurd.

'He insulted my little brother. What else could I do?'

'As long as you remember that he is Guthrum's little brother.'

'There is little love between them,' Leif said. 'I have witnessed this.'

'But they are brothers, nonetheless,' Asgrim said. 'The greatest grief a man can know is to slay a man he loves to avenge a brother he loathes. But he will do it, nonetheless. So be warned, both of you.'

They fell silent, each musing on Eohric and how they would might repay his malice without invoking Guthrum's vengeance.

Finally, as the sun set in a sky grown red as poppies, Sigurd turned to Leif.

'Has Aebbe bewitched you?' he asked.

'Yes, she has,' he answered. He took a deep breath. 'But I'm beginning to realise that it's no bad thing to be bewitched.'

The night grew dark, for the moon was still a crescent. Leif's eyes began to close and he had to force them open in order to stay awake. Finally, as the moon reached its highest point, he heard a noise in the distance, a long, low creaking sound.

'It's the gate,' Asgrim whispered. 'They're coming out.'

Leif raised himself on his elbows and stared towards the walls. By the glimmer of the stars he saw men slipping through the gate and heading to the north.

'That's the Northumbrian warriors,' Asgrim said. 'Let's go.'

'Where?' Leif asked.

'Where do you think? To kill them.'

They slipped out of the woodlands.

As his eyes got accustomed to the dark, Leif saw that the rest of the Vikings were pursuing the Northumbrians, as relentless as an incoming tide, but silent.

Finally, when the fugitives reached open fields three furlongs to the north of the walls, Halfdan sprung the trap. Hundreds of his men were hiding there and now they rose like ghosts from the earth and barred the Northumbrians' escape route. Halfdan ordered torches to be kindled, giving enough light for the slaughter work. Then, baying like fiends, the Vikings leapt to the attack.

'Keep close,' Sigurd said to Leif. He had no need to say it for Leif had no intention of getting any distance from his brother. Yet he did not fear the sword of any Northumbrian; it was the treacherous blade of Guthrum's brother which worried him.

The battle was short and vicious. The Northumbrians pleaded for no quarter and the Vikings gave none. In the end, only a dozen Northumbrian warriors remained alive. Halfdan ordered his men to disarm them but let them live.

Victorious, the Vikings marched back to their camp south of the city walls.

Ivar and Ubbe were waiting for them.

'The rest are dead?' Ivar asked.

'Every one of them,' Halfdan said, proudly. 'Wolves and crows will feast well tonight.'

Ivar gestured the prisoners closer. 'Which amongst you will serve as your spokesman?'

The Northumbrians looked at each other and eventually pushed one man forward. He stumbled from his many wounds.

'I am Ricsige,' he said. 'I am Captain of the southern wall.'

'Was Captain of the southern wall,' Ivar corrected. 'Now you're nothing but a walking corpse.'

The man did not respond, merely muttering an insult before the killing blow which he knew would follow. But instead, Ivar passed him a mug of ale.

'Drink up, Captain,' he said. 'I'm not going to kill you just yet. First, I'm going to bleed your brain dry of all that you know.'

The Viking army moved into the city later that morning. Leif was impressed by the size of it. It was bigger than Norwic, with a fine church and many stone buildings which, although ancient, were still habitable. A large central area contained scores of little booths for the buying and selling of goods. A dozen large storehouses contained grain and salted meats. It would be enough to feed the army for a several months.

There were a great many workshops and Sigurd wasted no time in commandeering the finest smithy he had ever seen for his own. A compact house was attached to it, big enough for him, Nerienda, Leif and Aebbe. It felt like a palace to them. Aebbe made it comfortable, bringing warm furs to cover the sleeping platforms, cramming the chests with food and ale, and settling some hens, a goat and a cow in one of the rooms to provide eggs, milk and warmth for the winter.

In the meanwhile, Nerienda laid claim to a large stone building, two stories high, with a small garden in the centre and dozens of small rooms each containing a bed and little else. She was told that it was a monastery, and the small rooms were the cells of the monks, where they slept and spent cold hours contemplating the mysteries of their faith.

'There won't be much sleeping here,' Nerienda said as she explored the place. 'And the only contemplating will be of the tits and arses of my girls.'

The whores moved in that afternoon and were soon doing a roaring trade.

Half a dozen local whores had not fled with the rest of the townsfolk, electing to stay behind and see what livelihood they could gain from the invaders. Things looked ugly for a while as the two group of women squared up to one another. But then Nerienda offered to house the Northumbrians in her own brothel and allow them to keep all their earnings, so the crisis was averted.

'You'll take no money from them?' Sigurd asked in surprise.

'Not for the moment. But when they get comfortable and complacent I'll give them a new choice. Pay up or move out and starve.'

'She's a good woman,' Leif said in admiration.

'Yes,' Sigurd said, proudly. 'I chose well.'

'Except you didn't choose her. She chose you.'

Sigurd looked disgruntled for a moment. 'I suppose she did,' he said at last. 'But that's because she knew I was a good catch.'

Leif was summoned to Ivar's hall four days later. He was surprised to see Deor sitting comfortably on a stool close to the fire. On the other side sat the Northumbrian captain, Ricsige. His ankles were chained but apart from that he seemed in a better state than when he had been captured. He had been given good food and ale and Deor had bandaged his wounds.

'Why are we here?' Leif asked.

Deor pointed towards Ricsige. 'Ivar wants to question this one and we're to be there when he does.'

'Why us?' Leif asked in surprise.

'Me because I can understand the man's speech better than you Danes can. And you, because Ivar values your intelligence.'

'Don't mock me,' Leif said wearily.

'I'm not. I've seen how you've impressed him. And don't say you don't know it. He's told you enough times.'

Leif gave a shrug. Deor was right, of course, Ivar often said he admired his cunning. But Leif often wondered if this was not really the case and that he merely said it to flatter him for some nefarious purpose.

'So you're here at last,' came a gruff voice from behind. Ivar and Ubbe had arrived.

They nodded to Leif and Deor and marched over to Ricsige, standing over him.

The Northumbrian squirmed in his seat. He had seen none of the brothers since his capture. This was a deliberate ploy on Ivar's part, intended to give him time to agonise over his fate. A man's own fearful imaginings can be far more effective than actual threats.

Leif was intrigued to watch the Northumbrian straighten and set his mouth firm as if expecting a killing blow to fall any moment.

Instead, Ivar handed him a golden armlet. 'I gather you've not been paid for several months,' he explained in a mild voice. 'Take it, it's yours. There are no conditions attached.'

Ricsige's hands shook as he took the armlet.

'Put it on,' Ivar said, encouragingly.

Ricsige gulped and did as he was bid, although reluctantly. Wearing a lord's armlet was tantamount to becoming his follower. Saying there were no conditions attached were mere words which could easily be lost on the wind. The visible sign of the armlet could not be gainsaid so easily.

'So,' Ivar continued, 'my brother and I would learn from you, Ricsige. We want to know about your homeland and its kings.'

'There is only one king in Northumbria,' Ricsige said. His tongue licked his lips nervously.

'And he is?'

'Some say that it is Aelle.'

'Not Osberht?'

'That traitor? He slew King Æthelred and seized the throne.'

'And a dozen years later Aelle seized the throne from him?'

'Another traitor.'

Ubbe chuckled. 'Northumbria seems a very nest of vipers.'

'So, if both Osberht and Aelle are traitors,' Ivar continued, 'they are false kings and should not be allowed to rule.'

Ricsige shrugged but did not answer.

'Then who should be king?'

'Few men have a good blood claim,' Ricsige said, 'though many pretend otherwise. My belief is that Echberht has as good a claim as any.'

'Do you know this Echberht and where we might find him?'

Ricsige nodded. 'I do. He is my cousin and lives in Bedlintun in Bernicia, beyond the great walls the old giants built

'Frost giants?' Ubbe said to Ivar. 'I didn't know they came to these lands.'

'If there's a wall built by giants I can't see who else it was,' Ivar said.

He turned to Leif. 'Hey, Skald, how would you like to go and see a wall built by giants?'

Leif appeared to ponder it for a while. 'I think I would prefer to remain close to you and your brothers so that I can compose tales about your mighty deeds.'

Ubbe appeared flattered by his answer but Ivar snorted with contempt. 'Don't be such a weasel,' he said. 'I'm sending you north to bring the heir to the Northumbrian throne here.'

'On my own?' Leif said in horror.

'A fool as well as a weasel. No, of course, not on your own. I'll send a chieftain who can impress this Echberht.' He pondered for a moment longer. 'Guthrum has brains and a thirsting spirit. You shall go with him and his men.'

'But not his brother,' Leif said hastily.

Ivar pursed his lips thoughtfully but did not reply.

THE NORTHERN LANDS

'I beg you, Ivar,' Leif said, 'don't send Eohric with us. He hates me.'

'I realise that,' Ivar said, grinning as he stroked the neck of Leif's horse. 'That's why I did it. You'll have to keep on your toes to avoid any unpleasantness. It will sharpen your wits still more.'

'It's not my sharp wits I'm thinking about. It's Eohric's sharp knife in the dead of night.'

'Then it will improve your fighting skills as well.' He clapped Leif on the shoulder. 'Don't worry. Guthrum knows you are my man and will keep his brother on a tight leash.'

'In that case, why bother sending Eohric at all?'

'Would you rather that he remain here when you are far away? I've seen how he looks at your woman.'

Leif's heart turned to stone. He had begun to harbour suspicions that Eohric lusted after Aebbe but Sigurd had tried to persuade him that he was being foolish. Yet if Ivar had noticed, there must be some truth in it. He took a deep breath. Better to have Eohric close to hand than in Aebbe's bed.

Not that he had any choice in the matter anyway. Ivar had made his mind up and would not be argued with.

Guthrum was already mounted with a score of his men beside him. Eohric was a little to one side, eyeing Leif like a cat eyes a mouse.

Leif climbed into his saddle, his face a picture of woe.

Thorvald smiled at him. 'Cheer up, Leif,' he said. 'A Skald needs adventures to write about.'

Leif felt like saying that he was no Skald but he knew better than that. Being Ivar's Skald was the only thing keeping him safe.

They headed through the gates and onto Dere Street, a road which stretched as straight as a spear to the north west. They travelled along it a fast clip for the rest of the day. There was open country close to the road but it grew more heavily wooded beyond. There were a few settlements but none large or prosperous looking. Unlike on their journey through Mercia they saw no sign of any enemy warriors.

'Are you Northumbrians content to have us ride across your kingdom?' Guthrum asked Ricsige.

'Some, perhaps. What difference does it make to people whose lands have been ruined by civil war and slaughter?'

'So, there's not much to plunder,' Eohric said. 'Ivar was a fool to make us journey hither when there are rich pickings in Mercia.'

'Mercia is powerful,' Guthrum said. 'Only a fool attacks an enemy he cannot hope to beat. Northumbria will be less of a foe.'

'And where's the glory in that?'

'Glory doesn't fill bellies or treasure hoards,' Guthrum answered.

Leif leaned towards Thorvald. 'I see Eohric still has no grasp of what is feasible,' he muttered.

'He's a mad dog,' Thorvald answered. 'Loki's beast.'

Leif shuddered visibly.

'What's wrong?' Thorvald asked. 'You have no need to fear Eohric while Guthrum and I are with you.'

'It's not that. It's the mention of Loki.' Leif glanced around as if the god were riding amongst them. 'I am cursed by him, Thorvald. He has signalled me out for his malice.'

'It does not seem that way to me. You have the favour of the greatest Viking who ever lived, a pretty wench, a house and good friends.'

'But Loki smooths a man's path so he slides more swiftly into the trap he has set for him.'

Thorvald raised an eyebrow but did not reply. If anyone knew about the machinations of the gods it would be a Skald. He just hoped that Leif was wrong about it. He had no wish for disaster to strike his friend but knew that all men are powerless against the gods.

They camped that night in the lee of a wood and headed north the next morning. The weather turned colder with the occasional downpour of rain. Most of the warriors seemed to hardly notice it. Leif drew his cloak and furs higher and shivered miserably.

Soon after noon they arrived at a sizable village.

'This is Catric,' Ricsige said. 'There are no more settlements until Alcleat, a score or more miles north. We should stay here.'

Guthrum needed no persuading. He was a tall and heavy man and his pony was trudging ever more slowly, making him ever more frustrated.

They commandeered the thegn's hall, booting him and his family out into the cold. He, in his turn, did the same to the miller.

The Vikings fed well that night, consuming much of the food the villagers had accumulated for winter.

They did the same when they descended upon Alcleat. The thegn there showed more spirit and ordered them to ride on. They slaughtered him and his family to cow his people and set fire to his hall when they departed next morning.

The land got wilder as they rode northward. High, bleak hills rose in forbidding ranks to their left and although the road mostly kept to the lower ground there were occasions when it climbed so steeply they had to get off their ponies and trudge beside them. It was a trial for them and Leif marvelled at the hardihood of the men who had built it.

But if he marvelled at the road that was as nothing to his astonishment when they reached the great wall two days later. It was built on a bluff and stretched east and west further than the eye could see.

'So this is the wall that the frost giants built,' Thorvald said, his voice awe-struck.

Leif could not answer. He was less convinced than the others that it had been built by giants for he had seen great edifices in his youth in the Frankish lands. But never anything like this.

Ricsige, on the other hand, seemed completely unmoved by it. 'We still have a day's journey ahead of us,' he said. 'We should move on.'

They cantered along another ancient road which ran parallel to the wall. It was in better repair than the one they had been travelling on and they made good progress. As daylight faded Ricsige called a halt at a huge square fortress which stood at the end of the great wall. The fortress walls were high but crumbling and the sound of bleating could be heard from within.

Guthrum listened for a moment and then turned to Ricsige with suspicion. 'Are there only sheep in there or are we likely to face armed men?'

Ricsige shrugged. 'It's sometimes used by warriors crossing the wall. We won't know if we lack the courage to find out.'

Guthrum glared at him for his insult and led the way through a shattered gate. The others followed. The place was deserted save for a flock of sheep and a shepherd boy who took one look at them and ran for his life.

'There's plenty of meat, at any rate,' Guthrum said. The men searched the fortress for wood to make a fire, while two of them killed, sheared and butchered the two plumpest animals they could find.

The fire was soon blazing and the meat threaded onto a huge spit. As darkness fell the scent of roasting meat filled the men's noses and they realised just how hungry they were. They feasted well that night. It felt like their long journey was well and truly over.

The next morning they crossed the wall and headed north to Ricsige's cousin's home. It was a small village on a ridge of land half a mile from the coast. They were spotted by villagers in the fields who ran back to their homes to raise the alarm.

When the Vikings reached the village they were faced by a score of men bearing bill-hooks and seaxes. Another dozen were better-armed with swords and shields. A man with long, black beard glared at them, the blade of his sword resting on his shoulder.

'Begone,' the man cried, 'unless you seek to manure my fields with your shit, blood and bones.'

'Thank you for your warm welcome, cousin,' Ricsige called, dismounting from his horse and making towards him.

The man peered at him in astonishment. 'Is it you?' he cried.

'As ever, Echberht, as ever.' Ricsige threw his arms wide.

Echberht sheathed his sword, pushed past his men and embraced Ricsige. Then he looked up, askance, at the Vikings on their mounts.

'Are these men from Deria?' he asked.

'From Denmark and Norway,' Ricsige said.

Echberht fell silent and regarded them more intently. 'What makes my little cousin ride with Vikings?' he asked. His voice was soft with menace.

'I am their captive. They are settled in York. A thousand warriors and more.'

Echberht whistled. 'And what of our brave King Aelle?'

'No sign of him. Nor of Osberht,'

Echberht shook his head derisively. 'Osberht is in the north, gathering an army to fight Aelle.'

'And you, cousin? Do you support Osberht or Aelle?'

'A snake or a rat. Why should I support either?'

Ricsige bent and whispered something in Echberht's ear. He straightened, glanced swiftly at Guthrum, then bent to listen more closely still.

Guthrum eyes narrowed with suspicion and he signalled to Thorvald. Both men silently drew their weapons, and when they saw this, the rest of the Vikings did likewise. Leif was the last to do so, concentrating on the two cousins, wondering what they might be saying.

'I don't think they mean to fight us,' he whispered to Guthrum.

'Why not?'

'For all his bluster, I doubt that Echberht is a hero. And he certainly isn't a fool. He may have a shield-wall but it's made up of farm-workers. He has no more warriors than we do. Any fight would leave most of his folk dead.'

'He looks at us with great doubt.'

'Wouldn't you? We Vikings are not loved here. And distrust seems to run in the veins of the Northumbrians. And is that not the reason we have journeyed hither?'

Guthrum chuckled. 'Ivar's right; you are a cunning man. Well, as you've guessed something of it, you may as well know the rest. Ivar wants me to bring Echberht to him. He means to offer him the kingdom or part of it.'

'Has he any claim to it?'

Guthrum shook his head. 'Have any of the men who have worn the crown? From what I gather Northumbria is a rotting carcase and the dog who gobbles fastest is named king. So why not Echberht?'

He climbed from his horse and strode towards the Northumbrian line.

'Greetings from Ivar the Boneless and his brothers Halfdan and Ubbe,' he said. 'They would have you journey with us to York where you will learn something to your advantage.'

Echberht stared at him in silence for a good while. 'I will come,' he said at last. 'Tell Ivar I will go to him after the Christmas feast.'

'You'll come now or not at all. Ivar is not a man to keep waiting.'

Echberht's warriors turned to him nervously, wondering what his response would be. Eventually he sighed and nodded.

'If I am to hear something of advantage,' he said, 'then I might as well hear it quickly.' He turned towards his steward. 'Saddle my horse. And find a dozen ponies for my household warriors.'

Guthrum shook his head. 'I said nothing of your warriors. You are to come alone.'

Echberht's eyes flashed with anger. 'A great lord does not journey anywhere without his men. Even a pirate such as you should realise this.'

Guthrum bristled and his fingers stirred as if itching to seize his sword.

'It is a fair comment, Guthrum,' Leif called. 'A lord who lacks followers lacks standing.'

Echberht looked Leif up and down. 'A savage with brains,' he said. He managed to sound impressed and contemptuous at the same time.

'But I'm sure that Echberht would not want to leave his village completely undefended in these dangerous times,' Leif continued. 'Perhaps half of his warriors should come with him, and half remain.'

Guthrum grinned at Leif's words. 'Six men, Echberht,' he said. 'That is what I allow you.'

'You will allow me?' Echberht said. 'It seems to me it is your follower who decided.'

'My brother makes the decisions,' Eohric cried bitterly.

Echberht glanced at him, then at Leif. He chuckled. 'Bickering in front of your foes,' he said. 'I shall feel at home amongst you.'

He turned once more to his steward. 'Seven mounts, then. And we leave straight away.'

The journey south was a miserable affair. The weather turned cold and a fierce wind brought icy rain from the north. Echberht was a past master at stirring up dissent and he played Eohric and Leif like harps.

Leif did his best to ignore him, knowing that the Northumbrian's jibes were designed purely for his own amusement. Eohric was less subtle, rising to Echberht's bait almost every time, cursing and threatening Leif. Then Echberht would laugh and insult him still more. Eventually Ricsige took his cousin on one side and persuaded him to guard his tongue.

And so, after seven gruelling days, they returned once more to York.

Ivar and his brothers welcomed Echberht and his men with great cheer and directed them to a comely house, promising a feast for the evening.

When they had gone out of earshot, he gestured Guthrum and Leif to him. Eohric made to follow but Ivar stared coldly at him until, cursing silently, he stalked off.

'What do you think of this Echberht?' Ivar asked.

'He's a trouble-maker,' Guthrum said. 'He goaded Leif and Eohric on the journey south, fanning the enmity between them. He did it for spite, nothing more. I do not trust such a man.'

Ivar glanced at Leif.

'Guthrum's right about this. He played me for a fool. He seems to know exactly how to winkle out any grievance or malice.' He paused and considered further. 'But I don't think he did it solely for spite. He was testing Eohric and me, using our reactions as a potential weapon for the future. When Eohric and I raged at each other he spent almost as much time watching Guthrum as us.'

Ivar rubbed his hands with pleasure. 'Exactly as I hoped. A vicious brute with just enough intelligence. The harder I ride him the more savagely he'll bite his countrymen.'

Guthrum frowned. 'Is it not dangerous to have such a man as King of Northumbria? Might he not try to bite us?'

'Northumbria is made up of two hounds, Bernicia and Deira,' Ivar said. 'When one hound is strong, it rules. But the other bides its time, sniffing out weakness, planning to seize power. I do not intend to make Echberht a powerful hound.'

Guthrum nodded although he still looked a little dubious.

'Northumbria is still a divided kingdom,' Ivar continued, 'with little love between the people of Bernicia and those of Deira. It is why I came north. A divided land is more easily conquered.

'And I will leave Jarl Osbern here to keep an eye on our new friend.'

Guthrum smiled. Leif, on the other hand, was less sanguine. Ivar might talk about setting up a new king but two other men, each with a better claim to the throne were still at large.

'Osberht is in Bernicia,' Leif said, 'and gathering an army.'

'To fight us?' Ivar asked. He seemed completely unconcerned.

161

'To fight Aelle for the throne.'

Ivar smiled. 'That proves my point, young Skald. Two dogs, each preparing to fight for a petty crown. Yet all the time a dragon is waiting to consume them.'

GATHERING STORM

The winter was as hard as any Leif had known. Frost came the day before the Yule feast and once it had its claws upon the land it refused to relent. The days grew ever more bitter and men walked in fogs of their own breathing. And then, a month after Yule, vast black clouds rolled in from the west and a blizzard fell upon the land.

'It's beautiful,' Nerienda said as she peered out of the shutters at the swirling whiteness.

'Aye,' Aebbe said, 'but it will be the death of many folk, I fear.'

'But not us,' Leif said. He stared at the storm for a moment and then returned to his stool beside the fire.

He was right. The English were going hungry but not the Vikings.

When they'd conquered York they had found the stores well stocked with food and ale. In the months since, they had plundered the land with systematic ruthlessness, filling the stores to over-flowing.

Ivar had ordered them to leave the immediate hinterland of the city untouched, reserving that for the worst days of winter when travel would be difficult. Instead they attacked a wide swathe of land between ten and thirty miles around. Not a farm escaped their depredations, not a herd of cows or flock of sheep still grazed, not an orchard bore fruit nor fish-pond remained stocked.

The Vikings took the strongest men and most beautiful women to the city as slaves. Some were loaded onto ships bound for the great slave markets of Dublin and Scandinavia but hundreds more remained in the city to serve the army. Sigurd now spent as much time forging manacles and iron collars as horse-shoes or swords.

Ivar and his brothers were delighted at the influx of slaves. Every ship's crew were given an allotment of half a dozen men and women. Even the poorest warriors began to think of themselves as lords.

The male slaves laboured in the freezing cold to repair the walls, make good any damage to the ships and assist their masters in hunts and wild-fowling. The women laboured to make wool for the fleet's great sails, to maintain the houses, cook and mend clothes and to satisfy the men's lust in bed.

The only ones unhappy at the arrival of the slaves were Nerienda and her whores. Nerienda charged the warriors good money, while the slaves were free. Inevitably her trade began to fall away. In the end, desperate to keep the business, Nerienda began to offer the best of food and ale in her brothel and made her girls offer ever more erotic and unusual services. Word got around the camp and it stemmed the exodus for a while. But in the end the men grew tired of paying for what they could demand for free from their slaves and her trade fell off once again.

Eventually she decided to buy those slaves who were prettiest or most celebrated for their bed-skills. Most of the warriors were persuaded to sell their slaves because of the price she offered.

'Why would any man sell their slave only to later pay for her services?' Sigurd asked her, bewildered.

'Because men cannot count as well as I can,' she said. 'A handful of coins seems a good bargain to them. They cannot see that I will recoup it from them many times.'

Her wealth was sore depleted but she remained one of the wealthiest people in the city and as time went on her wealth slowly but surely increased.

Throughout the winter a constant series of slave convoys arrived in the city, new blood to export abroad or expend within the walls. The slaves were treated worse than dogs, insulted and beaten on the slightest whim, forbidden to meet in more than twos or threes and given only enough food to keep them working. They had little shelter and the rags they wore were little use against the dreadful cold.

Many died in these months and their corpses were thrown outside the walls to be eaten by dogs and wild beasts.

This last practice caused great grief to the Christ-followers.

Their archbishop, Wulfhere, had remained in the city, making peace with the conquerors for the sake of his people. Eventually, as he watched the wretched slaves endlessly carting emaciated bodies for disposal beyond the walls, he found his courage and determined to speak with Ivar.

Leif was intrigued by the old man's bold move, wondering what he intended to do, and hurried after him to Ivar's hall. This might make for an amusing story, he thought.

'What is the nature of your complaint?' Ivar asked the archbishop incredulously, waving a half-eaten knuckle of pork in the air.

He listened to Wulfhere's long peroration with a bored half-attention but eventually lost any semblance of patience.

'Slaves die,' he growled, 'and their bodies can't be left to fester and rot in the city. When spring comes, the stench will become unbearable.'

Wulfhere closed his eyes and offered a silent prayer to his God.

'It is not about where the bodies are deposited,' he said. 'It is about how they are treated.'

'I will order that they are carried more respectfully,' Ivar said. 'They shall be covered in cloaks to shroud them from prying eyes.'

'But you still intend to dump them on the open ground, to be eaten by wild and savage creatures?'

Ivar shrugged and began to gnaw once more upon his meat.

'But these people are Christians,' Wulfhere cried. 'They need Christian rites, prayers, holy words, and burial.'

He paused both for breath and dramatic effect.

'Yes, they must be buried,' he continued, 'for if not, they will be devoured by beasts. And then how can they rise for the Final Judgement?'

'At Ragnorok?' Ivar asked in surprise. 'They rise up to fight for Odin?'

He exchanged a bemused look with his brothers.

'No,' Wulfhere snapped. 'Every Christian rises from the grave and stands in front of Christ for Him to cast eternal judgement upon them.'

Ivar's only response was a yawn.

'My lord,' Wulfhere said, 'I beg you to let my priests give a Christian burial to every man, woman and child who dies.'

Ivar sighed and looked at his brothers. They both shrugged, bored beyond words by the whole discussion.

'And if I agree to this?' Ivar asked, wearily. 'What do I get in return?'

Wulfhere had been expecting this and had his answer ready.

'I shall acknowledge you as lords of the city,' he said. 'And I shall levy a tithe upon every church and monastery in my province and this shall go to you.'

'I have no need of your help in taking money from your churches,' Ivar said. 'I take what I want, when I want.'

'But this will come to you without any effort on your part. And proclaiming you lords of the city will be a great blow to your enemies.'

'Then why would you do it?'

'For the sake of the dead. They must be given a Christian burial.' He got down on his knees. 'I beg you.'

Ivar stared at him in silence, pondering how to wring out the greatest advantage. 'If you must,' he said, at last. 'But no slaves are to dig the graves and no slaves are to carry the bodies. They work for us and us alone. From henceforward, these tasks must be done by your priests.'

Wulfhere swallowed. This was a harsh imposition and he knew that many of his priests would be unhappy at being forced to this work.

'I shall be the first to dig the graves,' he said, humbling himself still more by bowing low to the ground.

'I like that,' Ivar said. 'A man who leads by example. I shall come and watch.'

He waved Wulfhere away and returned to his pork knuckle.

Wulfhere was as good as his word. He helped carry the next slave to die, an old woman from a village near the coast. She was little more than skin and bones and even the aged archbishop had little trouble with the stretcher. A crowd of warriors followed him through the gates, a few cheering his efforts but most jeering.

Ivar stood beneath the walls, wrapped in a heavy fur coat and with a cup of hot wine in his hand. He had ordered Leif to attend, thinking this a fine topic for a song. Aebbe had insisted on coming along as well and watched proceedings anxiously.

The archbishop began to dig the grave. The ground was hard as rock and he made little impact with his spade. He changed it for a pick and resolutely chipped away at the soil. But he was an old man and unused to manual labour and he was soon panting from the exertion. A bevy of young priests who had accompanied him went to take the pick from him but Ivar bellowed to them to stop. Wulfhere had insisted he would dig the first grave and he intended to hold him to his word.

The crowd fell silent as the old man continued to hack at the unyielding earth. He staggered a few times but made the sign of the cross and continued with his task. But then his foot slipped on the icy ground, the pick dropped from his hands and he almost fell. The Vikings gave a loud hoot of laughter to see his arms whirling to keep his balance.

'This is terrible,' Aebbe cried. Before Leif could stop her she darted forward and took up the pick.

'I shall dig the grave, Father,' she said.

Ivar opened his mouth to stop her but thought better of it. He'd suddenly realised that if the old man completed the grave he would become a hero to his people. But if a girl had to finish his work for him he would be a figure of contempt.

But Aebbe was also having difficulty, so hard was the ground. She had made little progress when she stopped, leaning on the pick handle and gasping for air.

Leif could watch no longer. He strode forward, took the pick from her and began to chop at the ground. He realised it would anger Ivar but felt he had no choice. He cared nothing for the old holy man but did not want to see Aebbe exhaust herself fruitlessly.

But no matter how hard Leif swung the pick he could make little headway. The ground was more stubborn than Wulfhere had proved to be.

The sweat poured from his face as he worked, hot at first but icy cold within moments. He paused to see how far he had broken the earth. Hardly at all. At this rate it would take him until sundown to complete the grave. By then, he thought, he'd be so exhausted he might well fall into it with the corpse.

But then the pick was snatched from my hand.

'Out of the way, brother,' Sigurd said.

He spat on his hands, raised the pick above his head and sent it crashing to the ground with a thud which echoed against the walls.

Leif blinked in amazement. With one blow Sigurd had removed more soil than Wulfhere, Aebbe and he had managed in total.

He lifted the pick again and attacked the hole with unerring accuracy and strength. The onlookers marvelled at his strength and determination. In a surprisingly short while he had made a trench deep enough to take the corpse and keep it safe from the depredations of wild creatures.

Ivar watched for a moment longer, nodded his head once to give his agreement and headed back into the city.

The body was laid to rest and Wulfhere began the funeral service.

Sigurd threw the pick to the ground and smiled at Leif.

'That was easy work for a smith,' he said. 'You shall have a harder task to make a tale which will amuse Ivar and not drop you or me in the shit for helping the old fool of a priest.'

'He didn't do it for the priest,' Aebbe said. 'He did it for me. And I am glad for I am with child and do not wish to lose it.'

Leif's mouth fell agape.

'Lost for words, Leif,' Sigurd said. 'Now, there's a first.'

THE NORTHUMBRIANS GATHER

Aebbe's belly grew fatter as the days grew longer. Leif could not believe that a baby was growing there. Was it like a flower or a vegetable, climbing on a stalk? Or was it a tiny person, growing larger day by day as children and animals do in the world? He asked Aebbe which it was and she had no answer, nor did she seem to need one.

'When will he be born?' he asked, hoping that at least he would learn something.

'You're certain it will be a boy?' she said with a smile.

'I just thought it would be,' he answered.

Aebbe squeezed his hand affectionately. 'Time will tell. And the baby will be born in summer, on the longest day of the year, perhaps.'

Leif smiled, relieved for some reason. He could find nothing more to say, so he sauntered outside and sniffed the air. The days were still cold but there was a scent of warmth in the breeze, elusive but noticeable. A few bushes were budding, oak trees were starting to leaf and blackbirds and starlings were beginning to build their nests.

He walked to the smithy and found Sigurd hammering a horse-shoe into shape.

'So, you've finished with slave bonds,' he said.

Sigurd nodded. 'Halfdan asked me to make more horse-shoes. And more swords and spear-heads.'

Leif felt a little worm thread its way through his bowels. 'So we're getting ready for war?'

'Seems that way.'

Leif's lips grew dry. The mere mention of war sent his imagination spinning.

He saw himself in the midst of battle, hacking enemies in a shield-wall, falling maimed or fatally injured, or fleeing his foes in terror or standing stupefied by overwhelming fear. His nostrils filled with the stench of blood, shit and horror.

Sigurd whistled happily as he worked.

'Aren't you worried about going to war?' Leif demanded.

Sigurd shrugged. 'What's the point of worrying? It won't change anything.'

Leif sighed. His brother was right, of course. But it didn't make his words any use or comfort.

'I wish I was like you, Sigurd,' he said. 'I wish I didn't worry.'

Sigurd flung the horse-shoe on a pile beside the anvil. 'I like you to worry,' he said. 'It saves me the trouble. And besides, if you worry enough you might figure out how to keep us out of trouble.'

'There is that, I suppose. And it's important now that I'm going to be a father.'

'It's more than just that,' Sigurd said. 'I'm going to be an uncle. We don't want the boy to have an uncle who's been made useless by his wounds.'

'Aebbe thinks it might not be a boy.'

'Don't listen to her. What do women know about offspring?'

Leif did not answer for his attention was taken by a man racing to Ivar's Hall. He was breathing heavily and looked alarmed.

'Come on,' Leif said. 'Something's happening.'

The Hall was crowded with the chieftains of the army, Jarls and the greater thegns. Other warriors were streaming in behind.

Leif and Sigurd pushed their way to the front of the crowd and saw the messenger talking to Ivar and his brothers, his arms gesticulating wildly. He finished at last and Ivar rose to his feet, staring at the door of the Hall as though his gaze could pierce the timber.

'What's happening?' Jarl Sidrac demanded.

Ivar turned to him and gave a dreadful grin. Leif could not understand his look. Was it anxiety or excitement?

'The two Northumbrian Kings have put aside their differences,' Ivar said in a voice which carried to the furthest corners. 'Their armies have joined together and are marching south towards us. They will be here within days.'

There was an eruption of noise.

Leif glanced at the rest of the warriors. Most looked exultant although a few seemed concerned.

'Two armies?' said Jarl Osbern. He was a cunning man with eyes which roved everywhere except the face of the person he addressed. 'Can we fight such a force with hope of success?'

Ivar spoke quickly to quell any uncertainty Osbern's words might cause. 'How many warriors?' he asked the messenger.

'A thousand —'

'There,' cried Halfdan, in triumph. 'That's less than we have.'

The messenger gulped and spoke once more. 'In each of the king's armies.'

There was silence in the Hall. Even the most stupid of the men could do this sum.

'Twice our number,' said Jarl Frene, quietly. 'We will be slaughtered.'

A murmur went around the Hall, a worm of doubt and fear.

'Only if we go out to meet them,' Sidrac said. 'We can remain here behind the walls and defy them.'

'Until we starve to death?' said Frene. 'Such a course is folly. We should take ship and leave before it's too late.'

'You'd have us run away?' Halfdan cried. 'From English peasants?'

'They're not all peasants,' the messenger said. 'The majority are better equipped than we are.'

Ivar gestured to Echberht and Ricsige who were standing to one side of the hall. 'Who are these warriors?' he asked. 'Are they peasants or more dangerous?'

'We Northumbrians have been slaughtering each other for a century or more,' Echberht said. 'It has grown worse since the conflict between Aelle and Osberht and there has been a great increase in armies. These men are likely to be thegns or mercenaries.'

'Some looked like our kinsfolk in Ireland,' the messenger said. 'Others like Picts.'

'So they're mercenaries,' Ivar said. 'Men as used to warfare as we are.'

Or more, Leif thought although he did not voice it. The Vikings of Dublin were some of the most feared warriors in the world and the Picts as savage as rabid hounds. His stomach clenched in terror. He did not care much for Jarl Frene but he hoped that his counsel would prevail and they would take to the ships and leave.

Yet most of the men seemed to be unconcerned by this news, as were Halfdan and Ubbe, who were always ready for a fight.

But Leif kept his eyes on Ivar, knowing that he would make the decision and sway the army one way or another. He had fallen silent, his eyes narrowed, clearly in the deepest of thought. Finally, he seemed to awake from his reverie and stared at the warriors in the Hall. A moment later he raised his arm.

'We will not flee from our enemies,' he said in a loud voice. The men cheered at his words. 'But nor will we go out to meet them like lambs to slaughter. We will fight as Vikings always do, with guile as well as courage.'

'Does that mean we skulk behind these walls?' Eohric cried, giving a gesture of contempt to Jarl Sidrac.

Sidrac stepped towards him, his eyes burning with anger, his hand reaching for a knife, but Osbern restrained him.

'We fight with guile,' Ivar said, 'something you are too great an idiot to comprehend.'

Leif chuckled at his words and the reaction it caused in Eohric who snarled to himself in impotent rage.

'Jarl Sidrac is right, up to a point,' Ivar continued. 'We shall wait within the walls. But not in the way the Northumbrians expect.'

THE BATTLE FOR NORTHUMBRIA

Leif peered through the window of the merchant's house in which he was hiding. Everywhere he looked, the city was silent with not a soul upon the streets. He could see the great minster church with its doors locked fast. Inside were every Northumbrian in the city, save for Echberht and Ricsige. They were just behind him, talking in hushed tones to Ivar.

'What if Ubbe's men are killed?' Echberht asked. 'The armies of Aelle and Osberht will head to the city. We'll be like rats caught in a trap.'

'You might be a rat,' Ivar said in a sneering tone, 'but my men are wolves who will destroy my foes.'

'It is folly to divide your army,' Echberht continued. 'How many men does Ubbe have? Three hundred to fight two thousand.'

Ivar looked at him with disbelief. 'Ubbe is not going to fight them to the death, you fool. Just long enough to be defeated and flee. And he will flee quickly. He is not called Ubbe the Swift for nothing.'

'So your brother is renowned for his speed in flying from the enemy?' Echberht could not hide the contempt in his voice.

'He is renowned for following my plans and securing victory,' Ivar said. 'Now shut up and let me sleep.'

Leif exchanged a look with Asgrim who was silently honing his battle-axe. He grinned with pleasure, although Leif was not sure if it was at the exchange he had just heard or the thought of the coming battle.

A moment later they heard a horn braying in the distance, followed by an almighty thump as if of distant thunder.

Ivar's eyes flickered open. 'The battle has started,' he said quietly.

The men in the room leaned forward to hear better. The crash must have been the collision of shield-walls and it was now followed by fierce cries of men. This rose and fell like a winter wind, interspersed by a dull hammering noise as blades beat upon shields.

Echberht and Ricsige stared mutely at each other. Perhaps they were regretting their treachery, perhaps they were wondering how they could survive whatever the day brought.

The battle went on for a little while longer. Then a second horn blared and they heard the pounding of many feet.

'Ubbe's retreating,' Ivar said.

He pulled his sword Havoc from his belt and tested the edge of it with his thumb.

Leif realised that he had never seen Ivar use the sword he had bought from his brother at such cost.

At the same moment he recalled the sight of the fickle god Loki lurking in the spume of the smithy. His stomach crawled. Was the god here now, was he merely waiting to unleash doom upon them all?

He tried to dismiss the thought from his mind. He took a gulp of air. If he died he would try to make sure it was with a sword in his hand. Although he had no love of battle he decided he'd rather spend the afterlife in Valhalla than in the darkness of Hel.

He thought of Aebbe and his heart clenched. Together with all the women and children, she'd been evacuated downriver by ship. If the worst came to the worst the plan was for skeleton crews to take the ships across the sea, although to what fate no one could tell.

Leif had already told Aebbe that she should try to escape. She was English and the Northumbrians would be more likely to treat her better than the Danes. At least then his unborn son would have a chance of life.

The men fidgeted, the long wait seeming an eternity. Ivar moved next to Leif and stared every bit as intently out of the window.

'Will this make a good tale, Leif?' he asked, quietly.

'I'm sure it will, Ivar. If we survive.'

Ivar chuckled. 'Well, just make sure you do. Come what may I want a mighty tale to be told about this day. I want you to tell the world what a hero I am.'

'Even if you're dead?'

'Especially if I'm dead. With help from a good Skald, the fame of a man can last longer than his flesh.'

He gripped Leif's arm tightly. 'They're here.'

The main gate of the city was opening, and a dozen men slunk in. They walked stealthily across the open space beneath the walls, their eyes darting everywhere. After a few more steps they stopped walking, irresolute for a little longer, then turned towards the gate and called.

Scores of warriors began to stream into the city. They looked astonished to find it so empty, so silent, so desolate. And then there was a stir and a compact body of mail-shirted warriors marched in, followed by two men on horseback.

Ivar beckoned Ricsige to come to the window.

'Aelle and Osberht,' he said, almost under his breath.

'No doubt they're already plotting how to kill each other,' added Echberht.

'I shall save them that task,' Ivar said.

The two kings rode towards the church and turned to watch their men marching into the city.

The open space below was now already half full of enemy warriors. Even from this distance Leif could make out the tall blond Viking mercenaries and the short, swarthy Picts. But most of the men appeared to be Northumbrians, about half of them well-equipped warriors, the rest peasants armed only with spears and knives, many without even a leather breast-piece.

And still they came, until the whole great open space was filled with them. Most sheathed their swords. A number even began to take off their mail shirts.

And then they began to cheer their kings, exultant at winning back the great city. But neither king dismounted nor responded to the cries. They sat upon their horses and continued to scan the city. Then one of them, the younger one, commanded some of his guards to open the doors to the church.

They hurried to do his bidding and levered off the timber bars which had been hammered into the doors to keep them shut. They pushed the doors to open them but, to their surprise, they did not move. The two kings stared at the church intently, wondering what this might signify.

'Now,' Ivar cried, shaking Asgrim by the shoulder.

Asgrim put the ox horn to his lips and blew one long blast. It echoed across the square below, startling and unnerving the Northumbrians.

And then, with a mighty roar, the Vikings surged out of their hiding places and fell upon them.

'Come on,' Ivar cried, leaping down the stairs.

Leif followed reluctantly, hoping that Sigurd and Asgrim would keep up and stand beside him.

Girding his failing courage, he drew his sword and stepped outside. Ivar was to his right, with his personal guards swiftly congregating around him. These were the most skilful of warriors, hard and brutal, and Leif wriggled his way into the middle of them, knowing that he would be safest there. Sigurd and Asgrim pushed their way next to him.

And then they strode to battle.

The Northumbrians had been completely taken by surprise. They were unable to deploy a shield-wall, many unable to unsheathe their swords before falling to those of the Vikings. Their shrieks of fear and fury echoed off the walls.

Guthrum was to Ivar's left, smashing through the enemy like a fierce sea batters the shore. Halfdan was beyond him, raging like a berserker, drenched with the blood of his adversaries.

Ivar, on the other hand, fought more cautiously. He left his doughtiest warriors to fight the biggest and strongest of the enemy and dispatched easier targets with skilful thrusts. His willowy body swayed with every movement and Leif realised that his physical frailty meant he was no match for most of his foes. But he was the master in skill and cunning. These he displayed to good effect, killing two or three men and maiming half a dozen more.

Leif remained in the centre of Ivar's guard and no Northumbrians got close to him. The noise of screams and curses filled his ears as Ivar's men made their way, step by step, into the enemy ranks. Eventually the crush got so tight Leif had to use his sword, though it made little impact beyond the occasional slash wound that most warriors would barely notice. More by luck than skill, no blade touched him.

Leif glanced around. It seemed for a moment that they were in danger of being overwhelmed by the superior numbers of their foes. But as the Vikings hacked onward these numbers became a hindrance. The Northumbrians were forced back against the walls and became too closely packed to respond to the hammer blows of the Vikings.

And then, of a sudden, the Northumbrians broke. A few men at first and then many, many more, they ran for the gates. They fought amongst themselves to escape, pushing and battling each other in their desperate flight.

Both kings tried to rally them, bellowing to them to stay and fight. This slowed the panic for a moment with many of the seasoned warriors girding themselves to continue the battle. But most of the peasants took no heed and continued to surge through the gate.

Backwards and forwards the battle went, sometimes the Northumbrians having the upper hand, sometimes the Vikings. And then the sounds of blaring horns rang out beyond the walls, followed a moment later by shrieks and cries of woe.

'Ubbe,' Ivar yelled to Halfdan who grinned with delight. Their warriors cheered loudly and went back to the battle with renewed vigour.

The men trying to flee through the gates were now pushed back by their friends who had just left. Outside the walls, Ubbe and his men were slaughtering the peasants with ease and the survivors were now desperate to get back into the city.

In moments any semblance of discipline broke down amongst the Northumbrians. They were trapped and they knew it. Many threw down their weapons, seeking a mercy which was not given. The rest fought on grimly, although they knew that their lives were over.

Finally, the two kings were pulled from their horses and dragged out of the melee. Most of the Northumbrians gave up the fight soon after, falling to the ground and begging for mercy.

The Vikings drew off, conscious that there were still too many foes to kill, and turned towards their lords.

Aelle and Osberht were thrust towards Ivar and thrown onto the ground in front of him. The eldest was already badly wounded and blood was flowing from him. The younger, Aelle, shook with terror and pain.

The sounds of battle finally ended. The last of the Northumbrians threw down their weapons and the Vikings began to collect them and carry them out of reach.

The stench of death was overpowering. The earth was like a butcher's stall, strewn with severed limbs and guts, blood staining the soil and mixing with the shit and vomit of terror.

Ubbe pushed through the mob and joined his brothers. They stared at the death and destruction with grim satisfaction.

'Do you yield?' Ivar demanded of Aelle and Osberht.

The two kings forced themselves from their prone positions and nodded.

'Then I proclaim a new king for Northumbria,' Ivar called. 'Echberht of Bernicia is now your lord.'

None of the Northumbrians responded, they merely stared at Ivar with watchful, defeated eyes.

'Do you think they will accept him as their king?' Sigurd murmured.

'They will,' Ricsige said. 'Even now the thegns will be pondering how best to ingratiate themselves with him. It is dog eat dog in our kingdom and now it seems my cousin is the new leader of the pack.'

'Not Ivar?' asked Sigurd in surprise.

'Northumbria is a nest of serpents,' Leif answered. 'He deems it better to have a lackey suffer any poison fangs.'

'I doubt my cousin will be a lackey,' Ricsige said.

'Of course not,' Asgrim said consolingly. But he gave Leif and Sigurd a wink to say he thought otherwise.

Within moments, Ivar made clear what was to be the first task of the new King of Northumbria.

'What do you want to do with your predecessors?' he asked Echberht.

Echberht shuffled uneasily and glanced at Ricsige who refused to meet his eyes.

Not so the rest of the Northumbrians who stared at Echberht with eager curiosity. His reaction would give them an insight into how to act towards him.

'They are traitors,' Echberht said at last. 'They fought amongst themselves, heaped untold misery upon our people and caused hatred and dissent.'

He paused and glanced at the Northumbrian warriors to try to judge their reaction to his words. They gave nothing away, merely stared back at him with watchful eyes.

'So, my judgement is this…' He fell silent. It was clear that he had no idea what to say. Halfdan gave a snort of derision

'So, my judgement is this,' Echberht continued with faltering speech. 'All Osberht and Aelle's lands and those of their immediate kin are to be forfeit to the king.'

He gave an arch smile at the word, the first use of his new title.

'And they are to be exiled,' he continued, 'to a place of my choosing.'

A murmur rippled across the ranks of the Northumbrians. This was an act of unusual clemency. Previously deposed kings had been poisoned, had their throats slit or been starved to death. Some nodded in approval at his show of mercy, though many looked doubtful.

'No,' said Ivar simply. He nodded to Halfdan who seized an axe from one of his men and marched towards Aelle and Osberht.

Leif was powerless to turn his eyes away.

Halfdan stood in front of Osberht and smiled grimly. He held the axe high, took a swing, and severed the neck with one blow. Osberht's head fell with a thud upon the earth and rolled over, the eyes staring at Leif and his friends.

Aelle threw himself to the ground, screaming for mercy. 'Please, Echberht,' he cried, 'I was always good to you.'

Echberht looked horrified and turned towards Ivar.

Ivar folded his arms and considered the prostrate king for a moment. Then he made a savage, chopping motion.

Halfdan's axe swept down, burying itself deep into Aelle's back. Astonishingly, the man still had enough life to scream in agony, his hands reaching out, fingers working convulsively, still pleading for mercy.

Halfdan grunted and pulled the axe from Aelle's back, tearing off a slice of flesh in the process. Then he took another swing, aiming this blow on the other side of Aelle's spine. It cut deep, severing his ribs and revealing the pink, pulsating sacks of his lungs.

Still Aelle did not die; his fingers clawed the earth, his head shook from side to side in torment, spit and gore spewed from his mouth.

'I think he still wants to be king,' Ivar said with a chuckle. 'Persistent man.'

Halfdan plunged his hands into Aelle's body and pulled out his lungs, spreading them over his back where they throbbed and wobbled like a terrified beast.

Aelle had cried loudly before, but that was as nothing compared to the long wailing, shriek which broke from him now. Loud and high at first, it speedily slid into a whimper and then a gurgle. The lungs collapsed like a sail when the wind dropped.

'Time to feast,' Ivar said.

Halfdan nodded, holding up his gore-wet hands to the Northumbrians.

'Come and join us friends,' he called in a jeering tone. 'The dogs will dine on your kings.'

185

A NEW SWORD

The Vikings remained in York for a further half year. Archbishop Wulfhere crowned Echberht King although few of his subjects showed enthusiasm for him. All knew that Ivar and his brothers were the rulers of the land. Ricsige became his chief counsellor and he alone seemed to give Echberht the honour he demanded.

Leif strolled into Sigurd's smithy a month after the battle and found Sigurd hard at work on a strange weapon. He looked startled at his approach and told Leif to close the door.

'Why the secrecy?' he asked, bending to look more closely at the metal on the anvil. It was like no sword he had ever seen before. The blade was a little over half the length of a normal battle sword but that was not the most peculiar thing about it. For it was incredibly thin and not flat like a normal blade but rounded.

'It looks like a darning needle,' Leif said in confusion.

Sigurd smiled grimly. 'It's to be called Snake,' he said. 'You must have been sent by Odin for I was ready to call you to sing its birth song.'

'Who on earth would want such a weapon?'

Sigurd glanced around nervously and put his fingers to his lips. 'You must not breathe a word of this to anyone.'

Leif was intrigued. 'Of course not.'

Sigurd took a deep breath. 'It's for Ivar.'

'But why? He has Havoc. Havoc is a marvellous sword.'

'As this will be.' Sigurd held the blade up and examined it like a man might look at his bride when she shows herself naked for the first time.

'But the shape of it?'

Sigurd replaced the blade on the anvil. 'Havoc is too heavy for him.'

Leif frowned. 'But it's not heavy. You said yourself it's the best-balanced sword you've made.'

'But it's too heavy for him. He sought me out the day after the battle and told me that wielding it was proving too taxing. His strength is failing, Leif, although he wants none to know it. Not even his brothers.'

'And he thinks to fight with this?'

Sigurd nodded.

Leif picked up the blade and examined it closely.

'It makes sense,' he said, at last. 'I stood close to him in the battle and he barely used his sword. And when he did it was with great economy, as if to preserve his strength.'

'He will need little brawn to wield this,' Sigurd said. 'I designed it to be used with cunning and guile rather than muscle.'

'Then it's perfect for Ivar,' Leif said. 'Snake, you say. A fitting name, I think.'

Sigurd grunted. 'So come up with a chant which praises the hidden qualities of a snake and the dangers it presents to its foes.'

'And none are to know of this?' he asked.

187

'None.' Sigurd paused. 'Apart from us two. Ivar told me that you were to sing at its birth. And you are to take it to him tonight.'

Leif sighed, pulled up a stool and began to ponder the words for a chant. It was a challenging task.

At last he came up with something. An anxious glance showed him that Loki was nowhere to be seen, and he began to chant in time to Sigurd's taps.

He told of a snake that was sired by a dragon. It was so fiendishly clever it could curl up its wings to hide them and confuse its enemies or use them to soar the skies. So slippery-tongued it could make a man admit to any wrong-doing and any maiden invite it to lie with her. So powerful of mind that it could remember every slight or insult and feed them on the promise of revenge.

The brothers stopped hammering and chanting at the same time. They had created a masterpiece of venom and nobody was to know of it.

SLAVING

The walls of the city were made even stronger and new quays dug in the river to accommodate the fleet more easily. Word of the defeat of the Northumbrians carried across the sea and warriors and traders from Norway, Denmark and the northern isles descended upon the city. A flourishing slave market was set up and it soon proved competition for even Dublin's well-established trade.

Leif was told to join one of the many parties sent across the country to capture folk for the market. Sigurd refused to go, presumably because Nerienda forbade him to bring yet more pretty wenches to compete with her whores.

Aebbe was equally unhappy at Leif's going on these ventures; she had been a slave herself, if only for a little while.

'But the extra money will be useful,' he said, rubbing her stomach. It was now round and tight and he could sometimes feel the baby kicking.

'Don't you earn enough from being a Skald?' she asked.

'Enough for you and me. But we have my son to consider.'

She did not reply although she made it clear that she still opposed slaving and any part he played in it.

The women were not the only ones to argue against such ventures. Wulfhere pleaded with the Vikings not to send out the hunters, saying that it was more important to allow people to stay in their villages and tend the farms than to sell them as slaves. They would not listen to such seeming good sense. They

189

thought that money in the hand was better than crops growing slowly in the earth.

Ricsige was also opposed to it and tried to persuade Echberht to remonstrate with the brothers. But he had no stomach for such dissent and kept silent.

One thing Ivar did allow was to send the foraging parties as far distant from York as possible. But this was not due to the effectiveness of the English pleas, merely a continuation of his previous policy.

So it was that Leif found himself journeying once more along Dere Street, although this time with a dozen men led by Thorvald. Ricsige also travelled with them. Perhaps he was glad to get away from York, Ivar and Echberht.

At Catric they took a smaller road to the west and headed into barren uplands which remained cold and bleak even though spring had come. After a weary day's trek they began to descend from these high moors and the following day came upon a green land dotted with many lakes. A small village lay a little to the north of the nearest lake.

The people here were short and dark of hair and not of English stock.

'Brythons,' Ricsige said. His voice was full of contempt. 'They have dwelt in these lands for many years and are akin to fairy folk, hardly men at all. They were here long before my ancestors arrived and they claim they will be here long after we've died out.'

'And you let them say that?' Thorvald asked in surprise. 'Why haven't you Northumbrians conquered them? They seem a feeble people.'

'They might look feeble but they aren't. They are as hardy as thorn trees which stand against the snow and icy winds. Ugly, of little merit, but with strong roots. It is not worth our while to grub them up.'

'But they are strong?'

Ricsige nodded.

'Then they will make good slaves?'

'For a season or two. They are like stupid beasts and can be driven hard. Then, too often, they lose all taste for life and fall into a state of craven weakness. The secret is to work them to their utmost for a few years and then, when they have little strength left, sell them on cheap.'

'I think Ivar will find a use for them,' Thorvald said. 'Leif, take Skegg and Gorm to the top of the valley and, when I blow my horn, charge down upon the village.'

'And what will you be doing while I ride to what may prove to be my death?'

'I'll be waiting at the far side of the village to capture those who might make the best slaves.'

Leif gave a broad smile. Attacking a village unawares would be safer than waiting to catch a horde of fearful folk.

He led Skegg and Gorm to the top of the valley and they kindled torches. He had long thought that fire was more terrifying than any weapon made of steel and his experience of smithy work meant that he was far happier with flame than sword. They kindled one torch each and waited for Thorvald to give the signal to attack.

It felt like they waited for an age. Skegg and Gorm did not speak at all, merely sat their horses as placid as cows. Leif, on the other hand, studied the village keenly. It was made up of a dozen huts so poorly made they might well have been erected by foxes or bears. It would take no time for the flames to consume them.

On the far side of the village were a group of women, carding wool and singing. They little knew what doom was to befall them.

Thorvald's horn sounded and Leif and his men galloped down the slope towards the village.

The women were looking to the west, trying to see who was blowing the horn. Because of that the three riders came upon them unawares, waving their burning brands like demons and screaming at the top of their voices. The women looked petrified, threw down their work and fled down the long slope.

They didn't see the rest of the Vikings until it was too late. Nets were flung over the women, snaring them like a shoal of fish. Some managed to evade this and swerved, desperate to escape. But Thorvald had kept two men on horseback and they blocked their path. The women ran to right and left like hares cornered by hounds.

In a moment Leif was amongst them and Thorvald gestured to him to chase a handful of women breaking away to the south. It was the work of moments. Leif caught up with them and called them to stop. They could not understand the Viking tongue but they understood the menace in his tone, right enough. They flung themselves on the ground, their hands upon their ears, screaming at the top of their voices.

'Tie their wrists but don't harm them.' Thorvald ordered. He tilted the face of one of the women and scrutinised it. 'Not a beauty but good enough for a bed-slave, I think.'

'Take your filthy hands off her,' came a voice from behind.

Leif turned and gasped in surprise.

Standing to one side of a clump of trees was a tall woman dressed in mail-shirt, her cloak billowing in the wind, a slim sword resting upon her shoulder. Beside her stood another woman in leather hauberk, with a seax in her hand. A little further down the slope were a couple of dozen warriors with spears, battle-axes and swords.

Thorvald straightened and stared at the woman. His right hand moved slowly to loosen up his fingers, ready for battle.

'What's this woman to you?' he asked, gesturing to the peasant.

'She belongs to me,' the woman in the mail-shirt answered. 'They all do.'

Thorvald crossed his arms in a belligerent fashion. 'You're Norse?'

'Half-Norse. My mother was Irish. If it's any concern of yours.'

'No concern of mine,' Thorvald said. His eyes strayed to the warriors behind her, calculating their likely strength and the odds of any battle.

'If they belong to you then I apologise,' he said at last. 'I thought they were merely peasants for the taking.'

'They are. But I took them first.'

At that moment the sun broke through the clouds to reveal a longship drawn up on the shore of the lake.

Thorvald saw this and knew what he must do. 'My name is Thorvald,' he said, spreading his hands in an appeasing manner. 'I am the steersman of Jarl Guthrum and fight in the army of Ivar the Boneless.'

'I know Boneless,' the woman answered. 'And he knows me.'

'Then we are friends,' Thorvald answered.

'I did not say that Boneless and I are friends.' She did not sheathe her sword. Thorvald's hands flexed even more.

'My name is Kolga,' she said.

'The goddess of the icy wave,' he said.

She gave a smile every bit as cold. 'Better than a stream of piss.'

Thorvald half turned to Leif. 'You talk to her,' he muttered from the corner of his mouth.

'Why me? You're our leader.'

'You're a Skald. You have a way with words. I get the feeling she will skewer me with hers.'

Leif stepped forward reluctantly, as certain as Thorvald that this strange woman would best him in debate. Not that he minded that. His chief fear was that she would choose to attack and, if she did, they would either end up dead or join the women as her slaves.

He licked his lips nervously, wondering how to begin.

'I am Leif Ormson,' he said. 'Skald to Ivar the Boneless.'

'You I have not heard of,' she replied. 'His last Skald was Sigenoth who he flogged to death.'

It was the first time Leif had heard this alarming fact.

'My back is unmarked,' he said with a gracious nod.

'And what makes you think it will remain so?' she said. 'Dead men suffer wounds on their back. Slaves bear the marks of the scourge.'

He could find no answer to her words.

She gestured to her followers who strode towards her.

'It is one thing for Ivar the Boneless to scourge his Skald. Quite another for someone else to attempt it for him.' Leif said this with a hint of a threat. A tiny hint, not too much to alarm her, but hopefully enough to give her pause.

'Where is Boneless now?' Kolga asked.

'In York.'

'That's miles away.'

'Yet he sent us here. His reach is long. He has conquered the Kingdom of Northumbria and placed a yes-man on the throne.'

Her eyes narrowed at this, her mind calculating.

'How many warriors does Boneless lead?'

'A thousand men, my lady. But others join him daily, such is his fame.'

'And his brothers, the two fools?'

'Halfdan and Ubbe are with him. As are Jarls Sidrac, Frene, Osbern and Guthrum.'

'A mighty host,' she murmured.

She glanced back at her ship. 'I too am a Jarl,' she said. 'I am the daughter of Bjorn Blackbrow.'

Leif had heard of Blackbrow. He was a crazed killer of holy men and elderly goats.

'And is your father well?' he asked, although he had no interest in the answer.

'He is dead.' She stropped her sword and then sheathed it. 'We had a disagreement about a woman. She was too beautiful for him to bed.'

'But not for you?'

'I take what I want. Man, woman or youth.' She smiled. 'And you, Skald? Have you a woman? Or a boy, perchance?'

'A woman. She is with child.'

Her face lost something of its hardness. 'Freyja's blessing on them both.'

'I thank you,' he said. 'You're very gracious. I shall tell my wife.'

She clasped him on the shoulder. 'I would have you act as Skald to me, Leif Ormson.'

He swallowed hard. He had no wish to offend her but even less desire to anger Ivar.

'I cannot, my lady. I am sworn to Ivar.'

'Not for ever,' she said, chuckling at my discomfort. 'Only as long as it takes us to travel to Jorvic.'

'Jorvic?'

'It's our name for York. Yes. I have a mind to join with Boneless. It may prove amusing.'

Later that day they learned that Kolga was a more impressive leader than they had first thought. Eight more longships sailed in on the evening wind. She led two hundred and eighty men; more than most of the chieftains in Ivar's army, twice as many as Guthrum or Frene.

'It will take too long to sail around the island,' she said. 'We will journey with you across the moors.'

She glanced at the slaves who were tending the fires and cooking the food. 'If you're hunting for slaves you must have a market for them.'

'In York,' Thorvald answered. 'Ivar set up a market as soon as we arrived. It's flourishing.'

'Then I shall sell these slaves there rather than take them to Dublin. And a few I shall give to Ivar as a peace-offering.'

Leif wanted to ask why she needed a peace-offering but thought better of it.

He could not keep his eyes or thoughts from Kolga. Even more than Ivar, she appeared to have a natural air of power, it hung about her like a cloak and could not be gainsaid. At supper that night she was brought the finest cuts of meat and supped only the best wine. And when she retired to bed she took two people with her, the woman in the leather breast-plate and a huge man with vivid blue eyes and ready laugh.

They broke camp the next morning. Kolga's horse was brought to her from her ship, a fiery stallion she called Blood. Two men struggled to walk it up the slope for it kicked and snorted like a bull. But it quietened at once when she touched it and allowed her to glide into the saddle without a murmur. A dozen of her chief men were also horsed, including Vafri, her male lover and her female one, Asta.

Kolga bade Leif ride beside her and tell her of Ivar's expedition and all that had transpired since he led the fleet to England. Throughout the journey she never gave any indication whether she was impressed by his deeds or indifferent.

It took five days to retrace their route for the slaves were not inclined to hurry and needed constant hounding. Leif thought that Kolga would be incensed by this but it did not trouble her.

'I don't want them ruined or surly when we come to sell them,' she explained. 'That was just the sort of mistake my father made.'

They arrived at York late morning. Word had spread of their approach and as they entered the gates they were welcomed by Ivar, Halfdan, Ubbe and several of the jarls.

Kolga drew to a halt and regarded Ivar with an enigmatic glance. He looked discomforted but forced a smile upon his face.

'Welcome, Kolga,' he said. 'I had not thought to ever see you again.'

'Hello, Boneless,' she said. He winced at her using only his nickname. 'Clearly Frigg has greater wisdom in the matter of our meetings than you do.'

He grunted although it was unclear whether in agreement or dissent.

'You are welcome to tarry here for a space,' he said. His voice gave no sign of whether he desired the idea or loathed it.

'Tarry?' Kolga said. 'I do not intend to tarry, Boneless. I have come to join you in your escapade. I shall require a hall for my followers and me.'

She gestured to Vafri who led a dozen slaves to them.

'And here is a gift to you, my friend,' she said. 'Brythons, swart and stupid but good workers and willing bed-mates.'

'You would know about that,' Ivar said.

'What is good for the ram is good for the ewe,' she said, smiling at his sneers.

'And what if I do not wish you to join with me?'

'Your wishes hardly concern me. Besides, you have two brothers who I could ask.'

Ivar turned without a further word and strode away.

'You are welcome, Kolga,' Halfdan said, holding her horse while she dismounted. 'And your men and slaves even more so.'

'And what do you brothers have planned?' she asked. 'Destroying the north as you have destroyed so much else?'

'Milking it rather. Although Ivar has his eyes on a richer prize.'

'Wessex?'

'Not yet. Mercia.'

'That is a mighty mouthful to swallow in one gulp.'

'We shall see.'

Kolga shrugged. 'I can see that you will have need of my men.'

'Our numbers swell daily,' Ubbe said. 'But none have brought as many warriors as you.'

'Then I shall take my place at the council table,' she said.

Several of the jarls looked uncomfortable with this but Halfdan, Ubbe and Jarl Sidrac assented.

There is history between these men and Kolga, Leif thought as he turned away from them and headed towards his home and Aebbe.

KOLGA

Aebbe gave birth on the longest day of the year. Leif had been convinced that it would be a boy. He was half right. One baby was a boy, the other a girl.

'Twins,' Sigurd said, grinning happily. 'I didn't think you had it in you, brother.'

The boy was named Nefi, which pleased Sigurd as it meant both hand and nephew. 'He will make a great smith,' Sigurd said. 'See how he grips my finger.'

Aebbe insisted that they gave an English name to their daughter. Leif's friends demurred but he was happy to do so. They called her Godgyth and she was the delight of all.

Leif spent the rest of the summer going on slaving expeditions and crafting songs and tales for the forthcoming winter. He already had a good stock of the deeds of Ivar and the other chieftains, rooted in fact as so many of the warriors knew the truth of each tale, but with just sufficient embellishment to flatter the subjects of the tales and amuse the listeners.

But when his stock began to grow thin he decided that Kolga might be a good source of stories and sought her out.

She had spent the months since arriving very quietly. It was rumoured that she occasionally visited Ivar in his bed for this seemed to explain how some mornings he awoke unusually contented or abnormally enraged.

It was common knowledge amongst those who had no knowledge of her, that she was a fickle lover, demanding and demeaning on one night and loving and considerate on the next. But all agreed that, whatever her approach she was always passionate and abandoned. All agreed and all lusted. Not that anyone would make a move in her direction. They were all too aware of the jealousy of Vafri, Ivar and Asta. And all too aware of the cold and cruel nature of Kolga herself.

This was as welcome to Leif as mead to a warrior. He plucked up the courage to seek her out.

'Good morning, Skald,' she said as he approached. 'Have you come with some plea from Boneless which he's too scared to ask for himself?'

'No, my lady,' Leif replied. 'I come for tales which I can recount in the halls in the long winter months. Tales which will entertain and enthral and encourage men to do great deeds. Tales which I believe you can tell me.'

She closed her eyes and a little smile played upon her lips. He sensed that his words had flattered her.

'Pour me some wine,' she said, settling herself comfortably in her seat. 'What would you have me tell you?'

'The tale of yourself. Of your kin, your friends, your enemies, your deeds.'

'Ha. It would take more than one winter to tell all there is to know about Kolga Iceberg.'

'Iceberg?' he said. 'I had not heard that nickname.'

'Few dare use it and nor shall you. But it was given me by my father Blackbrow.'

'Bjorn Blackbrow, I presume?'

She nodded. 'A violent and vindictive tyrant, who amassed riches as he amassed victims. He slew one of my brothers in a rage and banished the other from his lands. So it is that I now own all he had. I loathed him.'

'And what of your other brother? Does he still live?'

She shrugged. 'He was a weak and stupid boy. Some say he dwells in England, others that he went to Francia to seek succour from my father's old friend Hæstenn.'

'Hæstenn,' Leif said, in surprise. 'My father was a smith to Hæstenn.'

'Now Hæstenn was a man to admire,' Kolga said. 'Deep and cunning, much given to plans and stratagems. You remind me of him, Leif, a little.'

Leif didn't know whether to be flattered by the comparison or appalled. Even amongst Danes Hæstenn was considered one of the most dangerous men alive.

'So tell me,' he asked, 'why do you admire Hæstenn but not your father?'

'Hæstenn is touched by Thor, my father by Loki.'

Leif swallowed at her words for a lump had instantly filled his throat. He saw once more the image of Loki in the mists of the smithy.

Kolga laughed suddenly, as if she had seen into his heart. 'Don't flatter yourself that any of the great gods should take an interest in one such as you, Leif. Bragi, god of poetry is the only one who might take passing notice of you.'

'Bragi was the enemy of Loki,' he said, trying to put a bold face on things.

'Only fools seek the enmity of the great gods,' Kolga answered. 'I do not take you for a fool.'

At that instant Leif realised for the first time the strange power she wielded for he felt it so keenly. She made him feel a bigger, more consequential, more powerful man. For the briefest moment he even imagined himself as her lover, then dismissed it. Some might wish to bed a dragon but he was alert to the peril of her fire.

'Tell me of your deeds, Kolga,' he continued, anxious to stop his galloping thoughts. 'It is rare to hear of a woman who rules so many warriors.'

'Rare but not unknown,' she said. 'There are more of us than you men realise. I myself have met three although none with so many followers as me, or as successful in battle.'

'Do you fight then?' he asked. He was aware of the surprise in his voice, and anxious how she might react.

'Why so astonished?' she said. 'You have seen my sword, my mail-shirt and how I ride my fierce horse, Blood.'

'Indeed I have. Forgive me.'

'I thought a Skald would have sufficient imagination to see me as a warrior. I suspect you see me battling in bed well enough.'

He blushed, hotter than he had for a long time.

Kolga chuckled. 'Perhaps if your songs please me, I shall let you fight such a battle with me.' She pursed her lips in a kiss.

'I am your servant,' he stammered.

She eyed him speculatively for a moment longer.

'If you must know,' she continued, 'I have been a fighter all my life, from the moment I could walk. My brothers and our servants can vouch for this. When I was little more than a girl I met Boneless and was bewitched by him. Such a tall, lean man, with power and calamity oozing from his pores.

'We bedded. I'm sure he'd say he bedded me but my mind is not so certain. He turned me from a farmyard brawler to a warrior. He won many great victories in Ireland before he decided to seek more glory by joining Hæstenn.'

'I didn't know that. It must have been after my father left Francia.'

'I care not about your father the smith,' she said. 'But I did care about Boneless, more fool me. I followed him to Francia and fought alongside him for three years. In the end I gained my own renown, much wealth and many followers. And then, a while after that, he left. Without a word of farewell. I returned to Dublin and have not seen him until now.

'My father had grown old, worn out by too many wounds and too fierce a bitterness. He was gaga, mumbling like a hen in the coop, drawling on his beard. I did him a great service by slitting his throat and sending him to Odin.'

Leif started at this revelation but she did not notice.

'And so,' she concluded, 'I inherited his wealth and warriors.'

She gave a broad smile, content with what she had told him.

'Thank you, my lady,' he mumbled. 'I will tell fine tales of this. Although I will not speak of the death of your father.'

'Why ever not? It does no harm to let others know. And it may serve as a warning to those who choose not to love me.'

Leif nodded and hurried outside. For the first time ever, he felt concerned about Ivar.

TO NOTTINGHAM

Once the harvest was safely in Ivar gave the order to leave York. Echberht and Ricsige remained behind. They had their own soldiers, of course, but Ivar insisted that two hundred Vikings remain in the city, lodging them in the tower. They were led by their jarl, Osbern who Ivar trusted to look after his interests and not risk his men in needless adventures.

He also left twenty longships in the city. The rest of the fleet was sent south with a third of the army, their supplies and women. The remainder of the warriors took horse and travelled south. This time they did not retrace the route along the western branch of Ermine Street but took the more direct, easterly route which headed straight to the river Humber.

Leif was fortunate because Ivar had decided to travel by ship and wished his skald with him to beguile the journey with songs and tales. Aebbe and their babies were allowed on his ship, and so was Kolga.

She affected no interest in the little ones, as if to make plain that she was too stern a warrior to do so. Yet, oftentimes, Leif found her watching them with a smile upon her face. Once, when they made camp, little Godgyth began to wail while Aebbe was at the cooking fire. Leif could not quieten her and began to despair. Then Kolga appeared and took Godgyth in her arms, rocking her gently and crooning until she was calm.

'Would you like a child?' Leif asked her gently.

'Are you offering to give me one?' she said sharply.

He raised his hands, seeking to calm her as she had soothed Godgyth. 'I didn't mean that.'

'Good,' she said. 'I may yet bed you, Skald, but I will be the one who decides, not you.'

She did not come near the children again.

The fleet sailed down the Ouse until they reached an islet close to the northern bank, a few miles west of the English ferry. They camped there for three days until the horsemen joined them. The horses were loaded into the ships and the army crossed the river. The Vikings had returned to the Kingdom of Mercia.

Ivar's ship led the fleet south along the Trent. There was a stiff northerly wind to fill the sails and no need to row, for which Leif was very thankful. His skin had never hardened enough to wield oars without peeling and he still found it difficult to keep time with the other rowers.

He leaned against the prow of the ship and watched the empty land beyond the river, content that they were moving at a gentle pace.

'Mercia will prove more difficult to subdue than Northumbria,' Ivar said, coming to stand beside him. 'It is rich and powerful, was once by far the greatest kingdom in the island.'

'It doesn't seem so now,' Leif said, gesturing to the flat marshes on either side. 'There are more wild-fowl than people here.'

'It will be different as we journey farther south. Mercia is full of folk and crammed with riches. You'll see.'

'But why do you seek to conquer Mercia?' Leif asked. 'You've always argued against it before.'

'Hunting dogs are vicious and if they aren't allowed to hunt they can turn against each other. So it is with we Northmen, and I fear this. It is folly to keep beasts on too tight a leash.'

He turned towards the crew of his ship and watched them thoughtfully as they lounged at ease on the deck.

'And Northumbria proved easy to conquer,' he said, 'and I deem that our warriors desire a more fitting foe. As, perhaps, do I and my brothers.'

Leif nodded sagely, sensing this was the safest response he could give.

'And where are we going?' he asked after a little while. He was surprised that Ivar was sharing so much information and was keen to make the most of it.

'To Repton,' Ivar said. 'The king of Mercia's great palace lies there and I have a mind to enjoy its hospitality.'

In the event they did not go so far. After a few days sailing they reached a large town a little way north of the river. It was well defended with a ditch and palisade and in the centre was a fine timber hall of large size.

A hundred of the Vikings leapt off the ships and raced towards the town, the inhabitants fleeing them like hens from a fox. A few resisted but were swiftly slain.

'Who dwells here?' Ivar asked an old man as they approached the hall.

'Thegn Wignoth,' he answered, struggling to keep his teeth chattering from fear. 'He is a doughty warrior.'

'We'll see,' Ivar said, with a smile as bleak as death.

He'd no sooner said this than a man strode out of the hall, carrying a sword in one hand and a spear in the other.

Wignoth did indeed look a mighty warrior, a tall, well-made man with massive neck and barrel chest. He stared at Ivar with a haughty, contemptuous look.

'Who are you to rampage through my town?' he demanded.

Ivar gave a pleasant smile. 'Ivar the Boneless and his brothers Halfdan of the Wide-Embrace and Ubbe the Swift.'

'I have heard of you,' Wignoth snarled. 'Danish scum, wolves and carrion-eaters.'

Leif shuddered. The man was a fool to speak to Ivar thus.

But Ivar merely laughed, as did his brothers. 'We, on the other hand, have not heard of Wignoth the Witless.' His tone had become harsh and challenging.

But it soon became clear that Wignoth was far from witless. While they were talking, four score warriors had sidled out of his hall. By talking to Ivar, Wignoth had bought them the time to don mail and grab shields and weapons.

Ivar's eyes flickered from the Mercians to his men. Halfdan was itching to attack, it had been months since he had dismembered the Northumbrian kings. But Ivar was more cautious, weighing up the odds. Despite his reputation for ferocity, he was not prepared to risk all in battle while he still had other choices.

'We have no wish to fight you, Wignoth,' he said, now speaking in a conciliatory tone. 'We come to trade, that is all.'

'From what I hear you trade only in death,' Wignoth replied.

'Not true. We have ended the civil war in Northumbria and put a true king on the throne. Have you not heard this?'

'I've heard a tale concerning it,' Wignoth said.

'This tale is true,' Ivar said. 'My skald will bear witness to it.'

Leif nodded mutely, fearing Ivar would ask him to spout the story in front of this suspicious Mercian.

'So,' Ivar continued, 'can we trade?'

Wignoth looked doubtful but then nodded slowly. 'Perhaps. What is it you wish to trade?'

'Food and ale. For gold and silver.'

'My people cannot eat gold and silver and winter is close.'

'We do not want much,' Ivar said. 'Just enough food to last a few days so that we can leave you in peace here.' He said the words in a friendly, reasonable manner but there was no mistaking the threat behind them.

Wignoth called one of his men and they whispered together. After a short while Wignoth gave him curt instructions then turned to address Ivar once more.

'My steward says we can sell you five hundred loaves of bread, two dozen sheep and eight barrels of ale,' he said. 'We offer a good price.'

'I'm sure you do,' said Ivar. He gestured to Asgrim and spoke quietly in his ear. Asgrim hurried back to the ships.

The opposing warriors stood facing each other for a good while, neither side prepared to move or relax their guard. At last the Mercians stirred and turned towards the river.

Two score Vikings were trudging up the path, bearing chests and bags.

'Have you no slaves to carry your goods?' Wignoth asked.

'No,' Ivar answered. 'We left them in Northumbria.'

The Vikings approached and Ivar signalled to them to open the chests and empty the sacks upon the ground.

Leif gasped. What was Ivar thinking? He was offering a vast amount of money for precious little in return.

The Mercian warriors had never seen such wealth, they pressed forward, mouths wide-open.

'There's enough for all of you,' Ivar said. 'Take what you want.'

'Hold,' Wignoth cried. But he spoke too late.

His warriors threw themselves on the ground, scrabbling for the coins and jewels cast before them. Almost immediately they began to quarrel, a few even threatening each other over the most valuable coins or gems. Their voices rose, some began to push and shove and all the while Wignoth shouted for them to stop.

Suddenly his voice was stilled. Ivar had thrust his sword into his throat.

Wignoth clutched at Snake's narrow blade, vainly trying to pull it free but Ivar pushed it deeper, turning it from right to left to open up a larger wound. At the same time the Vikings threw themselves upon the scrabbling Mercians.

Few had the chance to draw their weapons, most did not get off their knees. Within moments all were dead, their blood staining the ground, their hands grasping not their swords but the coins with which they had bought their deaths.

'I like this trade,' Ivar said, pulling Snake out of Wignoth's throat.

The Mercian toppled to the earth, gasping, wild-eyed, in agony; yet still clinging to the last moments of his life.

'Scum, are we?' Ivar said. 'Carrion eaters? Well it's you who are now the carrion, my friend.'

He watched until Wignoth breathed his last, chuckled and led the way to the hall, gesturing to Leif to follow.

'This will make a fine tale,' he said. 'Remember to include my jest about carrion.' He threw open the door and stepped inside.

Leif stopped on the threshold and whistled with amazement. This hall was almost as impressive as that of King Edmund's in Norwic. Like his it was white-washed to reflect the light. But it was also decorated, in glorious colours, red, blue and gold. The pictures were of animals, many of which he'd seen but some he always thought the work of men's fancy.

Three women sat at the lord's table, wide-eyed with terror, with half a dozen guards standing wretchedly by their side.

'Are you the family of Thegn Wignoth?' demanded Ivar.

The older woman nodded. 'I am his wife. These are our daughters.'

Ivar gave a curt bow of his head and then addressed the guards. 'You have a choice,' he said. 'Attempt to fight or put down your weapons. If you surrender, the women will live. If you fight, we'll disarm you and you'll watch them die. Very slowly. Very painfully. And you will follow them straight afterwards. But even more painfully.'

The guards looked at the woman but she ignored them, staring with horror at the door.

Halfdan strode towards her, swinging Wignoth's head by the hair.

'Put down your weapons,' she told the guards, her voice sounding as dead as was her husband.

'Sensible woman,' Ivar said.

He walked to where she was sitting, gazed in her face, and then at her daughters. He grasped each of their breasts in turn. The two daughters sobbed in horror but their mother bore it with grim determination.

'One for each of us,' Ivar said. 'Tell Ubbe he can have the mother.'

'I want the older girl,' Halfdan said.

'Too late. She's mine.'

'The young one has no tits.'

Ivar tore open her tunic. 'Yes she has,' he said. 'Nice little buds. If you want we can take turns with the daughters.'

Halfdan grinned and nodded, then threw Wignoth's head upon the table.

The eldest daughter took a step towards Halfdan and struck him across the face. He laughed and struck her back. She reeled but came back and struck him once again.

'This one's a feisty vixen,' he said. 'She'll be fun.'

'You'll regret this,' she cried. 'I'm Wynflaed, daughter of Wignoth and am betrothed to Beornulf, the nephew of King Burgred.'

Halfdan shrugged. 'We'll break you in for the boy. He'll be happy that we do so.'

Leif gnawed his lips, troubled that these ladies should be treated so savagely. Ivar saw this and gave a knowing smile.

'Take the women to some safe place,' he called to Asgrim.

'Concerned for the women, are we?' Ivar asked Leif, tauntingly. 'Or is it that you wish to bed them?' He clapped him on the shoulder. 'After we've finished with them, maybe. If you're a good boy.'

Leif turned away, fearing that his look of disgust, and desire, would betray him.

'This is a goodly hall,' Halfdan said. 'It must be a rich town.'

Ivar nodded. 'I think we should stay here for the winter. It will save us the trouble of taking Repton.'

'As you wish,' Halfdan said. 'As long as the town has enough supplies.'

'More than Repton,' said one of Wignoth's guards eagerly.

'Has it now?' Ivar said, staring at him coldly. 'And what is your name, lickspittle?'

'Leofric.'

'Leofric Lickspittle,' Ivar said.

'Yes, indeed my lord. Repton is small and consists of little more than King Burgred's Hall. But Nottingham is a great trading town. We have food and wealth a-plenty.'

Not for much longer, Leif thought, although he did not voice it.

'Then that's settled,' Ivar said. 'This will be our winter-quarters. This is our hall and here are our women.'

He threw a penny at Leofric. 'You belong to us now, Lickspittle. As do Wignoth's women.'

KING BURGRED OF MERCIA

News travelled fast in Mercia. Only fifteen days after the Viking took Nottingham a man raced in to the Great Hall where Ivar and his brothers feasted with Wignoth's wife and daughters at their feet.

'An army approaches,' he cried. His face showed alarm and fear.

The captains threw down their food and seized their weapons, running to the walls to see for themselves.

Leif wanted to make sure that Aebbe and the children were safe but Thorvald and Sigurd persuaded him to go with them.

'The city walls are strong,' Thorvald said. 'No army will take them.'

But when they reached the walls his words seemed to be tempting fate. The army which marched from the west was large, very large.

'Two thousand men and more,' Ivar calculated.

'We have fifteen hundred,' Ubbe said. 'And we are behind strong walls.'

His voice was confident, unconcerned. But Leif was not alone in having doubts. The Mercians can be reinforced, he thought, whereas we're trapped.

He had had been surprised when Ivar had changed his usual methods and ordered the lands close to the town to be pillaged. Now he saw the wisdom of it. Ivar was a wily commander and must have realised that the Mercian king would respond rapidly. He had wasted no time in building up their stores.

Nevertheless, Leif's heart sank a little. Mercia might well prove a harder nut to crack than Northumbria. He recalled Ivar telling him how wealthy the kingdom was and how difficult it might be to subdue. And unlike Northumbria it was united under one king, a king who had proved swift to seek battle.

And the king was no fool. He deployed his army between the city and the river, denying the Vikings access to their ships.

But Ivar was also no fool. He had left skeleton crews to man the fleet and it was already heading back up the river, out of reach of the Mercian army.

'Do you think Wynflaed's betrothed will be here?' Halfdan asked with a grin.

'Possibly,' Ivar answered. 'In which case, she may be of use to us.'

'I don't want her harmed,' Halfdan said. 'The vixen is too good in bed.'

'Do you think only with your prick?' Kolga snapped.

Ubbe laughed. 'I've always said it's the cleverest part of him.'

Halfdan bellowed with laughter, slapping Ubbe on the shoulder.

Ivar, on the other hand turned his steely eyes on the enemy, ignoring all jest and banter.

'Do you think that's their king?' he said. He pointed out a man riding a great black steed towards the walls, with a score of men behind him. They halted an arrow flight from the wall.

'This one's not a fool like Aelle,' Thorvald muttered under his breath.

'I am Burgred, King of Mercia,' the man called. 'Who is your leader that I may talk with him?'

Halfdan and Ubbe exchanged looks and then glanced at Ivar. He gave a grim smile and leaned upon the parapet.

'I am Ivar the Boneless,' he said. 'Our army is led by me and my brothers, Halfdan and Ubbe. Why do you disturb our repose?'

Burgred's face took on a look of rage but he swiftly masked it.

'You have no right to be here,' he said. 'Nottingham is held by my friend, Thegn Wignoth. I would speak with him.'

'You can speak with him but he won't answer,' Halfdan cried. 'His head departed from his body.'

Burgred froze. 'He's dead?'

'Pretty much.'

'And his family?'

'They're being well looked after,' Ubbe said.

'Especially the oldest girl, Wynflaed,' Halfdan added. 'She's got the appetite and skills of a whore. She wears me out day and night.'

A young man cried out and forced his horse forward. Burgred gestured him to remain silent.

Halfdan laughed. 'So you must be her promised man,' he said. 'She's as delectable a maiden as I've ever tasted. Except of course, she's no longer a maiden.'

The young man looked stricken by his words.

'And her sister, Eadburg?' Burgred cried.

'The little chit?' Halfdan said. 'She's sore from her riding lessons. But she's coming along nicely. She'll make a fine whore.'

'You devils,' cried the young man. 'You'll pay for this.'

'We haven't so far,' Halfdan said. 'Wynflaed is especially eager to try new tricks.'

The young man seized a spear and flung it in fury. It went surprisingly far but did not reach the wall.

'You have a feeble weapon,' Halfdan said. 'Wynflaed will be disappointed to hear it.'

'Enough games, Halfdan,' Ivar snapped. 'Let us hear what their king proposes.'

He placed his hands on the parapet and called out in a pleasant voice. 'We Northmen have a bad reputation, Burgred but it is not really justified. We are honest traders, nothing more. We come in peace and wish to remain here only through the bitter cold of winter.'

'You come in peace, you say?' Burgred gave a hollow laugh. 'Is it peace to slay the lord of a town? Is it peace to rape his wife and daughters? Is it peace to send your wolf packs across the land, thieving and despoiling?'

'This is purely a misunderstanding,' Ivar said. 'We killed Wignoth because he fought against us. We accept his women in our bed because they pleaded for us to do so. And we scour the land for food which we always offer to pay good money for.'

'You speak falsehoods as black as those of Satan.'

'You may fear Satan but you'll learn to fear us more,' cried Halfdan.

'I do not fear dead men,' Burgred said. 'And be certain of this, if you don't leave my kingdom, your corpses will litter the earth.' He turned his horse and returned to his army.

Ivar looked thoughtful as he watched him depart. 'Their king speaks brave words,' he said, at last. 'But I wonder if his deeds will match his boasts.'

Ivar expected Burgred to launch an attack immediately and summoned all his warriors to the battlements, fully armed and prepared to fight. But no attack came that day, nor in the days following. Burgred merely sat and watched the walls while the Vikings grew despondent and fretful. They hated the lack of action and craved a fight.

'Why doesn't Burgred attack?' Leif asked Thorvald after ten days of waiting.

'I think he means to starve us out.'

'We have plenty of food.'

'It won't last for ever and his army is too close for us to venture out for more. Our bellies will soon groan with hunger.'

'It's not only lack of food which will harm us,' Leif said. He glanced at the warriors prowling the town. 'This constant delay will eat away our courage.'

Ivar must have thought the same for he sought Leif out the following day.

'You have your ears open to the fears of our men,' he said.

'Do I?' Leif was alarmed by his question.

'You do. I've seen you watching and listening, watched your mind weighing up all you see. So, tell me now, truly, what is the mood of the men?'

He wanted an honest opinion but Leif realised he'd best not offer it without some sauce to disguise the worst of it.

'Your men are warriors,' he said. 'They like battle, action. As you recently told me, they do not take kindly to having their swords turning rusty.'

'Are they growing dissatisfied with my leadership?'

'Not at all,' Leif said, hurriedly, alarmed that he had failed to speak with sufficient cunning.

'What then? Do you suggest that I lead them out to fight against a much greater foe? I will not take such a risk unless I must.'

Ivar was clearly angry at being trapped within the walls and Leif feared he would vent his rage on him. He weighed his words before replying, searching desperately for something to deflect Ivar's wrath.

'I don't mean lead out the whole army,' he said. 'But send some men to forage. Perhaps others to make a swift attack on the enemy and then retreat to the safety of the walls.'

Ivar gazed at him thoughtfully and strode away without another word.

Leif was not greatly surprised when Ivar announced that Halfdan would lead a night attack upon the enemy while Guthrum took a foraging party to secure more food. The warriors, as one man, praised him for such a cunning idea. He didn't thank Leif nor so much as glance his way.

'A clever plan,' Kolga murmured in Leif's ear. 'It will keep the men busy and fill our bellies. You think like a leader.'

He looked at her in surprise. 'You know it was my idea?'

She nodded. 'Ivar told me. But he is too much a leader to admit that the plan is not his. But if it were to go wrong…' She grinned and strode off.

Fortunately, it did not go wrong. Halfdan enjoyed a killing spree and returned safely to the town with all his men and the weapons of many dead Mercians. Guthrum sneaked back in the dark of night with a dozen slaughtered sheep and eight barrels of ale. It was hardly a great haul but Ivar ordered a feast.

Everyone thought that he would repeat the raids the next night but he was too wily a commander to do this. He waited three more days before launching the next foray. The Mercians, who had been watchful for the two previous nights, were caught unawares and suffered more losses.

'At this rate,' Sigurd said, 'we'll gnaw the Mercian army to death.'

'Don't be too sure of it,' Deor said. 'Burgred is not like King Edmund. He comes from a long line of warrior kings and he will not watch his army bleed to death without a fight.'

His words proved more than prophetic.

Two days later Leif spotted signs of consternation from the sentries on the walls. 'I think the Mercians are attacking,' he cried.

Sigurd threw him a spear and thrust a helmet into his hands. They raced up the steps to the walls and gazed upon the scene. Leif's heart shuddered. But not because of the Mercians.

Marching towards the town came a second army, with more than twice as many men as Burgred had. Ivar and Ubbe lent upon the wall and beheld the scene in silence.

'See the golden dragon on that standard,' Ubbe said, pointing to a large flag at the head of the army.

'The dragon of Wessex,' Ivar said in a chill tone. 'So Burgred has sent to the Saxons for aid.'

The wild cries of welcome from the Mercian army proved his surmise to be correct.

The West Saxon army halted and a loud cry of 'Æthelred' echoed from their ranks.

Ivar gestured Deor to join him. 'Who is this Æthelred?'

'The young king of Wessex,' he answered. 'He has been king for only a year or so.'

And then more cries sounded from the Saxons. This time it was: 'Alfred, Alfred, Alfred.'

'They have two kings?' Ivar asked. 'Like the Northumbrians?'

'It's possible,' Deor said. 'In the past, Kent, the eastern part of the Kingdom, had its own king. Perhaps Æthelred has revived the tradition and given Kent to his brother.'

'Then there might be rivalry between them,' Ivar said hopefully. 'One king is a dangerous foe but two Saxon kings and a Mercian one may have divided counsel and be easier to defeat.'

'They have six thousand men,' Kolga said. 'You cannot hope to fight them.'

Ivar gave her a venomous look. 'Keep your thoughts to yourself, woman.' He glanced around uneasily at those men who were nearest, anxious that they may have heard her words.

Leif tried to look unconcerned although his heart felt like a stone.

A short while later three men rode towards the walls, followed by a hundred horsemen. Burgred rode in the middle. The man on his right was young, maybe in his mid-twenties. The third looked a callow youth.

'So, spawn of Satan,' Burgred called. 'You see now that my kinsman, Æthelred, King of Wessex has arrived with his army. You cannot hope to battle against us.'

Ivar spat over the battlements. 'If the puny creature beside you is King of the Saxons we'll have no cause to worry.'

Æthelred gave an angry glance. 'Sneering words do not make a great war leader,' he said. 'I swear you will eat them.'

'I shall eat you and your army, lord of Wessex. I have feasted on Saxon flesh before.'

'You have done so for the last time,' cried the youth angrily, spurring his horse in front of the two kings. 'My brother will destroy you utterly.'

Ivar laughed. 'What a vainglorious whelp. Go back to your mother, boy, and leave talk of battle to your elders.'

Æthelred gestured to his brother to return to his place next to Burgred. The young prince mastered his feelings and contented himself with staring silently at Ivar. Perhaps he thought his look threatening. Leif thought it looked childish.

'We make an offer,' Burgred said. 'Depart my kingdom and no harm shall come to you.'

'But you must leave within two days,' added Æthelred. 'Otherwise you will face dire consequences.'

Burgred stared at him in surprise. The young Saxon king's words had obviously not been agreed between them.

Ivar chuckled. 'You see, my friends, lots of kings make for divided counsel. We may yet turn it into discord.'

'We still confront six thousand warriors,' Kolga said.

'Not warriors,' Halfdan sneered. 'Most of them are peasants, wearied from getting the harvest in.'

'I don't think that's the case,' Kolga said. 'They have the look of fighting men, thegns.'

'Even so,' Halfdan said, 'they are unused to battle. They will shit themselves when we charge them.'

Kolga did not reply, contenting herself with an exasperated shake of her head.

DIPLOMACY

Ivar and the chieftains spent the next two days in fierce debate. The young hotheads led by Halfdan thirsted for battle and loudly argued that they should meet their foe beyond the walls. The older men were warier, pointing out the overwhelming numbers of the enemy and their fears that their own shield wall would be engulfed.

The wrangling went on incessantly but Ivar took no part in it. His mind seemed elsewhere, and Leif suspected that he was planning some devious stratagem.

He learned how right this guess was when Ivar summoned him in the middle of the night.

'You speak good English, Leif,' he said. 'Because of your friendship with Deor and your English wife.'

Leif nodded warily. When Ivar asked a question such as this it rarely led to a good outcome.

'I want you to go to the King of the Mercians,' he continued. 'Take Deor with you.'

Leif knew that to argue was foolish but, nevertheless, he found his head shaking in disagreement.

'You say no?' Ivar said, with a dangerous edge to his voice.

'I said nothing,' Leif mumbled. 'But I would like to know why you want to put me into the hands of our foes.'

'I want you to discuss terms with Burgred.'

'Terms?'

These were not the words of a great Viking leader, Leif thought. Perhaps Kolga had persuaded him.

Ivar nodded and then put a finger to Leif's lips.

Leif looked at him doubtfully. 'But what will your brothers say? And the jarls who are desperate for a fight?'

'Our enemies outnumber us more than two to one,' he answered in a low voice. 'And Halfdan is wrong when he thinks their armies are made up of peasants. Especially not the Saxons. If we fight them we will be badly beaten, perhaps destroyed. I came to England to win victories not to eat earth.'

'So what will you offer them? Treasure? Women?'

Ivar looked at him in astonishment. 'I won't offer them anything, you idiot. I will demand treasure from them and in return I'll promise not to attack their rich fat kingdom.'

'But why would Burgred agree to that?' Leif was puzzled completely now.

'Because I've heard that he's not had much success in war and doubts he ever will. If you can persuade him of the wisdom of it, he'll buy peace.'

Leif was unconvinced and when he spoke it was in a faltering voice. 'When do you want me to go?'

'Now, of course,' he said. 'Go to the north gate. You're expected.' He gestured towards the shadows where Deor was waiting silently.

Leif cursed while a guard inched open the gate at the north of the town. He gestured swiftly and Leif and Deor slipped through.

'This is madness,' Leif whispered. 'We'll be slain by the Mercians.'

'You're a Viking, so you might be,' Deor said. 'But I'll be fine because I'm an Angle.'

'But a traitor. Or that's what they'll think.'

'I'll rely on you to tell them different. And I'll do my best to keep you alive in return.'

Leif glared at him although Deor could not see it in the darkness.

They made a stealthy progress to some woods west of the town and then edged their way towards the river and the Mercian camp. Creeping in like this seemed utter folly. Leif couldn't understand why Ivar hadn't just asked Burgred for a meeting. He had sent them to their doom for no good reason.

After what seemed an endless time they reached the Mercian tents. Pale torches flickered from poles dotted haphazardly across the camp. The greatest number were near the centre, close to a tent which dwarfed the others.

Leif pointed to it. 'I think that's where we'll find Burgred.'

Deor nodded and took a deep breath. He reached inside his jerkin and pulled out two objects, thrusting one into Leif's hand.

'What's this?' Leif hissed. 'A dagger?'

'A crucifix,' Deor said. 'Hold it up before you and it should give us safe passage. Say that we're monks who've been captured by Ivar and made our escape. And we don't slink but walk upright as if we've nothing to fear.'

Leif groaned in disbelief at Deor's plan but there was nothing else to do but follow him. They got to their feet and strode towards the camp.

They'd only just reached it when they were surrounded by armed guards. Leif brandished his crucifix in front of him like a talisman, praying that it had the potency of a Thor amulet. To his astonishment, it did. The guards swallowed Deor's story without suspicion and escorted them to Burgred's tent.

Raised voices came from within, a curse or two and then, after a little longer, they were ushered in.

It was a large tent dominated by a camp table, a large bed and a brazier glowing with coals. They could hear the sound of someone pissing in a bowl. Then Burgred stepped from behind a screen, tying a cloak around him.

'What do you want?' he demanded. His eyes were heavy with sleep.

'We have come from Ivar the Boneless,' Leif said. 'We are Christian monks who were captured by the heathen in East Anglia. He has sent us here to discuss terms.'

'Terms?' Burgred repeated. He was fully awake now and curious.

'Ivar does not want a battle in which many men will die —' Leif continued.

'Why doesn't he?' Burgred snapped. 'I thought death and destruction is all the monster craves.'

Leif was lost for an answer for a moment and gazed at Deor who carefully avoided his gaze.

'For others, lord king,' Leif stammered at last. 'Ivar desires death and slaughter for others but not for him or his warriors.'

Burgred ordered a servant to pour some mead and savoured it thoughtfully before replying. 'So, he fears us, does he?'

'He is concerned by the size of the combined Mercian and Saxon war-hosts.'

'As well he should be. My wife is sister to Æthelred and Alfred. We are kin.' He beat his fist upon the chest. 'And we are stalwart in defence of each other.'

Burgred said this with greater vigour than was necessary, as if he were desperate to convince them of the truth of it. And perhaps to convince himself.

'So it is said,' Leif replied, in a doubtful tone. He waited just long enough for this to raise Burgred's interest before continuing.

'It is fortunate that you are kin,' he said. 'for the Saxons have a reputation for deceit and false-dealing.'

Burgred's eyes narrowed. 'What makes you say that?'

'Eadbald is from Kent,' Deor answered. 'Wessex has been a cruel master there.'

Burgred gestured for a second cup of mead.

'I expect you would have preferred the heirs of Offa to still rule your kingdom?' he said.

Leif nodded in full agreement although he had no idea what Burgred meant by it. He dreaded that he'd be asked more difficult questions and he'd be unable to answer.

Burgred downed the mead in a hasty gulp. 'So how have the Saxons played false in Kent?' he asked, quietly.

'They make many promises,' Deor said, 'and neglect to keep them.'

'As Æthelred's grandfather, Egbert did with Archbishop Ceolnoth,' Burgred said. 'Egbert persuaded him to abandon allegiance to the Kings of Mercia, promising him lands and honour for the church. But Ceolnoth got neither, poor fool.'

'Exactly,' Leif said. 'It seems that young King Æthelred is like his grandfather.'

'Untrustworthy?'

Leif nodded.

'And his brother even more so?'

Again, Leif nodded.

Burgred did not say more for a long while. Then he dismissed his guards and beckoned them closer.

'Does Ivar the Boneless suspect my kinsmen of treachery towards me?' he whispered.

'Not suspect,' Leif answered. 'The word suggests there's doubt concerning the issue.'

'And there is no doubt?'

'I have seen Saxons within the city,' Leif said.

Burgred smashed his fist upon the table. 'Damn them. I asked the Saxons for support and what do they give me? Treachery.'

His face became flushed and taut. 'And I did not request that they come with such a large army. Both brothers. Why would they do this? Why would both men leave their own kingdom and come to mine? Does Æthelred seek to supplant me with his brother?'

He poured yet another cup of mead and stared into it, until he began to calm.

'Yet, perhaps I have misjudged them,' he continued softly, almost to himself. 'They have gathered together a great army to come to my aid, risked their own lives as well. This is not the actions of traitors. They have left their own kingdom open to attack from the heathens. How could I doubt them?'

'How could you imagine that they would leave Wessex undefended?' Leif said quickly. 'They would only leave it if they were certain it was safe from attack.'

Burgred's eyes widened in horror. 'Because they have struck a bargain with Ivar?'

'I don't know, my lord,' Leif said, thinking it time to let Burgred fan the flames of suspicion for himself. 'Does it seem likely? Perhaps it's little more than a rumour.'

'Rumour flies on wings of truth,' Burgred cried. He was panting now, his hand gripped tight upon his cup.

Finally, he mastered himself. 'You said you have terms from Boneless?' he said.

Leif nodded. 'Do not attack the city and Ivar will leave your kingdom in peace. He will, of course, need food for his warriors and some small tokens of your regard: precious jewels, gold, coins, slaves. But withdraw your army and he will not attack Mercia.'

'Yes, yes, yes. But how can I do this? How can I conclude peace when the Saxons have marched to Mercia's aid?'

'You'll think of a way,' Leif said.

Burgred nodded, his mind already turning on various ideas.

'Do you have an answer for my master?' Leif asked after a long period of silence. Deor looked at him in surprise. He had used the term master, forgetting he was pretending to be English. But thankfully, Burgred did not notice.

'You have an answer,' Burgred whispered. 'I will pay him all he desires if he leaves my kingdom in peace.'

'He will,' Leif said in a decisive tone. 'Ivar is a man of honour, even though a heathen.'

'So I have heard,' Burgred said, though Leif guessed he had heard no such implausible a thing.

BATTLE FOR NOTTINGHAM

Two days later Leif stood on the battlements and groaned with frustration. All the negotiations he had undertaken with Burgred had come to nought. The Saxon and Mercian armies were marching towards the walls with grim determination.

Ivar gave him a withering glance but then turned his attention to the more pressing matter to hand.

'Stand ready,' he cried, drawing his sword and holding it high. 'We will repulse them.'

The enemy armies were only fifty yards from the wall now. Then a horn blew, they gave a huge shout and raced forwards.

The Viking archers sent a cloud of arrows amongst them while others launched a volley of throwing axes. This did some damage but not enough to trouble such a flood of men. Within moments they had reached the wall and were throwing ladders against it.

'Push them back, push them back,' Leif cried feverishly, grappling the top of a ladder and throwing all his weight against it. He was unable to move it but then Sigurd joined him and put his shoulder to it. The ladder began to teeter but the weight of the men clambering up it proved too much for the brothers.

But then Guthrum raced over, pushed Leif aside and began to heave. He was stronger than even Sigurd and together their efforts proved enough. The ladder swayed, the men climbing it cried with terror and then, with one last mighty thrust, Sigurd and Guthrum hurled the ladder from the battlements.

Leif glanced along the wall. Other ladders were suffering similar treatment but dozens more remained in place and the English warriors climbing these were now almost at the top. He ran to a second ladder and joined his friends in lobbing rocks down upon the climbing men. Many fell wounded but there were still more to take their place. Within moments strong warriors had clambered over the battlements, ready to do battle.

Leif drew his sword and parried at a large Englishman who watched his every move like a snake. He bore no shield, none of the attackers did, for fear it would have encumbered them upon the ladders. It gave the defenders their one slight advantage. They smashed into the Englishmen with sword, spear and shield, killing and maiming. Yet still they came, heedless of their deaths.

Leif wondered at this, for surely, they would never be able to get enough men on the walls to take the city. And then, out of the corner of his eye, he saw their plan.

The attack on the walls was just a diversion. Down below a body of men charged towards the gate bearing a heavy tree with which to batter it. They swung it once, the timbers rocked. It would take little time for it to shatter and leave the way to the city open.

'The gate, the gate,' Leif cried. He ran along the wall until he was directly above it and began to hurl rocks on the men wielding the ram. His first shots were lucky and a couple of men fell senseless. Then enemy archers came racing up and sent arrows over the walls.

Their aim was wild but it made Leif more cautious. 'Keep on throwing,' he said to the men as he ducked below the parapet.

There's no sense in us all getting killed, he thought. He realised that throwing rocks would not kill all the men smashing at the gate and they'd need another plan.

His eyes swept the walls, searching for Ivar or one of his brothers but they were too far away. The closest jarl was Guthrum and he bellowed out his name, gesturing him to come over to him.

'The gate will break at any moment,' he told him. 'We must have men below to secure it.'

Guthrum glanced at the gate and took in the danger in an instant. He summoned his followers, leaping down the steps with Leif following more slowly.

But the tardiness of his steps was more than compensated for by the swiftness of his thoughts. 'The battering-ram's the danger,' he cried. 'We should open the gate and let it enter.'

'Open the gate?' Guthrum cried. 'Are you mad?'

'Once the men on the ram are inside we'll slam it shut again. Then the gate will be safe.'

He had seen no sight of a second ram and prayed to Thor that the enemy did not have one to hand.

Guthrum considered his words for the briefest moment, clapped him on the shoulder and organised his men. Two placed their hands on either end of the bars holding the gate fast, a dozen stood in front of the gate to receive the enemy while a score stood on each side, ready to force it shut once the ram was inside.

At Guthrum's signal the bars were pulled back. The next blow of the ram opened the gates wide and the force of their momentum carried the English through at a trot. They looked astonished at their success but this turned to horror as Guthrum's men surged towards them. They dropped the ram and fumbled for their weapons but it was too late. They fell to the ground like barley before scythes.

In the meanwhile, the rest of the warriors were pushing the gates shut. A dozen Englishmen battled through the gate but that was all. With a final push the gate was slammed shut and the Englishmen inside slain.

'You did well to think of this,' Guthrum said, punching Leif on the shoulder. Then he turned and raced back up to the walls to continue the battle.

He was sorely needed. In the time he had been at the gate the situation on the walls had turned rapidly against the defenders. There were now hundreds of Englishmen upon the battlements and the Vikings were sore pressed to cut them down.

'Come on, Leif,' Thorvald cried.

Reluctantly, Leif followed him up to the walls. He doubted he would survive long there. He cursed Burgred for reneging on his promise and cursed himself for failing to make sure he kept it.

He reached the top of the steps and glanced over the walls. It was horrifying. The English armies swarmed against the walls like ants on a hot summer day. More and more ladders were being flung against the walls and men climbed swiftly up them, hindered less and less by the struggling defenders.

Leif looked to his left and saw that two dozen Englishmen had secured a section of the wall and were holding back all attempts to dislodge them. Then there came a mighty bellow and Halfdan led his warriors charging into them. It was a brief and bloody conflict. The Vikings were more experienced, more ferocious and more desperate. The English fell to a man and then Halfdan continued his rampage, slaughtering all who stood in his way.

He's done it, Leif thought. He's thrown them back. But then he looked more carefully. Halfdan had cleared this part of the wall but, nonetheless, their plight was hopeless. Some sections were completely in English hands and their warriors were already fighting their way down the steps. Leif realised that it would take little time for them to reach the gates and fling them open to the hordes beyond.

I'm a dead man, he thought. We all are.

And then a horn brayed in the distance.

Leif blinked in amazement as part of the attacking army seemed to shudder. Then, it broke off the attack and retreated from the wall with steady steps.

'The Mercians are fleeing,' Guthrum cried.

The Englishmen on the walls turned and looked in horror then, as a man, raced towards the ladders, trying to force their way back onto them. Few made it and those that did fell fighting with their fellows to make the speediest descent.

Most of their foes still raged against the wall, however, the dragon standard of Wessex flying high above their army. But their impetus had been broken.

Once more masters of the walls, the Vikings hurled rocks and axes onto the Saxons and followed this by the corpses of their friends. It was this last which had the greatest effect. A little while after this dreadful barrage a second horn called and the Saxon army made a slow, ordered retreat in the wake of the Mercians.

'We've won,' Halfdan cried in delight. 'They crumble against our courage.'

'Or maybe against your negotiations,' whispered a voice in Leif's ear.

Ivar was grinning quietly to himself. 'You did it, Leif,' he said. 'When he attacked I thought he had played us false but Burgred held to his promise after all. And tomorrow I expect him to fulfil the second part of our bargain and deliver us great gifts.'

TAKEN

The Vikings had suffered grievously in the English attack, with many dead and even more wounded. Their chief consolation was the thought that the enemy had suffered even more.

Some of the jarls wanted to pursue the advantage and attack the English camp but wiser heads prevailed.

'We will get all we desire and more, without battle,' Ivar said enigmatically. A few pressed him to say more but he maintained his silence.

He was not so silent with Leif who was summoned to his hall early the next morning.

'Why does he want you?' Aebbe asked. She looked alarmed. Despite her questions Leif had told her nothing about his dangerous visit to the enemy lines before the battle. He had explained his absence by saying that Ivar had kept him in his hall to beguile the long hours of waiting for the attack by telling tales. Aebbe hadn't believed it.

Now she pressed him even more forcefully.

'I don't know what he wants,' he said irritably.

'More tales? This early in the day?' She did not hide the disbelief in her voice. 'The only lords to ask for a skald while the sun is high are those in their dribbling dotage.'

'Well Ivar isn't that, believe me,' Leif said. He kissed her lightly on the cheek. 'Don't worry.'

'Now I worry,' she said, shaking her head miserably at his words.

It was a cold, dank day with a ceaseless rain which, although not heavy, seemed to sink right into Leif's flesh. He made his way through the narrow streets towards Ivar's hall. The townspeople stared at him with sullen, angry eyes, despairing at the failure of their king to relieve the town. Leif ignored them, his mind churning with suspicions of his own.

'Welcome, Leif,' Ivar said. He stood by a door at the back of the hall and gestured him to enter.

Leif found himself in a small chamber with no windows. The only light came from a stack of candles upon a table. As his eyes got used to the gloom he saw a number of people sitting on stools as if waiting for him: Halfdan, Ubbe, Sidrac, Guthrum and Kolga.

'Ivar has told us about the bargain you struck with King Burgred,' Ubbe said. 'You did well. I see now why he sets such great store by you.'

'Does he?' Leif muttered, staring nervously at Ivar. He had no wish for such high repute. It always seemed to come with a heavy price.

'I do,' Ivar said. 'And now you have the chance to win even greater glory. I want you to go to King Burgred and finalise the agreement.'

He nodded to Guthrum who pushed a piece of parchment across the table.

'These marks are words written in the English tongue,' Ivar explained.

'I have seen such marks,' Leif said. 'Deor can scribe them.'

'It was Deor who made them,' Ivar said. 'It is a demand for tribute from the Mercians.'

He gestured towards the shadows at the back of the hall and Deor stepped forward, took up the parchment and began to read.

'A thousand pounds of silver,' he began, 'five hundred head of cattle, one hundred stallions and two hundred mares, a thousand sheep, a thousand hogs, ten thousand bushels of wheat and the same of barley, five hundred barrels of ale and one hundred of mead, five thousand slaves, all young women, two thousand bolts of fine woollen cloth and four score barrels of salted fish.'

He rolled up the parchment and passed it to Leif.

'Are you coming with me, Deor?' he asked. He doubted that he would be able to manage the negotiations on his own.

'He's not but I am,' Kolga said, before Deor could answer. 'The leech is needed here to tend to the wounded,' she continued. 'I understand the Mercian tongue well enough.'

Leif gave a wan smile. He was not sure if she would prove a help or cause disaster. But he knew there was no point in arguing.

An hour later they entered the Mercian camp. The sky had cleared now and the sun shone brightly which was very different to how Leif felt. He walked in his own sodden rain-cloud.

King Burgred sat in front of his tent with scores of warriors standing guard and four men on either side of him. To his right was King Æthelred of Wessex and beside him a younger man who Leif recognised as the prince, Alfred. The young Saxon glanced briefly at Leif and then turned his gaze on Kolga, placing his finger on his lip in a rapt and thoughtful manner.

To Burgred's right sat Ceolred, the man who had led the Mercian forces that had shadowed the Vikings on their way to Northumbria. He looked at Leif with sharp eyes. 'Ivar's Skald,' he said, giving a nod of welcome.

'My lord,' Leif said, bowing his head. He comforted himself with the fact that Ceolred had dealt honestly with them on that occasion.

But then his heart hammered. He realised that he had told Burgred that he was Eadbald, a monk from Kent.

Burgred stared at him for a moment and gave a chill smile, as if this knowledge gave him power over Leif.

To Ceolred's left sat an older, wealthy looking man with locks well-groomed and hanging down to his shoulders. He was dressed in raiment almost as costly as that of the two kings and he wore it lightly as if it was his right and proper due.

'This is the heathen's emissary,' Burgred explained.

His words let slip that he had already met Leif but no one appeared to notice. None apart from the Saxon, Alfred, who gave the Mercian a look of surprise before swiftly masking it.

Burgred indicated Kolga. 'Is the woman Ivar's whore?'

The young warriors laughed although none of the men seated by the king did so.

'I am Jarl Kolga,' she said, putting one hand on her hip and eyeing Burgred as if she had a mind to cut out his tongue with her dagger.

Burgred's eyes narrowed. 'I have heard of you,' he said. 'The daughter of Bjorn Blackbrow, I believe.'

'You hear right,' she said.

'You claim to be a jarl?' Alfred said, leaning forward, his eyes shining.

'Not claim. Am.'

'I hear it said that you are not Blackbrow's daughter but Odin's.'

Now she laughed. 'Not true. I do not search the battlefield for dead warriors, as Odin's daughters do. I fill the battlefield with dead. Pray to your god that you won't be one of them.'

Alfred laughed quietly and received a stern look from his brother.

'What do you want, Skald?' Ceolred asked. 'Why have you come here?'

Leif risked a glance at Burgred who pretended to be equally curious.

'Speak up,' he said. 'I also desire to know why you have come.'

'Lord Ivar seeks only peace and friendship from the King of Mercia,' Leif began. 'He wishes to remain in this town for the winter months while travel is difficult. Then, in the spring, he will lead his companions back to Northumbria.'

'Why such giddy movements?' Æthelred asked. 'You've only just left Northumbria.'

'We came south because some of our men wish to return to their homelands.'

'Then why did you come so far into Mercia?' asked the old man beside Ceolred. 'My lands lie close to the river Humber. You should have followed it directly east to the sea. But instead you journeyed down the Trent.'

'Mucel is right,' Ceolred said. 'Explain yourself.'

Leif was lost for words for a moment. Then inspiration came.

'Although some of his men desired to do so,' he said, 'Ivar the Boneless had no intention of voyaging home overseas. He journeyed to Mercia to seek a treaty of friendship with King Burgred. He has long heard that he is a great and wise king.'

His eyes flickered towards Burgred. He was not so wise, Leif decided, for these honeyed words appeared to flatter him. Not so the two young Saxons who stared at Leif with sharp suspicion.

'A treaty,' said Burgred in a thoughtful tone. He hesitated for a moment and glanced at his two lords although not at the Saxons. 'This speaks wisdom on the part of Ivar.'

He turned his gaze on Leif once again, his face composed and serious. 'Peace is something wise lords desire for their folk, Eanbald.'

Alfred became still more intense and said to Burgred, 'It is truly a wise king who has never met an emissary but knows that he is called Eanbald.'

Burgred hesitated for a moment but quickly recovered. 'I had message from one of my guards,' he said smoothly and then turned to address Leif. 'I presume the guard was right in saying your name is Eanbald?'

'Yes, my lord,' Leif replied, nervously. He was alarmed that Alfred had seen through the pretence.

'Enough of talk,' Kolga said, sharply. She thrust the parchment at King Burgred. 'This is what Boneless demands.'

'This is what he requests,' Leif added quickly. 'Merely enough to keep his warriors well-fed and content.'

He decided there was no need to say how Ivar would react if he were not bought off in this manner. He had no need to.

Burgred studied the parchment swiftly and rolled it up. 'That seems very reasonable,' he said. 'A fair and just request.'

He leaned over Ceolred and handed the parchment to Mucel before anyone else could get sight of it.

'There is no point in your seeking to keep the document,' Kolga said. 'As a good Skald, Leif has memorised it and knows exactly what we demand.'

Alfred and Æthelred exchanged glances. 'You are a man of many names,' Æthelred said, at last.

Leif forced a smile upon his face. He decided it would be safest if he spoke the truth to the two sharp young Saxons.

'My name is indeed Leif,' he answered. 'I gave my name as Eanbald in order to make my way more easily through the camp.'

'I believe you,' Alfred said, his voice dripping with sarcasm.

'I should return to Ivar,' Leif said, unnerved by his tone. 'He'll want to know your response.'

'No,' said Burgred. 'We would have you stay here, friend, as our guest.'

Guards began to hustle Kolga and Leif away. They tried to protest but it did no good.

Leif looked back and saw that the Mercian and Saxon lords were already locked in bitter dispute.

'We came all this way at your request,' Æthelred shouted. 'Many of our men died in battle for you. Yet now you give up the fight.'

'I am King of Mercia,' Burgred cried, climbing to his feet. 'I do as I please.'

The Vikings heard no more for they were pushed along at still faster pace until they were out of earshot. Ivar will be pleased when I tell him of the discord between the two kings, Leif thought. If I get back to bring him the news.

They were lodged in a large tent with costly furnishings and a table laid out with food and drink. Leif was hungry but did not think it was intended for them. But being here calmed his fears, a little. If the English had wanted to kill them, he reasoned, they would have done it straight away and not brought them here.

He sank onto a stool and wondered how long Burgred would keep them captive. Presumably until he had considered how much of Ivar's demands he could meet. And until the Saxon's suspicions had eased.

A little later a figure entered the tent, with three warriors by his side. It was the older man, Mucel.

'Leave us,' he said to the guards.

'But Ealdorman,' one of them said, 'they are Vikings.'

'A woman and a wordsmith,' he said with a chuckle. 'I have no fear of them.'

Reluctantly the guards left the tent although they were careful to position themselves on either side of the opening.

'You are an ealdorman,' Kolga said. 'The same rank as me.'

'Don't flatter yourself, half-Dane. I am of the lineage of great men, stretching back into distant years. You're merely the child of a pirate.'

'And weren't your ancestors pirates?' Kolga said. 'This was not originally the land of your folk, and you know it.'

'True. But my ancestors wrested it from lesser people.'

'As we will wrest it from you.'

Mucel gave a derisive laugh. 'You may try. But the boastful killer who leads you is not the man to do it.'

'Then a woman, perhaps?'

Mucel chuckled. 'Perhaps. On the day the sun rises in the west.'

At that point the door to the tent opened and a young woman entered. She was dressed in a flaming red gown with a fur-trimmed cloak on top of it.

'Father,' she said. 'Why are you alone with these Vikings?' She tried but failed to quell the anxiety in her voice.

'I want to talk with them, is all.'

She shot him a dubious glance.

'This is my daughter, Ealswith,' Mucel said. 'She is betrothed to the young Saxon, Prince Alfred, and will wed him tomorrow.'

She looked astonished at his words. 'So soon?'

'King Burgred wishes to return to Tamworth,' Mucel said. 'Your mother and I will go with him. You, however, will go to Wessex with your new husband.'

'So you are to wed the prince with the lustful eyes?' Kolga said with a malicious smile.

Ealswith blushed. 'I did not know he looks at me in that fashion.'

'I'm not talking about you,' Kolga said. 'It was me his eyes devoured in such wanton fashion.'

Ealswith's face now turned white with fury. 'How dare you speak of my betrothed like this,' she cried.

She took a step towards Kolga as if she meant to slap her but Kolga moved swift as a pouncing cat, towering over her with a deadly dagger gleaming in her hand.

'Harm one hair of her head and I'll skin you alive,' Mucel said quietly.

Kolga did not respond for a moment, then sheathed her knife and sat down. Leif don't know if she believed the ealdorman's threat but he certainly did.

Suddenly there was a loud hubbub from without, the sound of voices raised in anger. Then one of Mucel's guards ducked into the tent.

'A thousand pardons, my lord,' he said nervously. 'But the Saxon brothers are here and say that the wedding must take place now.'

Mucel frowned. 'Why now? It was going to be tomorrow.'

'Because we're leaving today,' said Æthelred, pushing his way into the tent. He saw Ealswith and bowed courteously. 'Lady. I hope that this haste does not cause you any difficulties.'

'It does, actually. My ladies have not finished their preparations.'

'Then they must shift themselves. The wedding takes place before dusk.'

So, to Leif's astonishment, he was one of the few people who witnessed the royal marriage ceremony.

Ealswith had changed into a white gown which gleamed like the first snow of winter. Her hair was dark, almost black, which was in marked contrast to the rest of the gathering with their straw-coloured hair and pale faces. She looked strained, angry and fiercely beautiful.

Alfred was dressed in gleaming chain-mail with a dark blue cloak flapping in the breeze behind him. The ceremony was long and tedious, spoken by a fat priest in a language which neither Leif nor Kolga could understand and which, Leif observed, few of the rest of the assembly could either. He guessed it to be the language of the Christ God.

He was surprised to see that the only person with even a scrap of understanding was the young prince himself. The priest was forced to give instructions by gesture and in whispers in the English tongue. But Alfred appeared to understand a modicum of the strange tongue, responding to the words before the priest signed or whispered.

So, Leif thought, lustful, intelligent and holy. A strange combination.

At length the ceremony was completed and the couple were pronounced man and wife. But there was to be no feast of celebration. The Saxon army had already made preparations and were waiting only for the conclusion of the wedding to strike camp.

The young brothers were courteous enough to King Burgred but that did not hide the anger they clearly felt at his making peace with Ivar. The two kings gave each other a swift and cursory embrace and mumbled curt words of farewell. Ealswith climbed into a covered waggon and the army moved out.

Leif stood watching with Kolga, thinking that with the Saxons gone, they would soon be allowed to go back to the town.

But as he considered this he was seized by strong arms.

'You're coming with us,' said a voice in his ear. 'King Æthelred wants to know more about you and your bastard chieftain.'

Kolga fought furiously with the men who laid hands upon her but to no avail. They were overwhelmed and, as darkness fell, were carried off in the wake of the Saxon host.

THE ROAD TO WESSEX

The Saxon army pressed on for hours by the light of the moon. Leif wondered at this. Surely the King of Wessex could not think Kolga and he an important enough prize to justify this haste? It was a foolish notion. It was more likely that Æthelred had lost all trust in King Burgred. Perhaps he even feared that the Mercian would ally himself with Ivar and attack the Saxon army.

At any rate Æthelred drove his men forward at speed and it was only when clouds began to shroud the moon that he called a halt. He ordered pickets to surround the camp and told his men to keep their weapons close to hand. He was taking no chances.

Nor were the Saxons taking chances with their captives. Their wrists had been bound when they were captured and now that the army had halted their ankles were tied as well.

Leif could hear Kolga cursing as they bound her. It would go ill with the Saxons if she ever got loose.

He sat with his head bowed, cursing the fate which had befallen him, muttering angrily and miserably. Things had been going well with him, with ample money, a good woman, children, good friends and high standing with his lord and peers. And then this. He muttered even more angrily.

'What are you complaining about?' Kolga demanded.

'At my life,' Leif snapped. 'One day, everything is good and the next I am thrown into the dirt.'

'Some men are born unlucky. Perhaps you are one.'

'It's not that. I've been cursed by Loki.'

She fell silent so he knew that she was intrigued. So he told her all that had happened between the god and him since the day he caught sight of him in the smithy.

'I suspect it is Loki who curses me,' he said finally. 'I am his plaything.'

'Then what are you going to do about it?' she asked.

'What can I do?'

When she spoke again it was in a gentler tone.

'You can learn from him, Leif,' she said. 'Loki is a trickster god. He turns a smiling face upon a man while sharpening a knife behind his back. Learn from him. Become a trickster, yourself. Many men worship Loki. Perhaps if you do you'll reap the reward.'

Leif did not reply. But he spent much of the night pondering her words.

The army set out early the next morning. The captives were given ponies to ride; it seemed that they were considered worthy of some consideration. The straps on their wrists had been loosened sufficiently to allow them to hold the reins but they were still an encumbrance. It would be impossible for them to escape.

'Why do you think they want us?' Kolga whispered. 'Do they really think we have much to tell them about Ivar?'

'I expect that's part of it,' Leif said. 'We Vikings have always been raiders in the past; Ivar is behaving differently and they'll want to know why. But I suspect they also did it to annoy Burgred and cause him grief. They'll believe that

Ivar will be angry at our capture and may seek retribution on him.'

Kolga laughed. 'As if Boneless would bother that much about us.'

Leif nodded. 'Well it shows they don't know much about him.'

He fell silent, pondering his next words, anxious to say them right. 'But the Saxons will also be pleased that they have captured a jarl. Especially one who has Ivar's favour.'

'I take Boneless to my bed when it suits us both,' she said. 'I'm hardly a cause for him to stir himself to hunt for me.'

'I'm not so sure. He won't be happy that his woman has been so brazenly taken from him.'

She did not answer although Leif noticed a swift smile of pleasure cross her face.

They journeyed fast and next day passed through the Mercian town of Leicester where they took a good, straight, ancient road leading to the south west. From then on, they were able to make even swifter progress and the brothers forced the pace. They seemed to be in a hurry to get across Mercia.

The kingdom appeared to be a wealthy one, more like East Anglia than barren Northumbria. If Ivar were to see this, his eyes would grow huge with greed. It was no wonder that Burgred had been keen to buy him off.

But if Mercia appeared rich then Wessex was wealthier yet.

The army reached Æthelred's kingdom after a further five days of hard slog. Mercia had been heavily forested but Wessex was more open, with high downs dotted with sheep and cattle and small hamlets every few miles.

The mood of the Saxons lifted the moment they crossed the River Avon. The men had force-marched across Mercia with heads down and sour hearts. Now they were home they felt safe and relaxed.

Leif hugged this observation to himself. The English were more divided than even Ivar believed. The ancient enmity between each kingdom was living and potent. We could make good use of this, he thought.

Æthelred dismissed his army and headed west with his brother, their household warriors and the Viking captives. They arrived at the king's Great Hall in Cheddar as the sun was setting. Even in the failing light it looked huge, a slumbering fat beast of a building. Inside it was more richly decorated than the other halls Leif had seen. There were three huge fires and the air seemed made of the scent of meat and mead.

The Saxons were welcomed by Æthelred's wife, Wulfthryth and his two young sons, the younger only a babe in arms, the elder a toddler.

Wulfthryth made a great fuss of Alfred's bride who seemed sullen and unhappy. Little wonder, Leif thought. She must feel as much a captive as I do.

Except he soon found out this was not the case. There was a warm welcome for Ealswith but that for the Vikings was colder than ice. They were taken out of the hall and Kolga was marched off to a mean hut a little way distant with a guard placed outside the door. Leif was taken even further. Next to some kennels there was a small shed and he was forced into this.

He was no great size but the shed was barely large enough for him; he filled almost the entire space. He sat on the floor with his back to one wall and his knees raised high. There was no hope of stretching out his legs, let alone lying down.

He reached up in the darkness and felt the roof a little way above his head. His heart began to race. He felt trapped, unable to breathe.

Feverishly he pushed at the door but it was locked fast and only gave a little. A faint glimmer of light came through the crack but it was barely enough to even see his hand.

I'm doomed, he thought. I'll never see my friends again.

He had no idea how long he languished in the cell. Food and foul water were passed in through the door but he was not allowed to go out even to move his bowels. He pissed where he sat and had to scoop his shit into the corner of the cell. The stench grew unbearable but, after a time, he barely noticed it.

His only companions were unseen ones, the hounds in the nearby kennel. He spent each day listening to their noise: growls, whimpers, barks. After a few days he was able to distinguish them by the sounds they made. There were about a dozen all in all. Some he imagined to be tiny, little larger than kittens, while others were great brutes reared to fight bulls and wolves and bears. And me, he wondered? I am less than a hound, less than a brute.

He began to lose hope, his mind descending to an endless cycle of despair. Will I be left here to die? Is this the famous charity and compassion of the Christ-followers?

He knew well that the Danes had a reputation for savagery and, some, no doubt deserved it. Eohric and Halfdan, for example.

But not me, he thought. I never sought to be a Viking. Never sought the harm of others. And now I'll be kept here until I die. Why has this happened to me?

And then he realised. He saw again Loki's shadowy shape in the smoke and steam of the smithy. The god of tricks and falsehood had been biding his time, allowing Leif to enjoy life, to find a pretty woman, have children, rise high in the esteem of his lord and grow richer. And now this. Kolga had told him to make friends with the god and he had heard this and decided to play ever more false. Loki had thrown him to the wolves.

But finally, when Leif's body was continually burning with pain and he thought he was on the verge of madness, the door was opened and a gruff voice told him to get out.

He had no idea of the time but the light was so bright he felt blinded by it. He shifted himself to his knees and began to crawl out, each movement a fiery agony. As soon as he poked his head outside he swallowed great gasps of air. It tasted wonderful.

'King Æthelred wants you,' the guard said. He leaned closer and sniffed. 'Christ, you're disgusting. You can't go to him in this state.' The man pushed him towards a well.

Leif glanced into the kennels as he passed, eager to see if he had been correct in his picture of the dogs. He was, more or less. There were about a dozen of them, of all shapes and sizes. They watched as he passed by and he thought that they did so with sympathy.

It was now close to mid-winter but, despite this, Leif was ordered to strip naked and the guard threw bucket after bucket of freezing water over him. His teeth chattered so much he thought they would jump out of his mouth and he began to shake uncontrollably.

'Get him some fresh clothes,' the guard called to a servant. He kicked Leif's noisome rags away. 'And burn these.'

He was soon dressed in a rough tunic and thick woollen leggings. The heat gradually began to return to his body.

'I'm hungry,' he said. He was surprised how weak and frail he sounded.

'Do you think I care,' the guard said. He thrust Leif towards the hall.

To what, he wondered. My death?

He almost swooned when he entered. The warmth engulfed him like the thickest of blankets and the smell of food was a torment. At the back of the hall he saw a number of fires with meat turning on spits: beef, mutton, pork and game. He had to wipe his mouth clear of dribble.

'Bow when you get close to the king,' the guard grunted in his ear.

Leif forced his legs to cross the hall to where Æthelred and Alfred sat talking with great animation. Two brothers at heart, despite their great standing. Leif wondered if Sigurd believed him alive or dead. He thought of Aebbe and the children and his heart ached. Would he ever see any of them again?

He stopped in front of the brothers. Their conversation ended and they looked him up and down. He recalled what the guard had told him and bowed his head.

'How do you like your lodgings?' Æthelred asked.

Leif did not know how to answer. What did he expect him to say?

'I do not care for my cell,' he said finally. 'I think it might be the death of me.'

He said it lightly for he did not wish to antagonise them. But neither did he wish to hide the fact that he was suffering in a hell-hole.

'Well, clearly it hasn't done so, yet,' Alfred said. 'You look disgusting but still very much alive.'

'And for that I'm grateful,' Leif said.

'You'll be returned there,' Æthelred said, 'the moment we've finished with you.' He picked up a cup of wine and sipped it. 'Unless…'

The word hung on the air, so pregnant with meaning, so powerful, yet so devoid of any sense of how to respond.

'Unless?' Leif repeated.

'Unless you tell us what we want,' Alfred snapped. 'Your friend has been forthcoming as far as she's able. But she's told us that you are closer to Ivar and have been so since childhood. That you are more privy to his hopes and plans.'

Leif cursed Kolga for saying these lies. He wouldn't be able to tell the Saxons things that a man close to Ivar would know. But he realised she had probably done it for the best, to give him some chance of survival.

He tried to hold his sense of panic in check. And then he heard a voice whisper in his head.

It doesn't matter that you have no knowledge of Ivar's plans, the voice said. *Indeed, who does? It's doubtful if even Halfdan or Ubbe have more than an inkling.*

Leif gasped at this revelation. He could say anything and the Saxons would not know if he spoke true or false. The vital thing was to tell them things that they thought important. Important enough for them to wish to hear more. Important enough to keep him from being dragged back to the cell.

'I would answer fully,' he said, 'but my head is light from lack of food and drink.'

Alfred stared at him for a moment, his eyes sharp with suspicion. Then he glanced at his brother who beckoned to a servant.

'Sit, Leif,' Æthelred said. 'Eat and drink and then you will be in a fit state to answer us.'

'And if you don't,' Alfred said, 'we'll send you back to your cell.'

A fine Christ-follower you are, Leif thought. You're as ruthless as Ivar.

A WEB OF LIES

A servant brought Leif a plate of meat hot from the spit. His fingers burned as he tore it into chunks but he was heedless of the pain. He shovelled it into his mouth, wincing at the heat, chewed swiftly, swallowed and gulped a mouthful of ale to cool his mouth. Then, once more, he tore at the meat, shovelled, swallowed.

Æthelred and Alfred watched him in silence. Their former antagonism appeared to be fading. If anything, they seemed amused at the way he was wolfing down his food.

Casually, they turned towards their own plates and picked slowly at their meat. More slowly than Leif. They did not know what it was to starve.

Finally, the hole in Leif's stomach was filled and he leaned back and regarded the brothers. 'The food is good,' he said.

'You are no longer faint?' Æthelred asked.

Leif shook his head.

'Good. Then you can answer our questions.'

He glanced at his brother. Alfred's eyes were bright with anticipation and he leaned forward, cradling his chin in his hands.

'Why has Ivar the Boneless come to England?' Æthelred asked.

'He is a Dane,' Leif answered, 'a Viking. He comes as all Vikings do, to plunder and grow rich.'

'But he dwelt a long time in Ireland, or so the woman Kolga told us. Why did he not stay there where he held many lands and enjoyed great wealth?'

Leif took a sip at his ale. In truth he had no clear idea why Ivar had left Ireland. But then he recalled Kolga taunting him once about his enemies there.

'Ireland had grown less profitable for him,' he said cautiously. He saw that this had piqued the brothers' interest. So far, so good.

'There were rivals for his wealth,' he continued, more confidently, 'men from Norway and the northern isles as well as the Irish themselves.'

Even as he spoke Leif was thinking fast. His life might well depend on what he said.

He needed them to believe that Ivar was a powerful lord, and potentially a threat to them. But not too great a danger because that might turn their fear and anger against him. He wanted them to think that Ivar was the sort of man who could be bought off, controlled. But, of course, they must be made to realise that they could only achieve this delicate act if they had an ally who would work with them.

A man who knew Ivar as intimately as Kolga claimed that Leif did.

'So his power was waning in Ireland?' Æthelred asked.

'Not waning,' Leif replied. He was all at once the helpful ally they needed. 'But things were proving more burdensome.'

'And he thought there would be easier pickings in England?' Leif nodded.

'But why did he bring such a large army?' Alfred said. 'And why did he overwinter? Not just once, but now, a second year?'

Leif felt his teeth gnawing at his lips. This was not a question he relished. He dared not say that Ivar had come to carve out lands for himself for that would put the fear of the gods into them and make them savage with anger. But Alfred, he suspected, was not the sort of man to have the wool pulled over his eyes. He had to come up with something plausible.

Fortunately, he was given time for Æthelred asked a different question.

'You said he came to plunder? But a large host needs much plunder. Where was the sense of it? Why didn't he come with a smaller number of men?'

'Vanity,' Leif said.

'Vanity?'

'Yes, my lord. Ivar is vain beyond all measure. He does not wish the world to think him a common pirate, master of half a dozen longships and a crew of ragged vagabonds. He wants to appear a great and mighty lord, with more renown than any other Dane.'

'Like a king, perhaps?' Alfred said quietly.

Leif's eyes shifted to him. He was as watchful as a cat hunting a bird.

This was the most dangerous question imaginable. Leif had allowed himself to walk into a trap.

For a while now Leif had begun to suspect that becoming a king was what Ivar wanted deep in his heart. He had shown no evidence of it, as yet. He had demanded vast tribute from Edmund of East Anglia, slain the rival kings of Northumbria yet seemed content to place Echberht on the throne. But Leif sensed that this was no longer enough.

He suspected that Ivar's decision to leave Northumbria for Mercia was more than just a raid for slaves and treasure. Why else would he have taken so much of his army with him? The story he had told Burgred about his men seeking to return home was a blatant lie. But was his purpose to seek a kingdom? Leif closed his eyes a moment, as if by doing so he could glimpse the workings of Ivar's heart. Were his suspicions about Ivar's ambition correct? Were Alfred's?

Leif shook the question from his mind. It didn't matter a whit what Ivar's real wishes are. What matters is that I say something, anything, to keep me alive.

'More food, my lord?' he asked, playing for time. 'My hunger is still great.'

Æthelred looked annoyed at the request but gestured a servant to bring him more.

Leif eyed the plate carefully. There was less meat upon the plate this time, and much of it fat and gristle. But that meant it took him a while to chew the first mouthful. Time to come up with what he hoped was a good answer.

Finally, Alfred lost patience. 'I asked if Ivar desires to be a king?'

Leif took a deep breath, realising that a carefully constructed answer might satisfy all their questions.

'You see with clear eyes, my lord,' he said. 'Ivar hungers to become a king.'

Alfred glanced swiftly at his brother. Æthelred blanched. This was clearly a thing they had long debated.

'Of Wessex?' Æthelred asked. His voice seemed suddenly faint and weak.

'No,' Leif said as briskly as he could. 'Wessex is far too powerful for that. He seeks an easier prey. He aims for the kingdom of the East Angles.'

There was silence while the brothers digested this news.

'Then why did he go south into Mercia?' Alfred asked at last.

'To gain more supplies before turning to the east. And to surprise the East Angles by attacking overland from the west and not using his ships to land on the northern coast.'

Leif glanced at the brothers as casually as he could manage. Would they allow themselves to believe it? The alternative, that Ivar had set his eye on Wessex, was far too alarming.

'You are certain of this?' Æthelred asked at last.

'Not certain, my lord,' Leif answered. 'Ivar has also talked of taking the throne of Northumbria or of returning to Denmark. He is cunning and devious and it requires a shrewd man to ascertain what he plans.'

'A man like yourself, perhaps?' Æthelred said.

'I am his Skald, my lord,' he answered in self-deprecating tone. They could read into that what they would.

'We must ponder this carefully,' Æthelred said. 'In the meanwhile, you will be housed in a hut more to your liking. But your legs will be leashed so don't bother to think of escape.'

'I've no idea where I am,' Leif said. 'Only a fool would try to escape.'

'And you're no fool, are you?' Alfred said. His tone was a mix of admiration and suspicion.

'I believe not,' Leif answered.

Æthelred dismissed him with a gesture.

He was led out of the hall and taken into a hut by a couple of guards. They lashed his ankles together with strong leather bonds. They did a good job; without a knife it would be impossible to sever them.

'There's bread and ale,' one said gruffly, or at least that's what Leif thought he said. He spoke in a strange, sing-song, drawling manner, as did many of the Saxons.

The men left the hut and a wooden bar secured the door. Leif waited a little while and hopped over to the door, tugged at it but realised it would not give. There was no way he could open if from inside.

He cursed but then thought better of it. This was infinitely better than the murderous cell he had languished in. There was a pile of coarse blankets on the floor and a stool. Beside this was a beaker, a jug of ale and a platter with a large chunk of bread. They didn't mean him to starve.

He sipped at the ale. It was bitter and caught at his throat. The bread was dry and hard and would beguile his time here by lengthy chewing.

He settled himself on the stool and pondered what his fate would be. He knew that he would live only as long as he appeared useful to the two royal brothers.

And to do that he would need to weave a web of lies in which to trap their interest.

THE SPIDER CAUGHT

Thankfully for Leif, the brothers' desire for information about Ivar and his army meant that he was periodically freed from his hut to answer their questions.

He relished the freedom from confinement but was, nevertheless, disquieted by the experience. Æthelred and Alfred were shrewd and sifted his words with as much care as he used in uttering them. They had good memories too; early on they caught him out when he contradicted something he had said two days previously. He was more guarded after that.

They chiefly wanted to know what manner of men Ivar and his brothers were. Leif had to steer treacherous waters here. He wanted them to fear the Vikings but not enough to grow desperate and do something foolish. He also needed them to believe that he was important to Ivar and that he would seek vengeance if he were harmed. So he wove a tapestry of false-hoods, making them believe that he was not only Ivar's Skald but one of his closest companions, long time his friend, privy to his secrets and deep in his trust.

He also led them to believe that he was greatly esteemed for his wise counsel. Æthelred, in particular, was persuaded of this and began to seek him out for advice on other matters. He obeyed with all alacrity. If it kept him alive he would as soon serve the Saxon as Ivar.

Alfred, however, proved more suspicious and knowing. He was constantly trying to trip him up. And when he appeared to be simply asking for an opinion Leif suspected he had a hidden motive. One which he could not instantly quite fathom.

He came to loathe Alfred. Fortunately, he found that over time he began to understand his way of thinking and learned to be just as wily and devious.

Not that the prince spent that much time with Leif. His interests lay elsewhere, with any pretty girl who crossed his path. Although he was newlywed it did not seem to alter his need to bed slaves, servants and the daughters of peasants and thegns.

They left Cheddar four weeks after arriving there. Although it was one of the King's greatest halls and had vast holdings, there were limits to how long it could sustain him and all his followers. The stocks of food had run dangerously low. Even the game in the surrounding hills had been hunted until only the wariest creatures survived, proving hard to catch.

So the king and his entourage travelled twenty south to another of his halls at Somerton. It was a goodly place, although smaller than Cheddar, a low-lying land grazed by vast herds of sheep and cows. Leif had never seen so many and the king and his followers feasted hugely on their meat, consuming just enough to ensure that those left over would be able to survive the winter and keep fat on the store of hay.

Three weeks after arriving there they moved on for the winter rains had begun and Somerton was a low-lying settlement and prone to flooding. They headed to a town called Dorchester where they stayed for a week.

Leif marvelled at the wealth of the lands they travelled through. He had never seen so many farms and sturdy villages, so many large well-tended fields, so many herds of cattle, flocks of sheep and rooting pigs. It was a much richer land than Northumbria, or even Mercia. The people looked hale and well-fed and the thegns who welcomed the king on his journey lived in goodly halls in prosperous settlements.

The days grew cold and short and they left Dorchester and headed to Wareham, a large port on a sheltered inlet leading to the sea. This was a wealthy place and Æthelred planned to spend Yule here.

It was during Yule that Leif heard rumours that Alfred had fallen sick with some strange and ghastly malady which returned to him every day or so. No leech could cure it and, at first, even the most powerful of their Christ-wizards were at a loss as to the cause.

But then even Leif and Kolga began to hear rumours as to the reason. The first time Alfred had suffered this ailment was the night after he had returned to Wessex, bare weeks after having wedded the Mercian woman, Ealswith. It was not long before it was whispered that she was a foreign witch and had cursed him. Men avoided her and women grew wary.

Her only companions were those servants she had brought from Mercia, although it had to be said that Æthelred and his wife Wulfthryth were pleasant to her. How much this was genuine and how much diplomatic was not clear.

Alfred, on the other hand, appeared to show little compassion for his wife in her distress. He was polite and attentive enough but he kept his warmth for other women. His friends treated her with disdain.

Except for two. One was a young noble by the name of Ethelnoth. He was a big, bluff, hearty, good-natured man, always ready with a jest and as keen to chase women as Alfred. He was even friendly with Leif, taking the Viking as he saw him and not as an enemy. Ethelnoth and Alfred were bosom friends, closer than brothers or lovers.

Edgwulf was the second of Alfred's friends who treated Ealswith kindly. He was of peasant stock, a ceorl, not the normal sort to mingle with the thegns and churchman who thronged the king's hall. But he was Alfred's childhood friend and, despite Æthelred's attempts to persuade him that he was not a worthy companion, Alfred insisted in keeping him close.

Leif soon came to realise why.

Edgwulf was as loyal as only the most stupid ceorl can be when star-struck by a powerful, wealthy man. The sort who duped himself into believing he is more important to his lord than is the case.

Except Edgwulf was not stupid. Far from it. He was the cleverest man Leif had ever met.

Whenever the young Saxon was near Leif grew fretful. While he suspected that Alfred saw through most of his lies, he knew, for a certainty, that Edgwulf saw through them all.

Even though he knew that he was completely dependent upon Alfred, Edgwulf was not afraid to disagree with him and there were sometimes heated arguments between them. Yet Alfred never appeared to bear a grudge.

Because of Alfred's favour, Edgwulf was tolerated by the great lords and ladies. Tolerated but not liked. Few hid their disquiet that prince and peasant should be so familiar.

Yet how others thought made no difference. Alfred, Edgwulf and Ethelnoth were inseparable.

In the early spring the king and his entourage left Wareham and travelled to Winchester. It was an immense city with high stone walls, large and wealthy churches, numerous halls and many fine houses. The people there were well-fed and clothed and strutted the streets as if they were lords of the earth. It was a place built to be plundered and Ivar would have been delighted to hear about it.

It was here that Ealswith announced that she was with child. There was some celebration from Æthelred and his wife. But amongst his followers there was much talk that she would give birth to a demon. If Ealswith ever heard such comments she gave no sign.

The only people who showed genuine pleasure at the pregnancy were Alfred and his two friends. Ethelnoth, who appeared to have a woman in every town, was especially enthusiastic, while Edgwulf seemed more concerned to watch out for her to see that she had no mishap.

Alfred seemed as bemused and excited as any young husband at hearing the news. Leif often came upon him watching Ealswith's belly as if he sought to see who was growing inside. His former coolness to his wife disappeared overnight.

Not so the coolness of most people towards his two friends.

It was only a few days later that Leif came to understand why Edgwulf was so disliked.

He was summoned to Alfred's hall early in the morning. The guard took him to where Alfred and his two friends were warming themselves by a brazier.

'I have a question for you, Dane,' Alfred said, without any friendlier welcome.

'I am here to serve,' Leif said.

'I don't think so,' he replied. 'Let's not pretend.'

Leif inclined his head. 'Your question, my lord?' It already seemed like they were beginning to engage in sword-play.

'You Vikings are renowned for your mastery of ships,' Alfred said, 'ships which can move with utmost swiftness. So, tell me, why does your army have so many horses?'

'I'm not sure it has that many horses,' Leif said, playing for time. 'Not as many as your army, I think.'

'I believe it has more. Or so say our friends who keep watch on Ivar in Nottingham.'

Leif was astonished to hear that the Saxons had spies in Mercia and wondered who they were keeping watch on, Ivar or Burgred.

'Well?' Alfred said. 'Why does Ivar have so many horses?'

Leif was uncertain how best to answer. He had come to realise that large tracts of Wessex were not close to rivers and, therefore, comparatively safe from attack by ship. It seemed likely that Alfred had grown concerned that so many horsemen might indicate a threat to Wessex.

'Many of the horses are pack-animals, only,' Leif said. He watched Alfred narrowly to see if he would swallow this.

'Pack animals are necessary for an army on the move,' Ethelnoth said. 'Perhaps you plan to move against us.'

A spasm of annoyance crossed Alfred's face. He had learned not to give too much away to Leif when they sparred. Ethelnoth, clearly, had not.

'Across Mercia?' Leif said. 'King Burgred would not let us march across his kingdom.'

'But if he did?' Alfred said.

'I've said before, Ivar has designs upon East Anglia, not upon Wessex.'

'Then why not go by ship? Why the need for so many horses?'

Leif gave a warmer chuckle than he felt. 'Because men cannot eat ships. But when times get hard they can eat horses.'

Alfred leaned back in his seat, stroking his chin thoughtfully.

'That makes sense to me,' Edgwulf said. 'We do well to listen to Leif. He is, remember, more than merely a skald.'

Leif did not reply, wondering what was behind his words.

'That is true, is it not?' Edgwulf continued. 'I seem to recall that you assisted your brother in making Ivar's sword.'

'Did I say that?' Leif asked, nervously.

'No,' Ethelnoth said. 'It was Kolga. She told me when I was bedding her.'

Leif blinked in amazement at his words.

'Ah yes,' Edgwulf said. 'I recall now.' He turned to Leif. 'So you are both a skald and a smith?'

'My brother is the smith,' Leif answered, still pondering the news that Ethelnoth and Kolga had become lovers and wondering how best to make use of this.

'But you assist your brother,' Edgwulf said. He looked suddenly perplexed. 'Didn't Ivar think it odd that his Skald should also be helping make his sword?'

'I didn't know Ivar until he bought the sword,' Leif answered. 'He wanted a potent weapon for his move against England.'

Edgwulf appeared surprised. 'But how can this be?' he said. 'I thought you had long time been a friend and counsellor of Ivar. That you were as thick as thieves?'

Leif realised his mistake at once. He had secured his safety, his life, by pretending that he was closer to Ivar than even his brothers. Now Edgwulf had tricked him into revealing this to be a lie.

Leif glanced at Edgwulf. His look of surprise had disappeared and been replaced by a look of triumph.

'I'm sorry if I suggested this, my lord,' Leif said.

'I'm not a lord.'

'Nevertheless, I'm still sorry if I misled you. I have known Ivar only a few years but from the very first weeks he came to value my counsel. My friendship should I say.'

'Of course,' Edgwulf said. 'Of course.'

His voice was understanding, consoling. But he had caught Leif like a rat in a trap and all four men knew it.

Leif risked a glance at Alfred. His eyes were cold and watchful. 'Thank you for telling us about the appetite you Vikings have for eating horse-flesh,' he said finally. 'And for how speedily you heathens become the most intimate of friends.'

He dismissed Leif with a curt wave of his hand.

Leif got to his feet, bowed and left the hall. He hurried to the latrines, voiding his bowels as soon as he squatted down.

Loki has tricked me again, he thought, made me cock-sure and negligent. And I've completely under-estimated that bastard Edgwulf.

H pulled up his breeches and went in search of Kolga. She was in her lodgings, a far more splendid place than his hovel. It was warm and well furnished, fit for her status as a jarl.

'You look troubled,' she said

'I am. Alfred has found out that I'm not the great friend of Ivar that we've led him to believe.'

'Is that a problem?'

'It might lead to my death,' he said bitterly. 'I think I'd call that a problem.'

'Why are you telling me this?' she asked.

'Because they found out when you told your lover, Ethelnoth.'

'I told him no such thing. And how do you know he is my lover?'

'You might not have told him outright. But you told him that I worked in the smith with my brother.'

'What of it? Ethelnoth doesn't think deeply enough to make anything of it.'

'He might not but Edgwulf does.'

'Ah. The ceorl. He's clever, that one. More than the rest of them put together.' She frowned. 'Apart, perhaps from that pup of a prince he follows so loyally.'

'I don't care about all that,' Leif said. 'I care about my life.'

Kolga began to smile but then saw the look on his face and grew serious. 'So what are you going to do about it?'

'I'm going to run. I'm going to go back to Ivar.'

She blinked in astonishment. 'You must be mad. You have no idea where we are or how to find Ivar.'

'I only have to find the ancient road we travelled on. It's straight as a spear and will take me back north.'

'But what if Ivar's moved on?'

'He won't have done. Not in the depths of winter.'

She laughed. 'It's clear that you don't know him as well as you pretend. Ivar will move as swift as a wolf if he has need to. And you may not have noticed, but it's spring. He could be anywhere.'

'Nevertheless, I'm going north.'

He turned away but then paused.

'Do you wish to come with me?' he asked.

Kolga took a deep breath and glanced around the room. It was probably as comfortable as anywhere she had dwelt before.

'I suppose if you leave I might be blamed for it,' she said, quietly. She took a deep breath. 'I think you're a fool, Leif and this escape is madness. So, yes, I'll come with you.'

'Good,' he said and meant it.

ESCAPE

Leif and Kolga had been prisoners so long the Saxons' initial suspicions that they would flee had almost ceased. Even as they journeyed with the king across Wessex they were watched less and less. But Winchester was so large, so busy and with so many strangers they were hardly watched at all. They were expected to attend King Æthelred or his brother at meal times and guards took them to their lodgings at night and locked them in. But during the day they were free to wander the town.

And what a town it was. Leif dimly remembered seeing towns in Francia as a child but few seemed as rich and thriving as Winchester. It was surrounded by old Roman walls, although many stretches were ill-made and some almost derelict. It would take little effort to overrun such defences, he thought.

He particularly liked to wander among the small farmsteads which dotted the outskirts of the town. New-born lambs gambolled in the fields and ponds provided havens for huge flocks of geese and ducks. Even more pleasant were the many orchards, with trees already budding in the mild air.

Less pleasant were the tanneries on the edge of the city, near the river. Less pleasant but to Leif, gruesomely fascinating.

Boys from butcher stalls unloaded animal skins into vats full of piss which were replenished constantly by old women hauling pots and buckets from the town. The skins were soaked for several days, growing more noisome by the hour. Then men fished out the skins, heedless of how much they got drenched, scraped off the last remaining hairs and bristles and pounded dog or pigeon dung into them.

A few men preferred to pour the dung into a trough of water, climb in and knead the mess for two or three hours. Leif was amazed at how content they appeared, staring at the scene around them or chatting with their friends. The stench was overwhelming, catching so sharply at his throat he thought he would vomit.

But he was most interested in the smithies dotted along the edges of the built-up areas. Most of the smiths were local men although there was a Dane and a Norwegian who worked together as Sigurd and Leif had done. There were also half a dozen Franks, a man from Hungary with sharp, clever eyes and a youth who claimed he was from Rome.

But Leif was most intrigued by a dark-faced man from Cordoba who made the finest swords and knives in the city and was well rewarded for doing so. He was called Hisham and was very friendly. Leif occasionally helped him with his bellows and they exchanged stories of their homelands. It made Leif homesick and he yearned still more for his freedom.

Hisham was married to a Saxon girl although he still prayed four times a day to his own God and never drank ale or wine. After Leif helped him with a particularly intricate sword Hisham offered to pay him two silver pennies.

He asked for a knife instead. Hisham gave a knowing look but asked no question.

Two nights later Leif led Kolga to a small low door he had found in the western wall. It was sealed with a rusty iron bolt but he had spent part of the previous night smearing it with grease and he was able to slide it open without a sound.

He put his finger to his lip and listened for a while. The normal sounds of the city drifted over: cries of merriment, wails of children, barking dogs, lowing cows, the endless murmur of men and beasts. But no noise close by. They had not been seen or heard.

Taking Kolga by the hand Leif stepped through the door and pulled it shut behind them. The moon was full and low in the east so they'd have five hours or so of light by which to travel.

A furlong beyond the city was an ancient track which led to the west. Leif had found out that this was the path they must take if they were to find the long, straight Roman road to Mercia. He pulled his cloak close and headed west.

They walked until they were too exhausted to take another step. It was now close to dawn. Kolga led the way into the fringes of a forest, safe from any pursuit or prying eyes.

They slept until the afternoon and then debated whether to travel onward by the light of the moon or the sun. Leif was all for putting as much distance possible between them and Winchester and persuaded Kolga of the wisdom of it. They hauled on their packs and marched until the sun set and then on through the night until clouds shielded the moon and made walking treacherous.

The next morning they had good luck. They found an isolated farm with an ancient man and his infirm wife. They owned two donkeys. They wasted no time in relieving them of food, ale and the donkeys. They were too feeble to put up a fight and would not be able to swiftly seek help. So, in fine style, Leif and Kolga went on their way, always heading to the west.

Leif lost count of how many days they travelled the road. They ate all the food they had and he readied himself to steal more food. But then Kolga surprised him by producing a purse full of pennies and small gems.

'Where did you get that from?' he asked, running them through his fingers.

'I'm a Viking,' she answered. 'I took them.'

'Who from?'

'Anyone I could. Including the two smug brothers Æthelred and Alfred. And their bitches.'

Leif grinned at her words. It was what they deserved.

'I think we should pay for our food rather than steal it,' she continued.

'That's strange for a Viking.'

'A Viking who wants to live,' she said. 'If we steal we might get caught or injured or captured. I don't know about you but the sooner I get the stench of these Christ-lovers out of my nostrils the better.'

For the next few days they carefully selected their targets; isolated farms or small hamlets, and paid a fair price for food, drink and sometimes lodging.

A few people were suspicious of odd-sounding strangers but sight of a coin soon ended their qualms. Only once did Leif get alarmed when one cocksure young braggart said he would go to the nearest town and bring back a thegn to pass judgement on them. He was as good as his word, although he only got a quarter of a mile before feeling Kolga's knife slice open his throat.

Finally, more by luck than judgement, they stumbled on the town where they had arrived in Wessex all those months before. They were forced to ask directions and one young lad volunteered to take them to the road heading north across Mercia. He was a garrulous and excitable youth and begged that they take him with them. But Kolga deemed he had little knowledge of anywhere more than ten miles around and thought he would be no use to them. Besides, his near constant talking seemed likely to weary them beyond words. They paid him a farthing for his trouble and told him to go home.

It was late that day that Leif realised they were being followed. Something, some prickling in his neck made him suddenly anxious and he looked back. The road ran straight and level until it was lost in the distance. Yet he thought he saw a dark shape slip into the woodland on one side.

'So you've seen him?' Kolga said.

Leif blinked at her in surprise. 'You've seen something, as well?'

'For the past five miles. He's wary, keeps on the edge of sight.'

'This cursed straight road doesn't help,' Leif said sharply, annoyed that she had not seen fit to tell him. 'Whoever is following can see us for a mile or more.'

'If we got off the road we might lose him,' she said, glancing to right and left. 'But we'd be more likely to lose our way. One boy can't do us much harm.'

'One boy?' Leif said.

'The one who wanted to come with us,' she said.

Leif glanced back along the empty road.

'Well if we can't see him now,' he said, 'he might not be able to see us.'

He slipped into the shadow beneath an oak tree. 'You go on, more quickly.'

Kolga nodded, grabbed the reins of Leif's donkey and forced both beasts into a lumbering trot. Her speed had the added advantage of throwing up a lot of dust and their pursuer would find it hard to see who was on the road.

Leif turned his gaze to the south and waited.

A figure slipped from the distant trees and then started forward. He hastened along the road, keen to keep his quarry in sight, caution forgotten. Kolga was right. It was the boy who had pleaded to come with them.

Leif watched him more closely as he hurried past. He was about fourteen years of old, still more boy than youth. He was short with a layer of puppy fat which betokened a comfortable existence. His face was red and there was sweat on his forehead.

Leif let the boy get a few yards further and then lunged. He was alert as a thief and turned immediately. But he did not brandish a weapon. He merely covered his eyes with his hands and wailed.

Leif seized him by the arm and shook him.

'Why are you following us?' he demanded.

'Because I hate where I live,' the boy said, still clasping tight to his eyes as if by doing so Leif might disappear. 'My mother's dead and my father hates me.'

He sounded pathetic and Leif almost laughed.

'You're a bloody fool to want to come with us,' he said, trying to sound stern. 'Why would we think any better of you than your father does?'

The boy spread his fingers and peeked through them. 'Because you're not him.'

His voice sounded so hopeful Leif sighed. 'We're Vikings,' he said. 'Desperate and dangerous.'

'I guessed that. It's the reason I wanted to come with you.'

'Then you're an idiot,' Kolga cried as she clattered up. She leapt from the saddle and, before Leif could react, had her knife at the boy's throat. 'Either that or a liar.'

He wailed even louder now, his whole body shaking in terror.

'Don't kill him,' Leif said. 'Not yet at any rate.'

'No,' the boy whimpered. 'Don't kill me. I'll help you, I will.'

'How can you help us?' Kolga said. 'You're nothing but a snivelling little coward.'

'I know these parts,' he said.

'You're a liar,' she said. 'You couldn't tell us much about this road when we asked earlier.'

'That's because I wasn't sure of you,' he said. 'It's called the Fosse Way and goes all the way across Mercia. My mother was a member of the Hwicce people and we'd often travel to her family in Warwick. I know the road well.'

'So are you Mercian or West Saxon?' Leif asked.

'I'm both.' He took on a calculating, almost sly look. 'I can be whatever you want me to.'

Leif glanced at Kolga. 'He may be useful. If we can trust him.'

'We don't have to trust him,' she replied. 'Just keep him terrified.'

'I'll be loyal and true,' the boy said.

Kolga spat on his foot. 'I doubt it. Nevertheless, we'll take you with us. But the day you play us false will be your last. You'd better pray to your Christ-God at once, just in case I strike without warning.'

'Please don't,' he cried. His head shook so much it looked in danger of being loosed from his neck.

'You'll be safe as long as you remain useful and honest,' Leif said.

The boy beamed with relief. 'I'm called Higbald, by the way,' he said.

'I care not,' Kolga said, climbing on her donkey and trotting off.

Leif climbed onto his mount. 'Come then, Higbald,' he said. 'Try and keep up. And tell me where the next village is.'

'Ashley,' Higbald answered. 'It's just a farm and few huts. We should reach it by dusk.'

'Will it be safe for us to stay the night there?'

Higbald grinned and pointed to Kolga. 'With that she-devil? I think we'd be safe to stay anywhere.'

They were given a wary welcome by the farmer who sold them some bread and ale and allowed them to sleep in a cow byre. But he made sure that they left their weapons with him first.

'This has always been a disputed land,' Higbald said. 'For a long time it was the border between Wessex and Mercia. There's a lot of bad blood between the people here.'

'It sounds fit for you, then,' Leif said.

'Because of my bad blood?' The boy looked hurt.

'Because of your mixed blood. Are there many mongrels like you, half-Saxon, half-Mercian?'

'In the borderlands, yes. And sometimes further afield. I hear that the king's brother has taken a Mercian wife.'

'He has,' Kolga said. 'And the Saxons think she's a sorceress.' She snorted with laughter. 'Such brave heroes. They quake in their boots when she passes by, fearing her spells.'

'They think she's bewitched the prince,' Leif said.

Higbald shrugged. 'Well if she's pretty…'

'Get some sleep,' Leif said. 'We start first thing tomorrow.'

They made good progress the next day, passing through a goodly sized town called Cirencester and then onward to a village called Moreton. Higbald said that the people there suffered depredations from a village called Broadway where the people were notoriously crazed and dangerous. Hearing this they travelled a mile north and made camp in a wood to the east of the road. Leif felt bone weary from the long journey and Higbald was sleeping on his feet. Kolga, on the other hand, seemed unaffected by the long miles.

Leif realised the truth of this in the small hours when he felt someone undoing his breeches and then straddling him. Kolga groaned with pleasure. 'I've not had a fuck for a long time.'

Leif wondered what Aebbe would think of this but only for a little while. Kolga was a dexterous and demanding lover and mounted him twice more that night.

Leif came to grow quite fond of her as they rode across Mercia. She, on the other hand, treated him as little more than another donkey, something to make the journey less tiresome.

Leif had lost count of the days they'd spent on the Fosse. Thankfully, it didn't stray close to many villages so they were little watched. Higbald told them the road had been built by priests from Rome who were also great warriors and conquered the whole world.

Kolga laughed with derision. 'We Vikings are the greatest warriors the world has ever seen,' she said. 'And you will come to learn this. If you live.'

Finally, after two more days, they stumbled across the river Trent. They were a few miles east of Nottingham and, with great relief followed its banks towards their friends.

Except that their friends were no longer there. The moment they walked through the gates of the town they realised their mistake. The Mercians had retaken the town.

They slipped into a narrow alley so they would not be overheard.

'What's happened?' Leif asked even though he knew that none of his companions had any more idea than he did.

'Can Ivar have been defeated?' Kolga murmured. 'Has even his great luck turned?'

'The Mercians are a great people,' Higbald said. 'Not as great as the Saxons but still very powerful. A very dangerous foe for you Vikings.'

Kolga gave him a threatening look and he stepped beyond her reach.

'Instead of giving us your thoughts,' Leif said, 'go and do something useful. Walk around the town and find out what's happened.'

'You won't find us here,' Kolga said. 'We're leaving. Meet us where we crossed the river.'

Higbald nodded and hurried off. Kolga waited a few moments and then led the way back to the gate.

They waited for several hours at the river. Kolga grew ever more impatient.

'He'll have sold us to the Mercians,' she said at last. 'I never trusted him. We should leave.'

She tightened the saddle of her donkey and climbed onto it. 'Are you coming?' she asked. 'Or will you wait for our betrayer?'

Leif shrugged. 'I've no desire to stay here any longer,' he said. 'But we don't know which way to go. Ivar could have gone in any direction. My woman and children, my brother and friends, they could be anywhere. Where's the sense in blundering around this cursed country unless we know where we're going?'

She gave him a filthy look but, seeing the wisdom of his words, got off the donkey which whinnied in pleasure. She whacked it over the head.

'But with luck we may now have an answer,' Leif said, pointing back towards the town.

Higbald bustled up to them, his face shining with pleasure. He thrust some bread and hot meat into their hands.

'I've found out everything,' he said. 'The Mercians bought your people off a few months ago with great treasure. It seems that was enough to satisfy them and they left Nottingham and promised to leave the kingdom.'

'And which way did they go?' Leif asked, impatiently. 'North, south, east or west?'

'They went north. Most of the folk I spoke to said they were returning where they came from.'

'Denmark,' Leif said. His heart soared at the thought of home and safety.

'It's not my home,' Kolga said, 'but it will have to do.' She glared at the donkey. 'I'm sick of this stumbling little creature. We're on the river now, let's find a boat.'

They left Higbald with the donkeys and wandered along the river for a while. After half a mile they found exactly what they wanted, a small fishing boat, big enough for three and with two sets of oars. An old man was snoozing in it and they tipped him out into the stream.

They made their way back to Higbald, loaded the supplies into the boat and climbed aboard.

Higbald stood on the bank, shifting uneasily from foot to foot.

'Are you coming with us?' Leif asked. 'You don't have to if you don't want to. You've guided us through Mercia as you promised. You're free to go wherever you choose.' He reached into his purse and pulled out a handful of coins.

'I want to stay with you,' Higbald said. 'You're my friends.'

Leif heard Kolga give a snort of derision but he kept his gaze on Higbald.

'It's just that I've never been in a boat before,' the boy said. 'And I can't swim.'

'I can't swim either,' Kolga said. 'Which is why I'm careful never to sink a boat. Get in or stay there, it doesn't matter to me. But make up your mind.'

Higbald climbed nervously into the boat, making it sway dangerously. At last he settled, sitting upright and unmoving, his face a picture of terror.

'Come on,' Kolga said. 'The sooner we leave Mercia the better.'

They moved swiftly north upon the river, aided by a strong current. Nevertheless, it took two long days of constant rowing. Leif's hands were raw and bloody by the time they came to where the Trent flowed into the Humber.

'Now which way?' Leif asked.

He was still not convinced that the Mercian treasure would have satisfied Ivar enough to make him return tamely to Denmark.

They found out within the hour. A Danish trading ship appeared from downriver, heading west. They hailed it as it approached and asked the captain where he was going.

'York,' he answered. 'There's much good trade there. Ivar and his brothers have filled the town with gold and I want a piece of it.'

'Ivar the Boneless?' Leif said. 'Are you sure he's there?'

'I spoke with him forty days ago. There's said to be an English king in the city but even if that's the case, the brothers are the real lords. Some of the English are already acting like Danes, calling the city Jorvic and wearing Thor's amulet. It's almost like home.'

Leif pressed some silver into the man's hand and he welcomed them on board.

RETRIBUTION

Jorvic was every bit as prosperous looking as the trader had said. The quayside was crammed with ships of all sizes and with men of all types. Most were Danish or Norse but there were also many folk from England as well as the northern isles.

But Leif paid no heed to them. He wanted to see his family and he hurried towards the city walls.

The men of the army stood open-mouthed in astonishment. It was now May and they had been captured by the Saxons more than six months before.

'We thought you were dead or sold as slaves,' one man said. Then he looked a little furtive which Leif put down to shame at his words.

The rumour ran through the streets as they made their way to the centre of the city. A crowd followed them, chattering loudly, showering them with questions, slapping Leif on the back, although keeping a wary distance from Kolga. It was a wonderful home-coming.

And then Leif saw her. Standing in front of a little house, one hand on her breast, the other to her mouth. Aebbe. It was as if she had seen a ghost. Slowly, she came towards him and then, as she got closer, she sobbed and threw herself into Leif's arms.

His heart beat as fast as a galloping horse. He had never imagined he could feel so much for another person. And then he heard a roar of joy and Sigurd came racing towards him, yelling at the top of his voice. He grabbed Leif in a fierce bear-hug, lifting him off his feet and laughing so loud that Leif thought he would deafen all the people nearby.

Finally, when it seemed that he would squeeze the last drop of air from Leif he let go and lifted his head. 'My brother has returned,' he bellowed. 'Leif has returned from the Saxons.' His cry was so loud it must have carried throughout the city.

Aebbe put her mouth close to Leif's ear. 'I thought you were dead,' she whispered. 'We all did.'

'The Saxons treated me well,' he said. 'At least after a time. We were honoured guests of King Æthelred and his brother.'

'And they let you go?'

Leif shook his head. 'We escaped.'

'But why? If you were honoured guests?'

'Guests who had overstayed our welcome.'

Leif pulled her to him and kissed her fiercely. She tasted good, like berries new picked from the bush.

Two figures came running, leaping with pleasure; Thorvald and Asgrim, their faces bright with joy. Leif gulped in surprise. He had not realised how much he meant to them.

'You are right welcome,' Thorvald said fervently. 'Sigurd has been like a bear with a sore arse since the day you were taken.'

'And Ivar has been almost as bad,' Asgrim said.

'Ivar?' Leif said in surprise.

'He missed his Skald,' Asgrim explained. 'It's been a long, bleak, bloody winter.'

'But not for you, I see,' said Thorvald, prodding Leif in the stomach. 'You're as fat and as sleek as a jarl's daughter.'

'I am a friend of the Saxon king,' Leif said, tapping himself on the chest. 'I had all the food and drink I desired.'

'And women?' Aebbe asked, her voice quiet and shy.

'What woman would have him?' Kolga said. 'He's spent the whole time pining for you.'

Leif gave her a grateful smile. She grinned back and punched Higbald on the shoulder, sending him sprawling in the dust. Aebbe would be spared the pain of hearing about Leif's coupling with Kolga, it seemed.

He turned to Aebbe once more. 'The babies?' he asked.

But as he did so he detected a change in his friends. A terrible change. The words died on his lips.

Aebbe's closed her eyes, her face tight with pain and sorrow.

'Something's happened to them?' he asked, although he feared to hear the answer.

'To Godgyth,' she answered. 'To our daughter.'

'What? What happened?'

Aebbe turned away, tears welling from her eyes.

Leif felt Sigurd's iron grip upon my arm. 'Godgyth died,' he said. 'A few months ago.'

Leif stared at his brother in disbelief, not sure what he was saying.

'Died?' he mumbled at last. 'How did she die?'

Nobody answered.

'How?' Leif demanded.

Asgrim took a deep breath. 'She was killed,' he said.

'And the killer paid the price,' Thorvald said, hurriedly. 'Guthrum made sure of that.'

Leif stared at him in silence. His world was reeling. 'Guthrum?' he mumbled.

Thorvald nodded.

Leif shook his head, blankly, and then Aebbe reached out and took his hand. 'Let's not talk of it here. Not on the street in front of our neighbours.'

Leif followed her in a daze. Godgyth dead? He couldn't make sense of it. Surely it was some cruel jest?

He found himself in their little house. Tears were coursing down his brother's face. The sight of it made him feel weak and dizzy.

'Where's Nefi?' he asked.

'With Nerienda,' Aebbe said. 'She has a puppy and he loves to play with it.'

He slumped onto a stool and Aebbe sat beside him.

'How?' he asked. 'How did Godgyth die?'

Aebbe started to answer but could say no more than a few mumbled words. She glanced up at Sigurd who started to speak but then shook his head.

'It was Eohric,' Thorvald said quietly. 'He had been drinking heavily, more heavily than usual.'

'But that does not excuse it,' Asgrim said.

'I did not say that,' Thorvald continued. 'But it shows us something about him.'

'Tell me?' Leif whispered. 'Tell me what happened?'

'He came to your house,' Thorvald said slowly. 'He had conceived a great lust for Aebbe and sought to take advantage of your absence.'

He paused and gestured to Sigurd and Asgrim. 'The three of us were away, foraging in the east. He chose his time well.'

'He raped me,' Aebbe said. 'He was a beast, a brute. In front of the children. They were alarmed at the violence, at what they saw happening to me. Nefi tried to stop him, babe though he was. Eohric kicked him to the floor. Godgyth screamed and screamed. So Eohric picked her up, smashed her head upon the wall and flung her...' She pointed to the fire.

Leif stared at her. He wanted to reach out to her but he could not move. His body felt scraped clean and empty, his heart and mind suddenly frozen.

'I tried to get her out,' Abbe said, 'but Eohric knocked me to the ground. And then he raped me again. While my baby burnt to death.'

She buried her head in her hands, weeping uncontrollably.

Leif looked at Sigurd who bent his head.

'Sigurd tried to slay him,' Thorvald said. 'He tried to avenge you and Godgyth. But Ivar would have none of it, fearing a blood feud would spread like contagion. Nobody would believe Aebbe's word against Eohric's. He is the brother of a jarl while she is...' He did not finish his sentence, did not say that nobody would believe the word of a slave such as her.

'Several of your friends gave me money to support Aebbe,' Sigurd said. 'To my surprise Guthrum did so as well. I think, maybe he doubted his brother's word.'

Leif did not answer for a long while. His mind was awash with images of Godgyth: when she was new-born, of her sucking on Aebbe's breast, the first smile she gave.

But then, like shadows in the darkest night, he saw an image of Eohric slinking towards his home. Attacking Aebbe, raping her, smashing the little head of Godgyth and flinging her into the flames.

He sobbed but no tears came. Aebbe took his hand but he could barely feel it.

He began to shake as if he'd lain all night in the deepest snow-drift. He stumbled to his feet and heard the stool fall backwards, clattering on the floor. He tried to speak but no words came. He had lost all use of his tongue.

He went out to the street. A large crowd had gathered but he could not recognise their faces. He marched along the street towards Guthrum's hall. To Eohric.

Guthrum saw him approach and stepped in front of him to block his path. 'Don't be a fool,' he said. 'The wergild has been paid and accepted.'

'Not by me,' Leif cried, finding a strangled voice at last.

Guthrum grabbed him by the shoulders. He was huge and immensely strong. Leif pushed against him but it was like trying to move a hill.

'Don't do something you'll regret,' Guthrum whispered. 'There'll be a blood-feud. And Ivar won't condone it.'

'And in this feud?' Leif cried. 'Where will you stand?'

'Eohric is my brother.'

'And Aebbe is my wife and Godgyth was my daughter.'

Guthrum stared searchingly into Leif's eyes and then let him go.

'You are no warrior, Leif,' he said, 'but Eohric is. You are a man renowned for your wisdom. Don't throw that away.'

Leif looked at him, wondering what he meant and how he should respond.

Then he saw him. Eohric had sauntered out of the hall and was standing twenty paces away.

Leif's vision, until now hazy and unclear, became clear and sharp. He saw the sneer upon Eohric's face, the harsh set of his thin, cruel mouth. And then he laughed, a cold, mocking laugh, and spat at Leif.

'Looking for your brat, are you, Leif Ormson? Well you won't find her. Nor will you find Aebbe as loving a woman as when you left. You'd no sooner disappeared than she pleaded with me to mount her.'

Leif leapt at him.

Eohric moved aside at the last moment but Leif managed to swing at him, catching him on the temple. He staggered and came back, fists clenched, spitting fury. Leif turned swiftly and faced him, his rage building with every breath.

Eohric feinted, left and right, Leif dodged and ducked his sudden flurry of fists but as Guthrum had said, he was no fighter and every punch he aimed, missed. Eohric moved closer, then danced away, seeking for a weakness.

Suddenly, with a cry of rage, Leif leapt upon him. Eohric's fists hammered on his head but he felt no pain. All Leif wanted was to kill him.

The weight and fury of his attack sent Eohric crashing to the ground. Leif yelled in triumph and threw himself on top of him. His hands reached for Eohric's throat and began to squeeze.

Eohric kicked violently with his knees but Leif paid no heed. He increased the pressure on his enemy's throat, squeezing relentlessly. Eohric grasped his wrists, trying to tear them away but to no avail. He scratched at Leif's hands and arms, causing blood to flow from the gashes but doing nothing more.

Leif saw that he was choking the life from Eohric. He began to weaken, he gasped and coughed, his head shook back and forth, his tongue flicked like a snake's.

Then, suddenly, he let go of Leif's hands. Leif thought he had slain him.

But then a pile of earth and stones ground into his eyes. He was blinded and reached up instinctively to brush it away.

Eohric seized his chance. He grabbed a second handful and forced it into Leif's left eye. The pain was terrible, sharp stones pushing against the eyeball, the dry earth seeming to scour the socket.

Eohric yelled with exultation and ground the stones in still harder. Leif thought his head would explode. And then, he felt his eye give way to the onslaught, felt the soft, hot jelly dribble onto his chin. A woman screamed nearby.

Leif's sight grew dim, then black. And still Eohric forced the stones and earth into his eye.

Leif fell back on the ground. The world was dark but he could see, though only just. He saw Guthrum drag Eohric to his feet. He assumed that he would drag Eohric away but instead he held him upright and smashed his fist into his face again and again and again.

Eohric shrieked with pain and fury but Guthrum continued until, even with his failing sight, Leif could see his face was a red and ragged mess. Then Guthrum gave him one last punch, into his throat, which sent him careering across the street.

Leif felt strong arms lift him up, Sigurd he guessed and by the sound of it, Thorvald. And then he knew no more.

ONE EYED

Leif knew little of the next few days. He remembered that a leech had come and placed unguents upon his eye-socket and then bound his eyes with fresh, clean linen. He thought it might have been Deor but was not sure.

The agony was terrible. It was as if a fire had been lit in his head and that a dragon was at large within it and gnawing at his face. If he'd had more courage and the means of finding a knife he might have slit his own throat.

He was badly bruised from the fight and Eohric had broken several fingers on his left hand when he'd tried to prise it loose from his throat. But they were as nothing compared to the torment of his eyes.

The only comfort he had was in the gentle touch and soothing words of Aebbe.

'Nefi?' he managed to say towards the end of the first day.

'He's staying with Sigurd and Nerienda,' Aebbe answered. 'We didn't think he should see you like this.'

'Is he —?'

'He's safe. Quite safe.'

She fell silent and Leif sensed that she was uncertain what to say next.

'And Eohric's in no shape to do us any harm,' she said eventually. 'He's still coughing and retching from the fight and Guthrum has posted guards on his door to keep him there.'

Leif sighed with some small measure of relief, though he wondered if he'd survive long enough to see his son again.

But he did. He grew stronger day by day and was able to get out of bed, although he found it difficult to make his way around the cottage without banging into things. Higbald proved a great boon, guiding him around as if he were a baby taking his first steps, moving things out of his way and sometimes even catching him when he stumbled.

'This will pass,' Deor said. 'You need time to adjust to having only one eye but you will.'

Deor spent many hours with Leif, changing his dressing and using one of Nerienda's tweezers to pick out the fragments of stone and soil still in his eye-socket. It was the worst pain imaginable and Leif's hands grew stiff from grasping the arm of the chair. But gradually Deor removed each particle and the pain began to ease.

Deor also spent much time talking with Leif, telling tales of heroes who had lost one eye, both eyes, their legs or arms, and yet still gone on to greater glory and fortune. Leif found his stories irritating and hopeful in equal measure but sat and listened to them without complaint.

More interesting was the news that Sigurd told him. The army had been in great dissent in the spring over whether to remain in Mercia or move on to one of the other kingdoms. Ivar was all for ravaging Mercia, Halfdan and Ubbe for attacking Wessex. In the end a revolt in Northumbria against their puppet Echberht had forced them to put aside their quarrel and travel north to secure their position there. Jorvic was too great a prize to lightly relinquish.

Ivar showed then why he was a great commander. Within days he had defeated two rebel armies, slaughtering any man wounded or still defiant, and selling the rest as slaves. He insisted that they be sold to foreign merchants for he did not wish any to remain in their homeland and foment trouble.

He next sent his men on a spree of ruthless plunder to take the heart out of the country. By the end of summer, Northumbria was like a hound whipped into submission by a man determined to prove who was master. It was bloodied, beaten and broken, and became the most craven of beasts.

The Viking warriors, even the lowliest of them, were as wealthy and feared as lords.

'It's a pity you missed it,' Sigurd said, rubbing his hands with glee.

Leif wondered at his brother's new-found enthusiasm. Hitherto he had been a dutiful follower of Ivar and no more. Now he appeared as fervent as any other man in the army and would hear no word against him.

Will he still feel that way when Ivar sits in judgement of me, Leif wondered.

Aebbe fashioned him a patch to wear over one eye to hide his disfigurement. He felt better when she'd done so for it meant that Nefi could be brought home. At first he was curious about what lay beneath the patch but Leif moved his prying hand away so often that he eventually gave up.

Leif made up stories to explain his absence to the boy. He had been captured by a dragon, he had tricked it into allowing him to go free, then had tamed it so that it became his servant. He rode around the world on his dragon, seeing strange and marvellous places where people had blue or green skin, where some were ten feet tall and others no bigger than a finger.

'Where is Dragon?' Nefi asked.

'He's gone to live with his family,' Leif said. 'Just as I have come back to live with you.'

After a week Leif was well enough to wander outside although he did not go far and one of his friends always went with him. They said it was because he was still liable to blunder into things, which was true. But he suspected it was more because they feared what Eohric might do if he caught him alone.

He gained a new companion in a young man by the name of Ketil. He was Thorvald's son, about fifteen summers old, and very like his father in looks and temperament. He had come to Jorvic from their home village, keen to join his father who he thought the greatest man in the world. And keen to win glory and fame in battle.

The only way in which he differed from Thorvald was in his garrulousness. He was interested in anything and everything and assumed that everyone else would feel the same if only they let him tell them. Leif did not mind. Ketil often accompanied him as he walked around the city and he enjoyed having an engaging companion with keen mind and sharp eyes.

At last came the day which Leif dreaded. The day when Ivar and his brothers would sit in judgement upon him.

He had attacked Eohric and this had led to the savage beating Guthrum had dealt out to him. For some, Eohric was the innocent man and Leif the guilty one.

The trial would not, could not, go easy for him.

Sigurd and Thorvald helped Leif to the assembly. He was still having difficulty focusing, still in danger of tripping over and banging into things. Sigurd pleaded with him not to but he wore the patch over his missing eye. He knew better than his brother the power of such a talisman.

The whole army had congregated in the open space in front of the fortress, sitting or squatting on the ground.

Ivar, Halfdan, Ubbe and the jarls and chieftains sat on stools on a small platform. To their left stood Eohric with his brother and friends. To their right stood Deor and Asgrim. Two stools stood beside them. Aebbe was sitting on one, the other was empty.

A gasp came from the assembled warriors when Leif appeared. He shuffled like an old, frail man, his broken fingers were tightly bound and the patch on his eye spoke eloquently of all he had suffered.

He could have, as his friends well knew, walked more swiftly and surely but he was determined to display his injuries to the utmost degree. He needed every ounce of sympathy he could get.

Ivar told him to take the seat next to Aebbe and then rose to address the army.

'Fellow warriors,' he cried. 'We are gathered to hear judgement between Eohric, brother of Jarl Guthrum and Leif

Ormson. There has been much dispute about the events, and rumour has run as fast as fire amongst us. But I have ascertained the true facts and present them here, without gloss or comment.'

He surveyed the assembly for a moment, making sure that all attention was on him before continuing.

'These are the facts. Leif had been long a captive in Wessex along with Jarl Kolga. But they made their escape and returned to Jorvic after much tribulation. And here, Leif found out all that had transpired since he had gone.'

The warriors murmured, many of them darting venomous glances at Eohric for what he had done to Aebbe and to Godgyth.

'Leif listened to what had happened,' Ivar continued, 'and then, despite the pleas of his friends, he went in search of Eohric. Many of you saw what took place. Leif challenged Eohric for the attack upon his wife and daughter. Eohric laughed about the death of the child and claimed that Aebbe had invited him to her bed.'

The warriors glanced at Aebbe. She was an attractive woman and had turned the head of more than a few of them. Many wondered that such a woman should be the property of a man like Leif, poor, no warrior and with no renown. Of course, she was little better than a slave so likely to give herself to any man who happened on the scene.

'At that point,' Ivar said, 'Leif leapt on Eohric. It was a bitter, fierce struggle. Leif was the weaker in terms of strength and skill but his fury bore Eohric to the ground. But Eohric had more than just strength and skill. He had the cunning of a warrior, and the luck.'

Here Eohric smirked, basking in Ivar's words which he took for a compliment. But those who saw this were not as gleeful as he was.

'Eohric,' Ivar continued, 'clawed at a handful of earth and stones and plunged them into Leif's eye, gouging it out completely. It was then that Guthrum pulled Eohric from Leif and punished him, as many of you saw.'

Those who had witnessed the events nodded, remembering the power and fury which Guthrum had displayed. Those who had not seen it seemed envious. Eohric's injuries spoke eloquently of the dreadful punishment and it would have been pleasant to behold.

A silence fell upon the camp. The story had been told and retold many times and few had heard a version which agreed with any other. But Ivar said this version was the truth and so it was accepted.

'You must judge who is guilty of the crime,' Ivar cried. 'Leif for attacking Eohric? Or Eohric for raping Leif's wife and killing his child?'

Warrior turned to warrior in fevered debate.

Leif's heart grew cold as he watched them. What will happen to me if I'm found guilty, he wondered. Will I lose everything? My wealth, my standing, my position as Skald, my life?

And what will happen to Aebbe?

He knew that many men despised her because she was English and yet they lusted after her. They would believe she had invited Eohric to her bed. And, jealous and vindictive, they would want her punished as the cause of all the trouble.

At last the heated debate grew calmer. Eventually, one old warrior climbed to his feet. He was a wise and trusted man and all turned to hear his opinion.

'Eohric,' he cried. 'Eohric, is the guilty man.'

'Eohric,' echoed another close by.

Soon the whole assembly was baying out the same. Very few spoke up for Eohric and their voices were drowned out.

Ivar held up his hand for silence.

'Judgement has been made,' he cried. 'Eohric and Leif step forward to hear the sentence.'

Eohric stepped forward, his face arrogant and yet nervous. Leif pretended to struggle to rise and had to be helped by Deor. He trudged forward slowly and stood in front of the brothers and the chieftains.

'You wear a patch?' Ubbe asked. 'Is there good cause for it?'

Leif nodded and Ubbe gestured for him to remove it.

With a great show of reluctance Leif did so and turned to the assembled army. The warriors leaned forward to get a better look and a gasp of mingled horror and fascination spread amongst them. Those nearby grimaced. The eye socket was a charred and disfigured mass of blackened flesh. An empty void could just be glimpsed behind it.

Ivar allowed the sight of the injury to sink in before continuing.

'The army has concluded that Eohric is the guilty man,' he said. 'This is the punishment, the judgement of my brothers and me.'

The warriors fell silent and leaned closer. They looked forward to a juicy and controversial punishment.

'Eohric will pay wergild,' Ivar continued, 'for the attack upon Leif's wife, the consequent assault on his honour, the death of his child, the loss of his eye, his broken fingers and various other injuries.'

He stared at the assembled warriors, daring any of them to contest his judgement. None did.

'For this, Eohric will pay Leif one thousand silver pennies.'

Most of the warriors nodded in approval. This was a just settlement.

'In addition,' Ivar continued, 'Eohric must serve Leif as his thrall for one year and a day.'

Eohric heard this in horror and disbelief. He screamed in rage.

The army gasped. This was an immense penalty, more than any thought would be demanded, or was appropriate.

'For let us remember that Leif is no mere Skald,' Ivar continued. 'He is my sworn man and had left his woman here, in our care, while on a dangerous mission for us all, a mission which resulted in him being captured and treated ill by the Saxons.'

Each warrior pondered this and slowly, most came to see the wisdom of Ivar's judgement

'This has been decided,' Ivar said.

After a moment Guthrum stood and asked leave to speak.

'My brother has done much evil,' he said, 'and well deserves to pay a heavy fine. But he is the son of a Jarl and I cannot think it right that he becomes the thrall of a man who is the brother of a lowly blacksmith.'

'He may have started life as the brother of a smith,' Ivar said, 'but he is my sworn man now. He is also a valuable member of this host, more valuable, may I say, than your wastrel brother.'

Guthrum stared at Ivar. He knew that there was no point in arguing further. He nodded his head in acquiescence.

Eohric stared at his brother in shock and then cried out, 'You bastard. You traitor. You've always hated me.'

Guthrum's face reddened in fury but he mastered his rage and turned to Ivar.

'I accept your judgement on Eohric,' he said, 'for it is just and he deserves no better. But his punishment will shame my family. My father is an old man and news of Eohric's dishonour may prove the death of him. Is there any price I can pay to buy him back?'

'Do you want him back?' Ivar asked in surprise. 'I wouldn't.'

'My wishes are not important,' Guthrum said. 'I think only of my family's honour.'

Ivar gestured to his brothers and they spoke a while together. Then they summoned the rest of the jarls and spoke with them.

'Guthrum,' Ivar said at last, 'even though Eohric lacks honour himself, as a member of such a great and noble family, he is worth a great deal of treasure. We deem the price of his honour is a longship.'

He turned to Leif. 'Do you accept this, my Skald? Will you accept a longship as part of the wergild?'

Leif was too astonished to answer and could only manage a nod.

'But that's a sixth of our fleet,' Guthrum said.

'Then I suggest you take if from Eohric's half,' Ivar responded.

Guthrum shot a bitter glance at Eohric and nodded his agreement. He was just about to walk away when Ivar stopped him.

'That is wergild for Leif. But what about the insult to me?'

Guthrum swallowed visibly. 'What would you have from me, Ivar the Boneless?'

'Nothing more from you, Guthrum. But from Eohric I will take a second ship.'

'That leaves me with virtually nothing,' Eohric cried.

'You are nothing,' Ivar said. 'And you only have your freedom because of your brother's generosity. Be thankful to him, and to me.'

And with that he strode away.

A MAN OF GREAT STANDING

The whole army was agog for several days at this sudden reversal of Eohric's and Leif's fortunes. Most, who bore a strong dislike for Eohric, were jubilant. But there were a number of men who supported him and felt great anger at the judgement against him. Leif might be rich now but he felt anxious for his and his family's safety.

He was not alone in these fears. Kolga lent him Vafri and Asta, her two lovers and best warriors to guard him.

Many of the men from Eohric's ships had no desire to serve directly under Ivar and asked to serve with Leif. But he was nervous of making such a choice, fearing to make as many enemies as friends.

In the end, Thorvald informed him that he had decided to be his ship-master and would be happy to make the selection. 'I know better than you who to choose,' he said.

'I'm sure you do,' Leif replied in relief. 'After all, you made an excellent choice of yourself as ship-master.'

They laughed aloud. Both knew his words to be true.

Leif should have begun to feel less worried once his crew had been chosen. He now had thirty sworn followers while Eohric had few. But the thought of this merely alarmed him. He felt sure that, despite Ivar's words, it would lead to a feud.

Fortunately, Guthrum appeared to hold no ill-will against Leif. He would speak pleasantly to him when they met and once even asked how he liked being the owner of a longship.

Leif wondered at his good-humour for it did not seem natural and he sought the view of Thorvald.

'There are two reasons,' Thorvald explained. 'One is that Guthrum believes Eohric's actions brought shame on him and his father.

'The second is that he has a great appetite for power. He always has and now it waxes prodigiously. He seeks Ivar's approval and patronage and will do nothing to jeopardise this.'

'This means more to him than his brother?'

'Much more. Guthrum tolerates Eohric and will support him if he is in trouble. But only up to a point. And that point is where his own position and ambitions are at risk.'

The next day Leif decided that he would seek out Guthrum. If he had such a hunger for power then it was wise to keep on good terms with him.

He found him in even better humour than he'd hoped.

'Come,' Guthrum said, gesturing Leif to a seat. 'Join me at my meat.'

Leif thanked him nervously, his suspicions aroused. Maybe his former attitude to me was an act, he thought. Maybe he means to poison me.

Guthrum gave him a trencher and placed hot pork on it with his own hands. A female slave poured wine for them.

Leif waited until Guthrum had taken a deep swallow from his cup before taking a sip of his own. 'This is good,' he said.

'I prefer wine to ale,' Guthrum said, 'although I don't let my men know this. They might think I'm growing soft as a Frank.'

'I doubt any man would believe that. Or they wouldn't tell you to your face, at any rate.'

Guthrum laughed and raised his cup in salute. 'You know that I bear you no ill-will, Leif,' he said. 'I burned in shame at what my brother had done to your woman and child.'

'Not what he did to me?'

Guthrum shrugged. 'It was a fair fight between two men.'

Eohric's way of fighting did not seem fair to Leif but he thought it best to let it pass.

'You were lucky to receive such huge wealth,' Guthrum continued. 'Ivar meant to make an example of my brother. He cannot risk trouble amongst the men and wished to show the sort of penalty that will be meted out to those who cause it. It was a lesson that all took to heart. More than that, he wanted to make it good and clear that he leads the army and his word is law. He will brook no opposition.'

'But you suffered most from his judgement.'

He smiled. 'You think so?'

Leif frowned in surprise.

Guthrum laughed and gestured for more wine.

'Ivar gave me back the ship he took from me although he has not let this be known as yet. He'll wait until returning it to me appears a sign of his great magnanimity.'

Leif shook his head in confusion. 'But why would he take with one hand and give back with the other?'

'You're supposed to be the wise one, Leif. You tell me.'

'Because he doesn't want to antagonise you?'

Guthrum nodded. 'Ivar knows my worth. But he also wanted the men to know that he had power over me.'

'Did you know this was going to happen?' Leif asked. 'Did you and Ivar plan it this way?'

Guthrum smiled at the suggestion. 'No. I am not as cunning as that. I leave such complex strategies to the likes of you and Ivar.'

'I am hardly a man of great strategy. If I were I wouldn't have fought your brother.'

'You did that out of passion and anger. Out of a desire for vengeance for your woman and child. It is good that you did so. It shows you have as much heart as head.'

He gave Leif a curious look before continuing. 'One day, Leif, you might consider becoming my Skald. My man of cunning.'

Leif must have looked alarmed at the prospect for Guthrum laughed and took a deep draught of his wine.

'I don't mean now,' he said. 'Not while Ivar still rules.'

'But Eohric —'

'Will do exactly as I command. If I choose to take you into my service I shall do so. And Eohric will not be allowed to object.'

Leif inclined his head. It seemed too unlikely a prospect to waste any more thought on. But he was flattered, none the less.

'So, we at least are friends?' he said tentatively.

'We are friends,' Guthrum replied, taking Leif's hand. 'But a word of warning. Stay clear of Eohric. Don't fight with him and don't boast of what you have taken from him.'

'I didn't take it. I was given it. By Ivar.'

'Eohric does not think that way. I fear he will ever be your enemy.'

Leif spent the summer months recovering his strength and getting used to seeing with only one eye. To his surprise he found that his use of a bow improved greatly. He had always been an enthusiastic but indifferent bowman but now he found he had unerring aim. Thorvald told him this was not unusual and pointed out how many bowmen closed one eye when they aimed.

Whenever he could, Leif went out on his ship, taking Thorvald and Asgrim to give him guidance on how to act as a captain. Asgrim had asked Ivar to be released from his crew so that he could join with Thorvald in teaching Leif the skills necessary. He learned to play the part to some extent but all three men knew that in an emergency he would be worse than useless. But he knew he could rely on his friends to captain his ship, come what may.

Despite Leif's new-found wealth and position Ivar soon made it clear that his status in relation to him had not changed. Leif was still his Skald and still his sworn man. Not that he recalled ever actually swearing an oath. But he did not complain. The closer he was to Ivar the greater his safety from Eohric and his dwindling but malicious band of friends.

As the days wore on towards autumn he began to grow less worried about Eohric. He seemed like a wolf which had lost its teeth.

And then, one day, to Leif's surprise, Eohric stopped him in the street.

'I had a dream last night,' he said. 'Odin came to me and told me that the enmity between the gods would prove their undoing and would lead to their doom. I told him that this fate was long written. He agreed but seemed sorrowful, nonetheless. And then he drew me closer and said that the fate of gods need not be that of men.'

He looked at Leif and gave a rueful grin. 'I have wronged you, Leif. My dream of Odin made me realise this and vow to make all right between us.'

He held out his hand.

At first Leif was reluctant to take it but decided he had little choice. If he refused, word of it would spread and he would be deemed a craven.

Eohric's grasp was surprisingly warm and forthright.

Leif stared after him as he left, confused by what appeared to be his change of heart.

Later that day, he spoke to Aebbe about it. She was dismissive of Eohric's actions.

'He's doing it for his own purposes,' she said. 'To win back the favour of Ivar or Guthrum. He's a snake and I will never trust him. And nor should you.'

Sigurd listened more carefully and pondered for so long Leif thought he had fallen asleep.

'I think that Odin truly spoke to Eohric,' he said at last. 'Whether his change of heart is genuine or because of fear of the God, I can't say. But it is a change of heart and it behoves you to treat it as genuine.'

Leif did not seek advice from Thorvald. His long acquaintance with Eohric had only led to distrust and enmity.

In the end Leif decided that he would be civil to Eohric but nothing more.

TO EAST ANGLIA

That autumn there were many nights with a halo around the moon, the squirrels gathered acorns with unwonted frenzy and ducks and geese headed south earlier than usual. It looked like the coming winter would be unusually hard. Ivar and his captains felt that Northumbria might not sustain the whole army and decided that they would be better going to lands they had not ravaged for a while.

Ivar decided that a quarter of the army would be left in Jorvic to make sure that Echberht behaved and kept the Vikings' interests at heart. The rest were to head south.

But the captains were still undecided where to attack, with Halfdan and Ubbe in favour of Wessex and Ivar inclining to Mercia. Leif was summoned and informed of the dilemma.

'You spent time in the south,' Ivar said. 'What would you advise?'

Any answer would antagonise one or other of the brothers so, after a moment's hesitation, Leif decided it would be wise to say what he believed to be the truth.

'I would advise against attacking Wessex,' he said. 'It is a place of great wealth which makes it attractive. But it has a strong army and the king and his brother are astute and energetic. I don't think they will be easily defeated nor cowed. And they have very good advisers, who they listen to.'

'As we are listening to you,' Halfdan said.

Leif could not read what was behind his words, whether critical or admiring. He thought it best to continue as quickly as possible in order to get this dangerous questioning over with.

'As well as that,' he continued, 'Wessex is large, stretching many miles from east to west. But there is less distance from its northern frontier to its southern one which is the sea. If we attack the Saxons at any location they'll be able to move easily from one part of their kingdom to another.'

'This is as Kolga told us,' Ivar said. 'She too believes that Wessex is too strong to attack, at least for the moment.'

'But you could say the same about Mercia,' Halfdan said. 'It's as big as Wessex and, from what I hear, every bit as rich.'

'I don't think it is as wealthy,' Leif said. 'Or at least it didn't appear so when we travelled across it. The villages seemed smaller and the farms looked less prosperous.'

'Then we should attack Mercia,' said Ivar, giving Leif a look of thanks for supporting his option.

'But Mercia's still formidable,' Leif said. 'And don't forget that King Burgred is related by marriage to the young Saxon princes. They may well be persuaded to send help again if we attack Mercia.'

Ivar's smile turned to a frown. 'So, what would you advise, Skald?' he said. His tone was colder now. 'Where should we go?'

'A weaker kingdom,' he answered, 'but one which is still prosperous. East Anglia.'

'Are you sure that this isn't your woman speaking?' Halfdan said. 'She wants to go home and has told you to persuade us to return there.'

Leif held up his hands up as if he'd been caught out. 'Of course,' he said. 'She wants to send us to plunder her own land and kill her own people. I should have realised her plan.'

The jest made Halfdan laugh, as Leif guessed it would, and he slapped Ivar on the arm. 'Your Skald does not mince words,' he said. 'I like that in him.'

'Me too,' Ivar said. 'Leif makes sense to me. We shall go to East Anglia.'

Although winter was fast approaching, the autumn winds had not yet arrived so the captains decided to send half the fleet to make a dash across the sea for East Anglia. The rest of the army were sent to cross Mercia by horse.

The decision to cross the sea was the worst decision Ivar had ever taken.

The fleet made good progress for the first day and made camp on a spit of land where the river met the sea. The next day broke bright and clear with a steady wind from the north. The ships hoisted sail and coasted southward at a good speed.

Thorvald stood with Leif in the stern of the ship. After long consideration, Leif had named it Sea-Smiter in honour of his brother's trade. It was a good name, as strong and determined as Sigurd himself.

'She handles well,' Thorvald said.

'With you coaxing her, what else would I expect?'

'A poor attempt at flattery, Leif,' he replied. 'She's a good ship. Very fast, and swift to respond to my touch.'

Aebbe came struggling along the boat with Nefi in her arms. 'He wants to be with his father,' she said, thrusting him into Leif's arms. Then she turned and vomited into the sea.

'Go stand at the front,' Thorvald told her. 'Watching where we're going seems to settle most stomachs.'

Aebbe looked dubious but followed his advice and made her way to the bow.

'She's a fine woman,' Thorvald said. 'Has she got over what happened to her and the child?'

Leif sighed. 'Not yet, but she's recovering. Although I sometimes see her staring at Nefi, or rather, at a space beside him, as if she's looking at Godgyth.'

'Perhaps she is. Maybe Godgyth still shows herself to Aebbe.'

'Perhaps.' Leif was not convinced of this but he took some comfort from Thorvald's words. He tickled Nefi who giggled with pleasure. There was time for more children, he thought, and perhaps there would be at least another daughter.

After a few hours he noticed Thorvald glancing with increasing frequency over the side. 'Is something wrong?' he asked.

Thorvald pursed his lips. 'We're increasing speed, rapidly.' He pointed at the water breaking against the hull. It was moving fast, white and frothing.

Leif looked at the sail, which the strengthening wind had bloated into the shape of a gross belly.

'And look yonder,' Thorvald said, jerking his thumb over his shoulder.

Leif turned and saw a bank of thick, dark cloud gathering on the horizon. 'A storm?' he asked.

Thorvald nodded. 'A demon of a storm.' He shielded his eyes with his hand and peered at the ships surging ahead of them. 'I wonder if Ivar's seen it. I think we'll have to seek shelter.'

Except there was no shelter. The coast was barely land at all, a low-lying stretch of marsh and bogs interspersed with streams and little lakes. It was difficult to tell where the land ended and the sea began. The stench of rotting vegetation came from it like a fever. They could see no villages and there was no place firm enough to beach a ship. A ghostly, ghastly mist clung to it, dreary and disheartening, baffling the eye.

'I wouldn't want to land here,' Leif murmured.

'I doubt we'll have the chance,' Thorvald said.

Leif stared at his helmsman, startled by the urgent, fearful tone in his voice. Then he realised why.

The storm had swept down from the north with astonishing speed. It covered half the sky and was fast eating into the rest.

Within heartbeats, the sky turned a vivid, gruesome yellow and there was a flash of lightning with countless streaks ripping across the clouds. A moment later the thunder crashed upon them. The crew looked at the sky in terror.

'Thor is angry with us,' one man yelled.

The others groaned in alarm at his words. They were used to Thor fighting for them, not against them. Many men reached for the hammer amulets around their necks, muttering spells and prayers to protect themselves.

Another flash of lightning blazed across the sky and another roll of thunder, closer than before, louder than any Leif had known.

'He rages at us,' one man wailed. 'Thor is seeking our destruction.'

'No he isn't,' Leif cried, forcing his voice to carry across the ship. 'He is testing us, wondering whether we have the courage to ride his storm to glory.'

He didn't believe it for an instant but he prayed that the men would. To his astonishment they did.

Some even began to laugh and shook their heads as if, like Leif, they had been privy to Thor's purpose all along. A few cheered at this opportunity to prove their courage to the son of Odin.

Leif only hoped that Loki was not on board to hear his words.

He plucked Nefi from off the deck and clung onto him tightly. He did not want to lose a second child.

Thorvald ordered the men to furl the sail and they hurried to obey. Most of the other ships were already doing the same, although a few were more tardy.

The crew had only just lashed the sail to the mast when the storm broke.

The waters smashed on them with the speed and fury of throwing axes. The sheer force of it buffeted the ship and sent it spinning to the west. The noise was tremendous, a vicious, unending hammering on the timbers.

Leif's head smarted with the force of the rain, little daggers of unremitting icy cold. He wiped his eyes and peered through the storm in dread. Aebbe was struggling along the deck, head bent under the force of the wind.

'What are you doing?' he cried as she finally reached him.

'Nefi,' she said, taking the child into her arms. Then she sunk onto the deck, pulling her cloak over to shelter him as much as possible.

The next few hours were terrible. The Vikings were the best seafarers in the world and these men the best of the Vikings. But the storm threw their ships about like twigs and soon the fleet was scattered. Three ships were blown against the marshland to the west and stuck fast in its cloying maw. Two ships were thrown against each other, the noise of their collision echoing across the sea. They sank in moments and the sound of drowning men filled the air.

One of Leif's men climbed to his feet and waved his fist in defiance at the storm. The storm accepted his challenge and washed him over board. They saw him struggling in the waves for a moment and then he disappeared.

Finally, after endless hours, the storm began to slacken. The rain eased off, the wind dropped and little patches of sky appeared in the west.

Leif turned to Thorvald. He still had hold of the steering oar, though the skin of his hands had been torn off and were running red with blood.

'I'll get someone else to take over,' Leif said.

Thorvald nodded but was too exhausted to speak. He sank to the deck with a groan.

Leif called to Snorri Redbeard who was strong and experienced and he took Thorvald's place. The first thing he said was that they should unfurl the sail.

Leif gave the command and then bent and squeezed Aebbe's shoulder. 'Are you unharmed?' he asked.

'Sick to the stomach and terrified,' she said giving him the ghost of a smile.

'Nefi?'

He's fine. She pulled back the cloak she had covered him with. He was fast asleep.

'He is very brave,' Leif said.

'Or very tired.'

Leif straightened up and peered around. He could just make out the distant shapes of longships beginning to head towards each other.

'Steer towards them,' he ordered Snorri. He wondered how many had been lost to Thor's wrath.

It took until late afternoon for the fleet to gather. At a guess they had lost one in five ships with a good number damaged, most with broken masts or torn sails. Leif was relieved to see that Ivar's ship was not one of the casualties.

They rowed closer to the marshlands and dropped anchor-stones as night fell. Leif wrapped a blanket around Aebbe and the baby. It was going to be a bleak, cold, uncomfortable night. But so great was their exhaustion they fell asleep almost immediately and didn't wake until dawn.

The storm proved to have been the herald of icy weather and the crew's breath hung about the ship like a mist. There was little wind and it was almost with relief that the men took up oars. Rowing would at least keep them warm.

Thorvald's hands were still a raw and gory mess, the rough bandages wrapped around them black and stiff with his blood. Leif told Snorri to continue as shipmaster.

The one advantage of the storm was that it had blown them further than they had expected. By noon they made out land to the south-east and headed for it, reaching a large river soon afterwards. They followed this south for half a dozen miles and reached a smaller river heading east where they made camp for the night.

It felt good to be on dry land. Ubbe knew this place, having spent the first winter only twenty miles from there. He counselled that they take the easterly river next day for it led into the heart of the East Anglian kingdom.

Despite their weariness the men were pleased at his suggestion. Anything to get some distance from the savage sea.

The river was narrow and they had to journey in line, with oars sometimes clipping the banks. Once, as Sea-Smiter took a tight bend, it slowed so much that a line of ducks overtook her. It galled the men, though Nefi shouted in glee at the sight of them.

The landscape was flat, with fields full of sheep and only the occasional higher ground where a smudge of yellow showed where wheat had been harvested.

They saw no villages but plenty of farms and even more fleeing people.

'We could capture them for slaves,' Thorvald said.

'We'd never manage it,' Leif answered. 'This land is pitted with watercourses and pools. We'd never catch them or we'd drown in the attempt.'

Aebbe glared at them. Leif sometimes forgot that she had been taken as a slave. She never did.

That night, as they lay under a thick cloak beneath the shelter of a willow, Aebbe took Leif's hand and placed it on her belly. 'There's a little one in there,' she said.

'A baby?'

'A friend for Nefi,' she said, squeezing his hand.

And a replacement for Godgyth, he thought although he did not say it.

AEBBE GONE

They headed to Thetford where King Edmund had one of his great halls. He was not there but it contained a pack of well-fed servants who, shaking with fear, watched as the Vikings set up camp on the banks of the river close to the hall.

Ivar dragged the steward outside and ordered him to send a messenger to Edmund to tell him of their arrival. In the meanwhile, he and his brothers took over the hall and, with great enthusiasm, began to consume its stores. The jarls and captains took over smaller buildings.

To Leif's surprise he was given the hut reserved for Edmund's priest. Perhaps to Ivar, his Skald was the man most like a priest.

It was now early October and the leaves on the trees turned bronze with a number already skittering to the earth. The land around the hall was home to Edmund's livestock; thousands of sheep, hundreds of cows and pigs. The Vikings let them fatten on the accumulated harvests and sent out raiding parties to drive back still more. Ivar had no intention of letting his men go hungry.

Some villages resisted their depredations but this was quelled soon enough by hanging the ring-leaders and taking their kin as slaves. The country fell into sullen, resentful acquiescence.

The horsemen arrived twelve days after the fleet. They had travelled light, plundering only the villages nearest to their path and had been given no trouble by the Mercians.

'Perhaps we should have attacked Mercia, after all,' Ivar said, darting Leif an angry glance.

'Why run the risk,' said Guthrum, 'when we can gain all we want from easier prey?'

'I agree,' Kolga said. 'East Anglia is fat and rich. We will make a good winter of it here.'

Two days later Ivar received an emissary from King Edmund. It was the old man, Oswald, Edmund's chief adviser. Sending a man of his importance showed how great was Edmund's alarm.

Oswald came with great gifts: the choicest wine and food, thick furs against the winter cold, and panniers crammed with gold and silver. He made no complaint over the consumption of the supplies in the hall.

'You are welcome to stay in Thetford,' he told Ivar and his brothers. 'The land is well protected from the cold and frost, there is plentiful fish in lakes and rivers and the king has graciously ordered that his supplies be given to you.'

'That's very kind of him,' Ivar said. 'We'd be grateful if we hadn't already helped ourselves.' He roared with laughter but Oswald was not ruffled.

'I'm glad of it. We are friends to Lord Ivar and his captains. We intend to do our utmost to make your winter stay here as pleasant as possible.'

Ivar gave a cold smile. 'Winter stay?'

Oswald nodded. 'I presume you will not leave before the spring.'

'Of course not. But what makes you think we'll leave then? What makes you think we'll ever leave?'

If Oswald was surprised by these words he did not show it. 'You Northmen are the greatest travellers in the world,' he said smoothly. 'We know you are not the sort to settle in one place.'

'Things change,' Ivar said. 'Plans, people, dreams, they all change.' He smiled. 'Everything except nightmares.'

Oswald's urbanity slipped for an instant but he covered it with a smile.

He left hurriedly within the hour, with a long list of Ivar's demands for even more supplies.

The army spent the next week settling into their quarters and making all ready for the winter. Guthrum had a small hall close to Leif's hut and, because of this he saw more of Eohric than he liked.

In truth, Eohric's dream had changed his behaviour towards Leif. But Leif could not so easily change his. He received Eohric's cheery hellos with the slightest of nods, grunted in response to his conversation and always hurried to leave his presence.

On the other hand, Leif grew to like Guthrum more and more. He was open and honest, spoke his mind as he saw it and seemed not to be easily angered or hold a grudge. Leif wondered that two brothers could be so different.

But then he thought about Sigurd and himself. Most people considered them as different as brothers could be. Sigurd was the steady, dependable man, Leif the light-hearted, hare-brained one. But Leif knew that, deep down, they shared the same values.

And with that thought he grew suddenly warier of Guthrum. Despite appearances maybe he and Eohric were alike, after all.

Perhaps the same sickness ran in Guthrum's veins. Unless, of course, Eohric shared at least some of Guthrum's better qualities. It was a puzzle and one which he could not easily resolve.

'You need to show better attitude to Eohric,' Asgrim told him one day.

He was surprised for Asgrim disliked Eohric intensely.

'Do I?' he said. 'Why?'

'For two reasons,' Asgrim said. 'One is that Ivar told me he's grown weary of your attitude. He fears it will lead to bad blood amongst the men, a rancour which might spread.'

He eyed Leif shrewdly, as if to make certain that he fully understood the importance of his words.

'And the other reason?'

'You are a wealthy man now, Leif, lord of a ship and men. It behoves you to act like one, rising above grievance and petty quarrels.'

'You think that raping Aebbe and killing Godgyth are petty?' Leif felt his face grow hot with anger.

'Of course I don't. But people have poor memories. They will come to forget the cause of the trouble and see only that you rebuff Eohric's attempts at friendship.'

'So I will become the villain?'

Asgrim did not answer and that was answer enough.

Five days later, Aebbe and Nefi disappeared.

Leif searched the camp in frenzy, too panicked to even tell his friends what had happened. Now he cursed having only one eye for he wanted six or seven of them to look the better.

Word must have spread for Sigurd, Thorvald and Higbald appeared and joined him in the hunt. Soon, scores more were hurrying everywhere, calling out Aebbe and Nefi's names.

'They might have gone further,' Leif said and led his friends out of the camp and along the river.

It had rained a few days earlier and the river flowed more swiftly than before. They followed it for a mile north and south, searching for any sign of them. As well as the river, there were countless ponds where a person might drown.

In the end Leif slumped to the ground in despair. It was hopeless.

Sigurd stared at his brother for a long while, then stepped towards him. He placed a hand upon his shoulder. 'If they're anywhere nearby they'd have heard our cries,' he said. 'I'm sorry.'

Leif looked up at him, unable to give an answer. He could not say what he knew in his heart. They were gone.

Leif followed his friends back to the camp without being aware of his steps. His mind pulsed with the single thought, where, where, where? No answer came.

Deor came towards them the moment they arrived. His face was woeful.

'No sign here,' he said. 'Ivar has sent some horsemen to the east and rounded up some villagers nearby to see if they know anything.'

'And do they?'

He shook his head.

Leif waited the rest of the day in a silent, sick, despair. Things had been getting better, he thought, and now this. He found myself cursing Loki and then glancing around nervously in case he was hearkening. Would the god ever relent, ever allow him more than a glimpse of joy?

Most of the men that Ivar sent out returned by nightfall, none of them with any news. Two score, it seemed, had been sent further, led by Asgrim. Ivar would not say where.

The next day Leif resumed the search, even though he knew it was hopeless. Higbald went with him despite Leif telling him not to. They went on horse and ranged down the river for a dozen miles until they found its source. But they found no trace of Aebbe and bitterly, they turned back towards Thetford.

'Why is that man smirking at us?' Higbald asked as they approached the camp.

'What man?'

Higbald nodded towards a young man squatting in front of a tent. It was one of Eohric's friends.

'He's a bastard,' Leif said. 'And he's enjoying my grief.'

He pushed on though Higbald tarried, staring at the man a few moments longer. He looked troubled when he caught up although Leif could not summon the strength to ask why.

'Eohric's behind this,' Nerienda said the following day.

'That can't be,' Sigurd said. 'He daren't risk angering Ivar. And besides, he's made his peace with Leif.'

Nerienda snorted. 'Don't be such a fool. Eohric makes too great as show of friendship for my liking. You can daunt a mad dog but you can't tame it.'

'What makes you think he's got anything to do with it?' Leif asked. His voice sounded weary even to his own ears.

'Bed talk,' Nerienda said. 'My shrewdest girl, Burghild, said that one of Eohric's creatures boasted that he'd sold Aebbe. He clammed up when she asked him more.'

'Sold her?' His heart began to race. 'Who to?'

'He wouldn't say.' She sat down beside Leif and took his hand. Tears began to course down his cheeks.

Asgrim returned two days later. His face was bleak. Leif followed him as he went towards Ivar's hall but he brushed aside his every question.

Ivar and his jarls were in the middle of a meal when they entered.

Ivar placed his meat down. 'Any news?'

Asgrim glanced at Leif before answering. 'Yes. As you ordered, we went to King Edmund to see if he'd heard anything of Aebbe. He had that, right enough. He said that she'd been sold to him by a Dane. And that she was now his concubine.'

Leif felt the ground tip beneath him and only just kept his feet.

'Did you see her?' Ivar asked. 'Did you see Leif's woman?'

Asgrim shook his head. 'But I saw the child. He was playing with some other boys.' He turned to Leif. 'He was unharmed, Leif. I promise you that.'

'Then what?' demanded Ivar.

'I offered to buy her back,' Asgrim said. 'At double the price Edmund paid.'

'And…'

Asgrim licked his lips anxiously and took a deep breath. 'He said she was too good in bed to part with. At any price.'

He glanced at Leif and then returned his gaze to Ivar.

'Do you think he means it?' Halfdan asked. 'At any price?'

'He has no need of more wealth,' Asgrim said. 'Spiting us gives him greater satisfaction.'

Ivar's eyes narrowed and he turned to Leif. 'How much will you give to get your woman and child back?'

'Ten times what Edmund paid,' Leif said.

'And I will match it.' He turned to Asgrim. 'Return to the bastard and bring Leif's family back.'

'I'll go with you,' Leif said.

Ivar stared at him for a while and then nodded. 'Just don't make things worse,' he said. 'Swallow your wrath and pay him the money. And Sigurd, you go as well and help Asgrim keep an eye on him.'

KING EDMUND'S TAUNTS

It was a long day's ride to get to Edmund. He was at his hall in the port of Gipswic, a busy, wealthy town with scores of large potteries and a quayside crammed with ships. Leif and his friends arrived there in the late afternoon.

'Let me do the talking,' Asgrim cautioned as they approached the hall. Sigurd agreed immediately, Leif a moment later. He doubted he'd be able to keep silent although he realised it would be best if he did.

Edmund and his chief men were at their evening meal as the Vikings approached.

Oswald inclined his head in welcome, the young adviser, Hwita, gave them a mocking glance. Edmund did not look up from his meat.

'You have returned, heathen,' Hwita said to Asgrim. 'What is the reason this time?'

'I come on the same mission,' Asgrim answered. 'I seek to buy back the woman and child that were sold to your king.'

'I gave you my answer,' Edmund said. He belched and tore another slice from the mutton chop he was eating.

'And why is this Skald here?' Hwita said. 'He was silver-tongued enough in the past. Why so silent now?'

Leif went to answer but Asgrim gripped him by the arm. 'He is the husband of the woman and father of the child.'

'She may once have been his woman,' Edmund said. 'She's mine now.'

He put down his meat and picked up his wine-cup, swilling it in the air and staring at Leif above the rim. 'I can see why you want her back,' he said. 'She's a good fuck.' He licked his lips appreciatively.

Leif stepped forward angrily but the grip on his arm tightened.

'Oh look,' Hwita said, 'the Dane is indignant. Be careful, my King, he may seek to chastise you.' His voice was full of a sneering contempt.

'I seek only what is mine, Edmund,' Leif said, heedless of Asgrim's warning glance. 'And I will pay you twenty times what you paid for them.'

Oswald's eyes widened in surprise. 'Twenty times? You must value them highly, young man?'

'She is my wife and the boy is my son. Would you not value your loved ones as much as I do?'

'We might,' Hwita interjected. 'But we are Christians. You heathens are little better than the beasts in the field.'

'We do not buy another man's wife,' Leif said.

Hwita gave a hollow laugh. 'You jest. You bastards steal any woman you think of value. Wasn't your so-called wife taken as a slave? She was an innocent girl before you took and corrupted her.' He gave a mocking smile. 'And don't let's forget that it was one of your friends who sold her to us.'

'Who was it?' Sigurd cried, forgetting his promise to remain silent.

'Guthrum,' Hwita said. 'One of Ivar's jarls.'

Leif stared at him in horror. Guthrum? Who had acted like a friend and wished him to be his Skald. Guthrum? Leif groaned. He was every bit as vile as his brother.

'It matters not who sold the woman and child,' Asgrim said quickly.

His voice restored Leif to the moment. I'll plan what to do about Guthrum later, he thought. Right now, I need to concentrate on getting them back.

'I agree with your friend,' Edmund said, 'it matters not who sold her. All that does is that she was sold and now belongs to me.'

He picked up his meat and gestured towards the door. 'I have no need of more of your treasure, heathens. Be gone from my hall while I am still in good humour.'

He went to take another bite of his meat and then paused. 'I tell you what,' he said to Leif. 'I shall give you back your son, as token of my good will. I have no need of him.'

'I want my wife as well.'

Edmund shook his head and returned to his meat.

'Be satisfied with your son,' Oswald said. He looked thoughtful. 'Be sensible and leave now.'

Asgrim glanced at Leif and then back to Oswald. 'So be it,' he said. 'Produce the boy.'

They waited until one of Edmund's women entered, leading Nefi by the hand. He screamed in delight when he saw his father and leapt into his arms. Leif hugged him for a moment, passed him to Sigurd and took three swift steps towards Edmund.

'I want my wife back,' he cried.

Edmund raised his finger and the next thing Leif knew he was thrown to the floor. A burly warrior kicked him in the guts and another one joined in, striking his chest, arms and face. He rolled into a ball to try to protect himself but they were determined and accomplished. The pain was terrible.

Out of the corner of his eye Leif glimpsed the old adviser, Oswald, remonstrating with the king but to no avail.

'Enough,' Edmund said, eventually. 'He's lost one eye and one wife. Leave him his miserable life.'

His words were the last thing Leif knew as he lost consciousness.

He came too with his face crushed against the neck of his horse. He glanced around wildly. The position of the sun indicated that they were heading west, back to Thetford. There was no sign of Aebbe although Nefi was asleep in Sigurd's arms, wrapped in a cloak. Leif groaned and fell into a troubled sleep.

They rode for a few hours until the last daylight faded. They made camp in a sparse little wood, shivering in a cold, northerly wind. Leif was too weak and distressed to do anything other than sit blankly with his back to a tree. Nefi kept asking for his mama and Sigurd told him she was ill and would return in a week or so.

'You shouldn't lie to him,' Asgrim said when the boy had finally fallen asleep. 'He will be disappointed and will ever doubt your word in the future.'

'We will get Aebbe back,' Sigurd said, sharply. 'We won't let her languish as an Englishman's plaything.'

Asgrim did not reply beyond giving a non-committal grunt. Leif gave a wan smile of thanks to Sigurd.

'But in the meanwhile,' Sigurd continued, 'we have to think what to do about Guthrum.'

'I never imagined he would do that,' Leif said bleakly. 'I thought he was my friend.'

'He and his brother were spawned from the same foul nest,' Asgrim said. His throat retched, he hawked up a thick wad of phlegm and spat it on the ground. 'But he's a jarl and you're not. There's nothing you can do. You have no proof.'

'The king's adviser told us it was Guthrum who sold her.'

'And you think his word will count against Guthrum's?' Asgrim asked, astonished.

Leif shook his head, wearily. 'You're right. I'll never be able to prove it. But I swear I'll have my revenge.'

They arrived at Thetford shortly after noon. Leif was exhausted and every bone and joint in his body throbbed as if on fire. Nerienda welcomed them with cries of joy, taking Nefi from them and hugging him tight.

She gave Leif a questioning look, but Sigurd shook his head in warning. 'She's alive,' he whispered, 'but the English King has taken her to his bed and will not let her go.'

'Then there's hope, perhaps,' she said. 'Men grow tired of women.'

'But if he does he'll just sell her to some slaver,' Asgrim said. His hand went to his mouth, realising that Leif could hear.

Leif closed his eyes. His friends were right. There was now no chance of getting Aebbe back. He would never see her again.

'I won't have false hope,' he said, finally. 'Will you care for Nefi?' he asked Nerienda.

'Of course.' She paused and when she spoke her voice was so low Leif could barely hear it. 'Who did this?'

'Guthrum,' he answered. 'Guthrum sold them.'

'Then he'll rot in hell,' she said.

'I hope so. I doubt I'll get recompense on this earth.'

NEWS OF EDMUND

Leif's friends counselled him to avoid Guthrum, indeed avoid everyone as much as possible.

'Angry words fan flames of revenge,' Deor said. 'And they will burn you.'

'I'm no fool,' Leif said, testily. 'Guthrum's word is stronger than mine.' He rubbed his aching shoulder. 'Or the word of any Englishman, even that of a king.'

He closed his eyes. He may have given up any thought of revenge on Guthrum but ever since he'd returned he'd conjured up ways of harming Edmund and his advisers. He knew these ideas were naive and fanciful but they gnawed at his soul nonetheless. He would never see Edmund again and, therefore, he would never see Aebbe. He had lost daughter and now wife. The days ahead looked bleak and drear.

Then, in the middle of November, came alarming news. Edmund was heading north with an army of three thousand men.

To Leif's surprise he was summoned to a meeting of the war chiefs. Ivar took him to one side and told him that he must remember who said what in the forthcoming debate. He looked unusually concerned.

Ivar took his seat and Leif placed a stool next to Kolga so that he could easily hear all that was said.

'We should make the fortifications stronger,' Jarl Sidrac urged. 'Only a fool would attack a position as strong as this. I hear no suggestion that Edmund is a fool.'

'I agree with Sidrac,' Jarl Frene said. 'We defended Nottingham against the Mercians and Saxons. Defending Thetford against Edmund's rabble will prove easy in comparison.'

'Unless he starves us out,' said Kolga. 'There are over a thousand warriors here and even more camp-followers. We'll grow famished unless we can leave the camp to plunder more supplies.'

'I agree with Kolga,' Halfdan said. 'Edmund will seek to starve us into submission. I have no stomach for that.'

'Then what would you do, brother?' Ivar asked quietly.

'Lay an ambush for him when he's on the march.'

'I agree,' said Ubbe. 'We can move faster than they can. We'll strike them before they even realise we've left camp.'

'Ambush them? Strike them?' said Ivar. 'Which would you have us do, brothers? For we surely cannot do both at the same time.'

'And we don't know where they are,' Guthrum said. 'Asgrim and Leif saw Edmund in Gipswic four weeks ago but all we know is that he's left the town. He could be anywhere and he could be coming from any direction.'

He said Leif's name casually, as if he felt no guilt at having wronged him. He was as full of guile as he was of malice.

'Guthrum's right,' Ivar said. 'We'd be wise to send out scouts to find where Edmund is.'

'My men and I could do that,' Guthrum said.

Leif frowned. Surely Guthrum meant to betray them to Edmund? He pummelled his mind to think how to counter his plan. No ideas came.

'My brother is called Ubbe the Swift for good reason,' Ivar said to Guthrum. 'He will have found Edmund, returned here and bedded two women by the time your men have saddled horses.'

There was loud laughter which Guthrum joined in.

As if to prove Ivar's words Ubbe leapt to his feet and headed for the door.

'Come back as soon as you spot them,' Ivar called. 'Don't attack and don't let them see you.'

'The best place to start is on the track we took along the river Gipping,' Leif said.

'Go with him, Leif,' Ivar said. 'Show him the way. And seek out a good place for an ambush. In the meanwhile, Sidrac, strengthen the defences. We must protect the women and children while the warriors are away.'

Leif guessed why he had ordered Sidrac to do this. It was not merely to protect the women and children. It was to make sure the army had somewhere to fall back to if they lost the battle.

Sigurd and Asgrim wanted to go with Leif but he told them to stay to keep watch on Nefi. He feared that Guthrum might seek to harm him while he was gone.

'Then take Thorvald with you,' Sigurd said. 'I'd sleep better if I knew a good friend was beside you.'

Leif did not reply but hurried out of the hall.

'Hurry up, man,' Ubbe cried. He was already in the saddle and his men, used to his impetuous ways, were climbing onto their steeds.

Sigurd tightened the girth on Leif's horse and helped him mount. He groaned as he settled into the saddle. He was still stiff from his beating and the last thing he relished was a long, break-neck ride on horseback. But Ubbe was already leading the way out of the camp and he kicked his horse savagely to try and catch up with him. He glanced back and saw Thorvald feverishly struggling to ready his horse.

Ubbe slowed the pace a little to allow Leif to reach him. 'I'll need my men to spread out soon,' he said, 'so I'll order them to split up. But you're to stay with me.'

No sooner had he said this than Thorvald galloped up.

'Can my man ride with me?' Leif asked.

Ubbe nodded.

They had been riding an hour and were moving at an easy canter when Ubbe slowed to a trot.

'There's several tracks ahead, Leif,' he said. 'Which one should we take?'

Leif pointed out the route they had taken the week before and Ubbe ordered half a dozen of his men to ride in pairs along the other tracks. It appeared that as well as his famous speed, he had a good grasp of tactics. And he could read the landscape like a shipmaster read the sea.

Of the three brothers Leif knew Ubbe the least but over the next few days he came to like him the most. He was good-natured and cheery although without the overwhelming, bluff boisterousness of Halfdan. Neither did he have the watchful, cunning nature of Ivar. He would be a good lord, Leif thought.

They had ridden for about fifteen miles when they came to a place with numerous tracks. Ubbe sent men to the east and the south but to Leif's surprise he also sent some north and west, in the opposite direction to Gipswic.

'In case Edmund is a more cunning warrior than we think,' he explained. 'We Vikings would attack from any direction so why wouldn't he?'

'I think you give him more credit than he deserves,' Leif said.

Ubbe shook his head. 'Ivar has taught me never to underestimate an enemy.' He gave Leif a shrewd look. 'It is a lesson you would be wise to take to heart.'

A chill took Leif's heart. It seemed that his opinion of Guthrum was better known than he realised. Thorvald gave him a look of warning and he kept silent.

They stopped about an hour before sunrise.

'I have no wish to go blundering into the enemy in the dark,' Ubbe said. Then he beckoned Leif away from the men. 'What think you of this place?'

'To camp for the night?'

'To set an ambush.'

He pointed out a deep stretch of woodland. It was close to the track for much of its length but then the trees grew sparse to one side leaving a more open space stretching about a furlong away from the track. There were numerous tree stumps and signs of charcoal burning: kilns, both new-built and old, and logs piled up ready for use.

'We could lodge our shield-wall across the track,' Ubbe said, 'so both ends reach the trees.' Then he pointed to the open area and the treeline beyond. 'And we could hide an equal number of men in that wood yonder.'

'But isn't it risky to split our men?' Leif asked. 'We'd be pushed back by the weight of the English numbers.'

'Exactly. And when we are, Edmund's shield-wall will thrust after us. When they've advanced far enough their flank will be exposed. And our men in the wood will attack that flank.'

Leif gazed at the landscape. It was a good plan, he thought. As long as our wall doesn't crumble.

They rode south the next day at a slower, more cautious pace. Ubbe sent men in twos and threes to ride ahead of the main party.

An hour later one of them galloped back, his face bright with elation. 'The English are about two miles south,' he said.

Ubbe looked anxiously down the track. 'Did they see you?'

The man grinned and shook his head. 'I'm as wary as a farm-cat.'

'How many men?' Thorvald asked.

'It's hard to say for they're strung out for a good few miles. My guess is four or five thousand.'

'We'd better go,' Ubbe said. 'The rest of the scouts will make their own way back at the end of the day.'

'Let's hope none get captured,' Leif said.

'And let's make sure we don't, either,' Ubbe replied. He gave a grim smile, spurred his horse and led the way back to Thetford at ferocious speed.

BATTLE AND SLAUGHTER

Ivar responded swiftly when Ubbe returned to the camp, so swiftly that all thousand warriors were horsed and ready by the following dawn. The brothers led them out before the sun cleared the horizon and they thundered along the track as if being pursued by frost-giants.

Leif rode with his friends and his men close beside him. He made sure that he kept Guthrum in sight.

They soon neared the place that Ubbe had decided for the ambush. 'We're almost there,' he said, glancing at Leif for confirmation.

Leif pointed. 'That's the place.'

Ivar reared up in his stirrups and swiftly examined the site. 'You're right, Ubbe,' he said. 'This is a good place for an ambush.'

Leif had been surprised at how swiftly Ivar had set things going the night before. He was even more astonished by the speed with which he deployed his warriors now.

They hobbled their horses two hundred yards to the rear, leaving a small guard of the oldest men to keep watch over them. Five hundred of the younger, swifter men raced towards the woods beyond the charcoal workings and hid themselves there.

Leif cursed because they were led by Guthrum. He'd hoped that he might stumble in the shield-wall and then he could seize the opportunity to slit his throat. It seemed it was not to be. His vengeance would not come this day.

The rest of the army, perhaps six hundred strong, marched forward to where the trees grew close to the track and set up a shield-wall.

For a while there was a noise of cursing and grunting, and then the occasional sound of men pissing where they stood. A few slipped out of the shield-wall to crouch in the trees to empty their bowels. Ivar was tolerant of this. A man who had purged himself would fight all the better.

And then they waited.

After an hour Leif heard it. The unmistakable sound of a marching army. The English were careless, believing the Vikings were still in Thetford, fifteen miles away. Their foremost men reared to a halt when they saw that their route was blocked by a shield-wall.

There was a brief period of confusion and then half a dozen men rode to the front and stared at the Vikings. Amongst them Leif recognised Edmund, Oswald and the arrogant young adviser Hwita.

It seemed as if Edmund was pondering whether to talk but then thought better of it. Now that he had seen how few Vikings opposed him he ordered his army to form up for attack.

'How many English, do you think?' Ivar asked his brothers.

Ubbe was the first to answer. 'The scout who saw them yesterday thought four or five thousand.'

'Which means there will be three thousand at most,' said Halfdan. 'Nervous scouts always imagine two enemies for every man they see.'

'If it's only two thousand they are four times our number,' Ivar said. 'Let's hope Ubbe's plan works.'

Leif pushed his way towards the front rank, his eyes vengeful as a serpent's as he stared at Edmund.

'Where do you think you're going?' Ivar asked.

'Isn't it obvious?'

'It's obvious that you're heading for your death.' Ivar took Leif's arm. 'You're no warrior, Leif, never have been, never will. Get to the back where you'll be safer and can lend weight to our effort.'

'I don't want to.'

'It wasn't a request.' He held Leif's eyes but not with his accustomed ferocity, more a fatherly look. 'Take him to the back, Thorvald,' he commanded. 'And don't let him do anything foolish. A dead skald is no use to me.'

Thorvald grabbed Leif by the arm and dragged him through the crowd of warriors. He was only just in time for they were closing ranks, each man knowing that his life might depend on the two who stood either side of him.

Leif and Thorvald had only just reached the rear when the English shield-wall collided with the Vikings. There was an almighty boom as the shields crashed, an explosion of noise from thousands of throats and then the thump, thump of feet digging for a firmer footing.

For a moment the lines held without moving, then the Vikings pushed forward a little, causing the men at the back to cheer. Encouraged by this they strained still more and the English wall inched further backwards.

But then it stabilised and with a cry of, 'For Christ and his saints,' Edmund's men threw themselves forward.

Step by painful step the foremost warriors in the Viking wall succumbed to the weight of the superior English numbers. The only advantage they had was that they were retreating over dry ground, whereas the English were slipping on bloodied corpses. Yet still Edmund piled on the pressure and the Vikings fell back.

'I don't think we're much safer here,' Leif said to Thorvald. He nodded in agreement and unsheathed his sword.

Leif realised that his injuries meant he'd be more useless than normal with sword or spear so he'd equipped himself with a bow and a sheath of twenty arrows. Unbidden came to his mind the damage that Deor's archers had caused when they'd attacked Guthrum's ship long ago. He wished they had as many bowmen as Deor led that day. On his own he would be able to do little damage, if any.

The Viking shield-wall was thrust back until it was suddenly clear of the wood with the treeless area open to their left, leaving their flank exposed. Edmund would soon notice this and begin to lengthen his shield-wall to engulf them.

If Ivar doesn't do something, and quick, thought Leif, our men will be annihilated

But finally, when more than half of the English army were beyond the shelter of the trees, Leif saw them. Guthrum and his men racing across the open ground, silent as wolves in winter.

A few Englishmen saw the danger but they were too late. Five hundred fresh warriors rammed into their flank, shattering it as an axe splits wood. By the time Edmund realised what was happening, Guthrum was half way through the English army and closing in on him.

Edmund's household thegns saw the danger and formed a tight inner wall around him. While the rest of the English force began to split asunder the King's men held firm, repulsing every attempt to come at him. With astonishing determination they began to thrust their way forward. The rest of their army saw this and took heart. With a mighty yell, they smashed into Guthrum's men, sending those to the rear flying and surrounding Guthrum and the hundred men who were closest to him.

The ambush had failed.

Ivar saw the danger and ordered the shield-wall to thrust forward to rescue Guthrum and his men. But it was too late. They were trapped.

The English remorselessly ground on, slaughtering their foes by the score. The battle appeared lost.

The Vikings stood firm but they knew they would be overwhelmed; knew they would soon be meat for crows.

'No,' Leif cried, leaping forward. Thorvald made a grab for him but he was too late.

He ran to the left beyond the main battle, keeping Edmund and his thegns always in sight. There were several log piles beside the charcoal kilns and he scrambled on top of one. It was six or seven feet high and gave him a clear view of the battle.

He saw that it would be lost in moments. Somewhere down there, his friends and his brother were fighting for their lives.

He pulled the bow from his shoulder and reached for an arrow.

Time seemed to slow for him and the tumult of battle grew quiet in his ears. He notched the arrow, took a long, deep breath and pulled back the string.

He grew astonishingly calm and saw the arrow hunt for its target, almost as if it had a will of its own.

His one eye peered along the arrow shaft, waiting a few moments longer until it had steadied completely.

Then he released.

The shaft flew swifter than the fastest bird, straight and true. Straight at Leif's target.

Edmund cried out, staggered and clutched at the arrow drilling into his throat. For a few moments he remained on his feet, pawing at his neck, trying to pull the shaft out.

And then he fell.

A roar of dismay echoed from three thousand English throats.

It was over in minutes. The peasants who made up the bulk of the English army saw all was lost and fled. The thegns stood firm around their king and were hacked down.

Leif was unmoved by this. All he felt was a grim satisfaction at seeing his arrow slay Edmund in revenge for Aebbe. He clambered down from the wood pile and headed towards Sigurd.

Finally, only the staunch ring of the King's thegns remained, baying defiance at the Vikings, determined to give their lives in defence of their lord's dead body.

But Ivar called on his warriors to halt and approached the Englishmen.

'There's no need for you to sacrifice yourselves,' he cried. 'Your king died bravely; you do not need to emulate him.'

He sheathed his sword Snake and stretched his arms wide. 'You can go in peace and take the body of your lord with you.

You can bury him with only the one wound and send him whole and clean to your Christ-heaven.'

He paused for a few moments before continuing. 'Or, if you choose, you can die to the last man. And, as you fall, you can ponder how much your king's body will be defiled and degraded by my men.'

There was a long silence and then the old man, Oswald pushed his way to the front. 'You pledge this?' he asked.

'On my gods,' Ivar said. 'Odin and Thor.'

'Then let his thegns pass with the body of the king and I will stay here to seek terms from you.'

Ivar glanced at his brothers. They shrugged. The victory was theirs; it didn't matter to them whether Edmund was allowed a decent burial or hacked to shreds.

'You have my word,' Ivar said. 'Lay down your weapons and go in peace.'

Four of the king's thegns hoisted the corpse onto their shoulders and paced towards the Vikings. His nobles led the way.

Leif tensed as Hwita approached Guthrum, thinking they would acknowledge one another. But neither gave the slightest sign. If Leif did not know better he'd have thought the two had never met. They covered their tracks well.

But then Hwita halted and nodded at Eohric. 'You have the victory, Guthrum,' he said. 'But the girl you sold to the king stays with us. Perhaps I'll take her now.'

Eohric shook his head a few times as if to give warning to Hwita. But the Englishman merely looked puzzled and continued on his way.

'Why did he call you by my name?' Guthrum asked Eohric. 'And what did he mean about me selling a girl?'

'I don't know,' Eohric said. 'Perhaps he suffered a blow to the head.'

'As you will, any moment,' Sigurd said, hefting his war-hammer as he stepped towards him.

'What means this?' Ivar cried.

'That Englishman said that Aebbe was sold by a Dane,' Sigurd said. 'That Dane was Eohric, although he used his brother's name.' He took a step still closer to Eohric.

'Hold fast, Sigurd,' Ivar called. 'We need to know the truth behind this.'

Sigurd hesitated. But Leif did not.

He grabbed the hammer from Sigurd's hand and swung it at Eohric's head. It caught him on the side, tearing skin and cracking jaw and teeth. He slumped to the ground, groaning in agony.

Ivar stared at Eohric for a moment and then shrugged. 'I wonder how he got such a grievous wound?' he said.

'I've no idea,' Guthrum said. 'It must have been in the heat of the battle.' He took a few strides and straddled his brother, who cowered in terror.

'I doubt even Eohric knows who did this to him,' Guthrum said, glancing at Leif. 'In fact, I promise you that he doesn't.'

Ivar winked at Leif and gestured to him to return the hammer to Sigurd.

'Who shot the arrow that killed the king?' Ubbe asked. 'I didn't know we had any bowmen.'

The rest of the jarls and captains murmured in agreement.

'I can tell you,' Thorvald said. He indicated the bow on Leif's shoulder. 'His one eye has made Leif the most skilful of bowmen.'

'Then it was you who won the battle for us,' Ivar said, placing both hands on Leif's shoulder. 'You shall have rich reward.'

'The only reward I want is to have Aebbe returned to me.'

Ivar glanced at Oswald.

'That will be done, Lord Ivar,' he said. 'I will send messengers immediately.'

KINGS AND JARLS

Oswald was as good as his word and the very next day Aebbe was returned by the English. Leif swung her in his arms and kissed her passionately.

'How is Nefi?' were her first words.

'He's well. He's in Thetford with Nerienda.'

She sighed with relief. 'I thought I had lost you both.'

'I would never desert you. I would have brought you back, come what may.'

Tears filled her eyes. He brushed them away gently.

She smiled although he feared she did it to make him feel good rather than through genuine joy. She was too anxious about their son to do more.

'When can I see Nefi?' she asked.

'Ivar is negotiating with Oswald now. He wants the army to stay here until they've finished.'

'But not you, surely? And not me?'

Leif gave a quick nod. 'He said that we were both to stay here. He insisted.'

Aebbe groaned. 'He forces me to stay on a battle-field when I should be with my child. Haven't I suffered enough at men's hands?' Then she reddened and took Leif's hand.

She stood silently for a while, staring at the ground, as if she were looking there for an answer to a problem.

'I was forced into Edmund's bed,' she said at last. 'I did not choose it. I hated it.'

Leif put a finger to her lips. 'You don't need to speak of it,' he said.

'But I feel so ashamed.'

'There's no need for shame. You did what you had to in order to survive. In order to come back to Nefi and me.'

She forced a smile upon her face but he could sense the chill she still felt in her heart.

Then she squeezed his hand more tightly. 'I have been thinking about what happens now,' she said.

Leif looked puzzled. 'In what way?'

'I am with child again,' she began. 'And we have returned to the land I was born in. It seems to me that, perhaps, these are signs.'

'Leif, we could make a new start here, bring up our family in peace and contentment.'

'But how? I'm a Dane.'

'We could live in my village. There's plenty of land there, with pasture and good woodland. We could build a house, farm the land, fish the lakes, bring up our children.'

Her eyes shone as she spoke. 'You could even become a thegn.'

'But I'm a Skald, not a farmer.'

'Then tell songs and stories. You're a wealthy man, you don't have to plough fields and sow crops. Other men could do that for you.'

'But I wouldn't be welcome to your people.'

'Why not? Danes have always traded here, many live in Norwic and Gipswic, at peace with their neighbours. You don't have to fight and war. You never did before you came here.'

His face grew thoughtful. Maybe she was right, maybe he could settle here and live the life he thought he had lost for ever.

She saw his hesitation.

'After all, Leif, you're not really a warrior.'

'That I'm not,' he said with a wry smile.

'So why pretend? You've told me that you'd never have come to England if Ivar had not forced you. In some ways, our fates are the same. I was enslaved by the Vikings. You were enslaved by Ivar.'

He bristled at her words. 'No I wasn't. I'm his sworn man.'

But even as he said this he remembered that he could not recall actually swearing to be his follower. And journeying to England had been Ivar's choice, not his.

He let go of Aebbe's hand and began to pace up and down. Could this happen, he wondered. Could he leave the army, take his wealth and start a new life here, a life like the one he had enjoyed in his village back in Denmark?

It was a beguiling idea. But then he thought that it could never be. Loki would see his happiness and find a way to ruin it.

He felt defeated by the thought.

'You could even become a Christian,' Aebbe said.

He looked at her in astonishment. It was almost as if she had read his thoughts.

His mind began to race. Perhaps this was the answer. Perhaps he could become a Christ-follower and escape Loki's venom. But then he hesitated. It would also mean deserting Odin and Thor, swapping them for a paltry, sickly, half-dead god. No, that would never do.

But he could still do the rest. Still leave the army and settle with Aebbe. Perhaps Sigurd would come with him, and Nerienda. Maybe even Asgrim, Thorvald and Higbald.

His mind churned ceaselessly, as if it were adrift in a raging river. It was all too much for him to think about.

He was relieved when Sigurd appeared.

'Ivar and the Englishman have ended their jabber,' he said. 'The army has been told to assemble. And you're to come as well, Aebbe.'

She frowned in confusion but allowed him to lead her to the site of the battle.

The dead had been laid in two barrows, the Viking warriors in one and the English in the other, larger one. A Christ-priest stood by the English barrow. He was making odd gestures and appeared to be talking to himself. Perhaps one of the dead men was his brother and the grief had turned him mad.

Ivar and the chieftains of the army were seated on camp stools a short distance from the mounds. The English lords sat to one side of them, with the old adviser, Oswald a little apart.

When all the Viking warriors had gathered Ivar stood and raised his hand for silence.

'The King of the East Angles is dead,' he said, 'rightfully punished by Odin for his many sins.'

The Englishmen looked angry at his words but none dared raise their voice in protest.

'It has fallen to us, therefore, to look to the good ordering of the realm. It seems fitting that the new king of the East Angles should be Edmund's wisest adviser, Oswald.'

There was general assent from the English, general indifference from the Vikings.

Oswald showed no sign of surprise. He got to his feet and his eye took in every man there.

'I pledge to act as a wise King of the East Angles,' he said. 'I welcome our friend Ivar the Boneless with his strong arm and sense of justice. I feel confident that our two peoples will dwell peacefully together from this day forward.'

He paused as if he were expecting some approbation for his words. There was none.

'But I have a question,' he continued.

His voice took on a more intimate tone. Leif thought it almost a sly one. He placed his hands on his chest, as if he were a supplicant.

'Surely it is not possible for ordinary men to make me a king?' he said. 'Surely that can only be done by men who are already kings themselves?'

And here he turned towards the Viking lords.

'It seems to me,' he continued, 'that by the very act of appointing me king, Ivar and his brothers must, in fact, be kings themselves.'

Leif exchanged a glance with Thorvald. This was nonsense and everyone in the army knew it. But every man seemed convinced by the argument and they leapt to their feet.

'Hail to the Kings,' Jarl Sidrac cried.

'Hail to the Kings,' the warriors echoed with a show of enthusiasm.

The brothers stood to acknowledge the acclamation. The men began to cheer and pound their feet on the earth.

At last, Ivar raised his hand for silence.

'This victory belongs to us all,' he said. 'Every last warrior here. In recognition of that, each man will receive two slave women as his own and a pound in silver.'

The men yelled with even greater enthusiasm at this.

When the clamour eventually died down, Ivar drew his sword and grew more serious.

'The victory belongs to us all,' he repeated, 'but a few men played the greatest part in it. One is my brother, Ubbe the Swift, who tracked the oncoming English host, chose the site of battle and devised the battle plan. To him, to King Ubbe, we have agreed to give two hundred pounds of silver.'

The men cheered. This was a just amount.

'Jarl Guthrum led the attack upon the English flank,' Ivar continued, 'and that was vital in assuring our victory.'

There was less agreement with this opinion but none dared voice dissent.

'We have agreed that he shall receive fifty pounds of silver.'

Guthrum got to his feet and bowed in thanks to Ivar.

'But the greatest debt is owed to one man,' Ivar said. 'The man who slew King Edmund. For the battle was on a knife edge at this point and Edmund's death proved vital in our victory.

'Until now, few have known who shot the fatal, fateful arrow. But I now tell you that it was my Skald, Leif Ormson.'

The men got to their feet and cheered more loudly than they had done hitherto.

'Were it not for his arrow,' Ivar said, 'the English would have won and every man here would have ended the day as a slave or a corpse.

'So I give due and fitting reward to Leif. I give him two hundred pounds of silver and a new title. He shall not be known as Skald Leif anymore. He shall be known as Jarl Leif.'

Leif's jaw dropped. He could not believe what he'd heard. But the thumps on his back showed that his ears had not deceived him.

'Jarl Leif, Jarl Leif,' cried the warriors.

He turned to Aebbe. She looked crestfallen, imagining her plans would now come to nothing.

That might not be so, he thought. Most Jarls led their men in battle but everyone knew he was no warrior. Perhaps he could settle here with his title and treasure. Perhaps this was what Ivar planned all along. He could live here and keep a watchful eye on Oswald. Look after Ivar's interests.

He turned to look at the army. They were still saluting him, still chanting his name.

This will make a good tale, he thought in a daze.

And then Ivar did something even more startling. He gave Leif his sword, Havoc.

Leif looked at it, looked at Aebbe and shook his head in confusion.

Did this mean that Ivar wanted him to remain in the army, remain his Skald perhaps? Was his path set out for him forever?

'What does this mean my lord?' he asked nervously.

'It means I give you my sword,' Ivar said. 'You can do what you will with it. I did not use it much in battle but it was, nonetheless, a potent symbol. You can use it in either fashion, as you see fit.'

And with that he returned to his brothers.

Leif looked at the wonderful sword once more, wondering what decision he would take. Then he put the sword in his belt. He would decide tomorrow. Or maybe the day after that.

CHARACTERS IN WOLVES OF WAR

(Historical figures are listed in bold.)

Leif Ormson, Skald to Ivar the Boneless
Sigurd Ormson, Master-Smith and sword-maker
Aebbe, Leif's English wife
Nerienda, Sigurd's wife
Ivar the Boneless, son of Ragnar Lothbrok and leader of the great Viking army
Halfdan of the Wide-Embrace, brother of Ivar
Ubbe the Swift, brother of Ivar
Guthrum, a young jarl in Ivar's army
Eohric, Guthrum's brother
Thorvald, Guthrum's helmsman, a good friend of Leif
Asgrim the Traveller, crewman of Ivar and good friend of Leif
Deor, a healer
Jarl Kolga, daughter of Bjorn Blackbrow
Jarl Sidrac
Jarl Frene
Jarl Osbern
Burgred, King of Mercia
Æthelred, King of Wessex
Wulfthryth, Æthelred's wife
Alfred, Æthelred's brother, later King of Wessex
Ethelnoth, Alfred's friend, later Ealdorman of Wessex

Edgwulf, Alfred's friend, later his war-leader
Edmund, King of East Anglia
Aelle, King of Northumbria
Osberht, rival King of Northumbria
Echberht, Northumbrian nobleman, Ivar's puppet king
Ricsige, Echberht's cousin, later puppet king
Wulfhere, Archbishop of York
Oswald, Edmund's chief adviser, later puppet king of East Anglia
Hwita, adviser to King Edmund
Ceolred, Mercian lord
Mucel, Mercian ealdorman and father to Ealswith
Ealswith, daughter of Mucel, young wife of Prince Alfred
Higbald, West Saxon youth who becomes Leif's servant
Ketil, Thorvald's son
Klack, the lord of Leif's village
Asta, Kolga's lover
Vafri, Kolga's champion and lover

Thank you for buying Wolves of War. I hope that you enjoyed it.

The recommendations and comments of readers make all the difference to the success of a book. I would be very grateful if you could spread the word about the book amongst your friends. It would also be a great help if you could spend a few moments writing a review and posting it on the site where you purchased the book, Goodreads or any other forum you are active in.

To post a review please click here: mybook.to/WolvesofWar

OTHER BOOKS BY MARTIN LAKE

THE FLAME OF RESISTANCE

The Battle of Hastings is over. The Battle for England is about to begin. Edgar Atheling, the young heir to the throne must decide if he will battle William the Conqueror for the kingdom.

TRIUMPH AND CATASTROPHE

Edgar leads an English army into alliance with the Danes and war with the Normans. At first there is only triumph and glory. Then William returns and catastrophe ensues.

BLOOD OF IRONSIDE

Edgar is banished from Scotland and takes the war to the land of the Franks. But the death of his mother forces him to return. And there he faces death at the hands of the man who slew his father.

IN SEARCH OF GLORY

Edgar has been tricked into making peace with William. But when his old friend Cnut invades, Edgar takes up again the struggle against the Normans.

LAND OF BLOOD AND WATER

Warfare and warriors meant nothing to Brand and his family. But then King Alfred chose their home for his last-ditch defence against the Vikings.

BLOOD ENEMY

Ulf has risen high in King Alfred's service. But when he shows himself a berserker he loses everything. Can he redeem himself and return to favor?

OUTCASTS: CRUSADES

Saladin is marching to conquer the city of Jerusalem. Within the city waits only one nobleman, Balian of Ibelin, and four knights. In desperation, Balian knights thirty ordinary men of the city in to lead the defence. History says nothing more of the men raised so far above their normal station. 'Outcasts' tells the story of how they fare in a world grown more bitter and fanatical.

A LOVE MOST DANGEROUS

Her beauty was a blessing…and a dangerous burden…

As a Maid of Honor at the Court of King Henry VIII, beautiful Alice Petherton receives her share of admirers. But when the powerful, philandering Sir Richard Rich attempts to seduce her, she knows she cannot thwart his advances for long. She turns to the most powerful man in England for protection: the King himself.

Reveling in her newfound power, Alice soon forgets that enemies lurk behind every corner at court…and there are some who are eagerly plotting her fall…

VERY LIKE A QUEEN

The King's favor was her sanctuary—until his desire turned dangerous.

Alice Petherton is well practiced at using her beauty and wits to survive in the Court of King Henry VIII. As the King's favorite, she enjoys his protection but after seeing the downfall of three of his wives, she's determined to avoid the same fate. Alice must walk a fine line between mistress and wife.

She finds a powerful protector in Thomas Cromwell and Alice has every reason to believe that she will continue to enjoy a life of wealth and comfort at Court…until she puts everything at risk by falling in love with a Frenchman, Nicholas Bourbon.

When Cromwell is executed, Alice loses her only ally and flees to France. There she hopes to live in peace with Nicholas. But Alice is lured into a perilous game of treason and peace doesn't last long. Will Alice get back the life and love she's fought for? Or will she lose herself to the whims of a capricious monarch?

CRY OF THE HEART

She gave away her child to save his life. Another woman took him in, at risk to herself.

Viviane Renaud is a young mother living on the French Riviera in the Second World War. Times are hard but she is not the sort to be dismayed by circumstances. One day her life changes forever. A young Jewish woman, fleeing from the authorities, begs her to take care of her four year old boy, David. Almost without thinking, Viviane agrees.

Viviane's life is never the same again. She fabricates a story to explain how David came to be with her and must tip-toe around the suspicions of her neighbours, her friends and most of all her mother and sister. She and her husband, Alain, find allies in unlikely places, particularly an American woman, Dorothy Pine.

But then, the world crashes around them. Threatened by Allied military success, Hitler sends the German army to occupy the south of France. With them come the SS and the Gestapo. The peril for Jews and for those, like Viviane, who hide them, appears overwhelming. The challenge for them now is to survive.

WINGS OF FIRE: A WORLD WAR II NOVEL

A life and death struggle for control of the skies.

Claire Lamb believes she is as good as any man and being a member of the Women's Auxiliary Air Force gives her the opportunity to prove it. Harry Smith joins the Royal Air Force because he wants to fly. Frank Trent, an American pilot, risks prison to join the fight against Nazi Germany.

When Hitler invades Poland, he begins a conflict which eventually engulfs the whole world. Within eight months his army and air force conquer most of Europe. Only one adversary remains. Great Britain, led by Winston Churchill, refuses to surrender. Yet people fear that, in the coming weeks, the German Luftwaffe will bomb British cities to rubble and strew the country with poison gas. Worse yet. A huge German army prepares to cross the English Channel to conquer its last remaining enemy.

One foe stands in their way. The Royal Air Force remains defiant. Hitler is reluctant to attempt an invasion while the

RAF controls the skies above England. He unleashes the hitherto all-conquering Luftwaffe against it.

Throughout the summer and autumn of 1940, three thousand RAF pilots, the men Churchill called the Few, fight a grim life and death struggle for command of the skies. They are supported by the courageous and unstinting effort of thousands of others, many of them women. The Battle of Britain will decide the fate of the world.

A DANCE OF PRIDE AND PERIL

Four thousand years ago, Crete is a land of contrasts. The mountains are wild and forbidding yet on the coast, a new world is arising.

Mulia is famous for its thrilling and deadly acrobatic displays, where young men face the fierce charges of giant bulls, leaping over them or dying in the attempt. Talita is sold to the owner of the arena and trains as a dancer, her job to entertain the audience and goad the raging bulls.

Yet she wants more than this. Even as a child, she protected her flock from bears and wolves and was undaunted by them. Now she yearns to be a bull-leaper, a role reserved for men. Her friends believe she is foolish to have such dreams. Foolish, wilFul and dangerously reckless.

When she realises that she has a bond with Torq, the mightiest of the bulls, her ambition grows even stronger. Yet her dreams are thwarted when priests arrive from Egypt and steal Torq. Her enemies accuse Talita of taking Torq and she and her lover Pellon are condemned to death.

Will she find the strength and courage to escape? Dare she voyage to the distant land of Egypt and challenge the powerful, cunning, High Priest? Can she liberate Torq, prove her innocence and save her life?

THE ARTFUL DODGER

The further adventures of the Artful Dodger. After his trial Dodger is transported to New South Wales. He is taken in by a kindly family and learns to improve himself. But when he returns to England he finds himself stalked by a man who seeks to kill him.

PATHS OF TIME

We all live within the bounds of time and it marches on inexorably. Yet sometimes it has an elusive, subtle feel which makes us feel uneasy or perhaps exhilarated. On occasion time does not work at all as we expect. We are wrong-footed, confused, beguiled.

FOR KING AND COUNTRY

Three short stories set in the First World War.

NUGGETS

Fast fiction for quiet moments.

MR TOAD'S WEDDING

First prize winner in the competition to write a sequel story to The Wind in the Willows.

MR TOAD TO THE RESCUE

Mr Toad almost gets married but he has a lucky escape. The bride is kidnapped, not once but twice and Toad and his friends leave their familiar home to journey to the French Riviera on a desperate rescue mission.

THE BIG SCHOOL

Three light-hearted short stories about a boy's experience of growing up.

You can find my books easily by clicking here: viewAuthor.at/MartinLake

I have a mailing list with my new release, news and exclusive stories. To be the first to hear about new releases, please sign up below. I promise I won't fill up your mailbox with lots of emails. I won't share your email with anybody else.

If you would like to subscribe please click here: http://eepurl.com/DTnhb

You can read more about my approach to writing on my blog: http://martinlakewriting.wordpress.com

Or you can follow me on Twitter @martinlake14

Or on Facebook at:
https://www.facebook.com/MartinLakeWriting

Made in United States
North Haven, CT
14 April 2024

51305392R00221